Prison Snatch

Dear Reader:

Cairo has delivered his fifteenth novel and as usual, this one is a spicy and tantalizing read. Meet Heaven Lewis, a new addition at Croydon Hill who fast becomes the queen bee at the prison where everything goes behind the gates.

The vixen serving ten years for shooting her drug-dealing boyfriend is coveted by both correctional officers and inmates, and she relishes all the attention. She can be both adoring and vengeful as she moves back and forth from general population to solitary confinement. But wherever she goes, trouble and drama are at her heels. The luscious beauty with hazel eyes uses her body and wits to satisfy all her whims, including how to continue her preexisting lavish lifestyle.

Cairo takes erotica to a new level and offers an amusing and sinister look at lockup life with a zany cast of characters.

As always, thanks for supporting myself and the Strebor Books family. We strive to bring you the most cutting-edge, out-of-the-box material on the market. You can find me on Facebook @AuthorZane or you can email me at zane@eroticanoir.com.

Blessings,

Zane

Publisher
Strebor Books
www.simonandschuster.com

ZANE PRESENTS

Prison Snatch

A NOVEL BY

CAIRO

SBI

STREBOR BOOKS

NEW YORK LONDON TORONTO SYDNEY

Strebor Books
P.O. Box 6505
Largo, MD 20792
www.simonandschuster.com

ISBN 978-1-59309-663-2
ISBN 978-1-50111-964-4 (ebook)
LCCN 2016948696

First Strebor Books trade paperback edition November 2016

Cover design: www.mariondesigns.com
Cover photograph: © Keith Saunders/Keith Saunders Photos

10 9 8 7 6 5 4 3 2 1

Manufactured in the United States of America

For information regarding special discounts for bulk purchases, please contact Simon & Schuster Special Sales at 1-866-506-1949

The Simon & Schuster Speakers Bureau can bring authors to your live event. For more information or to book an event, contact the Simon & Schuster Speakers Bureau at 1-866-248-3049 or visit our website at www.simonspeakers.com.

PROLOGUE

Throw This Money On You . . .

As Heaven's hips naturally swayed, as she made her way down the near-empty corridor, CO Thurman rubbed a hand over his dick as he watched her on one of the zone-A monitors.

He was sitting behind the desk in central control, several large surveillance monitors strategically placed on the wall for easy viewing of the entire prison. He quickly—with the push of a button—zoomed in on the long-lashed, hazel-eyed beauty, his gaze caressing over her dangerous curves.

His tongue slid around his bottom lip.

"*Goddamn*," he hissed.

Everything about her did it for him. She fascinated him. A woman looking like *her* inside a prison could only mean one thing—*chaos*. Those eyes, that body . . . he was sure she'd end up causing a damn riot in the building if they didn't keep a close eye on her.

And, shit, he'd loved nothing more than to be the one to stand watch over her. He wanted to watch her back it up on his dick.

Watch his tongue glide around her clit, then push into (what he believed would be) her gushy slit. Fuck yeah.

And he'd love to see what was beneath that orange hip-hugging jumper she somehow managed to make look like something from off a Parisian runway. Prison couture.

He chuckled to himself. She definitely had a way of owning it—her sensuality, in the way she walked, in the way she carried herself. She walked like a woman who knew she had good pussy, like a woman who *knew* she was a bad bitch. And that shit in itself turned him on.

He loved dime-pieces, especially those sexy red-boned, long-haired, pretty-eyed ones.

The bow-legged, six-one, dark-chocolate CO with the big red lips had been working in corrections for almost twelve years, and he'd not seen an inmate as graceful or as beautiful as her. Sure, they had their share of pretty women come through the gates of Croydon Hill. But none compared to her thus far.

She was fucking mesmerizing. And every time he saw her, he found himself turned on by her presence.

Shit. He'd fuck around and dick her down, then trick up his whole overtime check on her fine-ass. He kept his gaze on her as she walked through the magnetometer on the right side of the hallway. He witnessed her roll her eyes up in her head as one of his colleagues, CO Clemmons—a stocky, big-breasted woman who wore her hair shaved bald—called back to her, and told her to go back through the metal detector again. She complied.

The machine must have beeped again. CO Clemmons walked over and said something to the inmate, and then she took the wall. Palms pressed against the wall, legs spread apart, her plump ass poking out just right.

He pushed out a hiss, massaging the head of his dick. He knew he'd end up with a nut-stain in his drawers, but fuck if he cared. He'd find some little trick-ass ho to suck him clean later (all the while thinking of *her*) once he clocked out.

Clemmons ran her hands over the inmate's body, sliding them over her back, down over her hips and then up and down the length of her outer and inner legs; her face mere inches from the inmate's ass.

He let out a groan, grinding his ass down into his chair as he discreetly squeezed and kneaded and rubbed his swollen dickhead. He felt the heat bubbling up around the sensitive gland and swallowed back a mouthful of drool.

"Yeah, Clemmons, what that ass smell like?"

Like sweet rainwater, he mused. Hell. He'd drink her piss water if she offered it to him.

Clemmons said something else to her, and the inmate gave her a murderous look, swinging her hair over her shoulders. There was disdain in her eyes.

The CO's gaze darkened. "What the fuck is you doing now, Clemmons?" he questioned as he continued to look on.

She must be up to her bullshit, again, he thought. She was known for trying to push up on inmates for pussy. But she had to know there wasn't shit she could do with a beauty like her. Nah. A woman like her needed a freaky muhfucka with lots of dick, like him.

He let out his breath in a long exhale. No inmate should be this fucking *bad*.

Bottom line, he planned on fucking her.

He didn't care how long it took—one year, two, three . . . he was getting inside her, and he was going to make it his mission to feel the stretch of her pussy over his dick before another CO got to her first.

Cash in her hand, or money on her books—whatever this hazel-eyed enchantress wanted, needed, he'd make it happen.

The question was, when?

ONE

Breathe You in My Dreams . . .

Fifty-five-year-old Lee Kateman—or Warden Kate, for short—sat behind her mahogany desk and fumbled with the button on her slacks, then undid it. Next she eased her zipper down, then slid her neatly manicured hand down into her opened slacks and cupped her pussy, but then she quickly shot up from her chair, knocking her knee against the desk. She grimaced, biting back a yelp as pain shot through her thigh.

She limped over to her door and locked it, then hobbled back to her desk and pressed the DO NOT DISTURB button on her desk phone, before easing back in her chair with a groan. Then she sighed. Now she could orgasm without any sudden interruptions.

She rubbed her knee a few times, then brought her attention back to the throbbing between her legs. She moaned in anticipation as she leaned back and spread her legs, her hand sliding back into the opening of her pants. She closed her eyes for a moment and moaned softly as she massaged her throbbing sex over the fabric of her white cotton panties. *Mmm, yes.* The ache between her thighs, which had started out as a slow burn over the course of the day, had now become an intense blaze.

She needed this release, this time alone, so very badly. Being the chief administrative official of a women's prison, which housed nearly nine hundred and fifty inmates in maximum, medium, and minimum security, along with another ninety women housed in the camps—coupled with the multiple personalities of nearly five-hundred-plus staff under her charge could be challenging in itself, some days more stressful than others. And today had been one of those days.

There'd been a gang fight on 5 East during breakfast, where eight women jumped two other women. And one of the women who had been attacked had had her eyeball nearly gouged out with a broom handle. Then an inmate coming out of classroom B had been caught with a brick of marijuana wrapped in cellophane. She and the teacher had been the only two in the classroom. And when she'd come out of the room ten minutes later, she'd tried to avoid being frisked. Hidden down in her jumper were the drugs. The little sneaky twat tried to run off from the COs, but they'd restrained her shortly after she'd given chase. Surprisingly, neither she nor the male teacher would say how or where she'd gotten ahold of the drugs—enough to light up a whole housing unit.

Then—as if her day hadn't already been shitty enough—another inmate jumped off the third-floor tier over on 8 North in an attempt to kill herself.

And all this occurred during *first* shift.

These crazy bitches had stressed her out today.

She'd already had three shots of pick-me-up by eleven this morning to take the edge off. *Mmmph. These nasty bitches trying to drive me to smoke crack.* She pinched her clit, and heard herself whimper as she touched herself. Her overly sensitive clit, all swollen and ready, protruded from beneath its hood, causing her whole body to shiver each time her hand stroked over her panties.

"Mmm, yes . . . ooh," she murmured.

As her hand slowly caressed her sex, she silently wished she had traded her granny panties—white Fruit of the Loom with pink flowers—in for something sexier, like a lacy thong. But she had been in a rush this morning, scrambling to get dressed and in on time for a nine o'clock meeting with the commissioner. And now she was reminded of the mismatched panty-set she'd been wearing beneath her designer pantsuit all day.

Not that she considered herself a sexpot, but there was something about the feel of silk rustling against her pussy lips that made her feel sexy. Even though that wasn't at all what she ever saw reflected in her husband's gaze whenever he looked at her.

Oh well.

Screw him! Her marriage was nothing more than a goddamn farce these days. So, she'd be damned if she was about to allow thoughts of him right now kill her vibe. She'd suppressed her need and longing for far too long. And, though, it was dirty desire, she was cognizant of what she was giving in to—of what she was stepping in to.

Fire.

And God help her, *she wanted it, craved it and ached for it*—with every breath in her quivering body. *Mmm, yes.* She pinched her clit again while staring at the computer screen that sat atop her sleek desk, and her breath hitched. The sight before her made her skin go hot. And her pussy instantly wet. She was slowly drowning in lust, drowning in want, drowning in fantasy.

The image filled her with conflicting emotions. Stark desire mixed with guilty pleasure. Then, always immediately after . . . came shame.

She and her fantasies were filthy. Dirty.

But—*damn it*—she needed a good fucking. Badly.

Still, she was a filthy, dirty, scandalous *bitch* for fantasizing over—oh, God help her—an inmate. But she couldn't help whom—and *what*—she lusted.

Or could she?

God, yes—of course she could. She'd done it for most of her thirty-five-year career. Kept her secret desires neatly tucked away in the darkest crevices of her filthy mind; that was. She'd mastered pretending. Maintained professional, healthy boundaries, and kept her private life just that—*private*.

But now she felt herself becoming more enticed, more driven, by her cravings, by the thrill, the rush, which surged through her veins every time she imagined herself taking a bite into the forbidden fruit of desire. Some days, she was so tempted to give in to spontaneity. To snatch the moment and revel in her most erotic fantasies, to indulge herself in debauchery.

It was almost as if she couldn't help herself. Sometimes she'd walk through the halls of her prison, and the smell of pussy would be clinging in the air, and her mouth would water and she'd become painfully aroused.

Maybe it was the flask of vodka she kept hidden in the bottom of her locked desk drawer that made her feel less inhibited, more daring of late. Maybe it was the fact that it'd been over five years since her husband had touched her, caressed her, or made sweet, passionate love to her.

Warden Kate grunted, her fingers greedily digging deeper, probing faster, stroking and stroking, desperately searching for that sweet spot. Her pussy needed some attention, some tender-loving fucking. A wet tongue licking over her folds would do her body so damn good right about now.

Her husband had robbed her of a good fucking, and she was angry with him for taking his dick elsewhere—giving it to some other bitch. When things first started to sour between the two of them, he had always been too tired, too stressed, too uninspired to even initiate sex. Initially, she'd have to beg him, practically plead, with him to at least let her suck his dick—anything to feel close to him.

Then gradually he'd come to bed long after she was asleep, doing anything he could not to share the same bed with her. And, over the last several months, he'd taken to sleeping in one of their spare bedrooms.

Still, she'd never divorce him. Othello. They had a long, rich history together. They'd started dating when she was eighteen. Then married at twenty. And they shared three beautiful adult children, two sons and a daughter—ages thirty-five, thirty-three, and thirty, respectively. And she had six grandchildren. Her daughter had four children, and her middle son had two.

Unfortunately, her firstborn—the apple of her eye, was too busy being a rolling stone to settle down and start a family of his own. He was a good catch. He was handsome. College-educated. Had fifteen years working with the state, and was making good money. But when it came to women, he just couldn't seem to get it right. He seemed to be a magnet for every wet pussy gone wild and wrong.

She grunted. She wished like hell he'd learn to keep his dick in his pants, or at the very least—stop giving it out so freely.

She loved him dearly, but he was a manwhore. Or at least he had been.

Of late, he seemed to be slowing down. Not going out as much, or tricking up his money on pussy. Maybe he was finally growing up. He'd been known to practically fuck anything with a pulse, if he thought he'd get away with it. And, once or twice, he'd gotten himself in some trouble with a few of those dogged-face bitches, leaving her to have to clean up several of his messes.

Truth be told, there wasn't anything she wouldn't do to protect her family. She was simply downright too loyal, too supportive. And not always goddamned appreciated enough. But she would always be there for them, including her husband, Othello, no matter how shitty he treated her. So tearing her family apart wasn't a part of her life plan, even if she had given it serious thought several times over the years. Bottom line, she'd stay stuck in a sexless marriage for appearance's sake. It was a benefit to them both. And, as he'd once told her, it was "cheaper to keep her."

Still, some hard dick plunging her cunt would be a nice treat from time to time, even if she did have her mind on something else—*someone* else. Ooh, yes, God. She had a taste for some pussy. And she wanted to taste herself on another woman's lips. Maybe even grind clits together while suckling on each other's tits. She moistened her lips with the tip of her tongue.

Hell. She was sure Othello had some Becky-looking bitch sucking his long, fat dick. There'd been a time, long ago, when she enjoyed the feel of him stretching her cunt, hitting the bottom of her well with all nine inches.

But now he was giving the dick to some sidepiece; he just had to be. Oh, sure. She'd found the text message exchanges between her husband and some lonely bitch he'd met on some social media site. *Veronica*. And she'd even found a few nude photos of the shameless hussy.

She'd become so sick and tired of giving a damn that now she simply didn't. Still, she'd invested too much of her time and life in her marriage. Lots of sweat and tears and sacrifice went into being married. So if he wanted out, he'd have to leave *her*. Period.

Warden Kate sighed, pulling herself from her reverie. She sighed regretfully. She'd given her troubled marriage enough thought for one day. Right now, she had a more pressing matter that needed her attention.

Her pulsing loins.

She licked her lips as her gaze flickered up and locked on the image in front of her on the Department of Corrections' inmate locator page.

"Mmm . . . ooh, yes . . . I bet you have a sweet, tasty hole . . ."

A soft moan slipped from the back of her throat as she winded her hips down into her chair, her fingers ever so lightly flicking over her cloth-covered clit. God how she wished she could feel her ass and the back of her bare pussy pressed down into the plush leather of her chair as she brought herself to climax.

If it hadn't been in the middle of the day, she would have pulled out her ridged "vibrator-friend"—the one she kept tucked in the back of her locked drawer in a satin black bag—and fucked her horny cunt real good with it. But, for now, she'd have to settle for her fingers and hand to take her to her happy place.

Hmm. Nirvana.

Oh how she longed for it. Yearned for it. The overwhelming need burned through her core. With her free hand, she unbuttoned her blouse, then slipped her hand inside, her fingers finding their way inside her bra—pink, cotton and . . . *boring*.

Why hadn't she worn the one with the scalloped, lacy edges?

Lee's hand moved languorously over her clit and lips until her juices simmered and slowly seeped into her underwear. She patiently teased herself, lightly pinching and patting her clit, her gaze fixed on her computer screen.

She pressed the palm of her hand down on her clit and moved her hand, harder, faster, creating a hot friction that set her pussy ablaze.

"Mmm, you degenerate bitch," she murmured. "You criminal. Mmm, yes . . . eat my pussy, you villainess whore . . ."

She hated herself for becoming so licentious, so loose . . . so damn greedy; potentially jeopardizing everything she'd worked so hard for her entire life—her career, her family—her reputation, for God's sake! She'd spent most of her career in corrections with an unblemished track record of being no-nonsense and by the book.

And, now, here she was.

Fantasizing.

Dangling over the edge of temptation. Oh, how she was tempted to throw caution to the wind, and do something uncharacteristically impulsive. Risqué. Of course, she'd never be foolish enough to do anything that might spoil her reputation, or ruin her career.

Still . . .

She toyed for a moment with the idea of summoning that sweet piece of ass to her office, to kneel before her, to taste her, to maybe have her slender fingers wedged between the inmate's slick folds, stroking into her silky heat until she climaxed.

She suspected the moment she'd laid eyes on the new inmate with the voluptuous body—firm, high breasts. Tight waist. Ripe, round ass—that she'd be trouble with a capital *T*. And, she'd been right. So far, half of her prison's population—and many of her prison staff—including custody staff—were seemingly enthralled by her.

Talking.

Thinking.

Imagining.

A woman *that* beautiful with *that* many curves had no business being in prison. *Her* prison. And she knew from experience that it was only a matter of time before inmate 22345C would manage to have most of the inmates here shanking each other up for a taste of her feminine nectar.

And—she also wouldn't be surprised if the hazel-eyed enchantress managed to have a few of her corrections officers' dicks roaring to life, surging against their uniform pants like a bunch of horny teenagers vying to be balls deep inside her.

Oh, yes. She'd already spotted more than enough appreciative male gazes from some of the COs to know that this little slut muffin was going to potentially wreak havoc in her institution. And she wasn't having it. Oh no. She wasn't about to let her turn her prison into her very own lair. Not if she could help it.

She knew she'd have to keep a close eye on this one. And, yet, she closed her eyes and blew out a blistering curse as her fingers slipped under the waistband of her panties, then skitted over the course strip of neatly manicured pubic hair before settling on her quivering clit, then to her slick entrance, then back to her clit.

And every nerve ending in her body jolted, and she gasped, opening her legs wider to her probing fingers. The golden brown lips of her pussy opened wetly to her fingers, allowing her to go in deeper. She moaned softly, and stretched herself more with two fingers—then three. She began stroking in and out, in and out, enjoying the wet clicking sound of her fingers, enjoying the silky walls of her cunt.

Her simmering pussy heated her fingers and its scent wafted up around her like a scented candle.

Hot. Sweet. Flicking fire.

And then came the creamy nectar, pooling out of her body, bathing her fingers and soaking her panties. But her fingers continued to skillfully fuck out another orgasm, causing her to go utterly limp.

She slowly opened her eyes, dazed, her body still shuddering, and glanced back at the computer screen. Heat stole over her body. Imagining the taste of *her*; the feel of her tongue sliding over *her* cunt nearly made her orgasm all over again.

She muttered a curse. Then clicked out of the browser.

Shit.

TWO

Desperado . . .

"What'chu readin', cutie?"

Heaven Lewis looked up from the book she was reading, and looked over toward the opened barred door of her nine-by-twelve cell. There, leaning up against its frame, stood a light-skinned woman sporting a Mohawk and a snake tattoo wrapped around her neck—a cobra. Droplets of blood dripped from its fangs.

The women housed in 3 West affectionately called her Snake because of her venomous temper when crossed, and the way her long tongue slithered all over her lovers' pulsing bodies whenever she crept into their cells for a salacious romp.

She had a raspy voice as if she'd been smoking cigarettes since the day she'd been born.

Heaven took in the burly, twenty-something-year-old with the handsome face and the spray of freckles across the bridge of her nose, and knew without having to say it that the stud wasn't the least bit concerned with what she was reading. What she was interested in was tucked away between her thighs beneath two pairs of white women's briefs and a pair of long johns. She kept her pussy triple-wrapped to stave off any easy attempts at getting to her good-good if some devious bitch tried to scheme on her pussy, that was.

"Just some book," Heaven calmly answered, and closed her book, placing it face-up beside her on the bunk. *The Power Couple.* By Allison Hobbs.

Snake smirked at her, the tip of her pink tongue peeking out from between her full lips. The stud had been trying to charm her way into Heaven's panties from the moment she'd stepped foot into Croydon Hill Correctional Facility—a woman's prison tucked away on 117 acres in Northwest New Jersey, twenty miles from the New York state line—nearly six months ago. And so far—without much hassle, she'd managed to keep her snatch untouched by the hungry advances of wolves like her starving for fresh cunt.

But the glint in the young stud's eyes told her that today she wouldn't be so easily dissuaded. Of all the females here, *she* had to pick *today* to fuck with *her*. She fought to keep from sucking her teeth.

Snake stepped inside the cell. Uninvited. Unwanted. Undeterred.

Long legs and large breasts swept through the small space in two steps. And then she was hovering over her, an arm up on the top bunk, looking down at her, casting her a hungry, primal look. She grabbed at her crotch in the way a man would, then pulled at the whiskers on her chin.

"So how is it?"

The hair on the back of Heaven's neck stood at attention. But she remained calm. "How is what?"

"The book."

Heaven shrugged. "It's okay." She kept her tone innocuous, not interested in engaging her with book talk. But she didn't want to be rude to her, either.

All she wanted was to do her bid. Period.

She was here on attempted murder charges. The aggravated assault and possession of a handgun—a Glock she'd used to shoot her cheating boyfriend—had been dismissed under the terms of her plea agreement. A ten-year sentence. And now all she wanted to do was her time so that she could return to her beloved Jimmy Choo stilettos and Birkin handbags. She missed all of her coveted pieces, along with her diamond studs and tennis bracelets.

But *this*—a one-piece stainless steel toilet/sink and a steel bedstead that held a thin mattress inside of a brick box surrounded by concrete walls and razor-sharp wire. And this God-awful orange New Jersey Department of Corrections jumpsuit—was her current reality.

The stud smirked. "So you like them nasty books, huh?"

Heaven gave her a blank look.

"Yeah, I read, baby," the young stud said, catching the surprised look on her face. She gave Heaven a lecherous stare. Then she lewdly slid the tip of her tongue over her bottom lip. "I like that kinky shit, too. I just finished reading *Vengeance* by that broad Zane. Yo, she wild as fuck. Reading her shit makes my dick hard."

Dick?

Was that what they were calling clits these days?

Dicks?

Heaven frowned. She'd never been friends with a lesbian, so she had no frame of reference to speak of—not that she was prejudiced or anything; she simply didn't hang in social circles where bisexual or lesbian women frequented—but one thing was for certain: she wasn't interested in becoming friends with her, or any other women who thought she had a dick hanging between her legs.

"I haven't read that book," Heaven simply stated. But what she wanted to say was, *"Why the fuck are you in my cell?"*

Snake glanced over her shoulder, then gave a slight head nod to her lookout, a tall lanky Dred about nineteen with bad acne and an overbite. The girl nodded back, then stood watch, like a faithful watchdog.

And then came the weight of the stud's body on Heaven's bunk. She smelled of Irish Spring soap, and Dial scented roll-on.

Heaven flinched, and inched away from her.

"I'm not here to bite you, baby," the stud said, reaching over and running the back of two fingers over Heaven's arm. "Not unless you want me to." She winked at her. "You pretty as fuck, baby."

The stud reached for the book lying on the bed and picked it up. She glanced at the cover, then she turned it over in her hand. "I bet reading this freaky shit got you real wet." She licked her lips again. "*Mmph.* I love a wet pussy. I'd tear that shit up. Make you forget all about the hard dick you wished you were still getting."

"Look, Serpent . . ."

"Snake," she corrected her. "It's. *Snake.*" She flicked her tongue out and rolled it several times for effect. Heaven tried not to look wide-eyed at its enormous size. It was six inches. And thick. It disappeared back into her mouth. "And this tongue lives up to its name, baby. Trust."

Heaven cringed. "Well, listen. *Snake.* Whatever it is you're selling, I'm not interested." She pushed up off the bed and stood. "So go do your soliciting, recruiting, or whatever it is you're trying to do somewhere else. Now I'm going to ask you nicely to please leave my cell."

"Nah, baby." Snake slowly licked the tip of her tongue along her top lip. "You fine as fuck." She made a tsking noise. "I bet that sweet thing between yo' legs is nice 'n' juicy. Tight too." She locked her gaze on Heaven. She saw the look on her face. Fear. She smelled it slowly seeping from her pores and it made her *dick* harder.

She wanted to fuck. Her. But she wouldn't take it. Not unless she really had to. She wanted this pretty bitch for keeps. Wanted to make her wifey. She wanted to hear her moan. Call out her name.

And beg her for more of her good loving. She wanted to feel her nails raking along her back, breaking skin. Drawing blood. Her legs up over her shoulders as she served her ass up right. She wanted to make this sexy bitch come over and over until her whole world spun out of control.

Heaven's tone was surprisingly strong when she pushed out, "You'll never know. Now I think it's best you get out of my cell. *Please*."

The stud smirked. She liked her sass. She flicked her tongue. "Yeah, okay. Good luck with that, ma. I'm not leaving until you and I come to an understanding."

Heaven frowned, and tilted her head in disbelief. "An *understanding?* Girl, bye. The only understanding there is between us is that I'm not interested."

"Not today, maybe. But you will be," Snake stated confidently. She reached over and grabbed an unopened bag of Doritos. Cool Ranch. "I'll wait, baby—for now." She tore open the bag, then began chomping on a chip. "But when I'm done waiting on you to get with the program," she said as she chewed, "I'll be coming to collect on what's mine."

Heaven's mind reeled. Who the hell did this wannabe man bitch think she was?

The truth was, she wasn't afraid of her. She was afraid of herself. She refused to be bullied, *or* manipulated, out of her panties. And she damned sure refused to be chased out of her own cell. No. This thug chick with the imaginary dick had to go, or one of them would have to be dragged down to the infirmary or carried out on a stretcher.

She was classy. A lady. But she wasn't new to a good fistfight. Sadly, many females mistook her long hair, light eyes, and pretty face for some girly-type who couldn't put in work. But her three brothers had taught her well growing up.

Still, she felt her heart banging against her rib. She'd heard the horror stories—seen the television shows—of inmates getting raped in prison. Real or not, she wasn't interested in finding out if any of the rumors were true. Nor was she interested in being strong-armed into a sexual relationship with some aggressive female with a chin full of whiskers, and a cunt bursting with testosterone. No, no, no.

She'd never played victim on the streets. And she'd be damned if she were going to start now. Even after everything she went through in her six-year relationship with Freedom and all of his lying, game playing, and his revolving door of bitches, she hadn't put up with any of his shit. She'd fought him—and, sometimes, them. No questions asked. And she continued to put up with his mess until she'd had enough of his bullshit.

Then she tried to blow a hole in his back when she'd walked in and found him fucking some other *bitch* in *their* bed. Missionary, her legs up over his broad shoulders, her hands cupping his muscled ass as he pounded his dick eagerly in and out of her; the white, eighteen-hundred-count sheet and comforter had been strewn to the floor. Heaven could hear his whore's moans as she writhed in ecstasy beneath him.

She'd been surprisingly quieted by shock as she stood and watched her man slay his bitch in *their* bed. The fucking nerve of that bastard! Without thought, she'd stepped slowly back out of the room, then turned around and headed for the gun case they'd kept in another part of the house. She'd punched in the code, selected a handgun, loaded it, then made her way back up to the bedroom, her hands shaking, her heart pounding her ears.

The moans had grown louder, more desperate.

She stood near the bed and pulled the trigger without blinking an eye.

And she'd do it all over again.

"Listen," she attempted to reason with the stud. "I mean no disrespect when I say this, but I'm not a lesbian."

The stud smirked. "That's fine with me, baby. I prefer straight women anyway; especially ones like you."

She frowned, and felt her patience growing thin. "Um, I don't think you're hearing me. I *said*. I'm. Not. Interested. Period. Now get the *fuck* out my cell. *Please*."

The stud's jaw clenched.

"Bitch," she snarled, hopping up from the bunk, nearly hitting her head. "Who the *fuck* you think you talkin' to like that? Huh, *bitch*?" She clenched her right fist, and pointed her finger at her. Then her neck cracked as she stretched it side to side. The stud felt her temper flaring. She didn't tolerate broads talking shit to her. She'd been running this unit for close to six years, and bitches knew their place. But this one here would need to learn the hard way.

She took her pointer finger and mushed Heaven in the forehead. "Don't you know who the fuck I am? I'll smack the shit outta you. I'm the King Bitch over here. I get what I want. Or I take it. You better ask 'bout me. You in *my* house." She stepped in closer, her tone threatening. "You're over *here* on this housing unit because *I* want ya stuck-up ass here." The stud took another menacing step, cornering her. "Fact three," she continued, gesturing toward her with one of her large, meaty hands. "*When* I make you mine, you'll be mine until I say otherwise. And when I'm done fuckin' ya conceited-ass inside out, you'd better hope I don't whore your stuck-up ass out to the rest of the prison."

Several thoughts came into Heaven's mind. Screaming for help. Pushing the stud backward, out of her personal space. Spitting in her face. Clawing her eyeballs out.

But, the bitch had put her hands on her, so in the end, there was only one thing that had to be done.

She whipped out her blade and went to work, painting her cell red.

THREE

Lick, Lick, Lick . . .

"**G**et on your fuckin' knees," the housing unit sergeant gritted out, his voice rigid and demanding as he pushed the young inmate down to her knees. She looked up at the very tall, intimidating presence standing in front, her frightened gaze sliding up his six-foot-six frame as he reached for his fly and unbuttoned his uniform pants.

Her eyes flashed wide, her heart beating fast as he lowered his zipper.

He smirked looking down at her. Yeah, the little bitch was scared, the way he liked 'em. He reached into his pants with his right hand and pulled out his dick.

A tear slid down her cheek as his thick, chocolate member jutted outward from a nest of hair. Her lips quivered. Not from anticipation, but simply from sheer fear.

His large hand gripped the base, and the thick-mushroom head was directed at her mouth. *God, please*, she silently begged. *Don't let him do this to me.*

He brushed his dick over her lips, glossing them with his precum.

"You open your muthafuckin' mouth and tell anyone about this," he warned, stroking his shaft, "and I'ma make your life a living hell. Understand?"

She blinked her wet lashes and nodded her head.

"Good. Now open that slutty little mouth of yours. And suck this dick. And you better not scrape my shit with them raggedy-ass teeth."

This hoodrat bitch better suck dick good, he thought as he watched her open her wide mouth. He'd been eyeing her for a minute. Hell. He hadn't gotten away with shooting his load in these prison hoes' mouths over the years by being impulsive or sloppy. He was calculating. He chose his prey methodically.

Bitches with low self-esteem.

Young.

Scared.

Vulnerable.

Emotionally damaged.

Broke bitches with little to no outside family support.

The ones with one or more of those limitations made for the best dick suckers. Preferably with low IQs—bordering on mental retardation was even better. He didn't want a bitch too smart, too mouthy, or too opinionated. Those types were harder to control, and were potential liabilities. The last thing he needed was some wannabe Prison Rights activist making anonymous calls to investigators.

Shit. He had a good thing going. He had close to twenty-three years on the job, made six-figures, and had a pension damn near four hundred thousand dollars.

He could retire in another four years and be set for life. He wasn't about to let some prison poontang fuck that up. Bottom line, he wasn't looking for a relationship with none of these convicted hoes, just some good prison head.

He knew he didn't have the longest dick. But it was thick as fuck, and more than capable of stretching the shit out of a hole. Most hoes couldn't even open their mouths wide enough to take him. And they tended to be the ones with the biggest mouths, talking mad shit about what they could do to the dick. Then they'd get it, and couldn't do shit.

Tiny-mouthed bitches.

Sometimes he wanted to unhinge them shits open by breaking their fucking jaws.

"Open wider," he warned, pushing the head of his dick between her lips.

Nervously, she opened wider and he slid inside. He was dangerously thick in her mouth, and his shaft—oh so rigid across her lips. "*Shiiit.*" His breath rushed out in a long hiss. He felt her trembling and stood still, offering her a chance to get her head game right.

"You better not gag or throw up on my shit. Or you going to motherfuckin' lockup tonight."

She looked up at him and nodded. And then closed her eyes taking him back inside her mouth, while she silently prayed that he wouldn't try to fuck her with all this beer-can thick dick. The thought alone motivated her to suck him as if her life depended on it.

And, sadly, in more than one way . . . it did.

"Hold that shit like an ice cream cone and lick it," he rasped. "Eat that dick up like you love it."

Like a good little dick sucker, she did what she was told and licked around the head of his dick, then lapped over the tip, taking away the precum that gathered there, her eyes falling shut as the taste on her tongue made her mouth water, and her pussy swell.

She ran her tongue over his dick once again before swirling a wet lick around the entire head.

"Yeah, that's it," he whispered, holding her face and stroking her cheek with his thumb. He surprised her with his gentleness, then he suddenly shook her from the illusion when he roughly yanked her hair back, his dick plopping out of her mouth and then slapping the heavy width of his dick across her mouth and face.

"Stick that tongue out."

She did and he slapped his thick cock all over it—until spit juice splashed off it, before ramming it back into her mouth. Her face flushed with heat as he muttered and cursed low above her as her head and mouth moved back and forth, rapidly sliding over his shaft.

"Yeah, you little naughty bitch. Uh, yeah . . . grab them balls."

She reached for his nutsac and timidly fondled them. They were big. Bigger than any balls she'd ever played with. Grown-man balls, full with lots of grown-man nut.

She was only twenty-three, not that experienced—and nowhere near as freaky as some of her friends back home in Boston. They'd been fucking since they were thirteen, fourteen. And yet she hadn't lost her virginity until she was eighteen.

And she'd only been with two guys—her age, of course—before she'd been arrested, charged, and brought to Croydon Hill for her part in two bank robberies in Jersey. One bank, down by the shore. The other bank, up in Teaneck.

That was three years ago.

So whatever she knew about sex, she'd learned from her exes—or from reading erotic books. But, now, here she was. Her knees pressed deep into the tiled floor, her mouth stuffed with big, thick grown-man dick. She moaned in spite of her fear lingering in the back of her mind that Sergeant Struthers could make the next twelve years of her bid a nightmare.

She knew, had heard, from other inmates what he was capable of. That alone frightened her. But he'd promised her fifty dollars' worth of commissary if she took care of his dick right. She needed that commissary. She had nothing. So sucking his grown-man dick was worth it. She'd hang from a ceiling fan if he wanted that too.

"Squeeze them shits," he breathed out, pulling her from her reverie. He pulled his dick from her mouth, holding it up in his fist by the spit-shined head, the shaft moving upward to lift his balls to her mouth. "Spit on 'em."

She did.

"Now lick 'em."

She did that too. Then sucked them into her mouth on command. A dick puppet, that's what she'd become. Another tear slid down her face.

"That's right. Cry, bitch." He grunted, yanking his balls from her mouth, then repositioning his dick to her lips. "Look at me, you little street tramp."

Slowly, she lifted her gaze to meet his.

"You like sucking this fat Daddy cock, huh?"

She nodded.

"Show Daddy how much you like it then . . ."

He palmed her face again and fucked her mouth hard, mercilessly, until her chest tightened and she was breathless. "Aah, fuck yeah. Suck it," he growled.

She opened wider, as far as her jaws would allow, then swallowed as the head of his dick brushed the back of her throat.

"Breathe through your nose," he coaxed. And she inhaled deeply through her nose. "I'm almost there. You want this nut?"

She knew to nod, so she nodded. Then moaned over his cock.

"Then swallow, fuck-face," he commanded. "Relax your jaw. And swallow with the thrust."

She cringed inwardly as she took heed—and gradually his dick slid in and out of her mouth with ease, rasping over her tongue. Spit splashed out of her mouth, then slid down her chin.

"F-f-uuuuck," he gasped out as a slight spurt of heat hit the back of her throat.

She moaned and swallowed, then kept greedily sucking him.

"Yeah, that's it, you greedy little cum slut. Swallow that shit."

He palmed her head like a basketball and grasped the base of his dick

"Hold still, fuck-girl," he said hoarsely. "Where you want this nut? Ya mouth?"

She nodded.

He grunted. Squeezing the top of her head, he snatched his dick from her wet, sloppy mouth and began jerking at his dick in rapid back-and-forth motion, its head slapping over her swollen lips—until a hot jet of cum shot into her eyes.

She shook, shutting her eyes as the thick cream coated her lashes, blurring her vision. He grunted again, his hand jerking over his incredibly thick shaft as he aimed another spray of his nut into her face. The creamy load slid down her nose, then dropped from her lashes.

Satisfied with his liquid paint job, he trailed two fingers over her face, collecting his cream. Then he held them to her lips.

"Open your mouth."

He smeared cum over her lips, then scooped more of his nut onto his fingertips and slid it over her tongue. "Suck it," he said huskily.

Her mouth closed over his fingers, and she tasted his musky essence and sucked at his fingers until he'd finger-wiped her whole face and fed her every drop. And then he slid his still-hard dick back into her mouth and pumped away until another nut flooded the inside of her mouth.

Her jaws burned. Her knees ached. But, she was surprisingly wet. And almost willing to let him fuck her too—if he wanted pussy too.

He stepped back, his limp dick flopping out of her mouth. She eyed him through cum-coated lashes as he stuffed his sticky dick back into his underwear and zipped his pants.

She quickly stood to her feet, then took the wet rag he handed her and washed her face. He waited until she was done, then reached for the two Burger King Whoppers and large fries sitting on his desk and handed them to her.

"Now get the fuck out," he snarled.

FOUR

Only the Strong Survive...

"**D**on't eat my *shit*. Don't touch my *shit*. And don't say *shit* to me unless I *want* to be bothered with you." Contempt coated the brown-skinned inmate's words like crackling fish grease. She stood in the middle of the cell in a white sports bra and men's white boxer shorts.

Heaven blinked.

She'd just stepped into the cell, and hadn't expected to be greeted with such disdain. She'd been in lockup—or the *hole*, as they called it—for the last sixty days for slicing Snake's face open over on 3 West. And now it seemed as if everyone over here was having a problem with her since the notorious bully had had her face split open to the bone, and a part of her ear sliced off. One hundred and fifty stitches later.

The woman stood in the way as Heaven tried to get to her bunk. Clearly, she'd been waiting for her. Wanting a confrontation.

Heaven held her breath. She didn't think she could do this. This, this . . . general population shit. She could already tell she would have problems over here. And the whole idea of having to constantly watch her back was a bit daunting. She'd either have to get off this housing unit or she'd end up back in solitary.

Lockup seemed like a much more suitable choice. At least down in the Dungeons (what the inmates called solitary confinement since it was housed over in another section of the prison where you had to walk through a long, winding tunnel to get to), she didn't have to deal with this type of shit. She was housed in a single cell, and showered alone.

At least with being on twenty-three-hour lock, she didn't have to deal with anyone, other than the guards who had to do their mandatory thirty-minute tours or pass out food trays with whatever inmate worked kitchen detail, or when the COs had to let her out for her daily hour.

During which time she came out to shower, and, maybe, write a letter. She was only allowed to make collect calls once every fifteen days (which she never did). And she didn't have access to a television, so she'd usually shower for twenty minutes or so, then return back to her cell to read a book. One of the female officers, Ms. Kimberly, was always nice enough—any time she worked overtime on that unit—to pass down her books after she'd finished reading them herself.

But now—*mmph*.

She'd have to share a cell with this cranky bitch. And be stuck using a shower with at least sixty other women over on this tier. She wasn't sure how this was going to work for her.

At least her time over on 3 West, as short as it had been, felt more like being at a country club compared to *this* shit she was currently assigned to. 4 East. The moment the housing officer had clicked open the door, she'd felt like she'd walked into the hood.

And she had.

4 East was clearly one of the prison slums. Every other female she'd seen in the day space had looked impoverished. Dirty.

Trashy. Prison misfits. Junkies and ex-addicts surrounded her. Many appeared to be women who looked like they'd been around the block a few times. Others appeared to have spent the majority of their lives lying on their backs, or from being down on their knees tricking.

She hadn't meant to pass judgment, but she didn't feel comfortable being around all these derelicts. She already knew the moment she ordered her canteen, her shit would get stolen. And, the last thing she was going to do was sponsor a bunch of broke-down bitches.

Heaven inhaled and blinked in the grim reaper. She hadn't done shit to this bitch, and here she was already on the defense barking orders. Heaven bit her tongue, though. She didn't want any problems. But she wasn't going to let this broad punk her, either.

She was doing her bid, alone. She had no friends here. Well, fuck. She really hadn't had any friends on the streets, either. Not any that she could honestly say she trusted, or knew would have her back.

She took another deep breath. "I'm Heaven."

"Bitch, I *know* who you are," she said nastily. "You the uppity bitch who cut my girl in her face. Try that shit over here 'n' you're gonna end up with your throat slit, and your guts spilling out ya ass."

Heaven cringed. "For the record. I didn't just up and cut your so-called *girl*. She stepped to me trying to get up in my pussy. I wasn't interested. And when I asked her nicely to leave my cell, she refused. She put her hands on me, *first*. So be clear."

Hand on her hip, the menacing inmate snarled, "Bitch, *for the record*. I don't. Give. A. Fuck about what she did to *you*, first. She ran shit over there, like I run shit over here. Period."

Heaven ran her tongue over her teeth. All she wanted to do was brush her teeth, and shower. Not argue. "Listen. I don't want any problems with you. But, do me a favor. *Please*. Don't call me a *bitch*."

"Sweetie, you over here in *my* space. I'll call you what I want. I heard all about you. Some uppity *bitch*, who thinks she's better than the rest of us. *Bitch*—yeah I said it. And *what?*" She stared Heaven down. "You ain't no different from anyone else; your ass is in a jumper with a state number like the rest of us. So that makes you a convict like the rest of us."

Heaven took her in. A platinum bob of hair brushed along her jawline. Her lean, toned body reminded Heaven of a dancer's. And though she had acne, she was still pretty. Pretty rough, that was.

Mindful not to touch her as she stepped further into the cell, Heaven sat her meager belongings, all neatly wrapped inside her bed sheet, atop her bunk, then smoothed nervous hands over her jumper pants.

She didn't want to be in this cell with her no more than *she* wanted her to be. That was the only thing they clearly had in common. Still, she wanted to be civil. Or at least, pretend to be.

"Keep your shit over on your side," her new cellie snarled. "And if you snore, I'll smother ya ass in your sleep. Got it?"

"Then I guess lucky for the both of us, I don't snore," Heaven replied lightly.

The inmate swung her bob. "No, *bitch*. Lucky for *you*."

Heaven scowled.

This shit was not going to work. And she was not sleeping in the same cell with this roguish bitch. Period. So before she went off, she politely snatched her shit off the bunk and proceeded out the cell.

"That's right ho, step!" the inmate spat, causing a few inmates within earshot to laugh. "Before you get stomped out."

"Coletta, you know you wrong for that, girl," someone said. "Chasing that stuck-up ho out your cell like that."

"Girl, fuck that bitch. She ain't welcomed up in here!"

"I know that's right," someone else said.

Heaven heard them, but refused to give any of them a second glance, even though she knew she should probably pay closer attention to her surroundings, in case one of them hoodrat bitches tried to attack her from behind.

Let 'em try it!

Admittedly, she was still trying to figure out the dos and don'ts of prison life, but one thing she was sure of: whatever the pecking order, she was not about to be *that* bitch at the bottom of the rung getting pissed and shitted on.

She tossed her hair—*real* hair—and stomped down the stairs.

Some of the female inmates sitting at various tables in the day space stopped playing their card and board games, mesmerized by her. Others eyed and tapped their homegirls gesturing with their heads over at Heaven—a few even whistled and suggestively flapped their tongues—as she marched her way over to the housing officer with her belongings in tow.

"Um, excuse me, CO," she said politely as she reached the desk.

The light-skinned woman, with the yarn twists in her hair, sitting at the desk ignored her as she wrote in the logbook.

Heaven glanced at the female officer's nametag. "Excuse me . . . Miss O'Neal. I don't mean to bother you, but—"

"Then don't," the CO replied.

Heaven narrowed her eyes. "Well, I have a problem."

"Back up away from my desk," O'Neal barked without looking up at her. Pen poised over one of the pages in her logbook, she waited for Heaven to take a step back. Then asked, "What's your problem?"

The CO not once looked up at Heaven, and Heaven thought it rude. *Bitch.*

"The *problem* is: I need to be moved from off this housing unit. *Now.*"

The CO finally peeled her eyes from the logbook, and slowly slid her gaze up to meet Heaven's hazel eyes, taking in her reddish-brown skin. *Oh, this Indian-looking bitch right here thinks she's all that*, the CO thought as she tilted her head.

The CO smirked, raising a brow. "And *where* exactly would you like to move to, Your Royal Highness? The Omni? The Waldorf?"

Heaven stood unmoved by the CO's sarcasm. "I don't care where you move me, ma'am, as long as it's out of here."

"Oh, sure," she said, closing her logbook. "I'll get right on it." She reached for the phone. "Let me see if the lieutenant can send over your glass carriage." She slammed the phone back onto the receiver. "*Not*. Now go take your ass back up to your cell. And get the fuck away from my desk."

A few inmates sitting within earshot overheard the exchange and laughed. And in turn, Heaven steadied her breathing. She dug her long fingernails into her bed sheet. Her nails had grown dangerously long during her time in lockup, and she hadn't had a chance to trim them.

Heaven dropped her belongings on the floor. "I'm not going anywhere. I want to speak to someone above *your* pay grade. Please and thank you."

The housing officer blinked. "I just gave you a direct order, Inmate." She stood up. "Now move the fuck away from my desk. NOW!"

Heaven sucked her teeth, snatching up her belongings. "*Bitch*," she mumbled under her breath as she stalked off.

"What the fuck did you call me?" the housing officer called after her.

Heaven kept walking toward the stairs.

"Get her, Miss *O*," someone said in back of Heaven. "That ho know she don't want it with you."

The housing officer grunted. "*Mmph*. You know that's right. I know if that bitch hadn't moved the fuck away from my desk, I was about to put my foot in her neck."

"Ha! Miss *O*, you shoulda dragged her ass," another inmate said.

"Who that bitch think she is, anyway, Pocahontas?"

"*Mmph*. She cute, though," another inmate said loudly. "But I bet her drawz real nasty. Y'all know it be them real pretty ones doin' the least to keep them drawz clean."

Laughter roared around the day space.

The housing officer eyed Heaven as she made her way back up the stairs, then reopened her logbook and went back to writing in it once Heaven reached the third floor.

Several inmates snickered as she walked by. A few others grunted.

Coletta, who had been watching Heaven the whole time, turned from the railing and leaned her back up against it. Arms folded, she smirked. "Well, look what the cat dragged back. Little Miss Uppity. I guess you couldn't swing your hair and bat your lashes to get what you wanted, huh?"

Heaven ignored her, stepping back into what would become her nightmare if she didn't do something. She tossed her belongings up on the bunk, then began tightly braiding her long black hair into two thick braids, while Coletta and her tier cronies cackled and loudly talked shit about her.

When she was finished braiding her hair, she unzipped her jumper and tucked the ends down into the neck of her jumper, then zipped it back up as far as it would go. She was not sleeping in here with that broad tonight, or any other night.

She kneeled, and tightly tied the laces to her Reebok Lady Classics.

She took a deep breath then stood and reached for the radio that sat atop her desk.

"Soon as we lock in, I got somethin' for that ass," Coletta informed her girls, "for what she did to our girl, Snake."

"I know that's right," a dark-skinned inmate named Lacy agreed. She and Coletta were codefendants, both born-and-bred criminals, incarcerated this time for carjacking an elderly woman driving a Mercedes-Benz CLK at a stoplight. The elderly white woman had been snatched out of her car at knifepoint and thrown to the ground. She'd had a heart attack during the crime, and had been pronounced dead the moment the paramedics arrived on the scene. That, coupled with the carjacking, was what had given the two women a twenty-five-to-life sentence.

"*Shiiiit*, fuck waitin' for tonight," another inmate who went by the name Goldie hissed. "Let's hop on that ass now." She was serving an eight-year sentence for four counts of burglary and endangering the welfare of a minor. Each time she burglarized someone's home or car, she'd taken her three-year-old son with her while she committed her crimes.

"No. I'ma handle this one my—"

Heaven had leapt out of the cell with her arm pulled all the way back and hit Coletta in the face with the radio, sending her head snapping to the left. Blood spurted everywhere. It happened so fast that it had stunned them all.

Pumped with high levels of adrenaline, she beat Coletta in the face with the radio, not giving her a chance to recover from the blows. She'd split her lip, and beaten her eyes swollen. Immediately, pandemonium erupted on the tier as four of Coletta's girls jumped in to help their homie, punching and kicking Heaven to get her off of her.

The whole scene was being captured on camera, causing the two COs manning the control center to take bets as to which inmates would be rolled out on stretchers as they watched on. The housing officer immediately backed up against the wall and radioed into central control for backup. A code was called.

Heaven was beat about the back and head with homemade clubs and fists and feet. But that didn't stop her from taking her razor-sharp nails and nearly gouging Coletta's left eye out, while she used her free hand and continued to punch the side of her face in. And, unbeknownst to her, Coletta Evans and her girls were members of a notorious street gang.

And she'd just taken on all five of them.

FIVE

Breaking Up Somebody's Home...

Warden Kate was livid!

She fell back into her chair in an angry daze. She'd just viewed the playback video for 4 East. What she witnessed on that tape made her stomach churn. It was appalling. Goddamn embarrassing. Women fighting like wolves.

The melee up on the third tier suddenly incited several other fights down in the day space, causing inmates to brawl, fighting and throwing plastic chairs at each other. One of those chairs somehow managed to hit Officer O'Neal in the face, causing blood to spill from her nose. And the one woman whom she'd struggled to keep her eyes off of so that she could view the entire fiasco was that fucking inmate Lewis. Hadn't she just been released from solitary? And less than one hour later, her ass was already in the mix of more shit.

The warden snatched open her bottom drawer and reached under a pile of folders, pulling out her flask filled with—this time, Stoli. She unscrewed the cap and sighed. She knew inmate Lewis was going to become the proverbial thorn in her goddamn side, one she would have to pluck out before it caused her a shitload of grief.

On a tier of sixty-eight women, twenty of them had been slightly injured. And another three were severely wounded—one of those being Coletta Evans.

She'd been beaten nearly unconscious, the lens of her left eye severely clawed.

Good for her troublesome ass!

Truth was, the warden couldn't stand her loudmouth, thuggish ass. Trashy bitch. She knew she had to have been the sole instigator in all of this recent mess, as she always was. Yet, she couldn't prove it. And, the fact of the matter was, she was glad someone had finally stomped her ass real good. Still, for appearance's sake, she had to appear concerned for the wretched bitch's welfare.

She sighed.

Two of the prison's most aggressive inmates had been hospitalized in two separate incidents, both at the hands of inmate Lewis. She honestly thought she'd be more of a problem by trying to seduce her COs, or fuck one of the civilian staff.

Not by fighting.

But it appeared the feisty bitch liked violence more so than she did cock. Fighting was probably how she got her rocks off, the warden surmised. After all, she'd shot her own boyfriend in the back. Three times.

Mmph.

Then she probably fucked herself with the butt of her gun afterward, the warden mused as she pressed play again, and watched the video for a second time. She fast-forwarded certain parts of the tape to get to other sections. When she got to the part where the housing officer had gotten hit in the face with the chair, the warden paused it, slamming a hand down on her desk.

"This shit is unacceptable," she hissed, finally bringing the neck of her flask up to her lips. If these convicts wanted to kill each other, perhaps she should simply let them all out in the yard with their shanks and homemade clubs and have at it like the savages they were acting like.

Millions of dollars had been invested into rehabilitation programs for the women at Croydon Hill. From horticulture and dog grooming to the prison's tailoring and shoemaking and cosmetology programs—along with treatment and educational programs and support groups, these women were afforded the tools to get back into society and be productive citizens, if they so chose to be.

But most of these women would rather *jail* than do something constructive with their time. So obviously many of them didn't want to be rehabilitated, so why should she give a damn? Obviously, these uncivilized bitches were living proof that they didn't give a fuck, either. Well, so be it. But she'd be damned if she was going to let them tear down her prison with their savagery.

Fuck it all to hell.

They were a bunch of damn cavewomen.

She took a quick swig of her booze. Then another. Each time she swallowed the vodka, she felt a warming in the center of her chest spread through her breasts. She closed her eyes and took a third gulp, before opening her eyes and then quickly twisting the cap back on her flask. She would have loved to finish off what was inside, but she didn't need to be staggering out of her office.

It was too early in the day for that.

"Captain Caldolini is here to see you."

Startled, Warden Kate dropped her flask on her lap as her secretary Susan poked her head in the doorway as she pushed open her door—with*out* knocking.

That was a close call. What if she had been caught with her

coveted flask to her lips? Then what? She made a mental note to remember to lock her door, first, before she engaged in her nip fests.

She stared at Susan for a moment before she said anything. She simply adored her. She'd inherited her from the last warden, Mr. Duncan. And, thus far, she had proven to be quite efficient in her duties. She was hardworking and dependable. And she knew prison policy like the back of her hand.

Warden Kate valued that about her. But she didn't appreciate the fact that this old bitch couldn't remember to knock before she walked into her damn office.

Susan fingered the pearls around her neck. "Ma'am, did you hear me? Is everything all right?"

Warden Kate speared her with a sharp stare. "No. Susan," she finally said, discreetly slipping her flask from her lap to her opened drawer, then sliding it back under the pile of folders. "Everything isn't all right. For starters, you not knocking before walking into my damn office is a problem for me. How many times must I tell you this? Knock. Then wait to be told to enter. Understood?"

The sixty-six-year-old secretary was speechless for a second. She felt chastised like some five-year-old and she didn't like it one bit. Mr. Duncan had never spoken to her in this manner. She wasn't accustomed to such disrespect. She had a mind to tell her so. Then put in her retirement papers first thing in the morning. But she needed the income. If she didn't need the money to pay for her husband's nursing home expenses, she'd tell the warden to kiss her tired, wrinkled ass, then slam the door in her face.

"My apologies, Warden. It won't happen again."

"I hope not," she said sternly. She saw the look on Susan's face, and immediately felt bad for being so brusque, but she was not in the mood to apologize. Follow damn instructions. Knock first.

"You can send the captain in."

"Is there anything else?"

"No. That will be all," she said as she stood. She smoothed her hands down over the front of her tailored skirt, and eyed Susan as she walked out the door.

A sigh left her. She couldn't deal with her hurt damn feelings right now. At the moment, all she could manage to think of was Susan walking into her office and catching her taking a drink. But to smooth things over with her, she'd have flowers sent up from the prison's florist shop.

She quickly reached into her top drawer and popped two mints into her mouth. There were two things she loved about vodka: it was colorless and nearly odorless. So she could drink throughout the day without anyone being none the wiser. She'd have a shot, or two, in her morning Starbucks coffee, then a little splash or two in her afternoon tea. Followed by several sips from her flask midday, depending on how badly these barbarians—or her staff, worked her nerves.

She swirled her tongue around the candy as it began to dissolve in her mouth.

Seconds later, Captain Nicholas Caldolini walked in. His olive complexion and dark-black hair—that always seemed tousled, along with those dreamy gray eyes of his, made most women swoon. He'd even had his fair share of prison pussy back in his earlier days. But he'd given all that up once he'd been promoted to sergeant.

In his early forties, the six-two MIT grad and former football star played running back in the early nineties for the Broncos. Two seasons later, his career was cut short due to a knee injury. Now here he was. A captain. Thanks to nepotism, he'd moved up the ranks rather quickly. Nonetheless, heat bloomed in her cheeks at the sight of him. Warden Kate found him irresistibly handsome and sexy. "Good afternoon, Warden. I understand you wanted to see me?"

Mm, yes. Naked would be nice.

She walked around her desk, gesturing with her hand toward the chairs situated in front of her desk. "Please, sit." His scent flitted across her nostrils as she waited for him to take a seat. He smelled heavenly.

Her mouth watered—and not from the mints.

As he folded his muscular physique into one of the chairs, the warden hiked up her skirt a few inches, then sat on the edge of her desk, her body positioned toward him.

She swallowed. "You're looking good these days, Captain." Her eyes roamed over his body. "Are you hitting the gym harder than usual?"

He flushed. Was she flirting with him? God, he hoped so. He secretly had a thing for older women, especially mature black women.

He smiled at her, then said, "No more harder than usual. Thanks, though."

She crossed her legs, and allowed the heel of her Prada shoe to dangle from her foot as she slowly slid her tongue over her lips, momentarily contemplating getting up and locking her door, peeling out of her skirt, sliding back on her desk and spreading open her legs, offering him up some of her lonely pussy. It felt so wet and empty.

God, she wanted so desperately to have it stuff full with cock.

She swallowed back the knot of lust pooling in her mouth. "So tell me, Nicholas," she said, throwing formality straight out the window, getting directly to the point. "What the fuck is going on in my prison?"

He shifted in his seat, somewhat taken aback by her abrupt change in tone. He looked at her, but suddenly seemed to become distracted by the sight of her toned calves. He'd always thought the warden was exquisite-looking for a woman her age. Chic. Sophisticated. She was like a fine wine that kept getting better with age.

Good black definitely hadn't cracked where she was concerned.

The warden noticed his gaze on her legs and uncrossed them, then slyly spread them slightly open, hoping he'd catch a whiff of her nearly convulsing pussy.

If he'd ever make a move on her, she'd fuck his white dick in a heartbeat. She'd let him swirl his vanilla all in her chocolate. She didn't care how big it was, as long as it wasn't pink, she'd give it to him in all three holes.

He shifted in his chair again, then placed his elbows on the arms of his seat and steepled his fingers in front of his mouth as if he was contemplating the right words to say. Then after long hesitation, he finally answered her question.

"From what the reports say, Warden, inmate Lewis had approached the housing officer in an aggressive manner, demanding to be moved off Four East."

Her brow furrowed. "And does the reports mention *why* she wanted to be moved?"

He shook his head. "I don't believe the housing officer asked. It wasn't mentioned in any of the reports."

She tilted her head, giving him a blank look. "Perhaps there was a legitimate reason *why* the inmate—who is still relatively new in this facility—wanted to be immediately moved. But we wouldn't know that since the question hadn't been asked. Now would we? And why exactly was she moved over on Four East in the first place?"

4 East—the Zoo, as it was called—was for the more problematic women.

The captain slowly shook his head. "Warden, I have no clue."

"Well, I suggest you *get* a clue, Captain. I don't want a repeat of this happening again. Has anyone spoken to the inmate?"

He nodded. "Yes. I believe the hearing officer did."

"And what has he said?"

"That she was insolent. Uncooperative. And based on his investigations, she was the instigator."

What a crock of bullshit, she thought, biting the inside of her lip. She fought to keep from rolling her eyes. She knew from her days of working with Officer Alvin on the housing units how shady he could be. He'd had numerous write-ups over the years for embellishing the truth and for his use of excessive force. He was also known for being verbally abusive toward some of the women.

Officer Alvin was crooked then. And she'd bet her entire paycheck and a bottle of her best vodka that he was crooked now. She'd love nothing more than to nail his cock to a stake and burn his ass.

"She's being charged with inciting a riot," the captain added, pulling her from her thoughts.

Warden Kate slid off her desk, pulling her skirt down. "I need to know exactly what went on over in that housing unit, *before* she gets that sort of charge. And if that is the case, then several others should be charged accordingly as well."

"Understood," he said, standing to his feet.

The warden extended her hand. "Thanks for coming in."

He slid his large hand over hers as his hot eyes matched her gaze, and she almost forgot to breathe until he smiled at her. "I'll keep you posted on the investigation."

"Yes, you do that." She walked ahead of him toward the door, and felt his eyes on her ass. She was tempted to give him a sassy shake with each step, but she had to remind herself that she was still his superior, even if her cunt ached for the feel of his dick sliding in and out of her. Ole Stoli was going to get her in trouble if she didn't rein her hormones in. "And in the meantime, I'll be paying a visit to inmate Lewis."

"She'll be in the infirmary for at least another day, before she's taken down to solitary."

The warden pursed her lips. "Then I'll wait until she's settled in."

The captain nodded as she opened the door. "Before you go down to see her, ma'am. I'm sure you are aware that she's been known to flash officers and become highly sexual. From what I'm told, she can be quite brazen."

The warden's breath caught in her throat as she gripped the door's handle. "Well, if Miss Lewis insists on conducting herself in such lewdly ways, then I guess I should prepare myself for the show."

SIX

What's In It For Me . . . ?

"Lewis?" the CO called out as he peered inside her cell through the tiny, rectangular window, tapping on the thick glass with his Folgers key. He couldn't completely see her from where she was in her cell, but he knew she was there.

The CO was glad she hadn't been injured too badly after that bloody brawl she'd had over on 4 East. A few lumps on the back of the head and multiple bruises across her back had been all she'd encountered. After two days of being in the infirmary, she was released. Thank God.

He'd been happy to see her back in lockup. Back in the same cell she'd left only a week prior. Where she belonged. He'd missed seeing her sexy-ass prancing around in her cell nude, dick-teasing him, and anyone else who dared to look.

She was a dime-piece, a freaky one at that. And he wanted her to himself.

"Are you dressed?"

She opened her eyes.

Of course she was dressed.

Dressed in her beautiful skin. Her bare-nakedness. Baring her birthday suit for all to see as she had done during her last stay. She wasn't ashamed of her body. In fact, she loved it. And why shouldn't she? She'd worked hard to maintain it, after all.

"Open it," she heard someone else say on the other side of the door. It was a woman's voice.

"Are you sure you don't want me to open the trap?"

"No. I said open the door."

And then Heaven heard the key slide into the lock. The lock turned. The steel-plated door swung open. Then came two sets of feet—a man's in shiny black boots, and a woman's in gray designer pumps—entering her cell.

The woman's heels clicked against the cemented floor as she stepped further into the cell. Very expensive pumps, she knew.

The CO stood behind the woman and slyly licked his lips as the woman blinked at the sight before them. There was inmate Lewis in a handstand up against the wall, her legs spread wide in a V. Her pussy exposed; her breasts, plump and perky.

The warden cleared her throat. "Miss Lewis, I'm Warden Kate. I don't believe we've had the pleasure of being formally introduced."

"*And?*" she said nastily.

"I'd like to speak with you for a moment, if that is all right with you?"

Heaven's eyes rolled upward, taking in the upside-down view of the warden and CO. She wondered if she worn panties underneath that fancy skirt she had on.

She grunted. "*Mmph.* Where were you when I needed you a week ago?"

Warden Kate crossed her arms over her blouse. "Well, I don't know. Perhaps I was in a meeting. But I'm here now. So can we talk?"

Right leg came from off the wall, then she extended it forward. Mygod, she's limber, the warden thought as she watched in amazement, as the inmate's pussy seemed to open up like a budding flower. Sweet, pretty petals in full bloom.

"Well, Warden Kate—or whatever the hell your name is. You're a fistfight too late. Thanks to that CO bitch, I had to take matters into my own hands."

"Yes. About that," the warden replied, stepping further into the cell. "I'd like to talk more in depth about the incidents that led up to Three East turning into a scene for the next *Hunger Games*."

"There's nothing to talk about. I asked to be moved. That CO bitch told me—and I quote—'get the fuck away from my desk' and I asked to speak to someone above her pay grade. And, then the bitch tried to shine on me."

"You're speaking of Officer O'Neal?"

"Yeah, *that* bitch! I came at her like a woman, and instead of that jagged-tooth bitch doing her damn job, she tried to be messy. That ho should have gotten more than a chair to her face. I hope the shit broke her nose."

The warden decided to let her vent.

"I'm done talking. Tell that GED-having bitch I said, next time an inmate comes to her with a problem to handle her business like a professional. If she doesn't like her job, then she shouldn't be here. That lazy bitch probably makes close to six-figures to sit on her ass and push buttons. The least she could do is, do her damn job with a smile."

"You're absolutely right," the warden agreed. "I will personally look into it."

"Uh-huh. Sure you will."

Right leg back against the wall, left leg off the wall. She extended it into a half split. The CO wiped beads of sweat from his forehead. The erotic sight made the air in the cell hotter than it already was.

"Why is it so hot in here?" the warden asked, giving the CO a dissatisfied look. Not once did she address him by his name, but he knew better than anyone that the warden was not one to toy with.

He shrugged. "I'm not sure, Warden." He suddenly felt sweat slide down his back. "I think it's the heat from the vents." *Yeah. The heat sliding from the slit of her sweet pussy.*

"*Whaat?*" she shrieked, glaring at him from over her shoulder. "In the middle of *May?* Are you kidding me? Are all the cells hot like this?"

"I believe so," he answered cautiously. He braced himself in the event she flew into one of her fits.

"I want maintenance down here, *now*. And I want this addressed immediately. This is unacceptable."

He let out a sigh of relief that she hadn't flown into a rage. "Yes, Warden. I'll put in a work order today."

"No. You'll call them and tell them *I* said to get down here. Not now, *right* now."

Nothing more needed to be said. Seconds later, he was pulling his radio from its holder, and radioing in for maintenance. The warden waited for him to finish, then returned her attention back to the naked beauty in front of her.

"Miss Lewis, do you mind coming from off the wall, and perhaps slipping into your jumper while you and I talk." She motioned for the CO to step out of the cell to give them more privacy. He obliged, but not before taking another sly glance at Heaven, his gaze zooming in on her beautiful, hairy pussy.

Heaven stifled a snicker. *I bet his dick is so hard I could crack walnuts with it.*

He shifted his gaze before the warden caught him, and reluctantly stepped out of the cell, standing by the door in case something popped off. He'd hate to have to yank the inmate up if she jumped up in the warden's face. He didn't want to have to choose one over the other. But he would.

It was his job.

His obligation.

"CO!" another inmate called out from cell four.

"*What*, Malone?" he snapped, annoyed. He couldn't stand her whiny ass.

"I need for you to tell the warden I wanna see her next."

Bitch, go sit your trick-ass down somewhere. "Yeah, a'ight," he replied. But he wasn't telling the warden shit. Fuck her. He saw the tape. Saw how she and her punk-ass homies jumped his future girl. But she'd put in that work. Beat the fuck out of Evan's ass.

Corny-ass hoodrats.

He peered inside the cell to check in on the warden. Lewis had come from off the wall and was now sitting on her bed, a sheet wrapped around her body.

"This is what I'm going to need from you, Miss Lewis," the warden stated. "I need you to stop all this violence."

"Tell me, Warden. Do you like pussy?"

Unflinching, the warden kept her eyes on her. "Miss Lewis, crudity is not acceptable. So if you're looking to get a rouse out of me, you're going to be sadly disappointed. You're much better than this."

"Lady, you don't know shit about me," Heaven snapped. Her tone was low, her voice calm. But her icy glare spoke volumes. "So you can kiss my ass with the rest of these bitches."

"Language, young lady," the warden calmly said, unfazed by her profanity. "I'm here to help you."

Heaven frowned. "Unless you have a dick underneath that skirt of yours, you can't help *me* with shit. Now do us both a favor, love, and see yourself out of my cell."

The warden didn't budge.

Heaven stared at her, long and hard. "Did you hear me? I said get the fuck out."

The warden didn't blink. "Miss Lewis, I'm not your enemy. And—"

"You're not my friend, either, so"—she flicked her hand at her—"go back to wherever the hell you came from. I'm good."

The CO reentered the cell, not liking how she was coming at the warden. His jaw tightened. He kept his mouth shut, though. After all her years as a corrections officer, he knew the warden could still handle herself, if she had to.

The warden sighed. "Though I am certain you didn't start what happened over on Three East . . ."

"You're right. I didn't. I *finished* it. That ho came at me from the moment I stepped in that nasty-ass cell. Trying to antagonize me. So I snatched her scalp. And beat her ass."

"That as it may be. You practically beat her into a coma."

"Good. Next time, it'll be the grave. I'm not here to be fucked with. I'm here to do my time and get the hell home. Period."

"And I'd like nothing more than to see that happen," the warden assured her. "However, for now, you'll be serving ninety days for your role in the violence that occurred over on Three East. Afterwards, when you're released at the end of August, you can start with a clean slate. But I am going to need for you to focus more on programming so that you can eventually return back to your community as a productive member of society, instead of being a problem in *my* prison."

Heaven narrowed her eyes at the warden. There was something remarkably familiar in her eyes. She'd seen it before. Many times.

"Lady, I'm *already* productive," she spat. "So maybe you should focus on *your* own problem, instead of focusing on *me*—or my return to society. Because, trust me, hon. I am no career criminal."

"Which is why I want you to program."

Heaven scoffed. "Maybe *you* should program."

The warden blinked. "Excuse me?"

"You heard me." She ran a hand through her hair. "I am *not* your problem. *You* are." She got up from her bunk and dropped her sheet. Then boldly sashayed her bare ass over to the far wall, looking out the tiny cell window.

The warden and the CO both willed their eyes from sliding a caressing gaze over Heaven's voluptuous ass.

The CO swallowed. He needed to shake the thoughts of him sliding his dick into her body from his mind. The last thing he needed was a hard dick in front of the warden. He took a step back, then shifted his eyes to the chipped paint on one of the walls.

The warden diverted her stare to the back of Heaven's head, folding her arms. *This rude bitch!* She pushed out a breath. "Tell me, Miss Lewis. What is it I can do for you to help you acclimate to prison life?"

"You see this?" she asked crudely as she faced the warden and pointed to her crotch. The warden gave her a blank stare. "It's hairy, lady. I want a razor and some cream so I can shave it."

The warden turned back and looked at the CO. "Make sure she gets what she's asked for." He nodded, silently disappointed that she wanted to shave her curly bush. He wanted to run his fingers through her pubic hairs before dipping them inside her creamy heat.

"I'll take care of it," he said, quickly shifting his eyes from the beautiful thatch of hair between her legs.

The warden turned her attention back to Heaven. "There. You'll have it here in time for this evening's shower. Anything else?"

Heaven pursed her lips, turning back to the window and staring out at the rosebushes that lined the edges of the perimeter, blocking her view from anything else.

She loved roses. She'd grown up all around them. Her father had an array of colorful rosebushes planted all over their neatly manicured yard in the suburbs of Northern New Jersey, where she'd lived most of her childhood. Clusters of red and pink and yellow rosebushes always scented the air. And, now seeing them outside her window, suddenly reminded her of her deceased father, Lincoln Lewis.

He'd died a little over six years ago. And she hadn't quite gotten over it. His death had been a shock. One moment he was alive; the next moment he was gone. He'd gotten behind the wheel of his Suburban and ran into a telephone pole en route to Loew's to pick up more rosebushes.

He'd had a heart attack behind the wheel.

Her whole family had been devastated. But his death had hit Heaven the hardest. He'd been her everything. He'd practically raised her and her three brothers singlehandedly, while working as a plant supervisor for Anheuser-Busch brewery. He, along with her overly protective brothers, doted on her, spoiling her rotten.

Their mother, Vivian, however, spent most of her days in a fog, and her nights passed out on the sofa, drooling. Other times, lying in her vomit.

As a young girl, she'd watched her father and brothers clean her up, then roll her into bed. For years, Vivian had hidden her—

Heaven turned her head and blinked the warden back into view. And then . . .

Suddenly, she knew what it was, that familiar look.

She saw . . . *her*.

"Yeah, Warden. One more thing," Heaven finally said.

"What is it, Miss Lewis?"

"Vodka, right?"

The warden blinked. "Excuse me?"

"Your drink of choice," she said. "It's vodka, right?"

The warden's eyes hid their surprise; she kept her composure.

"I have no idea what you are talking about."

Heaven gave her a pitiful look. "They never do. Denial is a terrible thing, Warden."

The CO shifted his weight from one foot to the other, as the warden stood there, eyeing her, her jaw twitching.

And in that moment, Heaven saw her mother's reflection staring back at her. Hidden behind expensive cosmetics and her designer suit, she saw the warden for who she was. She saw the woman beneath the mask.

A closeted-alcoholic.

Just as her own mother had been.

SEVEN

After The Candles Burn...

Shortly after the eleven-to-seven shift captain assigned to solitary made his one a.m. rounds, then signed the black logbook, he left the unit.

The CO waited another thirty minutes, then quietly made his way toward cell twelve. At the far end, tucked in the corner. He'd come in early for overtime.

And some pussy.

It'd been almost three days since he'd been inside her clutching heat, and he was practically going out of his mind with want. His dick didn't discriminate. He'd had his share of many flavors, attached to all types of women—white, Asian, Latina, Caribbean, German, Italian, Moroccan, Egyptian, French, and the notches on his bed-posts went on.

Good pussy was good pussy no matter who it belonged to. But *her* pussy was top-notch. In fact, it was banging. Even with a condom on, the shit was superb. Tight, juicy, deep, hot as fuck. Not many broads had been able to make his toes curl by just fucking. Yet, she'd managed to—not only curl his toes, but make his vision blur every time he bust inside her. Every time he fucked her, his release was an endless stream of nut, thick and hot, flooding his condom to capacity.

She undid him. Every time. Her whispers, her gasps, her low moans, begging for him to fuck her, harder, deeper, rang in his ears long after he was done with his shift.

He couldn't deny how he loved the way her body spasmed around him. Loved the way she bit his neck; clawed at his back, his ass, marking her territory. Fuck if he didn't want to know how she felt raw.

And tonight—if she'd let him, he would.

His heart pounded as his breath escaped in an excited rush. He could literally see her on her bunk, her legs spread wide, her sweet cunt already glistening with desire.

He knew the officers in central control, and the ones in the small control room outside of solitary were too busy doing their own dirt, to keep up with what was about to go down. He wouldn't be missed for at least another half hour. And he'd have his radio on low in case someone needed to reach him.

He'd already made it his business to sneakily keep her cell door unlocked when he'd had her out last for her shower, before the lights went out. He'd walked her back to her cell, then shut the door, sliding his key into its lock and pretending as if he were locking it.

The captain diligently came through to complete his rounds, but he never checked any of the cell doors. He trusted the CO to keep things running smoothly and all inmates properly secured in their cells.

He made another quick round on the unit, door-to-door, peeking in to see which inmates were still up. Everyone was in her bed, except Goldie Malone's fucking gang-banging ass.

Nosy bitch.

He shook his head, as he finished his rounds, then quietly entered his prison beauty's cell. His dick began to thicken and stretch the minute he slipped inside.

A predatory gleam flickered in his eyes as his gaze raked over her beautiful body. He couldn't wait to ravish her, with his mouth, his fingers and finally . . . with his dick.

"Come eat my pussy," she whispered, spreading her legs as he made his way toward her bunk. She pulled open her labia, sliding her fingers along her seam, smearing her juices over her clit and swollen lips.

She'd waited patiently all evening for this moment. The anticipation had her seeping with arousal. Her pussy became slicker by the moment waiting, waiting . . . waiting.

He'd been sneaking in her cell, almost every other night for the last two weeks, starting with the night after the warden had come to her cell. The purpose of that drunk bitch's visit was still a mystery to her, but her gut told her it wouldn't be the last time she and the good ole warden would be seeing each other.

Perhaps she'd been too curt with her. She should have been a more gracious hostess, maybe offer her a taste of her pussy as a little welcome treat.

Yeah okay.

Bitch bye.

She shook thoughts of her visit from the warden out of her head. She needed her attention—*all* of it—on the man quickly stepping out of his uniform pants. His dick sprung free as he tugged off his boxers and crawled onto her tiny bunk, between her legs.

She heard him suck in his breath as her flesh greeted him.

No words were needed.

In silence, he gripped her hips, then slid his hands around to her ass and cupped the globes in his big, warm palms. His head dipped and he ran the tip of his tongue over her clit, then French-kissed her pussy. He licked and licked and licked, lapping at her slit as if it was a delicious treat.

Oh and it was.

Holy fucking hell, it was.

Hot silk.

That's what her pussy was to him.

"So beautiful," he breathed out. Then his tongue swiped across her slit and upward to her clit.

"*Mmm*, yes," she murmured. "Let me come on your tongue."

He licked over her folds, tasting more of her. His tongue slid greedily back inside her body, and he groaned against her flesh as she clutched, her walls squeezing his tongue, her orgasm rippling out in tiny waves.

Her nectar filled his mouth, and coated his lips. Goddamn. She tasted delicious. She was warm and sweet, like honey. He sucked her long and hard, his mouth swiping over her cunt, from her slit to her swollen clit. Savoring all of her.

She moaned as he lapped between her folds, sweetly whispering over her clit. That felt delicious, his tongue on her clit, but still, she wanted more. Needed more. Her pussy was so ready for him. And, yet, she craved a taste of her juices, sucking on his lips, her tongue swirling over and around his.

"God, yes," she breathed out low. "Yes. Yes. *Mmm* . . ."

And then her hands were on his head; her fingernails raking over his waves, caressing his scalp.

He looked up at her. Her eyes were alit with fire and fixated on him, burning through his core. He loved how wild and uninhibited she was. So wanton, so damn freaky.

Precum trickled from the head of his dick, then glided down his shaft, slowly dripping onto her sheets. He felt his skin heat, felt it through his balls, which caused him to grind his hips into her thin mattress, his dick throbbing and swelling to maximum capacity.

He inhaled, wanting to breathe every part of her in. He wanted to wrap himself up into everything she was, connect to her soul, and become one.

Need.

Want.

His entire body hummed with it.

He reached up and cupped her breasts, his thumbs scraped across her nipples as he lightly bit into her clit. Tugged it between his lips. Then dipped inside. His tongue licked around her lower walls, and she gasped low in the back of her throat, her back arching and her pelvis thrusting upward.

"*Mmm*, yes. Fuck me. Ooh, yes . . . fuck me."

He sucked on her clit harder, his tongue sliding in and out of her juices. He groaned low as he absorbed her flavor melting on his tongue. He relished it with every swipe of his tongue. Just the taste of her had him leaking loads more of precum, and his dick harder than steel.

His hands slid back down her body, until they rested on top of her legs. He spread her thighs wider and then gently sucked her clit back into his mouth. His tongue moved rhythmically over her nub.

Yes, yes, right there, right there. Her pelvis tightened.

Almost . . . almost.

She was so close. God, so close.

She gasped.

Two fingers slid into her honeyed folds, and he stroked through her wet heat, spreading juices from her slit up to her clit. Then plunging them back inside. He watched himself fuck her that way, fingers gliding wetly and quickly in and out, in and out—

then he extracted them from her greedy cunt and lifted them to his mouth and sucked them clean.

"So good, baby," he rasped, thrusting his fingers back inside her. And then came his mouth, kissing her pussy all over again, sucking on her clit, this time harder, as his tongue slid back inside, fucking her slow and sensual, causing her ass to come off the bed.

Time was ticking, but he needed for her to get hers—all of hers, before he got his. He wanted to leave her spent, her head spinning long after he was gone. She writhed beneath him, pleasure searing through her pussy. She felt a scream catch in the back of her throat.

Sweet desire flowed through her veins as his middle finger caressed the inside of her cunt, while his thumb massaged her throbbing clit. Then he pushed further, finding her G-spot, causing her body to hum and shudder. Her nipples tightened, sending little tingles of pleasure ricocheting through her body. She came around his fingers.

He pulled out of her quaking body, wet fingers trailing from her pussy to the crack of her ass. And then he was kissing and licking her there, too.

And she loved it. God, she did.

Whispered sounds of pleasure escaped with each breath. No one had ever been *this* attentive, *this* loving with his mouth. She moaned and twisted restlessly, her body burning as his fingers danced over her skin, up her body, until they were cupping her breasts again.

Her juices splashed in his mouth, stealing his breath.

She let out a low whimper, more desire roiling over and around her clit, her breasts, the tender swell of her folds.

He was hard and aching, so aroused that his body nearly shook. His dick throbbed angrily, frustrated, that he had not, yet, sunk himself into her pool of juices. He pulled his fingers from her body as she softly begged him to fuck her.

"You ready for me to fuck you, baby?"

"Yes," she said breathlessly. "Where's your condom?"

"I'm clean, baby. Aren't you?"

Her eyes flared open. "Condom," she said sternly. "Or no pussy."

Shit. So much for going in raw. "You got that, baby."

"Then *fuck* me already," she hissed.

EIGHT

Truth Hurts . . .

That bitch. That self-righteous convict, Warden Kate thought as she burned a hole into her computer screen at the face staring back at her. It'd been close to a month since she'd seen inmate Lewis down in lockup. And, yet, her questioning words still rang loudly in her ears. How dare she try to insinuate she was an alcoholic?

She reached for her flask and gingerly took a sip.

"Yes, bitch," she hissed. "It's *vodka.*"

Who the fuck was that felon bitch to judge *her?*

She wasn't a drunk. She was a responsible woman who simply liked having a few cocktail sips throughout the day. Then if she wanted to, she'd have a shot or two before bed from the bottle she kept hidden in her nightstand, or the one in the back of her shoe closet.

That didn't make her a damn alcoholic. She could stop anytime she wanted to, she reasoned in her mind. But she didn't want to. She loved a good damn drink. Period.

Still, how had that little twat known?

"*Vodka, right?*"

She shuddered. Then her mind rolled back to images of Lewis in that sexy handstand, naked, baring her hairy cunt—the slightest hint of her mocha-colored flesh filled with a pinkish center—on display. God, it had been a sight to behold.

"*Tell me, Warden. You like pussy?*"

Subtle she was not. Yet, there was something refreshing about the inmate's bold, saucy attitude. The thought caused a slow ache to roil in the center of the warden's sex.

God, she'd love to be smothered in that wild, unruly cunt; her face glazed with her juices. Her mouth . . .

She swallowed. The tip of her tongue slid out of her mouth. She'd never licked a woman's snatch before, never even kissed one. But she found herself growing consumed with curiosity. Obsessed with sex. Any kind.

Twosomes, threesomes, foursomes—hell, a whole gaggle of men *and* women—she didn't care. She simply wanted sex. Wanted to be fucked the way she'd been seeing on those online porn sites.

Drinking, watching porn, and fucking herself to sleep had become her favorite pastimes. She was so lonely. She craved human contact. Yearned to know the taste of a woman. Ached for the stretch and burn of a dick bigger than what her husband had. He was eight inches hard. She sadly admitted to herself that she missed him fucking her. He'd always felt so good inside her. Good sex was always what they'd shared.

But *fuck* him now.

Now she wanted new dick. New experiences.

The ringing phone interrupted the dark desires floating around in her head, and she reached gratefully for it.

"Warden Kate here," she greeted.

"What time will you be home tonight?"

No *hello, hey* . . . nothing. The warden frowned. "Why?" she asked curtly.

"We have Reggie's retirement party tonight. Remember?"

What the hell? No, she didn't remember. Though she adored her brother-in-law, Reginald, she'd actually put it in the back of her cluttered mind. He was retiring from the New York City Police Department after thirty years of service, and his wife and children were throwing him an elaborate dinner party at TAO—an upscale subterranean restaurant in the Chelsea district of New York.

Midtown traffic would be hell. God, she hated being stuck in traffic. She almost hoped he'd go ahead without her. Never knowing what side of his bed he'd roll out of, she never knew what he'd do from one day to the next. Hell, she wouldn't have been surprised— or upset, if he had taken his floozy with him in place of her.

"Oh. That's tonight?"

"Yes, it's *tonight*," he replied, irritation coloring his tone. "I told you this over a week ago, Lee."

She bit her lip and squeezed the receiver of the phone. "I *know* you did," she snapped tersely. "It slipped my mind."

He huffed. "Yeah, like everything else."

She blinked. "And what exactly is *that* supposed to mean, Othello?"

He sighed. "Look. I didn't call to argue with you. I only want to know what time you'll be home? I don't want to be all night getting there."

She had the mind to tell him to go fuck himself. That she wouldn't be coming home. Instead, she glanced at the time. It was a little after one in the afternoon. "What time is his party?"

"Six-thirty."

Oh, great. Now she'd have to rush to do something with her hair, and figure out what to wear. Damn him. Why hadn't he reminded her last night when he'd come home from God knows where?

She looked at the flask on her desk. Then rolled her eyes.

"I'll be home by four."

"Do you at least know what you'll be wearing? I don't want you taking all night to get ready."

Her nose flared. "Then how about I meet you there, Othello. This way you won't have to worry about having me on some damn time clock. God forbid I make you late for the party, Mister Always First To Show Up For Every Damn Thing."

He hung up on her.

Bastard!

She snatched her flask from the desk.

"Vodka, right?"

She quickly tightened the cap and tossed it back in her desk drawer. But then she retrieved the flask again, unscrewing the cap and taking two more quick sips.

She wasn't a damn—

The knock on her door forced her to quickly screw the silver cap back on her flask, and tuck it back in her drawer. She slid the drawer shut, then reached for two mints, popping them in her mouth.

The person on the other side of the door waited several seconds, then knocked again, louder this time. "Warden?"

"Yes? Come in," she said, smoothing a hand over her arm as the sweet mints dissolved in her mouth.

The door handle jiggled.

Damn it.

She blew out her breath and stood, walking from around her desk toward the door. She opened it, and there stood—taking up the entire doorway—Captain Caldolini.

Where the hell was Susan?

He smiled, and his gray eyes twinkled at her. "Am I interrupting anything? Susan wasn't at her desk, so I took a chance to see if you were in."

The warden smoothed a hand along the side of her slicked back hair that she'd worn pulled back into an elegant bun. Oh how matronly she now felt standing here under his gaze.

She took a step back. "No, no. You're not interrupting anything, Captain. I was just going through some files." Her tongue clung to the remnants of her mints as the lie rolled from her lips. "Please. Come in."

He shut the door behind them, then followed behind her, his eyes on the sway of her hips.

She waited for him to have a seat, then asked, "So to what do I owe the pleasure of this visit, Captain?" She glanced at her desk calendar. "Did we have a meeting scheduled for this afternoon?"

He shifted in his chair as he chased images of her body from his mind. He was tired of wondering, imagining. He wanted, needed to know for himself how soft and feminine she was beneath those damn clothes.

A warm feeling skittered over her skin as she took a seat behind her desk. She knew he'd been eyeballing her ass, and she felt a fresh coat of desire slide over her cunt. It felt good, damn good, to be noticed, perhaps even desired by someone.

The corners of his mouth quirked up in a sly smile. "No, ma'am. No meeting."

Her sumptuously painted lips rounded into an "O." She crossed her legs under her desk. "Well, if there isn't a meeting, is there something you wish to speak to me about?"

He leaned forward in his seat. "Actually, Warden." He cleared his throat. "There is." He thrust a large hand into his hair, and she found herself grinning at the disheveled image. He was so rough, so rugged, so damn masculine and sexy.

She cursed the flood of heat sweeping through her body. God help her. She'd fuck him right here. No questions asked.

She eyed him curiously. "Well, Captain. What is it?"

"Well, ma'am. Forgive me for my forwardness. But I've noticed on several occasions that you haven't worn your wedding band to work in a while. And I was wondering . . ."

Self-consciously, she slid her right hand over her left, and raised her brow in silent question.

"I don't mean to pry. But I was wondering . . ."

She swallowed, feeling her cheeks heat as she intently focused her curious gaze on him.

"I mean." He scrubbed a hand over his face. "What I'm about to ask you is so inappropriate, I know. And if you throw me out of your office, I'd understand. But . . ." He shook his head. "Hell, ma'am. I was wondering, if you'd like to have dinner one night this week with me? I'd love to spend some time alone with you."

Her heart thudded in her chest. This couldn't possibly be happening. Not here. Not in her office. Jesus, God, was this man offering her a night of good fucking? Did he want to slide his dick into her pussy? Give her a night of hot, slow lovemaking?

Lee Kateman, stop this, she admonished. *It's only damn dinner.*

She blinked and refocused and saw that he was staring at her, waiting for a response. And another wave of heat crept up her neck.

"That was way out of line," he said apologetically, rising to his feet. "I knew I shouldn't have come. Forgive me, Warden. I knew this was a bad idea. I hadn't meant to offend you."

She leaned forward, giving him a slight glimpse of the mocha-chocolate mounds of her breasts, plumped up by the bra she wore, and a tortured groan lodged in his chest. He wanted to lick her there, kiss her there, slide his dick in between the delicate flesh and fuck her there.

Her face scrunched in what looked like dismay, and she shook her head a bit. Oh, hell. He'd gone too far. Shit. Perhaps he should have kept his fantasy of spending time with her to himself.

Her nipples tautened, and the muscles in her pussy tightened. She took a steadying breath, then pushed out, "Captain. I think you should leave my office"—she stood and walked around her desk toward the door—"before I forget I'm the warden and do something naughty. But tomorrow night"—she glanced back, catching his gaze on her ass again—"say, seven o'clock. I can be as naughty as I want to be."

His smile widened as his eyes burned into her, concentrating on her lips.

God, he wanted to kiss her, taste her lips. And she wanted him to.

In wet panties, her lips parted and she sucked in a minty breath as his finger trailed down her cheek. "I'm counting on it, Warden."

She swung open her office door and ushered him out. When she shut it behind him, she sagged against the door and closed her eyes, reaching for her aching breasts and pinching the tingling heat knotting around her nipples.

A groan escaped her as she hiked up her skirt.

NINE

The Saga Continues . . .

Heaven yawned and stretched sore muscles. She'd been doing calisthenics for most of the night as she'd been doing most nights if she wasn't getting that good CO cock. Holy fuck, yes!

Every chance he got, he was creeping into her cell fucking loose her pussy juices.

Mmm. She momentarily closed her eyes, relishing the thought of being dicked down almost every other night. All she needed was her television and commissary and she'd be fine.

She yawned again. She was exhausted. She hadn't been able to get much sleep last night, thanks to several rowdy bitches spending most of the night, well into the wee hours of the morning, yelling out their doors, while others banged on theirs.

She stretched again, kicking off the rough sheet that had covered her body. These fucking sheets felt like sandpaper across her skin, as did the toilet paper she had to use to wipe her ass.

A twinge of sadness nipped at her as she thought about all the simple things in life she'd taken for granted, like wiping her ass on cottony-soft toilet paper and the luxury of being cocooned beneath silk sheets.

She missed her bed. Her shower. Oh, God, yes, her shower, with the nine pulsating jets that flowed over her body in all directions. These prison showerheads here were worthless pieces of shit. But, at least she didn't have to worry about sharing the shower with a bunch of other women while in lockup.

She guessed that was one of the perks of being in solitary. She got to shit and shower in peace.

She missed her kitchen. The privilege of cooking what she wanted, when she wanted. Her stomach rumbled. Oh what she wouldn't do for a plate of scrambled eggs with Pepper Jack cheese, and several slices of turkey bacon right now.

She closed her eyes, sighing. Eighty-five percent of ten years equaled one hundred and two months.

Her heart panged in her chest. Eight-and-a-half fucking years of her life would be spent behind these concrete walls. That's if she were granted parole. So far, the way things were going, she'd end up doing her whole ten years behind bars.

Two violent fights in less than a year surely didn't make for an ideal parolee. She cursed under her breath, realization finally setting in. She needed to figure out a way to stay out of the crosshairs of crazy bitches. Or learn how to fuck them up, when they came at her sideways, without getting caught.

Being fake and kissing ass would never work for her. But, she was socially competent enough to manipulate others into getting what she wanted. The problem was, she'd made a lot of enemies in such a short time. And she already racked up numerous "keep separates" because she had so many hoes wanting a piece of her for her assaults on Snake and that Coletta bitch.

She was quickly learning that there were prison rules, and then there were the unwritten rules, rules that if broken could get your head bashed in, or worse—killed.

She hadn't come to prison to only end up leaving out in a body bag. No, no, no. These bitches were ruthless. She'd have to watch her back at every turn now, thanks to all her new haters.

She groaned inwardly.

There was nothing she could do about that fact, now. She'd already made a host of enemies and tarnished her prison record. And she damn sure didn't give a shit about any of these females hating on her. What else was new?

Yeah, she was beautiful and articulate and had a banging body. And? Since when did that become a crime? Obviously, since the moment she'd stepped onto the prison grounds. Well, these hoes had another thing coming if they thought she was easy prey. She wasn't a punk and she damn sure wasn't going to be punked.

Period.

Still, she knew she needed to do better, move better. Not let emotions dictate her actions. What she really needed was a contingency plan; some allies, and some sort of scheme to help her adapt to her current situation; to survive, in this hellhole.

But who, what, and how?

Her greatest fear was ending up broke, like some of these females in here. Having to beg for scraps, or sell her ass for a bar of soap and two soups.

Please God.

She had to wonder if coming in and out of lockup was going to become her MO during her whole prison stay. No, no. Hell no!

Well, shit. She hoped not.

She slid her hand beneath her pillow and pulled out the condom wrapper she'd held on to from three nights ago. She pursed her lips. She wasn't sure what she'd do with it. But one thing she knew for sure: it was surely a gift of sorts.

Unfortunately, she knew she couldn't leave it in her cell for COs to find, if and when they felt the need to run up in here and ransack it while she was in the shower, although she had nothing but her bra and panties, a pink jumper and her shower shoes in her cell.

Still, they'd come barging in at will and tearing up her bed and flipping over her mattress just for the hell of it. Miserable fucks.

She slid her hand between her legs and slowly rubbed her clit until she felt herself becoming wet. She licked the tips of her fingers, then continued swirling them over and around her protruding nub until she brought herself to orgasm.

When the rippling in her belly subsided, she rolled the condom wrapper, then slid it inside her pussy, her safe place, her personal locker for all things valuable.

She lay in her bunk, on her hard-ass mattress, for several long minutes afterward—thinking.

For some reason, Warden Kate came to mind. And she found herself wondering if she'd been too harsh toward her when she'd visited. She definitely hadn't won any congenial awards for her presentation. All she wanted to do was do her time, and get back to her life.

Still, a part of her toyed with the idea of requesting to see the warden so that she could apologize to her for the way she'd spoken to her. The warden had done her no harm, so she hadn't deserved her shitty attitude. The least she could have done was be civil.

But, if she were being honest with herself, seeing the warden had somehow drudged up old feelings and reopened wounds she thought she'd healed from. Staring in the warden's eyes and seeing her own mother staring back at her caused her stomach to churn. And she'd become pissed—and saddened—at that fact.

She hadn't thought of Vivian in years, not since her death almost eighteen years ago. Then in waltzes the warden in all of her fanciness, and there stood her mother all over again.

They'd never been close. Heaven grew up feeling abandoned

by her. And when she'd finally come of age to realize that it wasn't debilitating migraines her mother suffered from all those years that had kept her nearly incapacitated but hangovers, she'd been angry with her. Feeling betrayed and lied to. She felt as if her mother had chosen her drinking over *her.*

Her mother had hidden her drinking very well during the early part of her childhood. The falling down the stairs and breaking her ankle and even when she'd swerved off the road and hit a tree with young Heaven sitting in the backseat, it was due to her so-called migraines. Always, always, blaming shit on migraines she never had.

Heaven was fifteen when she'd found her mother's stash of vodka. Different brands and bottle sizes, stuffed beneath expensive panty-and-bra sets, hidden in shoeboxes, under her king-size bed—she had a bottle hidden in practically every room in their two-story brick home.

She'd been either *too* drunk or *too* hung over to pay attention to any of them, and Heaven resented her for it. Considered her worthless.

When the booze finally ate through her liver, Heaven was seventeen. Her mother died three days after her eighteenth birthday. She hadn't given a damn about trying to understand the disease of addiction. All she knew—and understood—was that Vivian Lewis was a fucking closeted drunk.

And she hated her for it.

Unlike the grief she'd suffered at the loss of her father, Heaven had felt nothing but relief when her mother had passed. Seeing her mother in her casket, her skin all weathered-looking and her face sunken in, she felt calmer than she'd ever been. The years of being neglected by her were finally over. And Heaven was glad.

While her father and brothers cried their eyes out, Heaven remained dry-eyed. She hadn't felt the loss or the pain everyone else felt. If anything, she felt a sudden sense of calm and relief.

As far as she was concerned, her years of suffering through her mother's silent drinking were finally over. And, long after her mother's departing, she rarely talked about her, or reminisced because what she remembered of her mother weren't good memories. So she avoided ever talking about Vivian Lewis.

And, now, here she was, linking the warden to her own mother.

She shuddered, then after several more seconds, she finally swung her legs over the side of the metal bunk and sat there. She glanced around her bare cell. *This is some fucking bullshit*, she thought as she stood buck-ass naked, and stretched. Just then she heard keys.

"Lewis," the CO called out. "Do you want to come out for your hour now, or wait until second shift?"

It was Officer Ferguson. She was a beautiful forty-two-year-old, olive-skinned woman with the prettiest doe-shaped brown eyes Heaven had ever seen. She was a very shapely woman with a big ass (rumor had it her ass was fake), which she always kept stuffed in extra-tight uniform pants. But she was one of the few female COs she liked. She was fair, and she didn't believe in doing inmates dirty. However, she didn't take any shit, either.

Out of respect for her, Heaven reached for her sheet and covered herself, then walked over to her cell door. "No. I'll take it now. I really need to shower."

"Okay. Let me finish my rounds, then I'll come back for you."

"I'm not going anywhere," she said lightly.

Heaven quickly slipped into her jumper, then stood by her door and waited. Ten minutes later, the CO returned and opened her door.

"Lewis, don't let these bitches in here get you caught up in any more of their shit," the CO warned as she walked her toward the showers. "They don't care if you don't ever get out, because a lot of these females are going to end up right back here the moment they get released."

Heaven nodded knowingly. "Trust me. I'm not thinking about any of these crazy broads. I'm trying to get home; that's it."

The CO gave her a side-eye glance. "Then you need to get focused."

"I plan—"

"Yeah, bitch. I see you!" the inmate Goldie Malone yelled from behind her door the minute she saw Heaven walk past her cell. She began banging on the thick glass window. "This shit ain't over, boo-boo. Trust."

Another one of Goldie's cronies began banging on her door too. "Hahahahaha! There go that uppity bitch. Yeah, we see you, ho. You dog food, boo! I put that on everything, *TRICK!*"

"Ohmygod!" someone else yelled out. "Why that bitch look like she trying out for *The Bachelorette*?"

"I bet that bitch suck a mean dick," Goldie yelled out.

Everyone on the unit laughed, except Heaven and Officer Ferguson.

"Ignore them, Lewis."

Heaven undid her ponytail, then shook her hair, letting it tumble down past her shoulders. "I'm not thinking about them," she assured the CO.

"Fuck that stuck-up bitch," another female stated. "But I'd smear this good-good all up over her face. Use her mouth as a tampon."

Lots of laughter.

Heaven frowned.

"All right, ladies. Enough," the CO warned.

"Hey, Goldie, y'all shoulda shanked that bitch," someone shouted out, disregarding the CO's warning.

"Don't worry. We got something for that ass," Goldie admitted.

Several more females began banging on their doors, calling Heaven out of her name and spewing threats of violence toward her.

She bit the inside of her lip. She wasn't about to do the back and forth, yelling and cursing at these hoodrat bitches. They were all irrelevant. Nonfactors. So she kept her eyes forward, and her mouth shut.

But her mind was made up. She'd have to take down that Goldie bitch next. And if she needed to hack her head off with a rusty blade, then throw it over the tier, she would.

"Yo, fam, that bitch really thinks she got that off," another one of the females who'd jumped her from behind yelled from her door. Her birth name was Laveenia Carver, but in the streets, she was known as Red Bull for her red hair and aggressive nature.

Goldie snorted. "Nah, God. Fuck that. I give credit where the shit is due. She *did* get her shit off on the homie. But that shit ain't 'bout nothin'. Chalk it up to the game, feel me? We go hard for ours. And that bitch on the menu."

"Uh-huh. She about to catch it, for real."

"You got that right," someone else yelled out. "You know how we do. All day!"

"That's right, baby," Goldie said. "We fucking gladiators. We fight to the death."

"Malone, you and your cronies had better shut the fuck up with that dumb shit," the CO snapped as she handed Heaven a fresh pink jumper—the color for inmates in lockup, "before I write your ass up for making threats and trying to incite a riot."

"I ain't tryna start no fucking riot," she spat. "All I said was that *that* bitch is good as got. Period. That ain't no *threat*. It's a promise."

TEN

Pussy is Mine . . .

"Oh, God, yes," she breathed. "It hurts *sooo* good."

In her mind, she heard Marsha Ambrosius angelically singing out, *"Your love's sooooo gooood . . ."*

God yes. And it was.

She'd had her share of big dick, but almost twelve inches was taking her to a new level of pleasure. And she was climbing, climbing, climbing. Rising over another wave, her orgasm building rapidly into a sea of pleasure-pain.

God, why did he have to look like a damn baboon?

Mm, but . . . but the . . . the dick—God, yes . . . it was everything.

Still, she wanted to be on top. Wanted to ride him deep into her guts. But she knew she wouldn't be able to stomach looking him in the face. She'd have to keep her eyes shut tight. And he'd want her to keep them open. She knew he would. Men loved staring into her spellbinding eyes, especially when they were glazed over by heated lust.

But she simply didn't have the stomach to stare back in his. The small space wasn't dark enough. And, money or not, he just wasn't worth the risk of puking up her breakfast.

So she contently lay on her side, her left leg lifted and bent, while he slow-fucked her from the back. A Sunday *dick*-down, he'd called it.

The weekends were the easiest days for debauchery. No administration, less chiefs, and lots of horny Indians.

"Uh, *mmmmmmm* . . ." She concentrated over her whimpers of passion and tightened her walls, grabbing him like a fist.

He growled. "Goddamn, baby."

Then he licked his index finger and found her clit, setting his wet finger on her clit. And then came those magical circles over her clit, around and around, while his dick slid in and out. His muscled chest was pressed into her back, and she could feel every twitch, every strain, of his flesh as he worked his hips into her body.

His eyes flashed fire and his jaw clenched tight.

"This pussy tight," he hissed, his thrust slow and deliberate so her body would gradually open to him—all of him. She was amazingly deep (gutless almost) and so fucking juicy. "Aah, *Heaven*, baby," he murmured. He closed his eyes, and red-hot lust swam behind his lids as she whimpered low in the back of her throat and came around him.

It had taken CO Thurman almost three weeks to bag her. He'd waited until she released from lockup, then got up in her ear when he'd seen her leaving medical.

"Damn, you pretty, baby."

"I'm *not* your baby," she'd hissed.

"Then what I gotta do to *make* you *my* baby?" he'd prodded around a grin.

She'd frowned and walked away from him, but his lusty gaze went straight to the sway of her sexy ass. And fuck if his dick didn't grow instantly hard. He knew he shouldn't have looked. But, shit, he was a man (one who loved to fuck) and she was sexy as hell. More beautiful up close than on any surveillance monitor.

The second time, he'd caught her in one of the corridors coming from the warden's office. And he'd tried to get at her again.

"Not interested," she'd hissed.

He'd stared at her mouth as if he wanted to tongue her on the spot. And he had wanted to. He'd wanted to devour every inch of her beautiful mouth with his own mouth.

"Well, what I gotta do to make you interested?" he'd countered over another grin.

The deep timbre of his low voice had sent jolts of unexpected desire through her, but she'd had no intentions of acting on it. The CO had been prepared for the chase. In fact, he was looking forward to it. He wanted to break down her resolve slowly.

But then by the CO's third attempt at trying to spit game at her, she'd surprised him (and herself) and had given in.

"Damn, you smell good," he'd whispered as she stopped at the corridor podium he was sitting at and handed him her movement pass. "You make a muhfucka wanna fuck."

"Two hundred dollars in my account," she'd stage-whispered shamelessly. "And you can."

He'd smirked. "I can what?"

"Fuck this pussy," she'd answered shamelessly, taking her pass, then walking off.

Her response had already fueled his rampant need, causing the tip of his dick to leak in his drawers.

"Yes, Oh God, yes," Heaven hissed, pulling the CO from his salacious reverie. She moaned, drawing him like a moth to a flame.

He could tell her body was on the verge of an orgasm, and he fought back his own desires for release, not willing to let go of this warm, wet feeling. Yet, he felt his animal impulses kicking up as he pumped his erection a little harder, a little longer. Her pussy spasmed, and a flash of searing heat blazed through him, causing his dick to throb wildly. He felt her inner heat rising hotter as he glided in and out of her body. And he began to move faster, harder.

"Damn you feel so good," he grumbled, and her mouth curled into a hint of a smile. Officer Thurman had made his intentions known with no pretenses. He wanted to *fuck*. Her. Period. And—after he gave her the dick, if *she* wanted it again—he'd give it to her anytime she wanted it.

All he wanted was thirty minutes of her body. No strings attached. Then he'd be on his way—unless she wanted more. And he was banking on her wanting it (the dick) again.

"This dick is good," he'd told her with such a confidence that it had made her instantly wet.

She liked that. His confidence.

And there was something sexy about his self-assured cockiness that she found endearing. So why not give him some pussy?

She was horny. And he was willing to pay. And the two hundred dollars in her commissary was another month she wouldn't have to pinch off her own measly coins.

So, ugly or not, it was a win-win situation.

She moaned. "*Mm, mm, mm, mm . . . mmmmmm . . .*"

"Come for me. Get yours, baby, before I lose it." His voice was hot, husky, and ragged.

She gasped. Went slick around him and he moved easier, pushing until she groaned at his depth—deep, toe-curling, soul-touching deep.

He felt himself floating in her wetness, his mind completely adrift.

"That's it, baby," he murmured. "Love all over this dick with that sweet pussy."

Her slick walls rippled around him, and she bit down on the sock he'd stuffed in her mouth to muffle her groans. There was no way around *not* moaning. He had too much dick. And the deliciously dirty act of fucking him inside a utility closet, surrounded by dirty mops and buckets only heightened her arousal.

CO Thurman lifted her hair from her neck and pressed his lips to the satiny skin of her nape, his mouth gently sucking there. He'd found one of her hidden spots. He ground his pelvis into her ass; his dick hitting spots and then more spots that she hadn't known existed.

"*Feel* what you've done to me, baby?" he murmured. "Got this dick harder than it's been in a long time. Aaah . . . shit . . . mmm." More slowly burning thrusts sent her body into uncontrollable shivers. "I wanna lick you in your asshole, baby," he crooned, his rich baritone voice vibrating off her skin.

The pain was sweet agony, like the bite of a whip lashing over her clit, over her cunt, his dick strokes seared through her body, burning her skin.

She felt the swell of her G-spot and then came a fiery ache that emerged from somewhere deep in the pit of her. She was throbbing and swollen and sopping wet. Her orgasm came scalding out of nowhere as she exploded all around his Magnum, mewling.

His nostrils flared and he hissed as her succulent scent filled the air around them. And then she had him gasping for air as need swept through him, heating his blood and making his heavy balls ache for release.

His movements grew fast and furious, still mindful not to hurt her. He wanted it to hurt sweetly, not kill her.

A trip to the infirmary for a savagely fucked hole would raise questions for sure. So he fought to slow his strokes, but she thrust her hips and slammed back on him with her own brand of desire and need.

She wanted to come again.

So he circled her clit again, spinning out another orgasm. She moaned and drooled over the sock, her teeth clamping down on the thick white ball of cotton, squeezing him, her soppy cunt thrumming and sending him over the same blissful cliff.

"Shit . . ." he gasped, his eyes rolling in the back of his head as he felt fire flick down his spine. She'd grabbed him and taken him into her tight-fisted cunt in a way not many women ever had.

His eyes grew drowsy with more desire. Goddamn. What the fuck?

He wanted to stay right here, her soft, wet pussy clenching and unclenching around him, her moans only fueling the flames already spreading through him.

The sex had been more than he'd expected. And somewhere around her third or fourth orgasm, Officer Thurman found himself feeling obsessively possessed by this vixen's hot cunt; already making plans in his head for another round.

ELEVEN
Catchin' Feelings . . .

Thirty-five-year-old Officer Austin Rawlings hadn't expected to fall in love, but shit . . . who did? The problem was, there wasn't anything he could do about it now. He was in too deep. And he didn't know what to do about it. No, no. Who was he kidding? He knew exactly what he needed to do—cut her off. Stop fucking her, period! Yeah, that was what he knew he needed to do.

But he couldn't. He didn't want to. She'd become his guilty pleasure. That fat pussy of hers had become his drug. And he'd become a straight-up love junkie for that wet, gushy shit. Straight like that. The freaky bitch had him under her spell. She kept his head reeling with images of her. Her taste, her touch, her scent . . . every part of her was stained on his tongue, his skin, his dick, his brain.

His dick stirred in his underwear.

Fuck.

He wanted some pussy.

Tight. Deep. Wet. Hot.

Her pussy.

He slid a hand down in his front pocket and discreetly shifted the bulge in his pants desperately throbbing for release, before pulling out a pair of red, laced panties. Contraband. But, shit. He couldn't have his baby wearing prison-issued cotton panties. Hell nah. She deserved better than that. That pretty cunt of hers was too damn good to be covered in cheap cloth. Victoria's Secret was the only thing he wanted her in. Well, truth be told. It was what she required of him. Lacy, frilly, expensive panty sets. That was, if he wanted to keep feeling the silky heat between her smooth, reddish-brown thighs.

And he did. Oh, fuck yeah—he fucking really did. And he didn't care how many pairs of the pricey undergarments he had to sneak in with him every shift to keep his woman feeling sexy and feminine.

Yeah, that's right. *His* woman.

The pussy—*she*—was worth every dollar spent.

He held the ones from the night before up to his nose and breathed in the remnants of her sweet, musky scent stained in the silky garment. She'd slipped them to him on the low—as a late-night treat—when he'd come to her tier to relieve another CO for his break. He swallowed the lust that began slowly pooling in the back of his mouth.

From the moment he'd laid eyes on her, he knew he'd have her . . . one day. Shit. He just hadn't expected it to be on the job. Again. Yeah, he'd gotten away with fucking an inmate once before. Some homely-looking bitch with a *phat* ass and big, juicy dick-sucking lips—about six years ago. He'd fucked her twice. Sadly, she couldn't take dick for shit. But her head game was the truth. So he swabbed her throat real good a few times a month, nutting down in her greedy-ass neck. But he had to cut off her dick supply when she started tripping; obsessing over him, acting all nutty and shit like she was his girl. So he had to fall back before the bitch blew his spot up.

He'd sworn then that he'd never fuck with another inmate. Shit was too risky. He couldn't afford to get caught out there.

Now look at him.

Strung out.

Pussy whipped.

In love—well, damn near close to it—with one of the baddest bitches he'd ever seen in a state penitentiary. He'd been working in corrections for well over a decade already, and he'd seen his share of bitches come and go. And several of them had been dime-pieces. But none had ever been as fine as this one here.

Fuck.

He blamed working the third shift; he blamed *her* for being in lockup for all those months, then coming back; he blamed the muhfucka in the control center for playing with his dick watching porn on his cell, instead of monitoring the cameras. He blamed everything and everyone else—except himself—for his current dilemma.

Had he been on days, had *she* not been in the hole—*again*, had his boy been more by the book, he wouldn't have been tempted. He wouldn't have been lured into her web of seduction.

He'd tried to fight it. Yet, by just the sight of her, she'd managed to break his resolve. To seduce him mentally, long before he'd ever touched her physically.

The first time he'd caught her playing in her sweet, juicy snatch, he had to blink several times to make sure he hadn't been seeing things. But when he'd looked again, his eyes caught hers, and she seemed to open her thighs wider, wanting him to see her.

All of her.

In all of her beautiful nakedness.

And, for a moment, when he'd shone his flashlight on her and their gazes locked, he'd thought he'd seen a soft, secret smile curve her lips as she worked her fingers in and out of her slit. Her pussy lips were glossed with her juices. And its mouth drooled around her fingers, sucking them into her body.

His gaze had been riveted to the scene before him so intently that he had to force himself to move from her door and continue his tour before he came on himself.

Yeah. She'd known what she'd been doing all those nights she'd lain naked on her bunk, legs spread, hand between them, slender fingers sliding over her clit, dipping inside her, then going up to her lips and inside that warm, silky mouth of hers.

He could still hear her strained moans of pleasure. Could still feel the way her gasps caressed his ears, driving him insane with heated desire.

"Mmmm . . . uhh . . ."

Yeah, she'd known what the fuck she was doing to him every time he did his fifteen-minute tours, every time he peeked in her cell, every time he'd shone the light on her, every time he'd opened the trap of her door and looked in—she'd been there playing with herself. Pulling open her sweet, puffy lips, revealing the deep pinkness, the wetness, of her slit, that winked come-hither with every movement of her hips and fingers.

She was brazenly inviting him in.

Licking her lips.

Taunting him.

Offering the snatch to him.

Shit. He was a man. And he loved pussy. So what had she expected him to do after months of viewing her? She had to know, eventually, he was going to tire of watching, of playing voyeur, before he made his way into her cell to get a closer look, then a quick feel, then a little taste . . . and finally fuck her.

Right?

That's what she'd wanted. Some dick. *His* dick.

Otherwise, she wouldn't have been spending all those nights giving him his very own private peep shows. Her ass would have been under her blanket, sleep. Not prancing around in her cell naked in the middle of the night, dirty dancing for him, not fucking herself in front of him, not on her bunk, legs spread for the taking.

She'd wanted him to pipe her out, to rock her to sleep with the dick.

And, eventually, he did. And she'd been so wet, so tight, so goddamn hot.

"Damn, baby," he'd murmured in her ear that very first night as he fucked her up against the cement wall of her cell. "This pussy so fucking juicy . . . *uhh* . . . so . . . *mmm* . . . fucking good."

She'd bitten into his shoulder, then nipped at his ear. "Mmm, yessss . . . fuck me. Oooh, yessss. Fuck my wet pussy . . ."

He'd slammed into her body, and she'd taking the pounding like a pro. Inch by inch, her warm cunt had hungrily, greedily, swallowed him in.

"Is this what you've been waiting for, this hard dick?" he'd said, his voice low and full of heat.

"Yes, yes, yes . . . mmm, yes . . . stretch my pussy . . . *uhhhh* . . ."

She'd come over and over, her juices splashing out as his dick slid in and out of her quacking body.

Her wet clutch had made him weak in the knees.

The problem was, he'd fallen hard after only the first time. First, with the pussy then he'd, somehow, fallen in love with her. What he felt was much deeper than lust.

It was supposed to be just sex, fucking her senseless, getting his nut, then going on about his business. But she'd turned him on beyond his wildest imagination. Though the sex between them was always wild, rushed, heated, he always felt satiated every time he came. More fulfilled than he'd ever been with anyone else.

And now he was hooked.

This shit was crazy.

She wasn't his side bitch. She was his *only* bitch.

He missed seeing her every night. Missed having her in his arms. Missed having his dick tapping the bottom of her well as many times as he wanted.

He sighed.

For three months—well, if he wanted to include the two months she'd done her first time in solitary, then it was five months. In any case, he'd had her all to himself on night shift, giving her long dick whenever she wanted it. They hadn't started fucking heavy until she'd returned to lockup the second time, and—as far as he was concerned—he'd stamped his dick all in it. The pussy was his. But—*fuck*. Now, for the last several weeks, she was back in general population, again, doing her own thing, probably enticing other motherfuckers.

His jaw clenched as he stuffed her panties back into his pants pocket. The thought of her giving another *muhfucka* her loving made his blood boil. He knew how grimy the dudes he worked with could be. He also knew of a few cats that were fucking several of the inmates already. So he knew it was only a matter of time before one of them shady motherfuckers tried to get a taste of what was his.

She was his, period.

He reached into his shirt pocket and pulled out a pack of Newport cigarettes, then reached into his pants pocket and pulled out a lighter. He lit a cigarette, tilted his head back, and let the sun hit his caramel-coated face. He inhaled. The world shimmered in front of his eyes, and, for a brief moment, he imagined a life with her outside of these concrete walls. The thought caused his erection to stretch, and liquid heat to pool in his testicles, and more than anything, he wanted to pull his dick out and stroke himself.

He groaned inwardly, then exhaled a long plume of smoke. He closed his eyes for a moment. What the fuck was wrong with him? He wasn't an ugly muhfucka. His six-one frame was gym right. His dick game was on point. He had paper in the bank. And he knew he had major swag. He could have any woman he wanted. And he had his share of them throwing the pussy at him left and right. So how the fuck had he gotten caught up falling in love with an inmate?

Fuck if he knew.

He took a deep breath. It was almost time for him to head back into the building. He'd taken overtime, just so he could be on day shift to see *her*, if only for a moment. Still, he needed to get her out of his head. Walking around with a hard dick all day was the last thing he needed, especially when he wasn't able to stick it deep into something tight and wet.

He took one last pull from his cigarette before flicking it to the ground and stepping on the burning tip with the heel of his boot.

Then he headed back to his post.

TWELVE

Sex with Me . . .

The cell doors slid open, and Heaven stepped out of her cell; her dark-brown hair tumbling to the center of her back in thick, bouncy waves. A cacophony of sounds swept around her. Other inmates yelled out to their homegirls across the other side of the tier, some rushed out of their cells to hit the showers, and those who didn't own a television of their own in their cells wanted to get to the first two rows on either side of the day space in front of the two fifty-inch flat screens anchored up on each wall.

The first inmate to the TVs' remotes was who controlled what everyone else watched. The TV bullies ran shit. So much for a democracy, it was nonexistent.

Heaven blinked.

Hazel eyes, full of mischief, rested underneath a set of ridiculously long lashes. Lashes that most women would kill to have. She dramatically shook her hair, sliding a hand through her luscious mane as if modeling for a Pantene commercial. Her lashes fluttered as she blinked in her surroundings. So much had changed, and so much had stayed the same, since she'd been dragged back to lockup.

Apparently being the sole reason for one of the prison's most notoriously vicious bullies on 4 East being ushered off the housing unit on a stretcher and, then, fighting her cronies singlehandedly had earned her respect, and had quickly moved her slightly up the inmate prison pecking order.

Whoopty-fucking-do.

All she knew was, the next time she—*if* there happened to be a *next* time—or any other bitch stepped to her crazy or disrespectful, or tried to put their hands on her, there'd be more blood shed.

And they'd need more than Hazmat and a stretcher.

They'd need a coroner.

Oh well.

That Snake chick got what she got. And that ghetto bitch over on 4 East had gotten what she deserved as well. So she wasn't about to worry herself over it. However, since the day of that bloody incident, she had changed. Solitary confinement—lockup—the second time had changed her. Hardened her. Made her more conscious of her needs. Of her wants, her desires, her sexuality . . . of what she *needed* to do in order to survive behind these walls.

In the beginning, she thought she might lose her mind. But she hadn't. Instead, she read books, lots and lots of books. Filthy books. Erotic books. Books that made her pussy quiver, and wet. Had it not been for her books, her time in the "hole" would have broken her. With nothing but time on her hands, she'd learned to turn her situation into her own personal playground filled with naughty seduction.

Reading passages of her books out loud, enacting scenes.

Openly masturbating.

Prancing around her cell naked.

Dirty dancing to the music in her head.

It all became a dirty little game to her, knowing someone would have to come by her cell like clockwork to check in on her. Knowing she'd be watched, or at the very least quickly eyed, had made her pussy tremble with excitement. The sultry acts heightened her awareness. Allowed her to hone her seduction skills. And it hadn't taken long—three, maybe four, weeks—before she'd finally reeled in her first mark.

Officer Rawlings.

Horny bastard.

Sure, he'd fought the urge best he could. But he was a man—for fuck's sake! Of course her womanly wiles—and nightly sex shows— would sooner than later play on his curiosity, and weaken his resolve.

And it had.

What man could possibly stand his ground against her wicked seduction?

The moment she'd heard the sound of his Folger Adams key opening the trap of her door, and his gaze locked on hers as she purposefully, methodically, brought herself to orgasm; the moment he was bold enough to open her cell door and sneak inside, the first time he'd slid his thick dick inside her and whispered her name over and over, and she'd melted around his every thrust, she knew then that she'd had him. That she'd, eventually, have him eating—not only her twat and ass crack, but out of the palm of her once paraffin-smooth hand.

And Austin Rawlings was fine as hell. And his lean, chiseled body was everything. But he wasn't shit for fucking her. An inmate. She could never respect him—or any man, for that matter—who thought with his dick.

Yes, the dick was good. Real good. But he was only a means to an end. And as long as she was locked up, she would do her prison bid comfortably, using any man's—or woman's—weaknesses for her own personal gain. No, she wasn't a lesbian, but she'd had a lot of time to think it over while in solitary confinement. And she'd come to the conclusion that crooked COs had needs too. So why not cater to them. Indulge their desires. Let them fuck her and lick her cunt clean.

Quid pro quo.

They'd have to give something in order to get something in return. And they'd need to make it worth her while. So as long as Officer Rawlings smuggled in the things she desired, he could keep on sniffing her panties, and fucking her. The tracker phone, her expensive Chanel cosmetics, and the lacy bra-and-panty sets he'd managed, thus far, to get into the prison for her were a start. But she desired so much more.

And, if she had her way, she'd have it all.

She deserved it.

She smiled slyly as she thought back to her closet rendezvous with CO Thurman. Two hundred dollars for a twenty-minute fuck was so worth it. It'd been one of her best fucks. Ugly or not, he could fuck.

She swallowed back the heated memory.

This wasn't about love. It wasn't about needing affection. It was simply about survival. Using what she had to get what she wanted. By any means necessary.

She almost laughed.

Pussy was the root of all things evil. Its grip, its pulsing heat, could damn near entice a man to consider giving up a testicle as long as he was granted unlimited access to its silky, wet heat. Well, maybe not to that extreme, but damn sure close enough. Pussy made a man willing to cheat on his woman. Made him willing to risk everything for the sake of getting lost inside of it.

And pussy—*good* pussy, that was, didn't always come free.

Heaven stepped up to the railing, and looked out over the tier. A wicked grin slid over her Chanel-glossed lips. She was so much better than that cheap shit they sold on canteen. The tangerine-orange color complemented her smooth complexion, and matched her uniform perfectly. Her crisp orange jumper was cinched at the waist, courtesy of her cellmate Sabina's tailoring skills.

Her twenty-seven-year-old cellmate was serving a fifteen-year sentence for drug trafficking. A sentence that should have been handed down to her boyfriend at the time, but love and loyalty had her unwilling to turn State's evidence against him. She'd rather take a bullet to the head, or rot in a prison cell, before she betrayed him.

Bottom line, she wasn't a snitch.

So far, she had three years in and another nine years and ten months to go before she was eligible for parole. With her long blonde hair, milky-white complexion, and eyes a lucid greenish-blue that matched the color of a tropical island, the women on the unit referred to her as "White Chocolate" because she had a sweet tooth for tall, dark, chocolaty men. To her, size didn't matter. Only that it was thick . . . and black. Her motto was: the darker the dick, the sweeter the nut.

And since being incarcerated, she'd already managed to screw at least two corrections officers thus far. And, from what Heaven gathered from her observations, Sabina had her sights set on, yet, another hard, black dick.

What a whore. She spent more time talking about all the fucking she'd done out on the streets that Heaven was convinced she was a horny, dick-crazed ho.

But she liked her.

"Lewis. You have a visit," said a voice approaching her from the left. Without thought, she felt her toes curling in her shoes. It was Sergeant Braddock.

The sound of his deep, raspy voice made her nipples strain against the lace cups of her bra. She stuck her chest out further, allowing him to take in the view. He stood well over six feet, and, as she looked up at him, she tried to envision what he'd look like without his annoying crisp uniform shirt on. She imagined a smooth expanse of brown skin stretching over his torso, his broad shoulders, his—what she imagined to be—rippled abs.

She looked at him. A neatly trimmed goatee framed his mouth and chin, and, for some odd reason, she stared at his dimpled chin, and wanted to swipe her tongue over it.

He wasn't someone she initially considered a potential mark, but standing here now, taking him in, in all of his manly delight, made her pause, and she almost forgot to breathe for a few seconds. Perhaps she would need to reconsider it as a possibility. It would be nice to have someone with a bit more rank—and pull— than a measly CO.

However, there'd been no rumors of him being shady or crooked. And she hadn't heard of any gossip about him fraternizing with inmates.

He always came across strictly by the book, but not overly rigid. And he was also very engaging and respectful, but never too friendly. She liked that. He typically treated the inmates fairly. She wondered what he was like outside of these walls, and out of his uniform. She wondered if he had a feral wildness that hovered somewhere beneath the surface.

Oh how fun it would be to find out. But she knew cracking his shell would be a challenge; one she wasn't so sure she was up for. Yet, by the way he was looking at her, with a simmering fascination, she had to wonder if he could be persuaded to step on over to the wild side with the right amount of mental foreplay. And, if she were able to find a crack in his chiseled armor, she'd happily oblige him in a night of forbidden sex, and gladly become a notch he could add to his pussy count.

"Who is it?" she asked, her forehead creasing. She wasn't expecting anyone. Sure, she'd finally put in her visiting card once she'd gotten out of lockup, listing the few people—only six—she'd want to come see her. So far, no one had bothered to visit.

He shrugged. "Hell if I know. I'm not on visit patrol."

But are you on pussy patrol?

His gaze locked on her breasts as he subconsciously licked his lips. In his mind's eye, he saw her reaching for his dick, rubbing her fingers along the edge of his zipper until he grew under her touch, long and hard.

Shit. He felt a tingling in his balls as he held on to the intimate visual for a few seconds more, before clearing his throat, his eyes darting from her face to the tops of her breasts practically spilling out of her uniform. Alterations to a prison-issued uniform were a violation of prison policy, and could ultimately result in institutional charges, but he didn't give a damn. He loved the view, as did almost every other male officer with a pulse.

But, fuck! He couldn't get caught up in any shit. Braddock had never fucked an inmate. A few female COs over the years, though. But if he thought he could get away with it, he'd pound the shit out of her sexy ass. He'd heard from COs assigned to the Ad-Seg unit how she'd blatantly masturbate in front of whomever was on duty.

Lucky bastards.

He wished he—

Whoa. What the fuck? He had to shake himself out of the lusty fog that was slowly beginning to cloud his mind.

"Why you fuckin' with me, Lewis?" he said in a voice so low that she barely heard him. He had to fight to keep his gaze from wandering over her body. And, despite the heat beginning to stir in his groin, he felt a shiver skid up his spine. Shit. Inmate Lewis was trouble. Feral, alluring, feminine trouble.

He swallowed, hard.

He'd need to keep his eye on this one, and deal with her with a long-handled spoon. He shoved his hands in his pockets as an attempt to keep himself from doing something reckless, like tracing a finger along her slender neck, then following it up with his lips and tongue.

His deep voice and his masculine, woodsy scent made her nipples tighten. "Oh, is that what I'm doing?" she asked coyly, pulling him from his thoughts.

He smirked, his gaze sweeping around the tier, before landing back on her. "Yeah, a'ight." His lips curved into a crooked grin. "You know what you're doing. Don't have me write your ass up."

Yeah, right. Lies.

Her gaze traced downward. To what appeared to be a bulge in his uniform pants that hung just right off his frame. "I have no idea what you're talking about, Sir," she replied innocently, batting her lashes. But then she gazed up at him, a smile hovering over her lush lips. She seductively licked over them, before pulling her bottom lip into her mouth. He eyed it hungrily.

"Yeah, okay." He pointed to her uniform. "You might want to go change before you get down to visiting."

She flashed him a sexy grin. "*Anything* for you, *Sarge*."

"You're a trip, Lewis." He shook his head, but he couldn't help giving her one last side-eyed glance as he resumed making his rounds through the unit.

THIRTEEN

Love Don't Love Nobody . . .

After being patted and frisked, the metal doors slid open, and, finally, Heaven stepped out into the visiting area. This was her first time in visits since her incarceration, and she had no idea it was such an invasive ordeal. It felt almost like intake, when she'd had to be crammed inside a room with a dozen or so other women who'd gotten off the prison van with her, shackled and chained.

Along with the rest of them, they'd humiliated her by having her strip, bend over and spread open her ass, and cough, giving officers a back view of her pussy while they peered between her legs. Supposedly to check for any potential contraband, such as drugs, money, and weapons, being smuggled in inside someone's anal and vaginal orifices.

Bitch, please. The only thing she would have been concealing inside her cunt was a hard damn dick. Or a long wet tongue. She'd wanted to tell them so at that moment, but had decided against it.

She'd even overheard one of the female COs comment on how fat her pussy lips were as she'd been bent over. She'd bit her tongue, but not before glancing back to get a glimpse of the officer's face. Officer Banks.

The same sick bitch frisking inmates today. Though she hadn't been the one to search Heaven, she still felt manhandled. Violated. Felt up on like some piece of ripe fruit. She swore the other freak-bitch, Officer Clemmons, who patted her down was trying to sniff her ass on the low, while trying to feel her up on the sly.

Mmph. She should have slammed her ass back in her damn face. Nasty ho.

And when she'd asked her for the time, the officer responded in a huff, "What time is it? Bitch, do I look like a damn clock to you? Get the fuck on before I cancel your visit." Again, she bit her tongue.

Fucking miserable bitch!

This place was crazy. She'd never been around so many so-called professionals who were simply downright inappropriate and fucked up. Since being at Croydon Hill, she noticed how some of the female COs either leered at her, or rolled their eyes on the sly as she passed by. Those ghetto bitches were worse than some of the male officers. Grimier. Disrespectful. And damn right jealous.

But, oh, well.

They could all kiss her ass.

She glanced around the large visiting room, and when she spotted a brown-skinned woman with a wrist full of silver bangles standing up and waving her hand in the air to get her attention, she knew who'd come to visit.

Kareema Daniels.

She would never consider Kareema a *good* friend. However, she'd been a step above an associate, so Heaven had loosely deemed her a friend of sorts. When she was out on the streets, free, they had been "turn-up" and travel pals—with Heaven always footing the bill because Kareema's money was always light, even after she'd started doing a little late-night tricking after a sweaty night at the club to keep a few coins in her purse.

Heaven made her way over to her, catching the eye of two male COs as she walked by. She overheard the chunky one say, "Man, look at that pretty bitch right there."

"Yeah, and I heard she a freak," his light-skinned counterpart replied.

She wasn't familiar with the tall, light-skinned one with the big nose, but she'd encountered the stumpy brown-skinned one a few times during her time over in Ad-Seg. Officer Alvin. He could literally pass as the twin brother of Eddie Murphy's character Rasputia in that hilarious movie *Norbit*.

He caught her eye and slyly winked.

She frowned. She didn't like his libidinous ass, but she'd love to learn his ass real good. She grinned as she envisioned the pudgy fuck stuffed in a black rubber suit with ass cutouts and a hole where his cock was supposed to go. She'd force him to bend over, then use a spiked paddle to whip his ass to shreds.

And if given a chance, she would. Hell. Maybe she'd stuff his ass with a gloved fist, too. Yeah, that's what she'd do. Fist-fuck the shit out of that fat fucker.

She felt a smile forming at the corner of her lips. But then she frowned, and shot a dirty look at him. She dared not say anything back or she'd run the risk of having her visit terminated. And the last thing she wanted was having her visit cancelled before she got the chance to find out what Kareema had been up to since she hadn't heard from her since her arrest. She'd written her three times, and the bitch had yet to write back. And, trust. The slight wouldn't be forgiven.

"Ooh, girl, work," Kareema squealed as she reached out and gave her a one-armed hug. The hug felt about as fake as her hair. Heaven cringed, but halfheartedly returned the gesture. Kareema stepped back and looked at her so-called friend. "Yes, *hunty*. Your face is *beat* for the gods."

Heaven swiped her bang from out of her eye. All she was wearing was eyeliner and a fresh coat of lipgloss, and this ho was acting as if she'd poured on a batter of face paint.

She raised a brow. "You say that like you expected me to come out looking all busted or something."

"Well, no. But I didn't know they allowed y'all to wear makeup, either," she said, taking a seat in one of the gray stackable chairs used in the visiting hall. She gave Heaven another once-over. "*Mmph*. You slay in that jumpsuit. Even in prison garb, you look runway ready."

Heaven gave her a look. "Hon, I don't care where I'm at, I'm going to *always* stay fly."

Kareema laughed, running her hand up the nape of her neck, through her weave. Synthetic. Mmph. Cheap bitch couldn't even spring for human hair.

"Girl, stop," she said as she sat across from Heaven. "You know your ass can wear the shit out of a trash bag if you had to." Kareema continued to assess Heaven's attire. "Even in those knock-off Nikes, you look cute. Ooh, I hate you."

Is this bitch throwing shade?

"Of course you do," Heaven replied nonchalantly. "What else is new? Everyone is guilty of being jealous of me at some point. It's inevitable. Cute weave, though."

"Ooh. You tried it," Kareema said. "*Jealous*, of who? *You?*" She snorted. "Honey, please. I'd never be jealous of *you*, especially now. Girl, your ass is locked up."

Truth was, she did, in fact, secretly hate on her. Was it that obvious? Oh well. Fuck her. She was glad the bitch was locked up. Served her stuck-up ass right. Shooting her man in the back like that. She could have paralyzed him, or worse—killed him. So what if she'd caught him fucking some other bitch. She should have jumped on that bitch instead. Heaven was a stupid ho, Kareema thought.

So what if he fucked other bitches? It came with the territory. Fucking a baller came with rewards and consequences. And there were rules to being his woman. The stupid bitch should have played her position, then she wouldn't be locked the hell up, missing out on all that good dick.

Yes, Lord. The man had amazing dick.

She'd fucked her man twice. And he'd made her come, *hard*, each time. Now she sucked out his tasty nut every chance she got.

And this bitch sitting here in prison garb was none the wiser.

Kareema smirked as Heaven eyed her, taking in her flawless makeup, perfectly threaded brows, and lush mink lashes. Kareema was an attractive, shapely female. However, Heaven wished she'd do something with that wide gap between her teeth and her obnoxious overbite. Her gaze dipped to the white-gold necklace, which hung around Kareema's slender neck.

"Ooh, I'm loving the necklace," Heaven cooed, feigning envy. "What type of stones are they?" she asked, baiting her. The oval cluster of white sapphires shimmered beneath the bright lights, giving off the illusion of being diamonds to the untrained eye. But Heaven knew better.

She knew diamonds. And she knew frauds. And this flat-ass bitch was a fake; from her scalp to her acrylic nails to the blue contact lenses in her eyes. If she was going for exotic, she'd failed terribly.

Kareema's hand went to her neck, and her fingertips gently

caressed her glittery necklet. "Diamonds, hon." She puckered her lips, then tilted her head. "You do know they're a girl's best friend."

Uh-huh. Something you'd never be.

Still, she smiled, her gaze quickly sliding over the rest of Kareema's attire. Cinched above her waist was a red Gucci belt over a black True Religion short-sleeved V-neck paired with a denim ankle-length skirt. She wore a cute pair of red Gucci pumps on her feet.

Kareema flipped her weave. "But, anywhooo. I didn't come to compare hair tips, or talk about my jewels. You ready to catch this tea, girl?" She tilted her head, and waited for Heaven's response.

"No. Not particularly," Heaven said dryly as their gazes locked. "But how about you tell me what's good with *you*, instead. Pour some hot tea on that."

"Ooh, girl. *Shade*."

Heaven tossed her hair again. "Well?"

Kareema waved her on. "Girl, I'm doing me. Just got back from South Beach with bae. And got wined and dined, then fucked down real right."

Heaven's eyelids fluttered. Bae? Since when did she start calling some man her *bae*? She gave Kareema a questioning look.

"Yassss, *hunty*," she continued. "And my young boy puts it down." She fanned herself. "All he fucks with is older women."

"So, your old-ass is out there robbing cradles now," Heaven said sarcastically. "How romantic. So where'd y'all meet? The playground?"

"No, bitch. Down at The Crack House," Kareema said.

Heaven frowned. Of course she'd find her true love down at some ratchet hood club where all the local thugs and wannabe ballers hung. Typical Kareema.

Heaven slowly nodded. "Oh, okay. So you've retired from the block now?"

Kareema frowned. "*The block?* Ho, you tried it. I ain't never been on no damn block."

"Mm-hmm, okay. So how old is this new boo of yours?"

Kareema tossed her weave. "Twenty-four, but he'll be twenty-five in a few months."

"Twenty-*four?*" Heaven frowned. "Girl, are you that damn desperate for a hard dick? You must be one lonely-ass bitch, fucking some boy that damn young."

Kareema snorted. "Yeah, okay. Says the bitch in prison. Don't judge me. Age ain't nothing but a number."

Heaven stared at her and wondered why she ever let this ho in her life. It was apparent they never had anything in common. "And what type of work does *bae* do? He *is* working, right?"

Kareema shifted in her seat. "Well, no. Not right now. He just got out of the county for child support, I think. Plus, he's on probation, I believe."

"Oh, so you *think* and you *believe?* Mmph. Great way to start a relationship."

"Heaven, get over yourself," Kareema snapped defensively. "Everyone falls on hard times at some point. So stop being so damn self-righteous. If I'm not bothered by it, you shouldn't be, either. All I care about is how Jah'Mel—*my* man—treats me. He knows how to handle his . . ."

Heaven fought the urge to yawn. She tried to pay attention to her prattling on about her unemployed boy-toy with the big dick and child support, who made her pussy cream all night.

Still, she smiled again, and tried to pretend to be interested, but—against her will—her mind kept drifting back to that night she'd caught Freedom in their bed giving some other bitch his dick.

"*Mmmm, yes, Freedom . . . mmm, fuck me!*"

"*You like this dick, baby . . .?*"

"*Yes, yes, yes. Hmmph. Uh. Oooh. It's so fucking big . . .*"

"*Yeah, baby . . . Gushy-ass pussy. Take all this dick.*"

Why couldn't he have fucked her at some seedy motel, like he tended to do with all the others? What had been so special about *that* bitch for him to fuck *her* down in their bed?

"Girl, are you listening to me?" Kareema's voice had derailed her train of thought, pulling her back into the moment.

"Huh?"

Kareema rolled her eyes, and said, "I asked you how you're doing in here?"

"I'm doing ten years, Kareema," she snapped, glancing around the visiting area. "I'm wearing some raggedy-ass state jumper, and sleeping on some cheap, wafer-thin mattress. And I'm sharing a cell with a white girl who snores like a damn man, and thinks she's black."

Her visual tour landed her eyes on Officer Rawlings who was looking over at her. She shifted in her seat, and pretended not to see him. *Mmm. So they have him working visits today; his fine ass.*

Her eyes landed back on Kareema. "So did you receive any of my letters?"

"Yeah, I got them," Kareema stated nonchalantly. "I've just been on the move; you know how it is."

Heaven twisted her lips. "Uh-huh. Yeah, I know how it is." She gave her a hard stare. "But I bet if I had a big hard dick, you would have been quick to press one, then be all in my ear about how much you miss me fucking you. Girl, bye."

Kareema sucked her teeth. "I'm here *now*, aren't I?"

Heaven stared stonily at her. "Hon, don't think you're here doing me some favor. I—"

"Wait a minute, ho," she huffed. "I ain't put your ass here. So I'm not obligated to jail with ya ass. We girls 'n' all, but you ain't my man." She didn't want to come see this bitch, any-fucking-way. But she'd been sent, so here she sat. *I can't wait for this shit to be over with*, she thought, glancing at her watch.

"Bitch, and even if you *had* a dick and *were* the last bitch on earth," Heaven snapped. "You could *never* be my man. Now be clear on that. And since we're talking so candid, know this: the only reason you stay halfway relevant any-damn-way is because of your mouth game. All you're good for is a backseat dick suck and some alleyway ass. So don't even come up here and try to shine on me."

Kareema's eyes widened. "What the—"

"Bitch, don't say shit else, except for why the hell you really came here."

"Well, since you wanna be all fuckin' rude 'n' shit. I really came up here to pass on a message."

Heaven blinked. "And what message might that be?"

There was silence a long moment before Kareema finally broke it.

"Freedom wants you to call him . . ."

FOURTEEN

It Takes A Fool . . .

By the time Heaven returned to her tier, she was literally drained. She needed a drink. A bottle of Moscato and a chilled wineglass would do her fine. Thank you very much. Better yet—a hard, deep fucking would do her even better.

She spoke to a few inmates as she moved through the day space, but had no interest in hanging around socializing, participating in of their *tea* parties (where they sat around gossiping) or watching them gamble on a card or board game. She needed a moment. Yeah, she was in the mood to brood and mull.

"Freedom wants you to call him . . ."

The fucking nerve of him!

Freedom.

How apropos. She'd lost her freedom by fucking with *Freedom*. And while he was free to still do his own thing—fucking whomever he wanted, she was locked up. The fucking nerve of it all! She'd allowed that motherfucker to take everything from her—her dignity, her heart, and now her liberty.

Caged in, like some damn wild animal.

She cursed Freedom, herself and this entire fucked-up situation. She should have left him alone a long time ago. Hell, she had no one to blame, but herself. She'd done this to herself. Not Freedom. Not the prosecutor. Not the judge. Only her.

And the sad thing was—if she really, really was honest with herself— that after everything she'd allowed him to put her through, she sadly still loved him.

But, physically, she was done with him. Emotionally? Well, not so much. The hurt was still fresh. She still felt the sting of his betrayal. Nevertheless, her heart was still burned raw from the pain, from all the love she still had for him. Still, she'd never take him back. Ever. And he'd be a damn fool to ever want her to.

Because the next time . . .

She'd kill him.

Heaven walked over to her cell window and looked out. The sky had darkened over the yard, and lightning struck. Then came the echoing boom of thunder. How fitting. The weather suddenly matched her mood. Shitty.

"Freedom wants you to call him . . ."

She grimaced as her pussy pulsed. *Fuck him.* She wasn't calling him. Period. She never wanted to hear from him, or see him again.

She knew she was lying to herself. Still, she repeated the lie over and over in her head, in hopes that if she said it enough times to herself, that it would eventually become fact. But, for now, her truth was this: as bad as she wanted to hate him, to wish him harm, her heart wouldn't allow it.

God, she wished she had shot him in his heart instead. Killed him. Put his cheating ass out of his misery, her misery. Then watched him bleed out.

Freedom.

Freedom.

Freedom.

Why the hell did he want her to call him? What could he possibly have to say to her? What, offer her an apology for being a grimy motherfucker? Tell her how much he still loved her? Promise to hold her down during her bid?

No. She didn't want his apology. She didn't want his bullshit-ass promises. What she wanted was, him gone from the crevices of her thoughts. She wanted him erased from her memory. She didn't hate him. She was deeply hurt by him. And, though, a part of her missed things about him, she wished he'd bled out when she'd shot him. She was feeling like she'd never be free of him as long as he was still breathing.

Heaven pursed her lips, sighed.

He was lucky she hadn't been a snitch. She could have easily brought down his narcotics operation in exchange for her freedom. Sent him away for life. But no matter how many times he'd betrayed her trust in him, she could never bring herself to turn his ass in.

Ever.

Freedom. Freedom. Freedom. His name kept running through her mind like a chant. She knew the real reason she wouldn't call him. She wasn't calling him because she knew the sound of his deep, sexy voice would weaken her defenses. She knew herself too well to pretend otherwise. A broken resolve would mean damp panties and, eventually, he'd—figuratively speaking—have her flat on her back with her legs up over his shoulders—right in the same compromising position he'd had his sidepiece in.

Dick dumb wasn't her middle, or last name.

No ma'am. No thank you.

So she wasn't going to ever play herself again with him. She'd always been good at reading caution and warning signs, and when she'd first met Freedom, he'd flashed a bright red warning that flashed: *Beware. Proceed with Caution.*

And she had.

Well, she'd tried to. Hard.

But, Freedom had been persistent. His representative had showed up and showed out on his behalf, wining and dining her until he'd eventually won her over. He'd treated her like a queen. He'd been attentive. Thoughtful. Witty. Very giving of his time and money. He'd been a true gentleman, not once pressuring her for sex—she'd been steadfast on not fucking him for at least ninety days.

And he behaved like a saint.

But on the ninety-first day, she'd given him some pussy, and he'd fucked her like a sinner. Fucked her so deep she saw stars. Fucked her long and hard until she tapped out.

At the time, he didn't eat her pussy, but his dick strokes and kissing had more than made up for his lack of oral enthusiasm. However, she'd refused to give him mouth service. If a man wanted to see what her mouth could do, then he had better want to clock in and put that work in too. She hadn't been the type of chick to suck a dick just to please a man. No, she sucked dick for her own pleasure. It made her mouth wet. Made her pussy wetter. Sure she'd licked over and around the head of his dick a few times, streaking it wetly with her tongue, but she'd refused to take him in her mouth until he willingly licked her cunt out.

Period.

It took almost six months into their relationship before he'd finally come around and put his mouth on it, and his tongue in it.

Anyway, Freedom had swag. Street swag. He was rugged. Confident. Articulate. Rough around the edges, but he also knew when to be refined. And those combinations, along with his deep, husky voice had made Heaven's pussy clench and her walls quiver every time she was with him. Whether in a well-tailored designer suit or Timbs and a hoodie, he exuded strength; he oozed raw sensual energy. The shopping sprees, the exotic trips, and good dick were all added bonuses.

"Freedom wants you to call him . . ."

The last time she'd spoken to him was the morning of that fatal shooting. Eight hours earlier. They'd been lying in bed, spooning; her ass pressed into his groin, the shaft of his dick wedged neatly between her cheeks. It was their morning ritual. To fuck like wild, hungry animals, then cuddle. Freedom didn't like to cuddle, but he'd done it with her every day since the first time she'd fucked him. She'd demanded it. And he'd obliged her, no questions asked. He'd rarely deny her anything.

So they'd lain there, her back against his chest, his hand slowly tracing over the curve of her hip. She'd shuddered against him, his cock swollen and rigid, straining in between the seam of her ass.

Her pussy had been still wet from their forty-five-minute fuck-fest. And had he'd slipped his hand up under her thigh and hoisted her leg up, and thrust back into her, she would had exploded all over him in seconds.

But he hadn't. Thrust his dick back inside her. He'd leisurely grinded his hips into her, and strummed two fingers over the rigid peak of her nipple, while they talked.

Pillow-talked.

"You know I love you, right?" he'd whispered. "You're my everything, baby."

He pinched her nipple for effect, and she let out a wail of both pleasure and increased hunger. Her pussy grew wetter.

"I know," she murmured, her eyes glittering from the heat roiling through her body. She wanted him back inside her. She rammed back against his pelvis, urging him, the slit of her cunt opening, trying to grasp the column of his thick shaft.

He pressed his lips to her head, breathed in her hair, then held her tighter.
"I love the fuck outta you, woman."
"Then fuck me," she said huskily.
And, then, in one stroke, he plunged inside.

Heaven closed her eyes against the sudden wash of emotion. She felt a headache slowly pounding its way to the center of her forehead. Gently, she massaged the area with two fingers. She'd played the fool once, but *never* twice; not where he was concerned.

Bottom line, she should have been whore enough for him. But, no matter how much pussy she'd given him, no matter how many times she'd sucked his dick and swallowed his warm loads, she hadn't been. Ever. So fuck you very much. She refused to get reeled back into his web of lies.

So like the lady she was, she was going to take several seats and stay as far the hell away from the likes of Freedom Lamont Banks.

FIFTEEN

Alone Together...

"Why you like fucking with me, Lewis?" Sergeant Braddock asked, eyeing her curiously. He'd called her down to the sergeants' office to confront her two days later after her visit with Kareema. She'd been on his mind. And he wanted to know why she liked taunting him. Well, that and the fact that she piqued his curiosity. He knew what she was incarcerated for, but he didn't know her deal. And he *wanted* to know what made this beautiful woman tick.

"You've been here for months, and you've shamelessly flirted with me every opportunity you get. Why?"

She tilted her head and coyly twirled a strand of hair around her finger. Then went that sexy bottom lip; pulled into her lush-looking mouth. The shit was fucking with him.

"Do you want the truth?"

He nodded.

"Is *my* truth going to somehow get me charges or land me back in lockup?"

"Absolutely not. I'm asking you because I wanna know your end game? What exactly are you after?"

She shrugged. "There is no end game with me. Well, there is. I'm a woman with needs, a woman who misses the comfort of a man. I'm not saying I'm looking for that from you. Male testosterone is good for the soul, especially when a woman like me is surrounded all day, every day, by a bunch of other women."

Something deep in his chest warmed. He sat back in his chair, a small smile curving his lips as he took in every part of her. She was fucking hypnotic. And he looked at her like he had no idea what to do with her.

Well, shit, he did. But that would require her being bent over his desk, and most likely costing him his career. Still, a man could fantasize.

"So, I don't mean to flirt with you," she stated, batting her lashes flirtatiously. "It happens because you are a man—lots of *man*, I might add. And in all of your fineness, you bring out that side of me." She paused, taking a deep breath. "And there's my truth in a nutshell."

He swallowed, shifting in his chair. "Oh, is that so?" he asked in his rich, deep voice. He felt his dick becoming erect, and he cursed under his breath. He wouldn't dare fuck with her (on the job, anyway). But he appreciated the looks of a beautiful woman, even if said beauty *was* an inmate. Shit. He was still a man, after all.

"And how exactly am I doing that?" he prodded, curiosity grabbing him by the head of his dick and tugging at it.

"Maybe," she drawled seductively, "it's because you're so damn sexy. Maybe because I have a weakness for fine, sexy men in uniforms."

He suddenly felt hot.

He had better get her the hell out of his office before, before . . .

Heaven licked her lips.

The sensual act caused him to groan inwardly. And in that moment, he saw himself getting up from his desk, scooping her up, knocking shit off his desk to lay her on it. Or maybe sitting her on his face, grasping the globes of her ass while he opened her up to him like a bowl of sweet cream and devoured her pussy with his mouth and tongue.

He'd continue to tongue her long after she'd soaked his face in her juices, lapping up every drop of her essence.

He swallowed again.

"And since you're allowing me to be perfectly honest with you, Sir," she continued, fighting the urge to lean over his desk and rub her tits in his face. "You have no idea how badly I would love to taste you. I'm horny. And if I thought for one moment I could get away with crawling under your desk and sucking—what I believe to be— your long, fat dick, I'd do it. Then swallow you whole."

Motherfuck. The sergeant bit back a hiss as he pressed his long legs together, then ground the palm of his hand down into his lap, desperately trying to tame the wild fire spreading in his groin.

"Jesus," he muttered. "You really know how to paint a descriptive picture."

Heaven smiled to herself, imagining his dick bulging tightly in his pants. In her mind's eye, she saw him with his pants draped around his booted feet, the length of him hanging out from the slit of his dick, her gaze locked on his as her tongue hovered slightly over its slit. Heat hummed through her body and her pussy hissed with an unfettered need for release.

For a slight second, nothing was said between them, and she knew he was giving thought to the idea of what it would be like having her cunt gloved around the whole length of him.

The fact that he'd allowed her to speak freely simply made her respect and desire him more. "Thanks for allowing me to talk openly with you," she stated, sliding both of her hands down the sides of her waist, then resting them on her curved hips. "I can tell you're one of the good ones."

He smiled. Damn, she was one sexy-ass woman. Too goddamn bad she was here.

She licked her lips again. "Maybe—another time, another place— we'll meet again and revisit this conversation."

She winked.

And then the phone on his desk rang out, snapping him back to reality, reminding him that he'd already crossed the line with her.

"I better get this," he said hoarsely.

She smiled at him. "Yes. Maybe you should. Thanks again."

He nodded. Then finally let out a breath as he watched her walk out the office, answering the phone. He knew for certain she would soon have her way with a few of these horny mofos at Croydon Hill. But he damn sure wouldn't let it be himself.

"Sergeants' office," he breathed into the phone.

"You want third shift tonight?"

"Yeah, I'll take it," he stated. Then he hung up and groaned. There was no way he could finish out his shift with a raging hard-on.

He stood to his feet and headed for the bathroom, with one thing—and one thing only—on his mind.

Heaven.

SIXTEEN

The Thrill . . .

"Yo, what the fuck is you doing, you fucking porch monkey. I said take the motherfucking wall . . . you dumb-ass bitches only good for sucking dick and getting fucked. And you probably can't even do that right."

Heaven blinked.

"Who is that?" she asked her cellie as she rubbed her eyes, then sat up on her elbows. She reached under her bed for her watch and glanced at the time.

One a.m.

Was this motherfucker serious?

Sabina sucked her teeth. "Sergeant Struthers."

"*Mmph*," she grunted. She wasn't familiar with him. "What's his deal, calling females bitches and porch monkeys? And making all that fucking noise?"

"*Psst*. Please. Those are his pet names. Piss him off and see what he calls you then."

Heaven felt herself reacting negatively to his so-called *pet names*.

There wasn't a damn thing endearing about his choice of names for those women—or any woman, for that matter.

"Why is he going off?"

"That pussy on the rag again . . ."

Oh.

"Flush that motherfucking toilet," Heaven heard him yell, "and I'ma drag your ugly-ass, along with this baldhead ho, to the hole."

Heaven grimaced. Not at the idea of someone going to lockup, but at the way he spoke to the two inmates. Regardless of what they'd done to get themselves locked up, they were still human beings. Calling them degrading names wasn't cool. She didn't like it. And she decided she didn't like him, either. Not one damn bit.

But she'd learned quickly if it didn't apply to her, to stay in her own lane, keep her mouth shut, and mind her own damn business. And she would.

Still . . .

"He's probably pissed he couldn't get someone over on Two East to suck him off tonight," Sabina continued, "so now he's over *here* looking for anyone he can send to lockup; ole stump-dick fuck."

"So he works nights?"

"Yeah. Third shift."

Heaven blinked. "Wait a minute," she stage-whispered. "Did you say he had a stumpy dick? How you know that?"

Sabina began making smacking noises with her mouth. "How you think?"

"Oooh, you nasty bitch," Heaven hissed, then started laughing. "You fucked him?"

"Hell no. You know my kitty-kitty only likes the taste and feel of dark-chocolate dick inside her. I sucked him."

"Say, what? You sucked *him?*"

Sabina giggled. "Like a Jolly Rancher. It was nice and fat, too.

But short as hell." She laughed. "All that muscled man—six-six—and he walking around with a short dick. A damn travesty."

"I'm not gonna ask you again," he barked through the tier. "Where the fuck is it? I know one of you crack whores got that shit hidden somewhere, probably stuffed up in one of your funky-ass holes."

"We don't have nothing," she heard one of the women say. She sounded young, and practically in tears. "I swear, Sir. I don't do coke. I only smoke a lil' weed."

"I never did that shit, either, Sarge," another voice chimed in.

"Evans, shut your lying ass up," he snapped. "Your knotty-headed ass still sniffing that shit; both of you stinking bitches probably in here snorting and eating each other's stank-ass pussies out."

Heaven's frown deepened. He was vulgar. "I wish he'd shut the fuck up."

"Good luck with that. Once he has it out for you, that mother-fucker can be ruthless. He's been known to storm through cells tearing up shit, looking for contraband—real or imagined. He's even been known to set up inmates, planting shit in their cells, fucking with their mail. Even getting them jumped."

"Say, what? Ohmygod, he's crazy. How come no one reports his ass?"

Sabina snorted. "And, what? Get labeled a snitch? Or end up with your face cut? *Not*. Ain't no one gonna say shit unless they looking for a long stay in the hole, or a trip to the infirmary. All that freaky motherfucker wants is his dick sucked."

Heaven licked her lips and her cunt clenched beneath the covers.

"What did you say his name was again?"

"Struthers," Sabina repeated. "Sergeant Harold Struthers the Third. And trust me. He's definitely not someone you want to piss off, or cross. He'll fuck your whole bid up. I've seen him do it. I'm telling you. That's one evil bastard."

Heaven slid her hand between her legs, slipped them down into her panties for a brief moment. She was wet. Her fingers flicked over her clit, and she stifled a low moan. She needed to know more about him.

She removed her hand, then brought it to her nose, and breathed in her arousal.

"Is he married?"

Sabina blew out a breath. "Hell if I know. If he is, he don't act like it the way he runs around here chasing after head."

Mm. Is that so? "And you said he had a fat dick?"

"Yeah, jaw-locking fat. But, short. Like six—maybe six-and-a-half on a good day."

"You measured it?"

Sabina leaned over her bed and shined her book light in Heaven's face, causing her to blink. "Unh-uh, tramp. What's up with the Twenty Questions? What, you want his dick stuffed in your mouth, too?" Her hair fell forward over her face, and she thrust her free hand through her hair above her forehead, pulling it tight against her head in a backward motion.

"Ohmygod," Heaven said, shielding her eyes with her hand. "Hell no." Maybe it was a lie. She wasn't sure yet. But she was sure she needed to figure out a way to lay her eyes on him. She needed a way to reel him into her web—she only hoped he wasn't some ugly fuck. "Now get that damn light out of my face."

"Mmhmm. If you say so." The light clicked off. She let go of her hair and Heaven watched as it flopped over her face once more. Sabina shook her head. "You seem too interested in his dick all of sudden, but okay. Annnnywho. Yeah, I measured it."

Heaven gave her an incredulous look once her eyes adjusted to the cell's darkness again. "You walk around carrying a ruler, measuring COs' dicks?"

Sabina laughed, shoving her hair out of her face again. "No, silly. I use my neck and mouth, and hands."

A lock of unruly hair fell forward over her brow as she dangled her arms over the side of her bed so that Heaven could see her as she closed her right hand into a small fist, then did the same thing with her other hand, placing them on top of each other.

"See, this right here is a five-inch dick." She spoke as if she were giving instructions on measuring a dick without using a ruler. "If the head peeks out over the opening of my fist, then it's about a five-and-a-half. Now if I stick it in my mouth and it only hits the back of my throat, then it's usually only six inches . . ."

Heaven stared at her in amazement. "And if it's smaller than five inches?"

Sabina gawked. "Then that's a damn Tic Tac, honey."

Heaven couldn't help herself from laughing. "Ohmygod, girl. Your ass is silly."

"Uh-huh. And I'm a dick connoisseur. I've sucked a ton of dicks to know the length of one."

"Wait. I thought you had a boyfriend."

"Yeah, and? Sucking dick was my side hobby. The bigger, the better; but don't get me wrong; I don't mind a short dick, if it's nice and chunky, like Struthers'. But if it's skinny *annnnd* short, hell no." She feigned a cough. "I'm allergic to little dick. The only thing a toothpick can do is, pick out the food between my teeth."

Heaven shook her head as she eyed her. "Now why exactly did you suck him again, knowing how ruthless he is?"

She scoffed. "Because when he asks you to suck his dick, you get down on your knees, and you suck it. Or feel his wrath. He doesn't take *no* for an answer."

"Oh, so he basically sexually assaults females?"

"No. It's more like creative coercion," she rationalized. "He coerces you, then creatively finds ways to keep you indebted to him. Interestingly, as nasty and horny as he is, he's very selective as to who he lets suck his dick."

Heaven sat all the way up. "Oh, how so?"

Sabina continued leaning down over the edge of her bunk, her hair falling into her face again. "He usually likes them real young and fresh, straight off the bus; especially the ones who've never been to prison before."

"Mm. Fascinating. So he's a predator," Heaven said, her mind swirling with all sorts of dirty thoughts.

She hadn't even seen what he looked like, and already she had him fucking her, bent over, feet in a wide stance, her hands up against the wall. Him in back of her, bent over, sliding his tongue down her spine—then giving her ass a heavy swat with one of his huge hands, the sting causing her pussy to tighten.

Her imagination started running like a wildfire. Hot, juicy images of him grasping her hips with those hands of his, yanking her backward as he plunged his hard dick inside her, burying himself as deep as his stumpy dick would possibly allow as he fucked her fast and hard, her pussy growing slicker with every thrust.

She couldn't help—

"Suck his dick good for him," Sabina continued, snatching Heaven from her salacious reverie just as a delicious thrill coursed through her body, "and he might bring you in some McDonald's or a chicken cheesesteak."

Heaven blinked out of her—hell, she didn't quite know what to call it. She frowned. Had she heard her right? A *chicken cheesesteak?* What the hell? *McDonald's?*

Mmph. These dumb hoes were definitely playing themselves too short, sucking dick for burgers and fries. So all they thought they were worth was a damn hot sandwich, or some burger joint?

She raised a brow. "And what did you get?" she asked Sabina curiously. "A burger too?"

Sabina grunted. "*Mmph.* Hell no. Don't even play me like that. I got three packs of Newport, and six mini bottles of Fireball."

Heaven blinked. So this bitch was sucking for smokes and 50ml nip bottles of cinnamon whiskey?

"Ooh, do it, girl. You ran his pockets, huh?"

"Unh-uh, ho." She pointed a finger at her. "Don't even judge me. It was my birthday, and I wanted to turn up. So, yeah, I sucked his dick. And I'd suck it again if I had to. Do you know how much a pack of cigarettes are worth up in here?" She didn't wait for a response. "A fortune, okay."

"Oh, okay. School me, then." Her tone was a mixture of sarcasm and sincere interest. She'd never smoked. All she knew was that they were ridiculously too expensive on the streets. She thought anyone stupid enough to spend almost sixty-dollars on a carton of cancer sticks were dumb as hell. Yet, as she sat up in her bunk, she suddenly heard cash registers ringing in her head as Sabina enlightened her on the prison cigarette trade.

"So be clear," Sabina added. "Prisons might no longer allow smoking, but an addict is gonna get his or her fix no matter what. And a prison bid isn't going to stop it. You have the pill poppers, the meth junkies, the coke users, and the nicotine addicts all up in here jonesing for their next hit."

She continued on about supply and demand in prison. Depending on the two, one single Newport could cost an inmate twenty-dollars or more. Sabina had charged twenty-five for one, netting nearly five hundred dollars on one pack.

"I made close to fifteen hundred dollars up in here, chickie. So don't knock the hustle. I sucked his dick, licked his balls, swallowed his baby batter, and let him call me every degrading name in the book. I did whatever I had to—and I do mean, what*ever*—to make a few dollars. Not one motherfucker out on the streets has sent me shit, not even that worthless fucker I'm in here for. So, I gotta make money however I can to survive. I'm not trying to be one of these indigent bitches in here begging for somebody else's scraps."

Heaven was quickly learning prison was a breeding ground for debauchery, and was a compound for a very lucrative black market trade. And it was filled with fiends and freaks. And—from what it sounded like—cigarettes, drugs, and sex was a seemingly hot commodity behind these walls, and—*yes, yes, yes*—she wanted in.

SEVENTEEN

No Angel...

Heaven shrugged out of her jumper, washed and pat-dried her face and then combed her hair, before pulling it up and fastening it with a black ponytail holder. Then she grabbed her seven-inch tablet from out of her locker and crawled up on her bottom bunk. She powered up her tablet, and waited for it to boot up. The one-hundred and forty-seven-dollar commissary purchase wasn't necessarily what she was accustomed to. She'd rather have her Apple instead of this nondescript gadget, but she had no other choice but to make do.

The money in her commissary account was slowly dwindling down to almost nothing from all of the purchases she'd had to make once she returned to general population. Hygiene products. Hair care. Skin care. Styling products. Cosmetics. Laundry supplies. Padlocks—so bitches wouldn't be tempted to steal her shit. Towels. Phone cards. Utensils. Radio. RCA flat-screen. Extension cords. Tablet. Table fan. And the list went on.

She learned very early on, if you wanted to jail comfortably, you had to have money. And before she knew it, she'd spent close to four hundred dollars, leaving her with a little under two grand left in her inmate account. Most of it money she'd already had in her purse when she'd been arrested and, then, some money that had been sent to her while sitting in the county jail.

Her bail had been too high to bail out—five hundred thousand, and her two bail motions filed on her behalf by her attorney had been dismissed. The two male prosecutors assigned to her case believed she was a flight risk, even though they'd forced her to surrender her passport.

So she was left with no other options but to sit in the county until her charges were disposed of. She didn't want her brothers taking on the financial burden of bailing her out. They had their own families, with their own encumbrances. So she'd sat in that disgusting hellhole for almost a year before she was finally sentenced. Then another two weeks before she'd finally shipped out, with her inmate check in hand.

She shook her head. This prison shit wasn't for her. She wasn't used to budgeting money. But without Freedom—*fucking Freedom*— no longer financing her, and the few friends she thought she had pretty much turning their backs on her, she would be penniless in no time if she didn't learn to pinch off her coins, and shop sparingly.

Sure, she had about eight thousand in a Chase savings account and about twelve thousand more of Freedom's drug money secretly stashed in a safety deposit box. She also had another few thousand tucked away in another hiding place, but there was no one trust-worthy enough to entrust with securing her coins and mailing in money as she needed it.

Her three brothers lived out of state, so she couldn't impose on any of them to fly in to collect her monies. And she didn't want them to. They had their lives. And she had hers. And, sadly, they'd drifted apart once she'd gotten involved with Freedom.

All three of her brothers had thought he'd end up being her downfall. Ha. They'd been right. Now look at her.

For a fleeting moment—one mixed with momentary insanity— she'd thought about asking Kareema, but quickly dismissed the idea. That bitch would run off with her money, then say someone had robbed her for it. She knew how grimy-hoes could be when it came to dick and dollars. And she knew exactly what kind of ho Kareema was. The type to fuck an ex's father while still fucking him, too; the type to fuck a man in his girl's bed, punch holes in condoms, lie about being pregnant, then trick men out of their money for make-believe abortions.

That bitch was as nasty as they came. Cum-swallowing anything with a pulse. She'd been known to . . . fuck raw, fuck married men and . . .

She frowned.

Wait one goddamn minute. Something suddenly churned in her gut. Had she missed it all these years? Had that scandalous bitch done her dirty too? Had she been smiling in her face all these years, while fucking *her* man—well, *ex*-man—right up under her goddamn nose?

Grimy bitches had no scruples.

Freedom had been a cheating dog, but she didn't believe he'd stoop *that* low and fuck Kareema. Let her suck his dick? Well, that was a possibility. But *fucking* her? She simply couldn't see it. He'd known how she was. Several of his boys had already run up in her; they'd played the pump and dump game with her, passing her around like a blunt. Then talked trash about her.

Then again—she'd never thought he'd stoop so low and have fucked some bitch in their bed, either. So, maybe he did fuck her.

Ugh.

Did (no, *should*) she even care? Hell no.

So why was she feeling as if she were about to have a panic attack?

There went her gut again; twisting in knots as she mentally noted the way Kareema would eye Freedom on the sly anytime he was around.

He'd laughed at her when she'd asked him if he'd been fucking her, pulling her into his arms. "Listen, baby. That broad can't ever get this dick. A'ight? This dick is all yours, baby," he'd assured her, before molding his mouth to hers in a hot breathless kiss that melted away any further crazy thoughts of him wanting to fuck her.

But, now—as the disc in her mind rolled backward over her life with Freedom, she realized more than ever . . . anything was possible.

"You got my heart, baby. Forever . . ."

"Fuck you, Freedom," she hissed, throwing her tablet across the cell. It hit the wall, then clunked to the floor.

Broken.

Just like her heart.

Yet, Heaven refused to cry. Shedding tears over a man who really hadn't given a fuck about her or her feelings wasn't going to change her current situation. He was living his life, doing whatever it was he was doing, slinging drugs and dick.

And now. She had to live hers.

Behind barbed wire.

And the one thing she knew for certain was, she wasn't going to do her time behind bars broke. She needed a plan. Money was what made the world go 'round, and she wanted her world to spin on lots of dollar signs.

Somehow, someway . . .

EIGHTEEN

Silhouettes . . .

"Excuse me," came a voice. Heaven looked over at her opened cell, and looked into the tear-stained face of a brown-skinned girl with slanted brown eyes. She was a young, attractive (a little dusty-looking with a tore-up weave), curvy-hipped girl with a small waist, and breasts the size of ripe cantaloupes.

In her left hand she fisted what was remnants of long weave hair.

Heaven sighed. She wasn't in the mood for niceties at the moment (couldn't this bitch see she was in the middle of having a *moment*?), but the young woman appeared distressed, and Heaven didn't have the heart to be rude. She didn't recall ever seeing the girl on the tier, so she surmised she'd been moved from another housing unit.

Heaven sighed inwardly. "Yes?"

The girl sniffled, swiping tears from her face. "Do you have a tampon I can borrow? I don't have any."

Did this little crazy bitch just ask me if she could borrow *a tampon from me?* Heaven stared at her. The poor thing had to be special needs, she thought. Bless her heart.

Heaven finally softened her stare. "No, I don't have any tampons you can *borrow*," she said, walking over to her locker, "but I have a few I can *give* you. We don't loan out tampons here, sweetie." *And what nasty bitch does?*

In good conscience, Heaven couldn't let her go without having sanitary napkins or something. Croydon Hill only gave women three to five pads a month, and two rolls of toilet paper apiece. After that, the inmate was on her own until the next month unless she had money to purchase her own hygiene products.

Heaven found the shit appalling, and inhumane. Some women didn't even have on any underwear and they were expected to attach a pad on the inside of their jumpers when their cycles came.

The girl sniffled again. "Oh, okay. Thank you."

Heaven opened her locker and pulled out an unopened box of tampons, then asked her how old she was.

"Nineteen," she replied.

Heaven blinked again. *Ohmygod, she's just a baby.*

"How long have you been incarcerated?"

"I got here last month," she answered, her eyes rimming with more tears.

At that moment, Heaven suddenly remembered her own anxiety when she'd first arrived at Croydon Hill, and found herself feeling bad for the young girl. She wanted to ask her what she'd done to end up here, but knew that was a no-no. You never asked another inmate why they were incarcerated. So instead she handed her the box of tampons and asked, "So why are you upset?"

Her top lip trembled. "Because I'm fuckin' pissed. I got jumped in visits." She opened and closed her hands into tight fists. "I wanna kill them bitches," she hissed.

What?

Heaven immediately zoomed in on the fresh handprint on the side of her face and the young girl's black eye and busted lip. She assumed it had come from another inmate; some bullying-bitch trying to intimidate the new girl.

Heaven could see where she'd easily become prey. Fresh meat. Young and tender. No one had had Heaven's back when she first arrived, but she didn't want this seemingly frightened girl to become someone's bunk bitch.

So she invited the young women into her cell, and allowed her to have a seat at the foot of her bunk. Heaven waited for the girl to sit, then sat on the other end, shifting her body and tucking a leg beneath her body as she faced the young woman. She made a face, smelling an odorous funk wafting from the young woman.

"Um, sweetie," Heaven said, trying to be thoughtful. "On second thought, I'm going to need you to sit"—*your funky ass*, she thought—"over there." She pointed toward the metal desk.

She tried not to frown at the young woman as she walked by, but she gave her the side-eye as she took a seat on the metal stool.

Heaven glanced over at the young girl's ass print still indented on her bed, relieved that she always used a second blanket as a covering for her bed during the day.

"Now tell me. Who jumped you?"

She blew out a breath, her hands shaking as she held onto the box of tampons. "My moms," she answered, taking a hand and wiping her face. "And her trashy, crazy-ass friend. Both them messy bitches got it comin', though."

"Your *mother?* Wait. Your mother is here, too?"

The young girl shook her head. "No. She was here visiting me."

Tears streamed down her face again. Heaven really didn't feel like taking on this girl's problems, but she looked like she needed a hug.

Wait. Well, she wasn't about to hug the stank girl, but she'd at least be an ear for her to bend, before she kindly put the girl out of her cell. Besides, curiosity had gotten the best of her.

"Well, why did they attack you?"

Her nostrils flared. "Because her ass still mad at me for stabbin' up her dirty-ass boyfriend."

Heaven blinked. "And why'd you stab him?"

Her nose flared. "Because I got tired of him beating her up." Now she was sobbing, snot sliding out of her nose. "I did that shit for her ass 'n' the bitch actin' like he the damn victim. I shoulda just let 'im beat her ass. Again." She sniffed back what sounded like a glob of snot. "Maybe I shoulda stabbed her dumb ass instead."

Heaven quickly stood up and retrieved a box of tissue from off her shelf and handed the box to her. She spat phlegm into the tissue, then grabbed more and blew her nose. Then she wiped her face with the same snotty tissue.

Ugh.

God this wretched girl obviously had very little home training.

The girl yanked out several more sheets of tissue, then blew her nose again. She looked up at Heaven, who was now leaning back against the frame of the bunks.

"That stupid bitch actin' like I killed his thievin' ass," she spat. "All he does is smoke weed and drink, then come in all hours of the night talkin' shit like he somebody's boss. Don't nobody wanna hear that shit all the time. He don't even work. All he wanna do is walk around in his dingy drawz scratchin' his big, ole nasty balls."

Heaven gave thought to asking her how she knew about the size of his balls, then quickly dismissed the idea. She really didn't want to know.

"I'm sure your mom will come around," Heaven offered, going back over to her locker and gathering some hygiene items for the young girl. The little bitch's odor was starting to really kick up the more she cried. And it was making Heaven gag.

"Fuck her!" the girl spat. "All that baldheaded bitch care about is drinks, dick, and dumbness."

Heaven frowned.

The girl's hand flew to her head and patted it. "Ohmygod! I hate that ghetto bitch. She really fucked my muthafuckin' scalp up."

Heaven gave her a sympathetic look. "Oh, I'm so sorry."

She grunted. "Don't be. All she cares about is Knutz's ugly ass. All he wanna do is go out and knock niggahs in they heads and rob 'em. She so fuckin' stupid."

Knutz? Heaven cringed. She didn't really know what to say to what she was hearing, but she needed, no wanted, to know who the hell was some man named *Nuts*.

"Wait, did you call your mother's boyfriend Nuts, as in a bag of *nuts?*"

The girl sniffled again, giving her a look. "No. Not like the nuts you swallow," she corrected. "It's *Nuts* with a *Kay* at the beginning and a *Zee* at the end. *Knutz.*"

Heaven truly felt sorry for the girl, but she had heard enough. And her stomach was starting to churn from the girl's atrocious breath.

She walked back over to her locker and began gathering personal hygiene items. Then she handed the young, distressed, stinky-ass girl a bag filled with two bars of soap, some deodorant, a tube of Colgate, a toothbrush, some cocoa butter lotion, a vinegar/water douche kit, and an unopened tube of Monistat cream to kill whatever fungus she was sure the nasty girl had between her legs.

"I'm sorry to hear that your mother and her friend fought you at—"

"Them dirty bitches didn't *fight* me," she snapped. "Get it right. They *jumped* me. Big difference."

Heaven bit the inside of her lip to keep from bringing it to the young woman while she was distressed, but she had better watch her volume.

"Look, sweetie," she said, thrusting the bag at her. "I don't mean no harm, but you smell awful. So I'm going to need for you to take this goodie bag and get out of my cell. Please."

The girl stood; seemingly embarrassed, but she quickly recovered, her eyes becoming glaring slits. "You ain't gotta try 'n' put me down, Miss Bitch," she hissed. She had the mindset to throw the bag back in this uppity bitch's face. She had enough shit to deal with. But, she bit her tongue. She had two friends already at Croydon Hill who'd been here for almost a year already, but she hadn't had a chance to see either of them.

So until she could get a few things from one of them, she decided to let this bitch live. Because the truth was, she couldn't keep stuffing her pussy with them hard-ass prison napkins. She really did need the care package. She had nothing. And her cellmate, some bird-ass ho from somewhere down past Cape May—shit; she didn't even know where the hell a Cape May was—was a broke bitch herself.

"I know my breath and cootie stink," she snapped, snaking her neck. "I don't need a bitch like you to remind me."

Cootie?

"You ain't gotta kick a bitch in the throat, when she already down."

Now Heaven felt bad. She hadn't meant to hurt the girl's feelings. But shit. She smelled like the back of a garbage truck. And the shit was offensive.

"I didn't mean—"

She cut her off. "Save it. I'm tryna stay classy as my auntie always says. But, trick. Don't let the tears fool you. I'ma grown-ass woman. And I'll take it to ya damn face."

Oh, no, this little stinking bitch didn't!

Heaven blinked, taken aback by her abrupt shift in attitude. "Now wait a minute, bitch. I'm trying—"

"To be goddamn messy," she snapped, cutting Heaven off. "That's what you tryna do, Miss Bitch." She gave her a cold stare as another tear rolled down her cheek, followed by another. It was bad enough that her mother and her mother's best friend had come up here and jumped her in visits.

And now this bitch was trying it with her. She felt like punching her in her throat. All she wanted was a goddamn tampon. Not judgment.

The young woman gave Heaven another look, but—this time—not too harsh. "You lucky I don't sling this bag in your fuckin' face," she hissed. Then walked out.

Heaven found herself standing there, blinking several times.

I don't believe this shit.

Had that little dirty hoodrat let her have it?

But what she didn't know was, the young woman wasn't as timid as she appeared. Out in the streets, she was wild and ran with two other young women. And the three went by the name the Switch-blade Bitches, who smoked weed, sucked and fucked, and sliced up anyone who came at them wrong.

Heaven stuck her head out of her cell and watched the girl as she stomped down the tier toward her own cell—a bloodstain seeping into her jumper right in the center of her bouncy ass.

NINETEEN

Midnight Lovers . . .

"Mmm, yes, yes . . . fuck me," Heaven moaned low into her burner cell, her fingers clicking away inside her wet pussy.

It was a little after one a.m., and Heaven and Officer Rawlings were on the phone, breathing heavy and talking dirty in each other's ear. They'd been on the phone for almost an hour, before the two of them had finally begun engaging in their nightly ritual of hot, nasty phone sex.

He'd been painfully stimulated most of the conversation, his dick jutting upward, stretching over his navel as he lay on his back and teased himself, slow-stroking it until he felt his nut roiling upward, then he'd let go of his dick. He waited a few moments, then began milking it again.

Liquid arousal seeped heavy out of the tip of his dick. His balls were swollen with nut. He wanted release. Needed it. Bad.

Shit. He wished he had a fresh pair of her cunt-scented panties so he could sniff them while he jerked himself off.

Listening to Heaven's sexy voice as she whispered through the phone, as if she were right there with him whispering in his ear, turned him on. She was addictive—everything about her was addictive. Her touch, her lips, her smile, her warm kisses, the feel of her skin, the warmth of her body, the way her mesmerizing eyes sparked fire every time he looked in them—everything.

He'd never get tired of her. She made him hungry for every part of her.

"You miss this dick, baby?"

Ever since she released from solitary—away from him, his dick—they talked on the phone late at night on his nights off. He missed her. His dick missed her. And she'd lie in her bottom bunk, listening to his voice, imagining being engulfed in his arms, while sliding in and out of her slick body.

She didn't love him. She loved all of the possibilities of using him. And, yet, she found herself conflictingly in deep like with him.

"Mmhmm," she cooed. "Yes, baby. I miss it . . . all of it. Yes, yes . . . mmm. My pussy's so lonely without you."

Rawlings smiled, languidly stroking his hard dick. He cupped his balls. "My nut sac is so heavy, baby. I can't wait to flood that sweet pussy with all this good nut."

Heaven rolled her hips and moaned, taking in more of her fingers. But it wasn't enough. She wanted to feel the weight of his hard body crushing her, his pelvis grinding into hers, the sound of flesh thump-thump-thumping. Kissing her. Squeezing her. Moving deep inside her.

"Close your eyes, baby."

"They already are," she said breathily.

"I'm kissing you, baby, my tongue sweeping over yours. Mm, baby. You taste so sweet; your lips, your tongue. Aah, damn, baby. I can kiss you forever."

"Yes, yes," Heaven whispered. A hand slid up to her right breast, a fingertip fluttering around the edges of her areola. "Kiss all over me."

"Now my lips are sliding to the corner of your mouth until I'm"—he puckered his lips and made kissing sounds as if his lips were sliding down her skin—"slowly kissing down your jaw. My tongue traces your ear, twirling around the shell of it. Then I'm sucking your earlobe between my teeth. I can feel your body shivering, baby. You like that?"

Heaven moaned low in her throat again. Her ear was . . . oh, yes, God . . . one of her weak spots.

"Yes. I love it. I'm so wet for you."

Rawlings groaned as he rubbed his thumb lightly over the crown of his dick, smearing the precum that drizzled out of his slit over it. His bulbous head was overly sensitive. He wanted to feel it between her lips, sliding over her tongue, hitting the back of her throat. She still hadn't given him head, but he knew it was only a matter of time before she'd be on her knees worshipping his dick, slurping and making love to it with that sweet mouth of hers.

"You gonna suck on this dick for me, baby?"

"Yes. I'm going to take it all in my wet mouth. Suck on your balls. Make 'em nice and wet, then slide my tongue up the underside, tracing that thick, pretty vein all the way up to the head of that thick, juicy dick."

He moaned softly.

In his mind's eye, he saw Heaven crawling on his king-size bed between his legs, her head dipping as she licked over his sac, rolling his balls with her mouth. He stroked his dick harder as if his hand were Heaven's hot mouth.

"Goddamn," he hissed, his hips shooting off his bed, arching up as if he were trying to push himself deeper in her mouth.

Rawlings closed his eyes, his imagination taking him places he'd never been, like feeling her tongue licking his asshole. He'd never had it done, never had the courage to ask a woman to journey there out of fear of being judged. He wasn't on some gay shit. But close-minded bitches, no matter how freaky they professed to be, would think he was if he came at them with some shit like that.

Still, he wanted the experience.

Heaven took him out of his comfort zone.

Made him want to be wild and uninhibited. He wasn't a prude. In fact, he was very open-minded. He enjoyed giving pleasure as much as he received it.

A lot actually.

And he wanted nothing more than to please his baby. But right now, he wanted his dick sucked, and his balls licked.

"Yeah, baby. Get up all on them balls. Lick 'em for me, baby . . ."

Heaven pulled her two wet fingers from her body and put them to her lips. She kissed the tips as if it was the head of his dick, swirled her tongue over them, then moaned. "Mm. I love this dick. It tastes so good."

"Yeah, baby. Suck that shit."

She slid her fingers into her mouth and greedily sucked him, her juicy mouth making sweet suckling sounds in his ear.

Heaven looked up at the mattress overhead and bit back her moan as Sabina stirred in her bunk. She hoped she hadn't heard her.

She held her breath for a moment. When all she heard was Sabina's growling snore again, she resumed sucking her fingers as she used her free hand and alternated between each of her breasts, toying with her nipples.

And then she told him, low and raspy, how her tongue was skirting along the ridge of his dick, then flitting tiny licks up and down his shaft, streaking it with her saliva, before taking it into her mouth.

Rawlings' dick jerked in his hand as he imagined the warmth of her mouth engulfing him.

"Mmm, daddy," she murmured. "My head is bobbing back and forth taking your dick deeper, deeper. Aah, yes . . . fuck my mouth, baby. Make it your pussy. Bust your batter down my throat."

Rawlings had gotten so caught up in the moment that he started panting hard, clutching the bed sheet with one hand, while he increased his hand speed, his hand swiftly moving up and down his shaft.

He growled out, "It's coming, baby . . . aaah, shit . . . aaah, shit . . ."

"Mm, yes. Give it to me. Flood my mouth, daddy . . ."

His hand pumped the base of his dick as he began groaning.

"Aaargh, aarrrrrgh . . . uhhh . . . take this nut . . ."

His body shuddered. His nut shot up in the air.

Long, thick streams of it, splashing over his chest and hitting under his chin.

Several seconds ticked by, both of them trying to steady their breaths, before Officer Rawlings blew a breath into the phone. "God. Damn, baby. I needed that. But I need you more."

Heaven smiled. "Me too."

She glanced at the clock. 3:17 a.m. She needed to hang up and get some sleep. Soon. The housing officer would be coming around to complete his tour, and she wanted to wash up and put her phone up, before she got caught with it.

She yawned. "I have to go."

"No doubt, baby. Thanks for the nut."

"No. Thank you. You made my night," she told him.

"A'ight, baby. Go get some sleep. I'ma need another pair of them panties, a'ight?"

She shook her head, smiling. "I'll have a pair ready for you."

And she would.

Fresh washed pussy in a pair of red-laced panties.

"My baby. That's what's up. You really know how to keep a smile on your man's face, don't you?"

"Always," she whispered.

She blew him a kiss, then disconnected, falling asleep around three a.m.

She heard the sound of running water and the depressing echo of cell doors sliding open before her lids fluttered open.

The time was six a.m.

Ugh.

She was exhausted.

Shortly after her call ended with CO Rawlings in the wee-hours of the morning, she'd drifted into what had started out as a peaceful slumber until she'd started dreaming of her first love.

Desmond.

Dez for short.

He'd been her first boyfriend, and her first love.

Tall, hard-bodied, dark-chocolate—everything fairytales and dreams were made of. The moment she'd laid eyes on him and his crooked grin, she'd become enamored. And he had wanted to have the young beauty, before anyone else sank their dick in her. And he'd snatched her up. Quick.

It'd been her freshman year, second semester, at UConn—the University of Connecticut. She was seventeen. Naïve. A virgin. And happy to be from under the overprotective thumbs of her brothers and father.

He was nineteen. Hood. Promiscuous. And obsessed with stacking money.

It had taken him almost a year, before she'd given up her virginity—his meaty, curved dick, stretching her tender cunt. He'd fucked her until tears burst from her eyes, until her burning pussy erupted in pleasure.

Afterward, he asked her how it felt. "Painfully good," she said, and he kissed her, then rolled her on top of him and showed her how to ride him, the curve of his dick hitting parts of her soul she never knew existed. She rode him—looking him in his dark-brown eyes, him instructing her how to change the rhythm, slowing down and speeding up; her ass clapping, her pussy coating his shaft until he slid in and out of her body with inexplicable ease and pleasure.

They kept at it—fucking, until she was skilled at it. Until her cunt became his personal sheath. He became her dark knight in shining jewelry. She—his arm candy, his sweet piece of ass. And, together, they'd been a beautiful couple. But, barely two years into the relationship, he began putting his hands on her. Mushing her in the head at first. Then came the snatching her up. Followed by open-handed slaps.

If another guy looked at her, he'd have a problem. If she looked over in some random guy's direction too long, he'd have a problem. If she wasn't accessible to him when he wanted her to be, he had a problem.

Suddenly, she'd found herself sucked into his world of danger, hiding her new life from her family, her grades failing, risking her freedom and her safety. All for love.

It'd taken her almost four years—and three STDs later, just shy of her graduation, to realize that the Hartford-bred thug was no good for her.

His drug dealing and weed smoking, she had been able to overlook. After all, he'd pamper her, buy her whatever she wanted; basically gave her the world. But the guns and his happy-handed attempts at controlling her, and all the other bitches in his life that she'd had to fight, had taken a toll on her. She couldn't put up with it any longer.

He'd been a liar, a cheater, and a damn woman beater.

She'd fought back—always. And stabbed him once. Suddenly,

things between them had gotten better, filled with almost six months of bliss. And then he slipped back into the streets and his old womanizing ways.

The only thing consistent was, him fucking her good. He was insatiable. No matter who else he'd give his dick to, he never had enough of her.

But she'd had enough of him.

So, with her college degree in hand—and three trunks stuffed with designer clothes and expensive handbags and heels—she climbed in the backseat of her father's Benz and cried her eyes out, leaving *him* and her broken heart behind.

Never looking back.

She'd left Connecticut nothing like the way she'd come. She'd arrived as an inexperienced girl from the suburbs, but left as a woman with a love for the hood.

And a voracious sex drive.

Heaven shook her head. She felt sudden disgust, plus anger at herself that she'd awaken with her panties wet.

Why, after all these years had he come into her conscience?

That had been a lifetime ago, the two of them. She hadn't thought of Desmond in years. But somehow he'd found a way to rob her—of what had started out as the ending of a very bliss-filled night, planting himself inside her head.

And then came the images of Freedom. Though he had never laid hands on her or given her an STD, he'd always reminded her, in many ways, of her first love.

Desmond and Freedom had a lot in common.

Hustlers. Liars. Cheaters.

And damn good fucks.

Consequently, they'd both made a fool of her time and time again until she'd reached a breaking point. One, she'd finally walked away from. The other, she'd shot.

She bit back a grunt.

Why couldn't she have walked away from Freedom's ass as well? If she had, she wouldn't be here. She'd be on the other side of this wall, living her damn life.

Fucking men!

Bottom line, her choices in them had always been fucking horrible.

Heaven finally opened her eyes. Bright sunshine flooded the cell. She groaned and shut her eyes again. A curtain. No, no. Blackout curtain. That's what that tiny cell window needed.

Heaven groaned again, catching a glimpse of all of Sabina's cosmetics scattered out across the desk. An open jar of Noxema. Hair spray. Styling gel. Tweezers. Emery board. Enough makeup to stock a cosmetics counter. Brushes. Pencils. Liquid eyeliner. Mascara. Bronzer. Eyelash curler. Eye shadow. Lipsticks.

"Good mornin'," Sabina muttered, hovering over the sink brushing her teeth.

Heaven sniffed and threw back the sheet. "Morning." Rubbing her eyes, she stood and staggered to the toilet to relieve herself, sliding the privacy sheet around the toilet.

She'd had to learn how to coexist with Sabina in such close proximity. Basic things like using the toilet came with some understanding. Growing up, she'd always had her own bathroom. So she'd never had to share one with other females, until now. Pissing was fine. Taking a shit—while your cellmate was still in the cell—was a no-no, unless you were locked in. Then it required complimentary flushes.

Heaven lined the steel commode with several layers of toilet paper, then slid her panties down over her hips and sat.

She heard Sabina rinsing her mouth, then spitting in the sink. "Bad dreams?" Sabina asked once she stepped away from the sink.

Heaven wiped herself, flushed, then pulled her panties up and slid back the sheet. "Huh?" she asked, washing her hands at the sink.

"You were tossing and groaning in your sleep, like around four thirty this morning. Dreams?"

Heaven grunted, looking over at Sabina as she swept her hair up into a ponytail. "Try nightmare."

"Care to share?"

Heaven shrugged slightly. "Not really. It's too early to rehash."

"Oh. That bad, huh?"

"Men aren't shit," she stated, wrapping her body into her robe, then peeling out of her panties. She neatly folded them, before slipping the lacy undergarment inside a small plastic Ziploc bag. She slid the zipper closed, sealing in her scent. She wanted CO Rawlings to get a burst of her essence the moment he unsealed the bag.

Sabina eyed her, wondering why the hell she was once again sealing her panties in a plastic baggie. But she let it go. She grunted. "*Mmph*. Ain't that the truth. Most of us behind bars are here because of a man in some form or fashion. Then abandoned and left to survive on our own while he's out there doing God knows what with some replacement bitch. Does that make us fools?"

Heaven gave her a somber look. "Yes. And dumb as hell."

TWENTY

Exchange . . .

"Lewis," Heaven heard over the housing unit's PA system. "Report to the podium."

She lowered her radio and frowned, wondering what she was being called down to the COs' desk for. She had no appointments. She wasn't enrolled in any of the prison's educational or vocational programs, although, for a fleeting moment, she'd considered signing up for the cosmetology program. But then decided she wanted no parts of running her hands in any of these bitches' heads.

Besides, she was already a cosmetologist. She'd gotten her license four years ago when she'd decided working for corporate America wasn't for her. She'd walked off a very lucrative job with Merrill Lynch after six years of employment, and never looked back.

Before Merrill Lynch, she'd spent three years on Wall Street. And that nearly drove her to self-medicate. The fast-paced, erratic, mostly male-dominated, hustle and bustle of the stock exchange wore her nerves thin. So, before she found herself locked in a bathroom stall doing lines of coke on a mirror, she gracefully bowed out.

Hell, work wasn't for her.

Life wasn't lived to suffer. It was lived to enjoy.

Sure she liked having her own money, but she didn't want to have to work for it. Not if it required her to be aggravated. Truth was, she liked having a man whose money she could spend more than having to work for it; hence, her attraction to ballers and top-level drug dealers.

She loved being pampered. Loved being spoiled. And loved knowing her man was able to offer her the finer things in life.

Was there anything wrong with that?

No, no—absolutely not.

Anyway.

She'd been invited to enroll in one of the prison's Home Economics programs, but she'd graciously declined. She wasn't interested in taking up crocheting, like Sabina, or culinary art. Making sweaters and scarves or baking cupcakes was not what she aspired for her life.

She didn't want to be in prison. But this was her reality. And the reality was, if this was where she had to be, then she was fine right where she was.

In her cell, watching television, reading a book, listening to her music, and minding her own damn business. She didn't need rehabilitation therapy. And, she damn sure wasn't interested in *working*. Free—no, *slave*—labor was not what she was signing up for. They could all lick her—

The CO called her name again, this time with a tone filled with annoyance.

Heaven rolled her eyes. *Bitch, I heard you the first time.*

"Hey, Lewis," an inmate named Greta said, standing at her cell in a white T-shirt and pair of sweats and shower shoes. Her blonde-dyed locks brushed over her shoulders. "Harris calling for you."

Heaven nodded. "Thanks, girl. I heard her."

"She wilding today, so you know."

Heaven shook her head. "What else is new. That ho needs a dick in her life."

Greta smirked. "Don't we all." She leaned her body into Heaven's cell, and lowered her voice. "I know this is TMI, but I'd kill for a long, thick dildo right now. I'm so tired of these fucking prison-made dildos." Some women made their dildos (if they were lucky enough to be in a pottery class) out of melted-down bars of soap that they'd mold into the shapes of a dick. Others simply used Maxi-pads wrapped and taped around toothbrushes, then covered in a plastic glove. And if an inmate were fortunate enough to get her hand on a tubular vegetable, like a cucumber, or banana, she'd wrap it in gauze, slide it inside a glove and then use that too.

Greta shrugged. "I'm a horny bitch right about now."

Heaven laughed, surprised at her candor. "Well, girl, if I ever get my hands on one, I'll be sure to keep you in mind."

"Girrrrrl," she drawled. "You could rent it out by the hour."

"You think?"

"Mmmhmm." She nodded. "I'd happily pay."

"And I'd happily do business with you. Anything for a horny, re-pressed soul."

The two women laughed.

"Lewis!" blared over the PA for the third time.

"Uh-oh. She's getting restless," Greta remarked.

Heaven sucked her teeth. "Let me go see what this damn CO wants, before she starts her shit."

Greta nodded knowingly. "Good luck with that," she said before walking off.

Heaven shook her head, and smiled. She'd had minimal inter-action with Greta, but from what little conversations they'd had over the last few months, Heaven liked the attractive, brown-skinned woman. She stayed out the way and minded her business.

Heaven slipped her feet into her clogs, then stood from her bunk. She had gotten comfortable. Jumper off, she was lounging in a sports bra and a pair of gym shorts (no panties, of course) that she'd altered into short-shorts.

All she wanted to do was chill.

Now this shit.

She locked her locker, then meandered out of her cell and down the tier. When she reached the podium, the CO rolled her eyes.

"You know I was about to write your ass up, right?"

Heaven gave the chunky-faced CO an incredulous look. "For *what?*"

"For taking your slow-ass time." She slung a pass at her. "Now go take your ass down to classroom C."

Heaven frowned. "Classroom *C*, for what?" She had a mind to refuse, but thought otherwise. A refusal could result in a write-up of some sort. And this CO obviously wanted Heaven to give her a reason to do just that.

Officer Harris huffed. "Lewis, get the fuck on; standing here asking me some dumb-ass question, like I'm some damn psychic. Do you see a crystal ball anywhere over here, huh? How the hell I know why they called you down there. Just go, so I can get back to my damn crossword puzzle."

Heaven snatched the pass from off the podium, then spun on her heel.

"I know one damn thing," the CO barked. "Snatch another pass off my shit, and see what I do."

Heaven ignored her rant, and kept walking. She was learning. Some of the COs were more fucked up than most of the inmates. And that bitch was one of them.

Shortly, there was a *click* of the door and Heaven opened it, walking off the housing unit. She glanced up at one of the cameras as she headed down the hall toward the educational department, wondering which COs were manning the control center, zooming in on her.

She'd heard how there'd been a CO who got off on zooming the cameras in on certain inmates in housing units, while playing with his dick.

If she were in the mood to go back to solitary, she'd peel out of her jumper and give whoever was inside the control center something to look at.

Instead, she tossed her hair and threw an extra shake, or two, in her hips, causing her ass to sway harder, faster. Oh how she loved thongs. The thin strip of material made her feel so sexy; so, so very naughty.

Heaven nearly bumped into an inmate with skin the color of cinnamon as she turned the corner. The inmate's short dark hair was slicked up with gel into a tiny ball on top of her head like a little rabbit's tail.

She reminded Heaven of a crack head.

Startled, she jumped backward. "Oh, excuse me."

The inmate looked her up and down, then slyly slipped her a tiny piece of paper. "Here," she muttered, before winding the corner and heading in the opposite direction.

Heaven blinked, but kept walking, gripping the note tightly in her hand. When she'd reached one of the camera's blind spots, she quickly opened the crumpled paper.

She immediately recognized the handwriting.

CLASSROOM B. NOT C. WAIT IN CLOSET.

Heaven crumpled the note, and smiled, her cunt clenching with every step.

TWENTY-ONE

Nothing in the Middle . . .

Almost immediately, Officer Rawlings eased up behind her. And . . . mmm, it instantly felt good—*too* good—to feel the heat of his body pressed up against her. She quickly turned her body to face him before she ended up grinding her ass up into his crotch.

"Damn, baby," he said low and deep, casting a wicked grin at her as she faced him. "I've missed you."

"I've missed you, too," she said softly. Well, her pussy missed him. Same difference, wasn't it?

"I need some pussy, baby."

"Is pussy all I am to you?" Her mouth curved into a sexy grin of her own before she slid her tongue over her lips. She loved the thrill of flirting. Loved the thrill of fucking . . . *him*. And fucking him was good. But she needed to know she had him wrapped around her finger. She needed him to prove his devotion to her, to show her just how far he would go for her, before she gave him any more of her warm, gushy cunt.

"Nah, that's not all you are to me."

"Oh? Then what am I?"

He wasn't one to often get serious with women. And he'd never been the sentimental, mushy type, but she was so fucking beautiful that his balls ached. He had it bad for her. And the less time he spent with her, the more consumed he became with her. She was his first thought in the morning, and the last thought on his mind before he closed his eyes at night.

Masturbation had become his new best friend since he'd given up fucking the horny bitches who eagerly threw him pussy. And God knew how much he loved being balls deep inside some wet pussy. But he'd given up all that—the late-night booty calls and trolling the strip clubs for sex.

The only thing on his mind was, *her*. And his thoughts of her last night—on his night off, had given him a hard-on he'd carried through the whole night, making it nearly impossible for him to sleep. Sex on the brain made for a hard dick. And it made for a very restless night. Still, it brought out every lustful fantasy he'd ever thought of, and even some he hadn't.

All he wanted to do was taste her, smell her, caress her with his tongue and hands, then fuck her deep. He could still hear her soft cries of ecstasy from the last time he'd been inside her, bringing her to orgasm, and every night, he replayed—while he sniffed her panties—having her back pressed up against the wall of her cell and her legs hitched up over his hips as his dick entered her body, losing himself in her wet, silky heat.

Yeah, she was definitely more than good pussy to him. She was what his fantasies had been made up of for the majority of his life.

She was everything he had ever imagined.

He wasn't desperate. He was deliberate. And he knew what he wanted.

She was whom he wanted to build a life with.

He wanted to take care of *her*.

And he'd wait for her, for as long as it took.

She made a huffing noise and glared up at him.

"Well? Are you going to answer the question?"

Desire flamed in his eyes. Then, without a word, he surprised her when he leaned in and gave her a slow, sensual kiss—they hadn't even gotten the closet door closed good, after all—but she couldn't stop herself from kissing him back, her tongue gliding over and around his.

He breathed her in, inhaling the very essence of her as he pulled her into him.

She emitted a soft moan and for a moment, her eyes closed and her hand leisurely eased up his back, over his uniform shirt.

The sexual tension between them thickened the air in the tiny space, making her lightheaded. She gasped for air but wouldn't pull away. The kiss consumed her. She consumed him. And their tongues continued to tangle until her mouth inched upward and her teeth nipped and caught his upper lip. She pulled outward and sucked it further into her mouth, greedily sucking. Her tongue licked and laved before she released his lip.

He groaned and pressed his thigh into her crotch, and she realized he was growing hard against her leg. A moan built deep in her chest as he nibbled back at her lips. And, then—kiss for kiss, lick for lick, bite for bite . . . it escaped from the back of her throat, and burst out in a sound of sweet agony as his hand slid between her legs, and he touched her *there*. Over the fabric of her jumper and the panties that had now become sodden with lust.

Her clit tightened and strained between her legs. *No, no, no.* She couldn't fuck him—not again, and not here, not now. But her body heated, and her cunt exploded in a rush of molten lava.

Her sensitive breasts rubbed against his chest through her jumper making her pussy tingle. And she heard another sigh of pleasure echo from her throat unbidden as his lips and warm kisses glided along the column of her neck, while his hands found her swollen breasts and cupped them.

"Oh, God, yes," she murmured.

"I want you so bad, baby," he muttered, his voice a hot whisper. She felt his arousal spreading down through her like warm fudge.

"*Mmm . . .*"

"Let me inside you," he whispered, reaching for her jumper's zipper and sliding it down. She caught his hand midway and stopped him, tearing herself away from his grasp.

"*Stop*," she whispered breathlessly, drawing back slightly.

He let out a low growl in response, pulling her back into his arms. "You don't mean that, baby. You have me so fucking horny. Just let me put the head in."

She looked up at him incredulously. She almost laughed at the absurdity of him only putting *the head in*. Yeah, okay. Good luck with that. She knew as well as he did that if the head went in, so would the rest of his dick.

So—*hell no*, she wasn't falling for that lame shit.

"C'mon, baby," he urged, rubbing his dick over his pants with his hand. "We gotta make it quick. I only have another ten minutes, or so. Let me bust this nut in you."

"No," she managed between thready breaths, trying to ignore the long, hard column that had grown in his pants. But without forethought, she reached down between them, wrapping her hand around it through the fabric.

Oh, he felt so thick in her hand.

So, so hard.

She licked her lips, anticipating the taste of him. She felt her pussy tremor at the thought of feeling his hard flesh over her tongue. It'd been over a year, before her incarceration, since she'd been down on her knees sucking a dick.

All the weeks in solitary, with him sneaking into her cell—dicking her down, not once had she given him head. She wanted to, but she restrained herself.

She sucked in a breath.

"No pussy for you," she pushed out in between pants. And as she protested, denied herself what hung between his legs, he dropped his head to her neck, kissing and biting at the skin under her ear.

A low groan left him before he said against her flesh, "You know you want this dick inside you. Don't you, baby?" His voice was thick, throaty, from arousal.

Mmm, God, yes. She wanted it inside her so badly, fucking her, ravishing her, wringing out an orgasm.

But she needed to test his commitment to her—further, first. "No pussy. But if you promise to bring me something, I'll give you the back of this throat . . ."

"Aw," he breathed. He was so, so ready to explode. But—fuck, head wasn't what he'd had in mind; still, he'd take what he could get. Bottom line, he'd promise her a mink wrap if it meant having her catch his nut. "Anything for you, baby; just let me feel them pretty lips around this dick."

She smiled. Then she reached for his fly and fumbled with his button and zipper. As his fly parted, she slid to her knees and shoved his pants down over his hips and then reached into his boxers and dragged his dick out of confinement. She licked the head and then suckled it inside her mouth, sucking gently.

"I want two dildos and a vibrator," she stated as she let the head slide momentarily free from her lips.

"Whoa. Wait a second," he stated unsure he'd heard her right. "You want *what?*"

"You heard me," she mumbled. "I want you to smuggle me in a few dildos. Nothing too big, though, just a ten-inch and maybe something a little smaller."

He frowned. "Nah, fuck that. You wanted a phone. You got it. You wanted expensive-ass panty-sets. You got that, too. And now you're asking me to bring you in some fake-ass dicks?" He shook his head. "Nah, baby. Ain't happening."

She looked up at him through her veil of lashes, and asked, "Do you want to keep getting this pussy?"

His jaw twitched, but his eyes flared with desire. Why the fuck bitches always gotta use the pussy to try and manipulate a motherfucker, he wondered to himself. That shit was a big turn-off when other hoes he'd encountered over the years tried it. But there was something about the way she'd tried it that made him want the pussy even more. There was no way he could *not* want to be up inside her, buried deep every chance he got.

"Don't play with me. Hell yeah," he breathed out. "But . . ."

"Then smuggle me in what I've asked for. Two dildos and a vibrator."

Before he could continue his protest, she held up his dick and slowly licked under and around his balls, before sucking them into her mouth. She wetly massaged them with her tongue.

She looked up at him through her thick lashes again; raw heat blazing in her eyes, she licked the underside of his shaft.

"Should I stop?"

"Fuck nah," he rasped, his hand tangling in her hair as he cupped the back of her neck and used his other hand to guide his dick to her mouth. "Suck it."

She flicked her tongue over the head of his dick, then swirled her tongue over and around the head. Then she slid her tongue along its head.

"Aah, fuck, baby . . ."

"Am I going to get what I've asked for?" she questioned, her mouth hovering over his turgid flesh.

He groaned. "Yeah, baby. I got you. Two dildos . . . *mmm* . . . and a vibrator." His arousal had risen to a fever pitch. Fucking her in the storage closet, while one of the teachers played lookout, sent him on the verge of losing control. "Now let me get in that throat, baby."

She opened her mouth and let him slide between her lips.

"Yeah, baby. Take it deep."

He inched forward, forcing her head against the wall, and placed both hands above her, leaning into her, his palms flattened up on the wall.

"Yeah. Suck this dick . . ."

He plunged deeper, forcing her throat open. She relaxed her jaws and his hips worked back and forth, the head of his dick brushing against her tongue over and over.

He looked down at her, her beautiful mouth wetly loving his dick. "Yeah, baby, swallow it," he said as he fucked her mouth in long strokes. "Take it all."

She closed her eyes and felt a rush of liquid desire burn through her veins as he swelled larger in her mouth. She hummed over the width of him and slid her hands around to cup his muscled ass, to take more of him—her mouth, her lips, her tongue, worked synchronously.

Oh how she loved the feel of his dick in her mouth. It'd been so long since she'd sucked a dick, and the feel and taste of him was an addicting combination.

His erection tightened even further, and she smiled, satisfied, taking him deeper into her wet mouth, his head slipping down in her throat, brushing over her uvula, filling her neck. With one hand, she reached for his balls and squeezed, and a warm spurt of his milk hit the back of her throat, and she swallowed quickly to keep from choking.

She kept on sucking him, her head feverishly bobbing back and forth as his hips matched her movements. She sucked and sucked until his knees buckled, until she had sucked his balls empty, and his semi-erect dick had finally, reluctantly, plopped out of her wet, greedy mouth.

TWENTY-TWO

Drunk in Love . . .

Love didn't just happen, did it? Wasn't it supposed to evolve over time?

Fuck nah.

It happened when the heart opened itself up to it.

Officer Rawlings took a swig of his Heineken. The thought of her made his dick hard. He swallowed the strong, bitter lager as he pressed the swelling between his legs together and turned on his computer. He stared at the green bottle with the lone red star, impatiently drumming his fingers as he waited for it to boot.

What the fuck was he doing?

Shit.

Fuck if he knew.

All he did know was that inmate Lewis had good pussy and had sucked the shit out of his dick. And that alone had set fire to his senses in a way that no other woman ever had. He groaned as his dick tightened at the memory of being slickly buried deep in her mouth, the tight grip of her throat milking the head of his cock. She'd sucked him wildly, greedily, and she'd come immediately without being touched, the sweet juices of her pussy flooding her panties.

And he had the proof to smell it.

He pulled her panties from his back pocket—pink and frilly—and inhaled the heady scent, before licking inside the crotch. He licked and licked, then sucked them into his mouth. Then he started chewing on them as if they were a big piece of pink, pussy-flavored bubblegum.

If he could blow a few bubbles with her panties, he would.

Goddamn. Fuck.

This was a fucking mess. She made him crazy with want. Made him twisted with kinky desire. He'd never done any crazy shit like licking and sucking the inside of a bitch's panties. And here he was laving away, his tongue practically licking out the seam.

And now he was, at eight thirty in the fucking morning, on a mission to shop—instead of crawling in bed and getting some sleep—for shit he'd never imagine buying.

Dildos.

He shook his head. He was bugging for sure. He removed her underwear from his mouth and pushed out a heated breath, then lifted his beer and pressed the opening to his lips and took a long, drawn-out swallow. He belched, setting the bottle back onto his desk as the computer screen lit up with his desktop icons. He clicked on the browser and went to a search engine page.

There, he typed in what he was looking for, and waited for the results. He almost fell out of his chair when pages and pages, link upon link, popped up on the screen. It was too overwhelming. The shit required too much thought: size, shape, color, material—jelly, silicone, soft skin (aka cyberskin), or acrylic or glass—vibrating (or not) . . .

What the fuck?

Ugh. He was tempted to click out of the browser, and simply

take his ass to bed. Instead, he kept browsing. When he finally clicked on the eighth link, he bit out a curse.

He didn't know the first thing about sex toys; let alone a fucking dildo or vibrator, but he was a man of his word. And it was what he'd promised his baby, though he couldn't understand why the fuck she needed one of those things any-damn-way when he was offering her up all the dick she needed.

Eight, thick, curved inches.

Fucking broads. One dick was never enough. So now he had to compete with a fucking fake-ass dick. He took another gulp of his beer. As the brew heated through his veins, the thought of some-one—or *something*—else fucking her made him feel murderous. He felt he'd seriously beat the shit out of a motherfucker, beat his skull down to the white meat, for even thinking about trying to press up on what was his.

Fuck, man. Get a grip. What the fuck is wrong with you? It's a damn dildo.

He laughed at the ridiculousness of feeling jealous over a fucking sex toy. There was no way a damn manmade cock could fuck her like the real thing, the way he could.

But, fuck it.

After she'd sucked his dick then ate his babies, she'd given him strict instructions as to what type of items she wanted. Big. And black.

He clicked on a link for sextoyfun.com and, after close to thirty minutes of perusing the products, he settled on some shit called Cockzilla, a black, sixteen-and-a-half-inch dildo.

His eyes widened when another item caught his attention. A Clone-A-Willy Vibrating Dildo kit. *Get the fuck out of here. Is this shit for real?* He read it again. The description said he could make an exact replica of his own dick. Hell, he had nothing to lose. Shit. He was proud of his thick, veiny dick. He'd give it a try, then give it to his baby as a surprise. Yeah, that's what he'd do. Then she could have access to his cock whenever she wanted it.

He took another swig from his beer, then added the kit to his cart, along with a vibrating jelly dong. He made his purchase, then, somehow, landed on another link. Zane's Pleasure Products. Shit. Now he was curious as fuck to see what this freaky broad had going on. He'd never read any of her books, but he'd watched her two television shows, *The Jumpoff* and *The Sex Chronicles* on Cinemax, so he knew what time it was with her.

There he purchased Heaven a seven-inch, multi-speed massager.

Rawlings blew out a curse when he was done, then clicked out of his browser, before standing to his feet. He stretched and yawned, then began stripping out of his uniform. Next he pulled his undershirt off, then came out of his boxers, leaving a trail of clothing as he made his way to the bathroom where he turned on the shower, full blast and steaming hot. He lathered up, then languidly stroked his soapy dick, dying to be back inside his baby again; him unleashing his seeds. In her mouth. In her pussy. He even wanted to feel it in her ass.

He closed his eyes to relish in the memory of her mouth on his cock, her tongue along his shaft, her fingers digging into his ass cheeks.

He pumped his dick in his fist. Threw his head back.

And growled.

Twenty minutes later, he walked out of the bathroom, towel around his waist, his balls half-a-pound lighter.

As he puttered around his bedroom, before climbing into bed, he gave thought to the purchases he'd made earlier. This was some twisted shit. Yet, he'd gotten his baby what she'd requested.

Now the million-dollar question was: How the fuck was he going to get all this shit into the prison?

TWENTY-THREE
Strange Fruit....

"Hey, there," Heaven said as she approached the young woman who'd come to her cell over a week ago. She hadn't seen her since that day, nor had she gotten the girl's name. But she'd heard from the prison vine (aka Sabina) that it was—*shit*. She raked her brain trying to remember what the gossipers said her name was. Tina something. She knew it was some crazy-ass name, but she couldn't remember it for nothing.

"Catina, right?"

The girl scowled. "My name ain't no damn *Catina*."

"Then what is it?"

"Why?" she asked defensively.

Heaven took her in. She looked different. Cleaner. She'd washed her hair and had the ends of a fresh weave curled. And it looked as if she'd put on a little makeup—eyeliner and mascara. She even had her nails painted. Yet, she still looked hard. Hardened. The streets, the hood, life choices, all had a way of snatching a young woman's innocence and youth away from her if she let it.

Heaven didn't need to know her life story to know she had it rough. Her gaze drifted to the young woman's arms crossed tightly over her chest, then she looked back up into her face. She was a pretty girl.

Heaven recalled that the girl had big breasts, but she hadn't really looked at them until now. They were beautiful breasts that many women would kill to have. Big, bouncy breasts made for tit fucking and lots of sucking.

Heaven shifted her gaze again. She'd felt bad for treating her the way she had, even if she had been generous enough to give the young woman a little starter kit. Still, she didn't have to treat her like trash even if she did smell like it.

Heaven glanced around the tier, then brought her attention back to the chick in front of her. "I wanted to have a word with you; that's all."

She crossed her arms over her chest, and gave Heaven a dirty look. "*What?* You want your tampons back?"

Heaven shook her head. "No, no. I gave those things to you. I actually wanted to apologize to you for the other day. I shouldn't have said those harsh things, especially when you were already upset. You didn't deserve that."

She clucked her tongue. "You right. I didn't. I ain't no low-class bum-bitch."

"I didn't say you were," Heaven replied.

"But you was actin' like it," she snapped. "Comin' at me all slick."

"I didn't mean to offend you," Heaven said sincerely.

"Oh no, boo-boo. You ain't offend me. You pissed me the hell off. But, trust. It's all good. I'ma pay you back for all the stuff you gave me when I get on my feet. Then after that, I'ma tell you to kiss my fuckin' ass. I might even fight ya ole stuck-up ass 'n' snatch out ya weave."

Weave?

Heaven flung her hair. She wasn't going to waste her breath schooling some little hoodrat bitch on what *real* hair looked like. Her shit was all hers. From her roots to her ends, there wasn't anything weaved up on her head.

"Listen, hon. I'm not looking for problems," Heaven assured her. "I only wanted to apologize to you."

She grunted. "Well, apology accepted. But I still fight old-ass bitches."

Heaven blinked. *Old?* She wasn't even forty yet. What the hell would she be called if she were? Ancient?

"Again," Heaven said. "I didn't mean to come at you like that. I was having a bad day. Haven't you ever had a bad day?"

Her brows rose in response.

"Well, I have," Heaven continued. "Many over the years. And I'm woman enough to apologize when I'm wrong. Anyway, I also wanted to thank you for coming by when you did . . ."

She tilted her head, and suspiciously stared Heaven down. "You wanna *thank* me for what?"

"You actually pulled me out of my mini meltdown without realizing it." Heaven chuckled lightly. "You saved me from tearing up my cell. So for that, I say thank you."

The young woman clucked her tongue, then twisted her lips. "Good for you. Anything else?"

Heaven frowned and took a deep breath. Usually, she said what she had to say, then kept it moving. She wasn't for a lot of back and forth with these females. But there was something about her that kept Heaven standing there.

"By the way, I'm Heaven." She held out her hand.

The young woman stared at her outstretched hand. "And I'ma hood bitch, so, in the future, watch how you come for me."

Heaven raised a brow, pulling her hand back and placing it up on her hip. She looked her up and down and smirked. "Well, nice to meet you, *Hood Bitch*. Now what's your real damn name, so I can go on about my day?"

Suddenly the young woman laughed, and Heaven could see the fillings in her teeth. "You *stooooooopid*. But, anyway . . . What you got in your hair, grade seven-A?"

Heaven scowled. "Excuse me?"

"Ya weave. That's that virgin Remy hair, seven-A, ain't it?"

Heaven ran a hand through her hair. "Oh, no, hon. My hair isn't a weave."

"*Mmph*. What you mixed with, Dominican?"

"No. Now are you going to tell me your name, or not?"

The young woman brushed by Heaven, flicking her weave over her shoulder. She waited until she got halfway down the tier, then turned around and said, "It's Clitina. Don't forget it."

"Ohmygod," Sabina said, walking into the cell. "Was that that girl Clit-something?"

Heaven flinched. "*Clitina*." The name felt dirty rolling off her tongue.

Sabina shook her head. "Who the hell names their child after genitalia, any-damn-way?"

"A woman who has a boyfriend named *Nuts*—with the first letter *Kay* and last letter *Zee*—unfortunately."

"Ohmygod. I have heard it all. You can't be serious." She gave Heaven a look.

"I wish I wasn't."

"So what she want anyway?"

Heaven waved her on. "Nothing. I wanted to apologize to her; that's all."

Sabina frowned. "Apologize to *her?* For what? It's her momma that should be apologizing."

Heaven chuckled. "I came off a little harsh toward her when she'd stopped by the cell one day last week asking for a tampon." Heaven shook her head. "She was tore up, weave pulled out, face lumped up."

"She's kinda new here, isn't she?" Heaven nodded. "And she got her ass beat already?"

"Yeah. By her mother and her mother's friend. They jumped her in the visiting hall."

Sabina's eyes widened. "Oh, she's the one everyone was talking about. I heard they tore her up, but she fought them both, even hitting one of them upside the head with a chair." Sabina laughed. "I heard they tore the place up. It took at least five COs to hold one of the women down. Some chick with a humongous ass, they said. And then it took another three COs to hold that Clit chick back." Sabina sucked her teeth. "I'm pissed I missed it. Nothing like a good ole family brawl."

Heaven laughed. "Girl, your ass is silly."

Sabina kicked off her Reeboks, then tossed her ID holder up on her bed. She pulled off her T-shirt, then grabbed her robe and slipped it on, tying it at the waist.

"Anyway. I apologized to her for not being more sympathetic to her when she was upset."

Sabina rolled her eyes. "I don't know why you were feeling sorry for her. I heard that girl is wild as hell. Anyway, moving on. Enough about chicks named after clits."

Both women laughed.

"Don't you ever get bored staying holed up in here, looking at these dingy-ass walls?" Sabina asked. "I don't know why you like staying up in this cell all the time."

Heaven swept an arm around the cell. "Look around you. How could I ever be bored with all this luxury around me," she said sarcastically. "There's flat-screen TV, a Sony radio, MP-3 player, three hot pots and a locker full of food. And a bitch has access to twenty-two basic channels from eight a.m. to eleven p.m. What more could a girl want?"

Sabina smirked, peeling off her ankle socks, then sliding her feet into her shower shoes. "How about some fresh damn air, smart-ass? You need to come out and play with the rest of us convicts sometimes," she joked. "Some of us are starting to think you don't like us."

Heaven tore her eyes away from the six-foot television cable. "I don't."

Sabina laughed, looking into her acrylic mirror as she applied Noxema to her face. "That's exactly what I told them."

Heaven shook her head. "Oh, I'm sure that went over well at the card table."

Sabina shrugged. "They'll live."

"I'm going to need another one of your jumper creations," she said, eyeing Sabina. "Ask your connect down in supplies how much it's going to cost me for two new jumpers?"

Sabina shook her head. "And what exactly do you want done to said uniforms?"

Heaven grinned. "I'll let you know when it comes to me. Maybe something crotch-less."

Sabina gave her an incredulous stare. "*Crotch-less?* Stop the press. Am I missing something? Is Miss Uptight planning to give up the cookie?"

Heaven smirked. "A lady never kisses and tells."

"Uh-huh. Whatever," Sabina said, leaning over the small sink to brush her teeth. "Anyway. I'll probably see her Thursday. She only comes out to the big yard Tuesdays and Thursdays to take orders. Speaking of which, you need to leave out this cell and get some sun. You're looking a little pale. Keep it up and you'll be as white as me. Then all the girls will be calling *you*, Becky."

Heaven laughed, opening a pack of salami slices. "Not." She popped two in her mouth, then offered her cellie some.

"Tramp. Now you wanna feed me. I just brushed my teeth."

"Fine. More for me."

"Speaking of feedings," she said, gathering her toiletries from her footlocker. "What's for dinner?"

Heaven sucked her teeth. "Oh, no, hon. Don't even try it. Tonight's your night to cook." The two women usually combined their commissary orders and took turns cooking their meals in their cell. "See if your girl in the kitchen can get us some chopped onions and peppers. I have a taste for some sausage and peppers with some brown . . ."

Officer Ferguson walked by and she suddenly lost her train of thought. "Hey, Miss Ferguson," she called out.

The CO backtracked her steps and peeked in their cell. "What's up, Lewis? Grover?"

"Hey, Miss Ferguson," Sabina said back, placing her shower supplies in her shower bag. "You doing OT over here?"

"No. I'm in outer control tonight." She looked over at Heaven. "Lewis, you staying outta trouble?" She narrowed her eyes. "No more lockup, right?"

"That's the plan. I'm staying far away from solitary unless someone else comes at me."

The CO gave her a look, then slowly shook her head, glancing over at Sabina. "Grover, keep an eye on your cellie."

Sabina sighed dramatically. "I've tried, Miss Ferguson. But this ho a wild child."

The three women laughed.

As soon as the CO left, Heaven turned to Sabina and said, "*Wild child*, huh?"

"Yup. You might have everyone else around here fooled, but I know you, boo."

Heaven gave her an incredulous look. "*What?* You know me how?"

Sabina started moaning low. "*Mmm. Oooh. Yes, yes,*" she cooed, rapidly moving two fingers in front of her crotch. "*Fuck me, baby. Give me that big dick . . .*"

Heaven's eyes widened, and her cheeks heated. "Ohmygod! And here I thought I was being discreet."

Sabina waved her on, seeing her embarrassment. "Girl, don't sweat it. I've known all about the little sex parties you have in your panties at night." She grinned. "I've heard you on the phone a few times in the middle of the night."

Heaven gave her a questioning stare.

"I might snore heavy, but when my ears are on alert, I hear *every*thing."

Heaven rolled her eyes. "Next time, I'll keep that in mind."

"Oh, no. Don't. The moans are sexy. Next time I might join in."

Heaven laughed. "Bitch, you silly."

She smirked. "Oh, no, hon. I'm very serious. What, you think I don't need a little late-night action sometimes, too?"

"So you want me to moan in your ear, too?" Heaven teased.

Sabina licked her lips. "That's a start, boo. I ain't no lesbian. But with the right incentives, I'm liable to do anything—once, or twice—for an orgasm."

And with that, she gathered her shower bag and trotted out the cell, walking down the tier to where the showers were located.

TWENTY-FOUR

Anticipation . . .

"Take ya dumb asses back to bed," a booming male voice barked, causing Heaven to quickly hide her cell phone. It was *him* again. She was wondering when he'd come back on their housing unit. The clinking of keys, followed by the sliding of metal, made her cringe. "Let me catch either of you bitches so much as breathing wrong, and I'ma have your asses in lockup so fast, it'll make your ugly-ass heads spin."

What a fucking asshole!

Heaven swung her feet over her bunk, slipping her feet into her shower shoes as she ran her fingers through her hair to give it a more tousled look. She tied her T-shirt in a knot at the small of her back, then stood up.

She sashayed her way toward her cell door in her pink, lacy panties, then called out, "CO."

"Lewis, don't do it," Sabina warned as Heaven called out for the CO again.

Heaven waved her on.

"I'm telling you," Sabina hissed. "You're playing with fire, and you're gonna get burned fucking with that nut."

"I'm a pyromaniac," Heaven teased over her shoulder. "I love playing in the flames. CO!"

"Yo, what the fuck you want, *Inmate*?"

"I *need* to see you," she yelled back. "*Please.*" She added the last part—*please*, for emphasis. It seemed men liked it when women begged. It seemed to be an ego booster, or some shit. Well, hell, she'd happily stroke his ego since it sounded like it was bigger than his dick, any-damn-way. She giggled to herself.

Sabina shook her head, shutting off her book light, and shutting her magazine. She settled herself against her pillow, then pulled the sheet up to her chin. "Okay, then," she whispered. "Play on, and get burned if you want. But you've been put on notice."

"I'll keep that in mind," Heaven said, rolling her eyes up in her head. Who the fuck did this bitch think she was, putting *her* on notice? *Bitch, bye.*

Sabina shook her head. "Goodnight, then."

"Yup, sweet dreams," Heaven snidely replied.

Sabina's jaw tightened. That self-righteous bitch deserved whatever she got fucking with Struthers. Right then, she decided she wanted no parts of whatever it was Heaven was scheming up. So she was done with it.

She liked things the way they were—quiet. And she wanted nothing to do with having her bid disrupted behind some wet-behind-the-ears chick who obviously didn't know shit about jailing.

She'd been sent to lockup once for having a lighter and rolling paper—contraband that wasn't even hers—hidden in a pair of her Reebok sneakers that a CO had found during a random shakedown on her tier. The items had belonged to her cellmate at the time. And, instead of her sneaky-ass stepping up and claiming the contraband, she'd kept her mouth shut and watched Sabina get led off the tier in handcuffs. She'd received an institutional charge, and ten days in lockup behind that.

It had been absolute hell there. And she'd be goddamned if she was going to let this bitch get her hemmed up in whatever dumb shit she had going on in her pretty little head. She didn't need another reckless bitch in her life. Right then, she found herself considering putting in a request for a single cell over on 2 South. Hell, she'd even try to get over to the dorms on 7 North if possible. Shit. She'd paid her dues sharing cells with crazy bitches. She'd been charge free for the last year. Now it was time she finished out her bid away from these reckless bitches.

Still, she liked Heaven, but she had to look at her sideways at the moment. She'd told her in so many words to fall back. Don't go fucking with Struthers. But—*noooo.* This whore just had to go and do the opposite. She lifted her head from her pillow and looked over at her cellie.

Just look at her, Sabina thought—frowning, standing over there with all of her ass hanging out like she's some damn video vixen. If she hadn't been so annoyed at her, she'd probably get off at the sight of all that big, juicy ass.

Maybe tomorrow she would.

But before her head hit the pillow again, she had to admit she looked sexy as fuck. She sighed. Heaven was cool, she reasoned. But she thought the chick was too stuck on herself, like her shit didn't stink. Some of the other women on the tier didn't particularly care for her, either, but they respected her for slicing up Snake, then for fighting Coletta.

Snake.

God, she'd done good *not* thinking about *her.* She had been a terror on the tier, a troublemaker and a bully.

But—*mmm, yes*—she had been a damn good lover, too.

Sabina felt her pussy quivering at the thought of Snake's tongue snaking its way inside her walls as she attempted to lick out her ovaries. Ooh, she had known her body better than she did. And, every night, she'd make love to her with her mouth, tongue and hands. And she'd made her cum, heavy and hard.

Sabina swallowed at the memories. She hadn't let Snake fuck her—per se, but she'd come damn near close on several occasions to letting her stick her dick in her. Kissing, grinding, and lots of pussy eating had been their nightly pastime.

God, yes.

They'd been cellmates for almost a year. And from the moment Snake had stepped over the threshold, into the cell, she'd made her intentions known. *"I'm gonna be fuckin' you by nightfall. I know how you white bitches love good dick."*

And there had been—all-night fucking. With her tongue and fingers.

Sabina hadn't minded playing *wifey* as long as she respected her. And she hadn't minded her having other lovers as long as she was coming *home* (to their cell) to her. But, somehow, she started putting her hands on her, choking her, and smacking her up.

Then, out of the blue—after almost a year—Snake had managed to get moved out of their cell, and into the cell of some ugly black bitch on the other side of the tier without so much as a *goodbye*. And, as if that hadn't been enough insult, she'd run off with all of her commissary; stole her shit while she was out in the yard.

Just thinking about how she'd done her made Sabina's blood boil. Her nose flared. Thieving bitch! She didn't know why she'd ever fucked with that ghetto black bitch in the first place. Broke bitch was only good for licking her asshole and sucking her pussy walls clean, any-damn-way.

Oh—and toe sucking.

And, and . . . God, yes . . . licking all over her breasts.

Still, she had loved her once—or at least had wanted to. But, now, she was glad someone had the heart to take her ratchet-ass down a notch. Heaven had sliced that bitch real good. She—

"CO!"

Sabina shook her head again, her thoughts returning to the present moment. "This dumb bitch still fucking yelling," she mumbled under her breath as she shifted in her bunk and rolled over on her side, facing toward the wall.

She shut her eyes, holding her breath, before the storm came.

"Yo, why the fuck is you hollering out your fucking cell, huh, *Inmate?*"

His booming voice alone made Heaven's insides shudder. Her gaze drifted down to the center of his crotch, then down to his long, booted feet before she craned her neck upward and took in the menacing face of her next mark.

Around his waist hung from his duty belt were a radio, flashlight, handcuffs positioned at the small of his back, and a set of keys.

He wasn't exactly what she'd envisioned. And she hadn't expected her cunt to respond so excitedly, either. She had expected him to be some old, greasy-looking, big-bellied fucker. Not this handsomely groomed man with skin the color of sun-kissed copper and a beautiful set of full lips.

She slowly licked her lips. "I wanted to ask a favor, CO."

He scowled. "It's *Sergeant*," he corrected. "Now what the fuck you want?"

She hesitated for a moment, holding her breath deciding whether she wanted to risk disrupting her bid. But Sabina had piqued her curiosity, and she wanted to see his dick for herself.

Shit. She thought she had a strategy in mind—well, sort of—but the plan hadn't unfolded in exacting detail. And now he was standing at her cell in all of his six-foot-six glory and she felt momentarily dumbfounded at what to do next.

His overwhelming presence had totally disarmed her.

Shit, shit, shit . . .

TWENTY-FIVE

Playing with Fire . . .

"That motherfucker!" she hissed, walking into her cell the next morning. She felt blood rush to her head, making her ears burn. Her flat-screen TV was gone. And the lock on her gray footlocker had been cut off. The lid was up, and all of her commissary and extra hygiene products were gone, along with the hygiene products she'd had on her shelf.

Everything *gone!*

Sabina removed an earbud from one of her ears and shook her head, giving Heaven an I-told-you-so look.

She wanted to fall to her knees and scream, but her jaw was too sore. And she probably would have broken down in tears had her eyes not been still swollen and red, and stinging from being Maced.

She managed to choke back a sob instead. "What the *fuck* happened to my shit?"

Sabina shrugged. "COs took it in the middle of the night. Waking me up." She blinked. "Wait. Why are you back? I thought you went to lockup?"

No. I went to get face-fucked.

She'd managed to get what she wanted—his dick in her mouth. And she couldn't believe her eyes. There was thick dick . . . and then there was humongous. And Sergeant Struthers had a severely thick dick. It was, it was . . . God—she couldn't even describe what it was.

No, no. She knew what it was. It was a damn jawbreaker! And she'd thought for sure tackling that thing was going to fracture her jaw, and knock all of her teeth loose.

She decided her cellmate didn't need to know all that. Liking Sabina didn't mean she trusted her. But Sergeant Struthers and that undercover lesbian bitch Clemmons had escorted her out of her cell in the middle of the night in handcuffs. But before she could be brought down to solitary, the sergeant and Clemmons dragged her to a classroom out of view from any cameras.

She felt her body shiver at the memory.

He'd been rough and dirty and vulgar.

And she'd become shamefully wet . . . so, so wet . . . at the filthy names he'd called her. Slut. Bitch. Cum-sucking whore. Prison trash.

And the list of degrading names went on.

"So you like taunting motherfuckers, huh, you slutty bitch? Trying to get a motherfucker all hemmed up 'n' shit. Isn't that right?"

"No. That's not what I do," she'd said quickly. "I . . . would never do something like that."

"You'se a lying-ass bitch, you know that, right? You light-skinned, pretty bitches aren't nothing but a bunch of sleazy-ass, stuck-up whores; undercover sluts. Didn't you say you wanted some hard dick? You fucking troll."

Troll?

She'd fought the urge to laugh. Surely he couldn't have been referring to her as such. She bit her tongue, and then her bottom lip.

"No. I mean, yes. But I didn't mean I wanted it from you."

"Shut your fuckin' cum-hole. Your horny-ass want dick wherever you can get it, by whoever's willing to give it to you. Flaunting your pussy 'n' ass and them pretty-ass titties all up in motherfuckers' faces. I know what the fuck your scheming-ass is doing. Trick-ass slut."

She feigned insult. "All I want to do is, do my time." She'd blinked her eyes and, then came, another tear. Then another. Growing up being the youngest and the only girl, she'd learned very early on how to manipulate her father and brothers with tears. And she'd perfected the art of crying with the right amount of facial distress and lip quivering so that it bordered on sexy. "Please. Don't send me to lockup. I hated it there."

He'd glowered at her. "Bitch, your whore-ass loved it down there. Playing in your stank-ass pussy every motherfucking day, like you were some fucking porn-star. Nasty bitch."

Waves of heat had crept up her neck, and she'd felt her pussy tingle.

"I didn't mean any harm," she'd said softly, her voice near a whisper. "I swear I didn't." She forced herself to think about all of her fabulously expensive designer heels she'd left behind and wouldn't be able to wear for a long time, and began to sob. "Please," she begged. "Sometimes things blurt out of my mouth, before I have a chance to think."

His dick pulsed at the sight of her wet, tear-streaked face. Some men hated tears. But tears turned him on. It meant fear. It meant control. It meant pain. It meant these bitches knew who had the power to shut their motherfucking worlds down. And here he had thought this bitch was strong-willed and confident. Shit. She was just as weak and pathetic as the rest of them.

"Then maybe that big-ass mouth of yours needs to be stuffed to teach you when to keep it the fuck shut." He ran his large hand over his crotch. His dick—the *Beast*, as he called it—was slowly awakening.

She'd stared back at him, unblinking, fresh tears streaking her face.

He looked over toward the window, where Officer Clemmons stood on the other side, looking in.

"I'll tell you what," he'd said, kneading his cock over the fabric of his pants. "I won't write you a charge, or send your ass to lockup, but suck this dick, or I'm going to have my counterpart, Clemmons—you do know who she is, right?" Heaven nodded. "Good. So you either suck this dick, or I'm going to have"—he nodded his head over in her direction—"her come in here and fuck you with her baton until you pass out, and then I'm going to haul your ass off to lockup."

Hands cuffed behind her back, she'd slowly eased down to her knees, then replied, "I'm all yours . . ."

"So how'd you manage to escape solitary?" Sabina asked curiously. She suspected Heaven had gotten off because she'd sucked his dick, but she didn't want to assume anything. Still, this was prison. Anything was possible.

Heaven blinked and refocused and saw that Sabina was staring at her.

"What?"

Sabina removed her other earbud and tilted her head. "I asked you how you managed to get out of going to the *hole?*"

Heaven took a deep breath. "He's hanging it over my head. A *suspended sentence*, he called it. Fifteen days." She rolled her eyes. "The bastard, still wrote up some bogus charges, and that fat, stumpy bastard . . ."

"Who?"

"That ugly-ass hearing officer . . ."

"Oh, Officer Alvin."

"Yeah, him—that *Rasputia* lookalike; fat-fuck. And the whole time his nasty-ass sat there leering at me. His dick was probably hard as a rock watching me."

She'd had her disciplinary hearing first thing this morning, surprisingly. Disciplinary hearings usually only occurred on Tuesdays and Thursdays. Only to find her guilty of willfully disobeying a directive and soliciting a bribe to an officer, which were both Class C violations. And his lies resulted in a thirty-day loss of canteen privileges and thirty hours of extra duty.

She huffed. "What type of bullshit is that? The motherfucker took away my canteen privileges knowing goddamn well he'd robbed me of my shit. *Everything!*" She paced the cell. "I didn't willfully *disobey* that motherfucker." *I sucked his dick willingly.* "And I damn sure didn't solicit him for shit. I asked if he wanted to see me make my ass clap. How the hell is that solicitation?"

Sabina shrugged. "Be lucky that's all you got. It could have been worse."

Heaven felt the back of her eyeballs burning. She closed her eyes and pinched the corners of her eyes with her thumb and pointer finger. It felt like her brain was about to explode. That bastard didn't have to fuck with her canteen. But he had. And now she was on fire.

Sabina shook her head. "I warned you. But you didn't wanna listen."

Heaven stopped her pacing and shot her a nasty look.

"Anyway," Sabina continued, dismissing her glare. "Struthers and Alvin are real tight. Whatever Struthers wants, he gets."

Heaven started pacing again, her fists opening and closing. Her knees practically buckled when she looked over at the empty space where her television had once been. Two hundred and forty-two dollars down the goddamn drain!

Sabina stared at the rosy blotches on Heaven's face and her swollen eyes, and asked, "Who Maced you?"

The muscles in her jaws tightened, and she almost winced in pain. "That Clemmons bitch."

Sabina gave her a sympathetic look. "She's another one you'll need to try and stay away from. When she has it in for someone, she'll fuck with you every chance she gets. Until she breaks you."

Heaven snorted, slamming a hand on her hip. "That ho can *try* to break me all she wants, but she'll be the first to learn that I'm *not* easily broken. I might be new to prison, but I'm *not* new to bitches like her. You shit on me, you had best believe, I'll shit on you three times harder."

Sabina grimaced at the visual, but managed to give her a distasteful look mixed with humor. "Gee. Thanks. Just the image I need planted in my head; you squatting over Clemmons and shitting on her." Sabina pursed her lips as she scrutinized Heaven. At least their disdain for the roguish CO was one in the same.

"So why'd she Mace you?"

TWENTY-SIX

Drop It Like It's Hot . . .

Heaven huffed.

She'd been on her knees with her mouth stretched to capacity around Struthers' dick. He'd started out slow and easy, thrusting leisurely into her mouth until her mouth dripped like a waterfall and her jaws loosened. He withdrew and then pushed in again . . . in, out . . . in, out . . . each time deepening his thrust as his fingers tangled into her hair and he palmed her head with his hands.

"Yeah, slutty bitch, take all this fat-ass dick."

He'd pulled out, then began smacking her lips and face with his dick. The slaps fell heavy against her face, almost like a miniature billy club. He'd beaten her face and lips up with it, then demanded she opened her mouth—wide, and then slammed back in.

"You better not scrape my shit, either, or I'm going to take my radio and knock your front teeth out. Understand, bitch?"

It was hard to speak with her mouth crammed with cock, so she shook her head and grunted. She'd found herself almost choking on her spit as his dick brushed back and forth over her tongue, then hit the back of her throat, clogging her airway.

His dick had reminded her of a huge plug. Ass plug, throat plug, pussy plug . . . he'd plugged her mouth, tightening the grip on her head as his thrust became more aggressive, more urgent.

"I'm going to fuck the shit out of this mouth," he muttered. "Uh . . . *mmm* . . . shit . . ." He pounded harder, fucking her mouth in a way he'd fuck a pussy. He wanted to see her choke and gag, but she'd refused to give him the satisfaction of seeing, either.

She'd focused on her breathing; her nose smashed into his coarse pubic hairs as he grinded his pelvis into her face.

"Aaah, shit . . . motherfucking mouth good as fuck . . . dick-sucking bitch . . . aaah . . ." Unbeknownst to her, he'd become spellbound by those pretty lips of hers, and that warm, silky mouth. Her tongue had felt like heated velvet over his dick. And she'd impressed him with her flexible jaw and magnificent dick-sucking skills.

She'd proven herself a champion dick sucker, worthy of a nut down her throat.

Yes. She'd dropped to her knees, unashamed—ready and willing—to worship him. And her reward had been a fresh spurt of cum, warm and thick.

It splashed the back of her throat.

Her body had shuddered, surprising herself, her nipples and clit swollen and tingly. If she could have gotten a hand loose to slide between her thighs, she would have orgasmed on the spot. She'd pressed her legs together, her knees sinking deeper into the tiled floor as she thrust her own pelvis, trying to press her clit, as his dick slid over her tongue again and again.

"Swallow it all," he rasped, his balls bumping her chin. She gulped. "Yeah, that's a good, greedy bitch . . . aaah . . . get all that good nut . . ."

And then he thrust hard. Harder. Harder. His fingers so tangled in her hair she thought he might snatch her scalp from her head. She grunted, groaned, and nearly growled in pain and excruciating pleasure.

He'd grunted. Pounding her mouth, gripping her head, harder, tighter.

And then she felt another explosion of liquid heat hit the back of her mouth and quickly flood her mouth. Her pussy flared with even more arousal as she shut her long-lashed lids as his semen bathed her tongue and she swallowed every drop of his essence.

He cast his gaze downward and watched the erotic sight before him. He groaned in pleasure. He would have thrown her over the desk, yanked her panties to the side and fucked her had he had a condom with him, and more time. But it was getting late, and he needed to get her down to solitary, before someone radioed in, checking for his whereabouts.

She'd swallowed him again and again as more semen filled her mouth. He'd come back to back, emptying another fresh load of heat into her mouth.

"Hurry up and suck this fucking dick clean," he'd ordered.

And she'd obliged him. Then when he slowly pulled his dick from her mouth, she began wetly bathing him with her tongue, licking it clean of his release, she'd licked the remnants of his nut as if it'd been creamy white frosting.

He'd yanked his dick away from her, stuffing it back into his pants and zipping his fly as he motioned for Officer Clemmons to come in.

She'd entered the classroom, jaw tight—pissed that this prissy bitch got to suck his dick instead of being impaled by her baton. She snatched Heaven by the arm roughly, and when Heaven had stumbled from her knees buckling, she'd taken that as a show of resistance.

"Oh, you wanna resist. I said get to your feet, *bitch.*"

When Heaven hadn't stood fast enough, Clemmons pulled out her canister of Mace and sprayed it in her eyes, causing her to howl out in pain.

"She said I was resisting," Heaven finally answered, her thoughts drifting back to the present moment. She took a deep breath. "So the bitch Maced me. And that motherfucker stood there and let her."

A brow rose in question, but Sabina said nothing. She simply stared at her, and shook her head. She'd warned her. But some bitches were simply too fucking hardheaded to listen.

Oh well.

Maybe she'd listen the next time.

Heaven finally sat on her bunk, kicked off her shower shoes, then scooted back, pressing her back against the wall, seething. She swallowed, then coughed. Then took two fingers and slowly pulled out two strands of curly pubic hair from between her teeth.

She stared at them, then swirled her tongue around them as she held onto them with her fingers. Slowly, a sadistic grin eased over her still puffy lips.

Later that evening, Heaven stared up at Sabina's bunk as she thought back over the early part of day and parts of last night. It had been one hell of a ride. Her eyes were still red and itchy from her date with the can of Mace. And her jaw still ached from being skull-fucked.

"Yeah, slutty bitch, take all this fat-ass dick."

"Swallow it all . . ."

She angrily blinked back the memory. Yet her cunt still clenched. God, the filthy whore in her had loved it. She would never admit it out loud, but the memory made her breasts ache with need as her cunt pulsed.

But the shit still pissed her off. She hadn't maintained control of the situation properly. *Fuck.* She'd come on too strong. Had been too damn aggressive. Strong-willed women easily intimidated arrogant fucks like Struthers. He needed to always feel in control. And she'd stolen that from him when she'd boldly thrown herself at him.

She groaned at the memory of arching her and shamelessly shaking her ass at him. *"You wanna see me make it clap, too?"*

What a damn tramp!

In retrospect she came off acting and sounding thirsty.

God, she hated that word, *thirsty.*

Horny, *yes*; but parched she was not.

Thirsty felt desperate. Hell, it *was* desperate. And desperate women usually made reckless decisions. They moved impulsively. He had her all kinds of fucked up if he thought for one second that *that* was who she was.

Oh no fucker. Anything she did, she thought out before doing it—well, with the exception of shooting Freedom's ass. But that didn't count. He'd earned those bullets to the back. She hated him. Because he'd turned her into a fool. Because she had loved him once—okay (shit), she still did.

But he'd been her mistake.

She sighed. She wasn't going there again. It was done and over with.

Sergeant Struthers the goddamn Third was her primary problem at the moment. He needed a dose of his own medicine. Inmate or not, she was going to tear his little dirty playhouse down.

She reached for her phone, hidden inside the seam of her pillow, and pulled it out. She was thankful for Sabina's snoring ass. It gave her motivation to stay awake, researching every-and-any-thing she could find out about Mister Dirty Six-Six.

She powered it on, then punched in several digits, unlocking it. Then she pressed the icon for the Internet. Next she opened a tab in the browser and then typed in his name.

Mmm. He had Facebook and LinkedIn pages. She clicked on the link to his Facebook page. And *voilà*. There he was. Stupid fuck didn't even have his page private.

Her eyes zeroed in on the INTRO section:

ABOUT MY $$

STUDIED CRIMINAL JUSTICE AT MORRIS BROWN COLLEGE

WENT TO SNYDER HIGH SCHOOL

FROM JERSEY CITY, NJ

LIVES IN WEST NEW YORK, NJ

MARRIED TO ANGELICA K. STRUTHERS

Married? Oh, this dirty-ass, no-good motherfucker!

She clicked on his wife's page. *Mmph. Well, at least she's smart not to have her page open for public viewing.*

Heaven stared at her profile photo.

She had very intense brown eyes. And she was beautiful.

But what pissed her off more than anything else was the fact that he came to work and abused his power over female inmates, mostly on the young black women.

And here he was . . .

Married to a white woman.

TWENTY-SEVEN

Last Chance...

"Yeah, what is it, Lewis," Sergeant Struthers asked on a sneer. "Don't you have toilets to scrub?"

Heaven swallowed. "I'm done for the day," she stated calmly. But inside she was boiling over with anger. She wanted to punch him in the throat. She inhaled a deep breath, unfortunately breathing his masculine scent into her lungs.

She swallowed again.

God, she had a mind to ask him how Angelica—his *wife*—was. She wondered how well the Mrs. would take to knowing what kind of twisted sex games her husband was up to while at work. Then again, maybe she knew what type of debauchery her husband got off on.

Back arched, hand on hip, she slid her tongue around her teeth, then said, "I'd like to know what I have to do to get my commissary and personal property back?"

His expression hardened. "You'll get your shit back if/when *I* feel like letting you have it." He gave her a hard stare. "Anything else?"

Heaven stared at him for a long moment and then her eyes narrowed. "Is that your final answer, *Sergeant* Struthers?"

"I *thought* I already made myself clear."

Heaven forced a smile, but inside she was seething. Yet, she knew enough to not piss him off, either. But sooner than later, he'd get his.

"You did. *Very*," she said dryly. "Safe travels to you tonight, Sergeant."

"Inmate, did you just fucking threaten me?"

She smirked. "No, Sir. I simply wished you safe travels."

The muscles in his jaw tightened. "Get the fuck out of my office, Lewis, before I write your ass up."

"Good day," she said and headed for the door.

Sergeant Struthers eyed her as she stalked out and shut the door behind her. Then with a muttered curse, he rubbed his hard dick.

Heaven fought to bite back her temper, but that motherfucker had her hot like fire. Yet, she had to keep reminding herself not to move off emotions. Another stay in lockup was not what she was going for at the moment. She only—

"Lewis, where are you going now?" came a voice in back of her.

She sighed, rolling her eyes. Not this bitch again. Heaven gave thought to ignoring her, but she wasn't in the mood for a big production. So she simply said over her shoulder, "Back to my tier."

"Let me see your pass," Officer Clemmons said.

Heaven stopped walking and sucked her teeth. "Here," she said, thrusting a white pass at her.

Clemmons snatched it from her, then glanced at it. "Maybe if you started being a little nicer to me, I wouldn't have to be such a hard-ass all the time."

Heaven nearly laughed at the absurdity of the CO not *ever* being a hard-ass. "Mmph. Imagine that," she said sarcastically, taking her pass once the CO handed it back to her.

Clemmons frowned. "Did you snatch that fuckin' pass from my hand?"

Heaven scowled. "No. I took it."

"Take the motherfucking wall."

Heaven gave her an incredulous look. "Are you kidding? For what?"

"For being a stuck-up bitch," she hissed. "And for ruining my fucking day. I was in a good mood until I saw you. Now take the wall."

Heaven sucked her teeth. "Ohmygod! You have got to be kidding me."

"I'm tryna be nice, Lewis, but if you want me to put ya ass on paper, I will."

Heaven bit her tongue and reluctantly complied with the CO's directives.

"Now spread them legs wide for me," Clemmons stage-whispered. "I bet you love it from the back."

Heaven huffed. "This bitch," she mumbled under her breath. She cringed the minute she heard the snap of rubber gloves, and then felt her gloved hand slide over her shoulders.

"You need to start playing nice, Lewis."

Heaven rolled her eyes. "Play nice how?"

Clemmons continued frisking her. "Don't play. You know what I mean."

"Uh, *no*. I don't."

"Yeah, okay. Play dumb if you want."

Heaven sighed. "No. Tell me," she coaxed. Not that she gave a damn. But she wanted to hear her say it. That she wanted to lick her cunt.

"You show me yours," Clemmons said. "I'll show you mine."

Heaven made a face. *I think not.*

Clemmons' hands went up over Heaven's breasts, and then she pulled in her bottom lip; if there hadn't been cameras up, the CO would have pressed up against the inmate and humped her ass.

Clemmons stepped back. "Now, get the fuck on."

Heaven felt her blood boil. She was sick of this bitch fucking with her, and finding any excuse to cop a feel whenever she felt the need to. Nasty bitch. She gave her a dirty look and proceeded toward her housing unit. She wasn't about to let her miserable ass get under her skin. Not today.

One day this bitch has it coming, she thought.

And so she whistled and swayed down the corridor.

TWENTY-EIGHT

This is What You Came For...

S he rubbed her eyes. She hadn't gotten much sleep the night before. Sabina's snoring had reached an all-time high, and it had kept her up practically the whole night. Well—that wasn't completely true. Though Sabina had been growling like a bear, Heaven had spent the better part of the night on her cell talking to CO Rawlings on his night off.

Their ritual of hot, steamy phone sex had been initiated once she'd slid her hands down into her panties and started playing with her clit. His deep voice had heated her skin, and caused her cunt to clench hungrily.

She wanted some dick. Hard dick. Thick dick. Thrusting dick. Dick that would stretch her pussy and give her multiple orgasms. But all she'd had at the time was her vented brush with a rubber handle. So she'd used that to get herself off—sliding the handle in and out of her clutching snatch—while CO Rawlings spoke low and dirty, and whispered sweet, naughty nothings in her ear.

She'd moaned and talked dirty back.

He'd come, hard. And she'd come soon after. Twice.

And then, two hours before the sun rose, they'd planned their next sexual rendezvous, inside one of the custodian closets.

"I need a Taser," she'd whispered before their conversation ended.

"Say, what?" he'd asked incredulously. First she'd asked him for a *smart*phone—and he was still trying to figure out what was wrong with the one she already had. And now this shit.

"I *said* I need a Taser."

"And how on earth you expect to get one of those, and keep *muhfuckas* from finding it?"

"I have a plan."

"And what plan is that?"

"Get it to me, boo," she cooed. "And leave the rest to me."

"You're bugging, you know that, right? There's no—"

She cut him off. "Please, baby. I wouldn't ask if it wasn't important."

He huffed. "I need you to tell me what exactly *you* need with a *Taser?*"

"I need justice," she'd whispered.

Silence greeted her. Then Rawlings said, "Let me see what I can do," and ended the call.

Batting her eyes a few times, Heaven took in the last three stalls and cringed. She leaned her mop up against the wall, and stretched. This was her fifth day sweeping and mopping bathroom floors and cleaning dirty toilets, all which were a part of her punishment orchestrated by the sergeant and that fat-fuck Alvin.

She hadn't had Struthers' dick in her mouth again since that night she'd been dragged out of her cell in handcuffs, but she'd seen him a few times in the corridors. Twice, she'd caught his gaze on her and she'd rolled her eyes at him, which only caused him to smirk at her.

He'd gotten under her skin, and she'd let him. And it pissed her off. She'd done this to herself, and yet she blamed *him*—Struthers—for her current predicament. Hustling for snacks and personal hygiene items was not a good look. She wasn't a begging bitch.

She wasn't used to having to barter for shit. But here she was—thanks to that motherfucker—eating prison slop and washing her ass with soap that they gave out to the poor bitches. Her skin felt scratchy because of the harsh chemicals.

Without canteen privileges for another few weeks, she had to mooch off Sabina, who had very little her damn self. Nevertheless, she did what she had to do, knowing that this too would pass. The only bright spot in this fucked-up situation was the fact that she still had Struthers' cock hairs.

What she planned on doing with them, she didn't know. But what she did know was, somehow they'd become, along with the condom wrapper, very useful. So she had his coarse hairs tucked away in between the pages of her Bible—King James Version, Psalm 105:15.

Blasphemous, yes . . .

But she'd purposefully hidden his pubic hairs there because he had disrespected her. And, she twisted the context, *"Touch not mine anointed, and do my prophets no harm"* to suit her own sick need for payback. And, make no mistake. He was going to pay dearly. She believed she was one of the chosen ones. Chosen to shut his motherfucking ass down.

She planned to run this prison if it were the last thing she did. And when it was time to swoop in and snatch her throne, these motherfuckers wouldn't know what hit them. She smiled.

Oh how sweet it would be.

But before she gave that scandalous six-foot-six motherfucker a taste of his own medicine, she wanted another go at his enormously fat dick without the handcuffs, and without that Neanderthal twat, Clemmons, window-watching.

She closed her eyes for a brief moment and took a deep breath. She needed to not allow emotions, particularly her anger, to take control of her. Whatever she did from this point forward, it had to be done methodically. It had to be well thought out. And it had to be dirty.

Period.

Her lashes fluttered open and she looked at the yellow "Wet Floor" sign and sighed. *Thank God, this shit is almost over,* she thought as she glanced up at the wall clock. She turned to one of the row of mirrors along the wall. She looked a hot mess. This manual slave labor was aging her.

Irked, she reached for her mop again, then tightened her grip on the handle and swung the mop wide across the floor, back and forth. She had another hour before she could break. And then she'd have to come out again second shift to clean another set of toilets. She was assigned to clean one-and-a-half hours in the morning, and another one-and-a-half hours in the afternoon.

Three hours a day.

Fifteen hours done, and too many more to go!

She hated it. But she was almost at the proverbial light shining at the end of the tunnel. She was one day closer to being finished with this ridiculous bullshit. She'd never seen so many pissy, shitty, or bloodstained toilet seats in her life.

And someone had gone as far as shitting in one of the showers.

Her knuckles began turning red from squeezing the mop's handle so tightly as she mopped over the floor in wide figure-eight circles.

These bitches were filthy. Half wiping their asses. Not properly disposing of tampons. Not flushing toilets. The whole ordeal was nothing short of humiliating. And it made her contempt for Struthers and Clemmons that much deeper. It churned inside her like a river of battery acid.

She wanted them both to pay for trying to fuck her over. It was all she thought about since walking into her cell and finding all of her shit gone. *Stolen.*

The thought aroused her. Made her wet. And if she had the opportunity to place her finger on her clit, she'd mewl out.

And come.

TWENTY-NINE

Beat That Bitch With a Bat...

Hair in a loose ponytail, and a white headband around her forehead, Heaven—donned in a white sports bra and a pair of white gym shorts, which had been cut shorter in the back so that her ass cheeks peeked out from beneath the bottom of her shorts—stretched in the yard. Her crisp white Nikes gleamed in the sun.

To avoid unnecessary drama, she rarely came out to the yard. But, today, she agreed with Sabina. She needed some sunshine and to breathe in some fresh air for a change. Besides, she felt like running; something she hadn't done since her incarceration. She did several yoga stretches to loosen her already limber limbs. Then, once she finished, she held her head up to the sky for a few moments, and let the sun shine down on her face. She needed the vitamin D.

Clusters of women huddled together talking and laughing as the air flooded with different types of music floating out of a variety of portable speakers.

She scanned the yard for any signs of trouble, then took off running. Although no one had come at her crazy lately, she still had to watch her back. Her only ally thus far was Sabina, but she doubted White Chocolate would be any real help if some major shit popped off.

The yard was huge, with a full outdoor basketball court, two tennis courts, and it even had an in-ground swimming pool that never got used. The grounds looked more like the surroundings of a country club more so than that of a women's prison.

As she rounded the track, almost completing her first lap, she spotted Sabina sitting over on the bleachers holding court with a mixed group of mostly black and Latino women, either sharing tales of her dick-sucking escapades or gossiping about which female officers were fucking the male officers.

Over to the left, she noticed a group of women playing a game of hoops on a smaller basketball court. Then there were three younger women with headphones on, dancing provocatively to what Heaven believed to be some form of reggae as they dropped their asses, then eased them back up, then rocked their hips and thrust their pelvis.

One of the girls danced the raunchiest, her tongue darting in and out of her mouth as she made erotic faces, while her hands traveled over her body. Another girl came behind her and slapped her ass.

The others laughed.

Heaven squinted. One of the young women dancing all nasty-like looked like . . .

She rounded the bend.

Ohmygod. It was . . . *her*.

Clitina.

Just thinking her name made Heaven cringe. But what surprised her was, she'd taken her weave out and was now sporting six thick cornrows, the ends sweeping past her ass. Heaven hadn't seen her since she'd apologized to her on the tier, which had been almost three weeks ago. And the way she moved her body, Heaven couldn't help but think what a lucrative gold mine she'd be at somebody's strip club. Still, all she saw in her mind's eye was the young girl in a pair of cruddy, bloody drawers.

Heaven frowned, wondering if she'd used the Monistat she'd given her.

Still, it amazed her at how quickly the girl had acclimated to prison. It was as if she were hanging on the streets with her girlfriends without a care in the world.

Heaven shook her head, and kept moving around the track. She tried to focus on her run, and not the nasty ways of some of the women she was surrounded by, or the number of days, months, years she still had left on her prison sentence.

She missed being home—badly. The nights went by quickly. But the days seemed to drag on forever. She'd be an old bitch by the time she'd hit the streets. At least that was how it felt to her. Ten years, felt like a hundred instead.

Two laps, three laps, unaware of the burning gazes on her, Heaven pushed herself to run as many miles as she could. Lungs burning, legs aching, she increased her pace as her feet pounded the graveled outdoor track, her ass bouncing like two basketballs as her feet hit the gravel.

Her body screamed. She was practically on fire. Her skin felt like it had been lit by a blowtorch. Sweat rolled down her neck and soaked into the shirt that clung to her body like a second skin. Yet, she continued to push herself.

Another lap later, she finally forced herself to slow down until she was practically speed walking. She took the towel she had draped around her neck, then took one of the ends and mopped her sweaty brows as she slowed her pace even more, bringing herself to a normal walk.

As much as she hated taking showers in an open shower area, her body longed to be under the spigot, so she planned to head back inside the prison to get in the shower before the rest of the women started pouring back inside from the yard.

She was about to pass by Clitina and her friends again, when Clitina spotted her, and waved.

Heaven waved back.

Clitina blew a large pink bubble, then popped it back into her mouth. She said something to the three other girls, who in turn looked at Heaven, but she didn't pay it—or them, any mind. One of the girls—a small-waist, wide-hipped girl with spiky dark hair, and intricate tattoos that covered one entire arm—cut her eye over to the right, and frowned.

Out of her peripheral, Heaven saw someone walking in her direction, so she turned to see who the girl was frowning at. The approaching figure was the tall, lanky girl with the dreads who'd played lookout on the day Heaven had to slice up the stud, Snake—months ago.

And she wasn't alone.

Shit.

This was exactly what Heaven didn't need in her life right now. More drama and another damn fight. But she'd do whatever she had to do to defend herself.

To the left of Dread Girl was a young redbone with red dyed hair. She was lean and toned like a track runner, and wore a menacing look on her face. While on the Dread's right side stood a cute, slim, brown-skinned girl sporting a short, boyish cut.

Both girls looked like former hole-in-the-wall strippers, with sexualities that swung either way the wind blew.

Heaven's pulse ticked upward, but she kept her composure.

Dread Girl sneered. "Yeah, I thought that was you with all that sweet ass bouncing. You remember me?"

Heaven feigned ignorance, quickly glancing over at Clitina and her three comrades who were now watching the action unfold with their arms folded.

Realizing she was on her own, once again, Heaven knew this encounter would end real ugly. But she'd fight all three of them with no hesitation. She just needed to brace herself.

Heaven stared at Dread Girl, then looked her up and down. "Should I?"

"Yeah, bitch," Dread hissed. "What you did to my girl, Snake, was mad foul. Hope you didn't think we was gonna let you get that off."

Heaven shrugged. "I'm sorry about what happened to snake girl, but she deserved every stitch she got to her face for how she came into *my* cell, and tried to push herself up on *me*. You should know that, since you were there."

Dread Girl sneered. "I thought you said you didn't know me."

"I *don't*," Heaven snapped. "But what I do know is, your little friend was pissed that I didn't want to give her freaky-ass any of this pussy. And, for the record, she put her hands on *me*, first. So, I did what I had to do. And I'd do it again," Heaven stated vehemently. "So either do what you came to do, or please get the hell out of my face."

"Fuck all the talk, Lea," the redbone snapped, glancing at her watch. "Let's beat this bitch's ass and be on our way. Shit."

What Heaven didn't know was, a big brawl had been staged on the other side of the large yard to distract the COs while the young dread and her friends quickly handled her.

"Let's get this bitch, now," the redhead snapped as she lunged forward.

Heaven quickly stepped back. But before the redhead could get anywhere near her, she was unexpectedly met with a homemade club to the right side of her head, knocking her to the gravel, giving Heaven enough time to pull her razor from her sports bra and slash Brown Skin across the face.

The girl screamed out in pain, grabbing her face. Blood poured out through her fingers, causing Dread Girl's eyes to open in sudden shock. She hadn't wanted to confront Heaven, but she'd had no choice. She'd been forced to. Now it was too late to back out.

"You fuckin' bitch!" she yelled as she reached for her shank she'd hidden under her shirt, charging toward Heaven. But Clitina and her three friends pounced on her, slashing her with razors they'd suddenly spat out of their mouths. The blades sliced into Dread Girl's face and neck, causing blood to splatter everywhere.

Stunned at how expertly each girl used their blades, Heaven quickly stepped back from the attack trying to keep blood from getting on her. She'd already gotten blood on her hands and arm from slicing the chick with the boy cut across the face. She didn't want blood splattering on her clothes and sneakers, too.

Then, in a wild rush, one of Clitina's friends—an attractive, dark-skinned female—reached down and yanked Brown Girl's head back and sliced her across her neck in one swift motion, leaving her to bleed out.

Heaven gasped in shock.

"Let's get the fuck out of here 'fore the COs get here," two of the girls said as they pulled Clitina by her arm. The four girls ran off with their bloody razors, laughing as they ran in the opposite direction, leaving Heaven standing there with three bodies at her feet.

Then it hit her.

Ohmygod!

She had to get away from the scene before the COs realized

another fight had taken place, and charged her—*again*, for yet another bloody brawl. But this time there were bodies, *dead* bodies—well at least one body, which potentially meant more criminal charges and spending the rest of her time in prison on twenty-three-hour lock.

Heart beating fast and hard, Heaven took off running. She'd pray for her sins later, she thought as she scattered away from the blood bath; losing herself in a sea of women.

THIRTY
We're Gonna Tear This Mother Out...

Warden Kate couldn't wait to get back to the confines of her office, behind her locked door, to her coveted flask. She needed a damn drink. These bitches had gone too damn far. Again. And now she had the commissioner breathing down her neck. He wanted answers. Like, "How the fuck had one woman gotten severely sliced, another's head bashed in, and a third's throat slit, while another two women were being badly beaten on the other side of the yard, and not one breathing, goddamn soul saw a damn thing?"

And the one camera that could have shed light on the head-bashing and slashings had no footage. None! Somehow, the camera had malfunctioned.

How convenient.

What the hell was going on inside her prison?

The whole compound was shut down. All movement, all activities *shut. The. Hell. Down.* And she'd shake this motherfucking prison upside down, and inside out.

With so many women with diverse backgrounds, criminal histories, and personality clashes, there was bound to be violence. It was inevitable and—yes, a daily occurrence on some level. But that still didn't make the shit acceptable. The warden knew that for many of these women, solving problems with fists and weapons was all they knew how to do.

She sucked in her breath and snatched her desk drawer open and pulled out her flask, frantically twisting off the cap and taking a long swallow. Truths or not, she was sick of rationalizing and making excuses for these wild-ass boorish women.

If they couldn't find a way to get along and coexist instead of acting like a bunch of barbarians, then she would make their lives a living fucking hell in here. She'd make it a living hell for any of them to jail in her prison.

Try her.

She slid the opening of her flask to her lips again, and swallowed a mouthful of her most trusted friend. Belvedere. She inhaled, then exhaled, savoring the way the alcohol spread warmth down in her chest, then fanned out into her stomach.

She couldn't let these unruly hyenas get to her. But, with the commissioner now breathing down her neck, they'd really fucked her nerves raw with this most recent shit.

Oh, those bitches were going to suffer. And suffer well!

So far, with the water shut off since the prison yard attacks, no one had been able to shower or flush their toilets—to prevent anyone from flushing drugs, weapons, and any other contraband. And many of the women were starting to feel the effects.

As far as the warden was concerned, it was unfortunate—but if inmates wanted to act like wild animals, then they could stay locked in their damn cells in filth, funk, and squalor, inhaling their shit and piss.

She needed to sort through the drama, and clean out the trouble-making trash. And fast.

The search teams were in full force, turning every housing unit upside down—with explicit orders to not destroy any inmate's personal property. Any cell found with contraband would result in both inmates being charged, and sent to solitary.

So far, over the last several days, the raids had confiscated a number of cell phones, weapons—ranging from shanks to hammers, and drugs; lots and lots of drugs from weed, cocaine, heroin, and hundreds of ecstasy pills.

Her damn prison was a damn drug den.

These junkie bitches probably been attending NA meetings higher than kites. She took two small sips from her flask.

"I'll tell you what. I want this situation handled. Now either you get this mess under control," the commissioner had warned her, "or I'll find someone else who will."

Then he was up on his feet, heading out her door, leaving her at her desk with her jaws slack.

She shook her head in disgust.

She had plans to retire in another three years, and she'd be goddamned if she was about to let any of them fuck over her pension—or her plans.

Period.

There was a knock at her door.

She sighed.

"Give me a sec," she called out, quickly twisting the silver cap of her flask back on. She reached for two cinnamon mints and tossed them in her mouth, then walked around her desk to open her door.

"Yes, Susan?"

Her secretary blinked, startled by her brusqueness. "You have your 'Do Not Disturb' on."

"Oh, right. Yes. I forgot. After having my ass chewed out and handed to me, I needed to steal a moment to myself."

She nodded knowingly. Susan smiled to herself. *Good for her ass.* Ever since she'd gotten promoted to warden, she'd become this moody, snappy-mouth bitch. And Susan didn't appreciate the level of disrespect and disregard she suddenly tossed at her.

"So what can I do for you?"

Susan blinked. A tiny spark of irritation shot up her spine. "Nothing, ma'am. I only wanted you to know that the inmate you requested is outside."

She glanced at her watch. "That was over an hour ago. Send her in."

Hand poised on the door handle, Susan said, "I'll send her in."

The warden nodded.

As Susan began to walk out and close the door, the warden called out, "Oh, Susan."

Her secretary popped her head back in. "Yes?"

"Thank you."

Susan gave her a puzzled look.

"I don't tell you often enough how much I appreciate you. But I do. So thank you for all you do."

Touched by the gesture, Susan simply smiled, then backed out the door. A few seconds later, the door opened again.

And in walked the thorn in her side.

"Miss Lewis, please. Have a seat," the warden said, forcing a smile to spread over her lips. She eyed the inmate as she sauntered into her office. Her breasts were sitting up high, nice and plump, and somehow she managed to wear the orange jumper like it was Department of Corrections couture.

The warden swallowed. Their last meeting hadn't gone well, but this time, she hoped they could have a productive, adult-like conversation.

The warden's gaze drifted lazily up and down Heaven as she took a seat across from her desk. She flopped in the chair across from her desk, emitting a seemingly annoyed sigh as her long, shapely legs crossed.

"How can I help you, Warden?"

The warden gritted her teeth. She had to rein in her temper before she said or did something that would cause her to toss office decorum out the window. She took a breath and stretched her arms out and clasped her hands in front of her.

"Well, Miss Lewis. I'm sure you might be wondering why I had you brought to my office today . . ."

Heaven tilted her head, and gave the warden a *really bitch* look. "Um. No. Actually, not," she flatly said. "But since you have me sitting here, I'm *wondering* when you're going to lift this lockdown ban. I haven't showered since the day you enforced this mess."

"And that's unfortunate," the warden stated calmly.

"*No*, what's unfortunate is a bunch of grown-ass women having to stay locked in their cells with no running water. You get to go home and wash your ass every night, don't you?"

"Miss Lewis, I understand your frustration."

"No *War*. Den," Heaven snapped. "I don't think you do. Is your snatch washed every day? Or do you like a little stank on it?"

The warden fought to keep her expression neutral. But Heaven's lips distracted her a little. She shifted in her seat and forced herself to keep her eyes fixed on Heaven and let her rant. She actually found her sass disturbingly refreshing.

"Are you walking around in dirty drawers right now, huh, Warden? No, of course you're not, unless you're just nasty. Unless you've missed the memo, we're women locked up in a tight-ass space. Smelling each other day in, day out. And as females we need to wash our asses."

Heaven hadn't signed up to become a mouthpiece for the prisoners, but since the warden had summoned her, it was only right she gave her an earful.

"I can't speak for everyone," she continued. "But I'm not some trashy ho. I get it. This is prison, and we all did something to put us here. But, unlike some, I like getting waxed and pampered. Not walking around with a bunch of whiskers sprouting out of my damn snatch."

The warden nodded, and listened intently. "Miss Lewis," she said calmly. "I hear your concerns. Now I need for you to hear mine."

Heaven grunted in return and shifted in her seat.

"Over the last several months, there has been more violence in my prison surrounding one inmate than we've had in years. And the common denominator in each incident, thus far, has been *you*. So do you see my dilemma here?"

Heaven gave her a probing look. "What *exactly* are you implying, *War. Den?*"

"What I'm implying, *Miss* Lewis, is this: since you've walked onto the grounds of this prison, you've not only sliced someone with a razor, causing her to need hundreds of stitches . . ."

"And *she* came into my cell—uninvited—trying to push up on me. Trying to tongue-fuck *my* pussy. No bitch. I'm not interested. Period. Point. Blank. So she slapped me. And I sliced her. Next."

The warden gritted her teeth. She was slowly losing her patience with this bitch and her nasty attitude. "And then *you* attacked another inmate over on Three East, beating her unconscious. Would you like to explain that?"

Heaven swung her ponytail over her shoulder. "And I was punched, kicked and beat with sticks. Like I told you, when you paid me a visit in lockup: I went for help. And when the CO bitch gave me her flat-ass to kiss, I took matters into my own hands.

What was I supposed to do? Wait until that bitch got at me while I slept? No, thank you. You got the wrong one. I'm not a gang-banger or some hood-trash chick, but I'm damn sure not some goofy bitch, either, who's going to let some female threaten me, bully me, or put their damn hands on me. Trust. If a bitch steps to me—here or out on the streets—she has to get dropped before she drops me. And *that*, Warden, is a promise."

The warden glanced at her watch and grimaced. She had a date with Captain Caldolini and she'd wanted to be out of the building by three so she could get checked into the Marriott in downtown Brooklyn, then prepare for her date.

They'd made dinner plans the night before, and she was looking forward to seeing him again. This would be her third date with the sexy, hard-bodied captain—and tonight she planned on sitting on his face while getting a taste of that Italian sausage that hung between his strong, hairy legs. Kielbasa or sausage link, it didn't matter. She wanted to smother herself in his pubic hairs while sucking his dick.

It'd been so long—too long—since she had a dick sliding over her tongue. And tonight, she planned on changing that.

Maybe then she'd stop having dark, dirty fantasies of sliding her clit over—

"Are we done here?"

The warden blinked out of her salacious reverie. "No. We're not. I listened to you rattle on. Now I need for *you* to hear me. And here me good."

Heaven flicked imaginary dirt from beneath her fingernail, then looked at the warden.

"Now I can't prove it, but I know in my gut that *you* were—no, are—somehow linked to what happened out in the yard with those three women last week."

Heaven frowned. "Try again, *War. Den*. Like I already told *you*. I'm not gang involved, so I would have no reasons to entertain a bunch of dusty birds, or be involved in what happened to any of them."

The warden tilted her head. "No, you're not gang affiliated, but—dusty bitches or not, one of the young women who had her throat slit was a friend of Shareesa Lyons . . ."

Heaven gave the warden a blank stare, then feigned ignorance. "I don't know a Shareesa Lyons."

"The young woman whose face you sliced. They called her, *Snake*."

"Oh," she said nonchalantly. "I thought that was a man. But, anyway . . . what does one thing have to do with the other? I was nowhere near that girl, or her friends. So try again. Next."

The warden stared her down. But Heaven refused to back down. So she stared back. The warden suddenly felt conflicted. A part of her wanted to reach across her desk and slap the inmate's beautiful face. She was a smug bitch. Yet, she was equally breathtaking. Then there was another part of her that wanted to bite out her jugular. The one between her thighs. She cursed herself for wanting to kneel between her legs and sniff her unwashed cunt, wondering what she smelled like.

She fought to keep her gaze from drifting to her breasts; so goddamned perky and full. Several silent moments passed before the warden shifted in her seat and finally spoke, still keeping her eyes locked on Heaven's.

"The water will be on by next shift," Warden Kate stated. "But, understand this, Miss Lewis. I will not let *you* or any other inmate turn this prison into a battlefield. It stops *now*. One more incident that comes across my desk with your name on it or anywhere in it, and I promise you this: I'll have *you* so hemmed up with street charges that by the time the judge finishes with you, you'll be rotting under this prison. Now get your shit together, Miss Lewis. Get a grip on your life. And get the fuck out of my office."

Heaven stared the warden down. Although she wanted to fill the room with a bunch of expletives and tell the warden to kiss her ass, she bit her tongue. The warden's tone was calm, but there was a bite to her words and an icy glare in her eyes that let Heaven know she meant every word.

As Heaven stood to her feet and tromped to the door, she could feel the warden's gaze taking her in. She felt like bending over and shaking her ass in the warden's face.

Instead, she left the office, slamming the door behind her.

Then the dark desires swept in, and the warden wondered if she had touched her, would there have been magic. Heat. Fire.

She pressed her thighs together, then closed her eyes and shuddered.

Oh, she'd been tempted.

Her lashes fluttered, and her eyes slowly opened. She glanced at her watch.

God, she couldn't wait to get laid.

THIRTY-ONE
Wild, Wild, Wild . . .

A week later, the prison ban was completely lifted and all was well in the world behind bars. And Heaven found herself entertaining a new friend in her cell. She didn't believe in coincidences. This unlikely union had to be fate. Still, she never thought in a million years that the same nineteen-year-old girl who'd come to her cell in tears almost two months ago, bloody drawers and all, would become a bona-fide ride-or-die.

Heaven walked over and handed her a large microwavable bowl of tuna salad that she'd made using two packs of tuna, mayo, garlic and onion powder, and relish packs.

Clitina's stomach growled. She didn't have any money on her books, and the only food she'd been eating, besides what was served in the dining hall, was food Heaven had graciously started sharing with her after the prison ban had been lifted. The two women were oddly indebted to the other. And, while Heaven had promised herself she'd look out for the young girl, Clitina had already sworn to have her back as well.

The young woman was in awe, transfixed, by Heaven's beauty. She secretly idolized her, and thought she should be on a runway somewhere instead of a prison cell. She was pretty and classy, but not some soft-ass bitch.

Clitina despised those types.

So when she saw Heaven being confronted by those three chicks out in the yard, she knew from her own experiences in the streets that it was about to go down. One of her girls had slid her a wooden club that she'd made in her carpentry class— the one she'd smuggled out to the yard (the same one she'd planned on using on someone else who owed her three soups). Clitina knew those bitches had to get it to the head. And she was ready to put in some work. She'd been looking for a reason to brawl. She missed being home on the bricks, jumping females with her girl, Day'Asia and sister, Candylicious. Chicks knew The Switchblade Bitches were not to be fucked with. But when they fought, they didn't always use blades. Sometimes they used their fists. Other times they used bats, hammers, and, even, crowbars.

"Mm. Thanks," she said.

Heaven reached in her locker and pulled out a sleeve of wheat crackers and handed them to her. "Here's some crackers."

She watched as Clitina opened the crackers and packed salad onto one, then slid it in her mouth. Her eyes rolled up in her head as she chewed. "Mm. This is so good."

Heaven smiled. She surprisingly liked her. And the wild, young woman intrigued her. "So, have you spoken to your mother?"

She shook her head. "Nope." She answered with her mouth full, then swallowed. "That trick ain't even acceptin' my collect calls. But I talked to my sister, Candy." She scooped more salad onto another cracker, then stuffed it in her mouth. "She said she gonna send me, like ten dollars—maybe more, as soon as she gets her SSI check."

Heaven frowned. Ten dollars? *What the hell was this poor soul going to do with ten damn dollars in here*, Heaven wondered. She felt bad for her. "Oh, that's nice of her," she said lightly, but she was really being sarcastic. "Not to be in her business, but why is she getting SSI, if you don't mind me asking?"

Clitina shrugged. "I don't know. I think she was dropped on her head or sumthin' when she was a baby 'cause she a lil' slow-actin' sometimes. She ain't even finish high school until she was twenty."

"Oh," Heaven said.

"Unh-huh. She gets almost five hundred dollars, but by the time she buy her weed from the weed man, then get her nails did, and buy this boy, Killah, she be fuckin' clothes 'n' stuff, she be broke in like three days."

Heaven blinked. *Killer?* She didn't have the stomach to ask her how he got his name. "Yeah, Candy fuckin' Knutz's nephew," she answered as if reading Heaven's thoughts. She shook her head. "She dumb as hell. All he doin' is fuckin' her 'n' usin' her. But she can't even see it. But he do gotta big dingaling, though."

Heaven raised her brow in silent question.

"Me 'n' Candy used to sneak out into the living room mad late at night 'n' watch him playin' with it," she said. "Candy don't know, but . . . me 'n' Day'Asia gave him some sloppy top in one of the stairwells a few times." She smacked her lips together. "We tag-teamed the shit outta his ole nasty ass. But Day'Asia's dumb ass ain't even swallow him when he came." She shook her head. "That bitch stupid as hell. How you not gonna swallow?"

Heaven gave her a blank stare. This was all too much information for Heaven to take in. And she felt a headache coming on.

"Anyway, Miss Heaven. You looked out for me when I first got here," she said, changing the subject. Then she broke out laughing. "Ooh, I wanted to go off on you when you told me to go wash my ass 'cause my cootie stank. But I couldn't even be mad at you 'cause I know it did."

Heaven chuckled. "Lord, yes. It sure did. I tried to pretend that it didn't. But, girl, your ass stunk worse than rotted meat. It smelled like an open grave, girl."

Clitina laughed harder. "Oooh, Miss Heaven. I know I was smellin' a lil' raunchy, but I ain't *stink* that damn bad. Did I?"

Heaven gave her a raised brow. "Like rotted skunk meat. You had roadkill pussy, boo."

Clitina screamed out in laughter. "Ohmygod. Lies! But, whatever. I'm springtime fresh now. Thanks to you. So kick rocks, Miss Heaven."

Heaven laughed, then became serious. "Tina"—she shook her head—"I know it's *Clit*. Tina. But, uh, I'm having a problem calling you that. So forgive me."

The young woman shrugged. "It's cool. You can call me Tina, if you want. At least you're not callin' me Dickalina, or something shitty like that."

Heaven winced. "I can't even imagine what it was like having a mother who everyone called Dick . . ."

"A. Lina," Clitina finished for her. "Mmph. Well, my name ain't no better than hers. Growing up, bitches stayed calling me Clitty Clitty Tina until I started fuckin' them up. I bashed this one ho dead in her ugly face with a brick when I was in six-grade. I bet the rest of them hoes left me alone after that. But, anyway, no one ain't really mess with my moms 'cause they knew she would fight them 'n' if she couldn't beat 'em, she'd get my Auntie Booty to fight 'em with her."

Heaven shook her head, not believing what she'd heard. "Wait.

Wait. Wait. So let me get this right. Your mom's name is *Dickalina*. And you have an aunt named *Booty*?"

Clitina nodded. "Yeah. Well, it's Big Booty in the streets. But her real name is Cassandra. Sometimes I call her Auntie Cass. Depends on how I feel. But I ain't callin' that bitch shit now. Not after what them bitches did to me out in visits. Fuck both them crazy bitches. All that ho like to do is chase young dingaling 'n' get fucked in the ass. Fuckin' trick."

Heaven blinked. She'd heard enough. Yet, she wanted to know more.

"I see. So before you got locked up, what did you like to do for fun?"

She shrugged. "Nothing really. Smoke. Drink. Chill wit' my girl, Day'Asia 'n' my sister, Candy. Boostin'. We sometimes would go into Macy's 'n' Walmart 'n' light they asses up." She laughed. "We'd come out with mad shit. But, anyway. Most times me 'n' Candy 'n' Day'Asia would get us a pound of weed, a few boxes of condoms 'n' a room 'n' turn up all weekend."

Heaven kept from frowning. What the hell? "Why'd y'all need so many condoms?"

Clitina tilted her head, and gave her a blank look. "Uh, damn, Miss Heaven. Why you think? Ain't nobody got time for fuckin' raw. Bad enough Day'Asia stayed havin' nasty infections. That's my girl 'n' all, but sometimes her pussy be stinkin'." She laughed. "That's my ride-or-die ho, though. But she one fishy bitch." She laughed again. "Oh, she so nasty sometimes. This one time we had a room with some niggas from Irvington 'n' me 'n' her were drinkin' Henny 'n' walkin' around in our bra 'n' panties. We got liquored up, then started bendin' over grabbin' our ankles 'n' shit, shakin' our ass. And Day'Asia nasty-ass ain't even know she had a shit stain in her drawers."

Heaven's jaw dropped open. This was really just too damn much to take in.

So this girl was a cum-swallowing thief, a brawler, *and* a certified ho who hung out with nasty bitches, Heaven thought.

"And what about your father?"

"*Psst*. Please. Fuck him. I don't even know who he is; Dickalina was fuckin' some old-ass man 'n' his two sons all at the same time. Then got knocked up with Candy, then me. So me 'n' Candy is sisters 'n' cousins, too."

THIRTY-TWO

That's When I Knew . . .

"Ohmygod! Are you *serious* right now?" Heaven asked. She was stunned by what she'd just heard.

Clitina nodded her head. "Mmhmm. Serious as a hard dingaling."

Heaven shook her head. "Wow. So how many years do you have to do for stabbing your stepfather?" she asked, quickly shifting from any further talk of incest, or Clitina's fucked-up family tree.

Clitina frowned, jerking her neck. "That big-dicked niggah ain't none of my step*fahver*," she said indignantly. "That's my moms' bum-ass boyfriend. Ohmygod, Miss Heaven. He is such a fuckin' clown-ass. He don't even have his damn L's. And my moms' dumb-ass be thinkin' it's cute when he takes her out on his bike."

"Oh, he rides motorcycles? That's cute."

Clitina frowned. "Oh no it ain't cute. He ain't ridin' no motor-cycles. *Psst*. Please. He be ridin' her on them old-ass ten-speed bikes with them ugly-ass straw baskets in the front 'n' the back."

Heaven blinked.

"Unh-huh. What kinda niggahs you know ridin' they bitches on handlebars?"

None. Heaven shook her head.

"*Exactly.* Nobody. Anyway, I gotta do four years. They acted like I sliced his nasty shithole open. But, anyway, I might get out on parole in like three. And I can't wait. I'ma turn the hell up. My sister done already got me a big bottle of Hen-dog on deck. I tol' her to put it up in my room until I get out."

"Hopefully, it'll all work out for you," Heaven said. "But you're going to need to make sure you don't get caught up in any major infractions and end up going to lockup while you're here."

She shrugged. "Maybe."

Heaven stared at the young girl, wondering why she ended up at Croydon Hill, anyway, when there was a prison for girls her age about two hours away, farther south from where they were. She didn't have to wonder for long. She shared with Heaven the numerous assault and weapons charges she'd racked up since she was fifteen, along with things she'd done and hadn't gotten caught doing.

"And this one time," she stated excitedly. "Me 'n' Day'Asia busted up in my ex-boo's house 'n' caught him fuckin' some other bitch. We beat her ass real good with crowbars. Beat her face wide open."

Heaven blinked, her mouth dropping open. "Ohmygod! Were the two of you arrested?"

"Well, yeah. That rat-ass bitch snitched on us. She knew who I was 'n' how I get down 'n' the ho still tried it. Even *after* I told that bitch on Twitter 'n' up on the *Book* that I was gonna come for her if I ever caught her ass. I Snapchatted that ho 'n' tol' her ass what it was gonna be, so she shoulda been glad I came at her lady-like. I coulda just ran up on her ass. But, no. I kept it classy, like a hood bitch does it."

Lord Jesus. I can't. "And what did your mother say about all this?"

She sucked my teeth. "Her 'n' my Auntie Cass fought me 'n' Day'Asia in the courthouse. And they both got arrested."

Heaven's eyes widened.

"But, whatever. I told the judge that that bitch should'na been fuckin' my man."

Heaven shook her head, dumbfounded at the fact that she took no responsibility for taking a crowbar and beating that girl in the face. If anything, she should have beaten his ass instead.

Right at that thought, the warden's voice licked at her ear. *"One more incident that comes across my desk with your name on it or anywhere in it, and I promise you this: I'll have you so hemmed up with street charges that by the time the judge finishes with you, you'll be rotting under this prison . . ."*

Heaven quickly shook the voice from her head. The last thing she needed was that bitch haunting her. Still, she knew she couldn't afford to get caught up in any other beefs. She needed her own little stomp-out crew. A group of females who knew how to move, yet, didn't mind getting their hands dirty if need be.

A sly smile eased over her lips as she eyed Clitina taking her finger and swiping it around the inside of the bowl, then bringing her fingers to her lips and sucking them into her mouth.

"Mm. That tuna salad was good as hell."

Heaven smiled. "Glad you enjoyed it."

Clitina handed her the empty bowl. Heaven took it from her, then set in the sink.

"Listen, girl," Heaven said, lowering her voice. "I didn't get a chance to really thank you for what you and your friends did . . ."

Clitina shrugged it off. "It was nothing, Miss Heaven. I like to fight, so it was a win-win." Her eyes lit with excitement. "We took it to those bitches' heads. Ooh, I wanted to bust that skinny bitch's eyeballs out."

Heaven cringed, feeling a smidgen of guilt for the loss of that one girl's life.

"So who were those girls, anyway?" Heaven inquired, getting up from her bed and reaching under her bunk for a mesh commissary tote that she'd filled with pecan swirls, iced honey buns, chocolate cupcakes, tropical punch drinks, strawberry Twizzlers, assorted Now and Laters, BBQ corn chips, cheese puffs, and cinnamon graham crackers.

"Oh, two of 'em my hoes from the bricks. The dark-skin one with the long weave is my girl Weena . . ." Heaven cringed at the girl's name. "Well, it's Roweena, but we call her Weeena for short."

Oh.

"And the one with the one with the short, spiky hair 'n' tats is my girl, Samara. And the other chick is some chick Weena knows from around the way. Plus, they over on Three East. They told me how you beat that ho's ass over there, too."

Images of blood splashing from the girl's throat flashed in Heaven's head, and she cringed inwardly. "Why did your friend, uh . . . *Weena* . . . why did she cut that girl's throat? Slicing her up was good enough. But *killing* her?"

Clitina gave her a look. "Because that's what she does. That bitch be on them mollies. And she do what crazy bitches do. She all burnt out on that purple drank."

Heaven frowned.

"You know, cough syrup mixed with Sprite and Jolly Ranchers."

"Oh," was all Heaven was able to say. She had no understanding why anyone would want to drink a prescription cough syrup with codeine in it trying to emulate what he or she heard on rap songs. She simply couldn't wrap her mind around it.

Clitina shook her head. "Damn, Miss Heaven, you stay lost. Anyway. Weena's here now 'cause she beat up her moms, then stabbed her up, like ten times, with a screwdriver."

Heaven gasped. "Ohmygod. She killed her?"

"She might as well had; she a crackhead anyway. Her life been over."

Dear Lord. She couldn't imagine having a crackhead for a mother. A drunk was bad enough. "How old is that girl?"

"She just turned nineteen last Sunday."

"And the other girls?"

She slid a finger in her mouth, gliding it from back to front over her teeth, getting the last of her meal. "Samara's like twenty-three. I don't know how old that other chick is. She probably around my age, or sumthin'. Why?"

Heaven shrugged. "Oh. No reason. Here," Heaven said as she handed the bag to her new ally. "This is for you."

Clitina's eyes lit up like a kid at Christmas. "Ohmygod! For *me?*"

Heaven nodded as she said, "Yes."

Clitina took the bag of goodies. "Yassss, boo, yasss . . ." She quickly frowned. "Wait. I hope you ain't givin' me all this stuff 'cause you tryna get me to lick your cootie or sumthin' 'cause I ain't with that freaky licky-licky shit. I suck dingaling, Miss Heaven. I don't fucks with lickin' cooties. Sorry."

Heaven laughed. "Little girl, relax your delusional ass."

"Oh no, hon. I'ma grown-ass woman, boo. Trust. Ain't nothin' lil' on me."

Heaven waved her on, dismissively. "Girl, bye. Grown woman my ass. But, anyway, *hon*, you are *not* my type. Trust me. It's simply my way of showing you my appreciation for having my back."

Clitina clutched her bag of treats to her chest. She couldn't wait to get back to her cell to flop on her bunk and eat herself into a sugar coma. "I fought those bitches for free. But, hell," she said, shimmying her shoulders. "What a bitch gotta do to get a bottle of Henny, Miss Heaven? Set a ho on fire?"

Hmm. That's a thought.

Heaven couldn't deny it. She liked her new young, reckless friend. She was ratchet and hood, but with a little—hell, a *lot* of—coaching, Heaven saw potential.

And she saw opportunity.

All she needed were a few more crazy bitches like her on her side.

Then there'd be nothing—absolutely nothing—she wouldn't be able to do.

THIRTY-THREE
Don't Look Back...

Heaven awoke to another morning behind bars, wishing (as she always did *every* morning) that she'd somehow be able to turn back the clock. Start anew. Wipe the slate clean and simply start over. But, there were no do-overs, no stage rehearsals. Once it was done, it was done. There were no retakes. No taking shit back.

She grabbed her pillow and put it to her face, and then screamed in it.

The monotony of prison life was slowly killing her. Being around a bunch of women all day, every day, was too much. All this estrogen flooding the prison walls was toxic at times. It was breathing in mold. And somewhere, she believed, there had to be studies on the detriment of one's psyche from being around a bunch of crazy-ass bitches.

She was slowly starting to feel like she was being programmed and someone from behind a hidden control panel was controlling her.

Heaven put her pillow back over her face, and screamed again.

The shit was maddening.

It seemed like as hard as she tried—and Lord knows, she tried—to stay in the present, to not focus on the past, somehow it always found a way to drag her right back to it.

Last night, she'd dreamt of Freedom. It hadn't been a bad dream. Nor was it a good one, either. He was just there, everywhere in her conscience. His face. His smile. His hands. Stalking her dreams. Hijacking her in her sleep.

Fucking Freedom! He was everywhere he shouldn't be.

And Heaven knew that the only way she would be able to finally free herself of that part of her life would be by finally confronting him—*that* part of her past.

She stared over at the privacy curtain covering the bars of her cell, and sighed. There was no escaping this, or the nagging reminder of why she was here—because of herself. And that angered her.

She swung her body around and slid her feet into her shower shoes, before standing. She looked over at Sabina's bunk. It was empty.

She hadn't heard her leave, or the door slide open. She'd literally slept through the ruckus.

I must have been exhausted, she thought, lining the toilet with napkins, then sitting.

A part of her was relieved Sabina was out. She needed the time alone. Needed the space to do what she had to do.

"Freedom wants you to call him . . ."

She relieved herself, and then washed her hands. She stared at herself in the mirror. "Bitch, look at what you've become," she whispered at the reflection staring back at her. She shook her head. "He didn't deserve to be shot. And he didn't deserve *you*. Yet, you let that bastard bring you to this point. Why didn't you just fucking leave?"

She turned from the mirror, not waiting for the answer, and went to retrieve her phone hidden in the seam of her pillow.

She couldn't believe she remembered the number after all this time. With a wildly pounding heart, she dialed the number; partly hoping he wouldn't pick up.

"Yo," came the low growl on the other end of the line.

Heaven quickly sat on her bunk before her knees buckled. She closed her eyes, gripping the cell. She hadn't heard his voice . . . God—forever.

"Yo, who the fuck is this?" he barked, snatching Heaven from her thoughts.

"It's . . . me," she whispered.

"Hol' up." There was rustling in the background. *"Heaven?"*

"Yeah."

"Oh, shit. Damn. You good?"

She nodded as if he could see her through the phone, a lone tear sliding down her cheek. "Yes."

"It's good to hear your voice, baby . . ."

Heaven cringed. *Baby.* She felt something inside of her unsnapping.

"Yo, where are you?"

She rolled her eyes. "Prison." *Where the fuck else I'm going to be?*

"Oh, right, right." He let out a sigh. "Damn. I've missed—"

She couldn't do this—go *there*—with him. And yet she clung to the phone, imagining his mouth moving in slow motion as he spoke.

"I'm sorry," she blurted out. She needed him to know that before she threw up. "I shouldn't have shot you."

"Yo, c'mon, baby. That shit wasn't about nothing, only a few bullet wounds. I survived. But, dig, you need anything?"

She shook her head. *Yes.* "No."

"You get that money from Kareema?"

Heaven frowned. "What money?"

"I gave that broad a stack to put on your books."

Heaven frowned. That bitch hadn't given her shit. And she could have definitely used the thousand dollars. It was the least he could do for all of her heartache.

She bit back a string of expletives. "No, I didn't get it."

"Yo, what the *fuck*," he snapped. "I gave that bitch that paper over a fuckin' month ago. Stupid bitch." He took a breath. "I'ma get at her grimy-ass, though."

"No, don't worry about it."

"Nah, nah…that fuckin' broad real foul. I knew I should'na trusted her grimy-ass with no paper. But it's a'ight. I got something for that ass; word up."

"That's what you get for fucking her ho-ass," Heaven heard her saying in her head. Instead she asked, "Why did you want me to call you?"

"'Cause I needed to hear your voice; that's all. I pulled some real grimy shit on you. And I ain't gonna front, baby. It kinda had me fucked up for a minute. You know I didn't wanna press them charges on you, right?"

Heaven felt the beginning of tears welling in her eyes. "Yeah, I know." He hadn't cooperated with the police, but the prosecutor's office proceeded anyway. Plus, the naked bitch beneath his body was alive—and traumatized, let her tell it—and had been able to give the prosecutors everything they needed to convict her.

"I shoulda never brought that broad to our crib."

Heaven blinked, then scowled. Was that supposed to be an apology? "No, Freedom. How about you should have never been *fucking* that bitch in the first damn place?"

"You right."

"*Mmph.* Well, I hope her pussy was worth it."

"Nah, that shit was fuckin' trash."

That was definitely not the answer she was going for. She shook her head again. "You know what, Free—"

"Baby, come back to bed," cooed a woman in the background. "I miss my *daaaaddy*."

"Yo, what the fuck," Freedom snapped. "Get up off my dick. Damn. You know what, matter of fact. Get ya shit, yo, and bounce."

Heaven recoiled. Sadly, she heard the woman apologizing, begging to stay.

Disgusted, Heaven ended the call. She wasn't mad. She was relieved. He was still no damn good. Out there being who he was—a womanizing bastard.

She slipped the phone back in its hiding place as Sabina was coming into the cell.

"Ohmygod! Have you heard? Wait," she said, sounding almost out of breath. "This is for you." She handed Heaven a white crocheted pullover. "I finished it this morning."

Heaven took the crocheted dress/pullover shirt thingy and placed it up to her body. "Ooh, this is cute, girl. Thanks."

"Well, I hope you can fit it." She craned her head back to glance at Heaven's ass. "But, uh, I don't know. There might be some complications trying to stretch it over all that"—she pointed—"wagon you got dragging back there."

Heaven rolled her eyes dismissively, then laughed. "Girl, *what*. Ever. Now what was it you were asking me if I'd heard?"

Sabina kicked off her clogs. "Oh, yeah, right. Wait?" She eyed her. "Are you okay?"

Heaven feigned ignorance. "Yeah. Why?"

Sabina shrugged, grabbing her MP3 player from her locker. "I don't know. You seem, like down or something."

Heaven waved her on. "No, I'm fine."

"Oh, okay." Sabina climbed up on her bunk. "Anyway. Did you hear anything about what happened to that Angelica chick in the showers last night?"

"Who?"

Sabina tilted her head. "You, know. That loudmouthed chick with the birthmark on the side of her face."

Heaven knew whom she was speaking of—the Spanish chick always sneering and giving her dirty looks. "Oh her. What happened to her?"

"Somebody snuck her in the showers."

Heaven's eyes widened. "Oh no. That's awful."

Sabina shook her head. "Yeah, and whoever did it also bit her in the face."

"*What?*" Heaven screeched. "What the hell is wrong with these women? Who the hell would bite someone in the face?"

Sabina shook her head and said, "Some wild fucking animal."

THIRTY-FOUR

When It's All Over . . .

"Hey, are you Lewis?"

Heaven peeled her eyes away from the book she was reading, *Mistress*, by James Patterson and stared into the blue eyes of a punk-rocker-looking chick with pink hair and several pieces of white and pink striped straw slid through the three holes in each ear.

She held two new blankets in her hand the way a server would a tray of drinks.

Heaven laid her book facedown on her bed. "Yeah. Why?"

"These are for you," she said, thrusting the items inside the cell.

Heaven's brow rose. "I didn't request—"

"Listen, lady," the girl hissed impatiently, her eyes flashing in irritation. "I'm not here to go back and forth with you. I have other things to do. I was *sent* here to deliver these to you, so you *need* to take them. *Now.*"

Heaven huffed, sliding her feet into her shower shoes, then standing. She walked over and took the items from the girl. And, then, as quick as she had come—she'd disappeared.

Heaven frowned carrying the blankets over to her locker, but then she thought to check to see if there was anything hidden in them.

She gasped as her pulse raced.

Inside one of the gray blankets was what she'd asked for.

A Taser.

And smartphone.

She smiled. It had taken him a week to get them to her, but somehow—once again, he'd managed to make it happen. *I'll have to remember to suck his dick real good next time I see him*, she thought, sliding her hand in between one of the blankets and caressing the Taser. She knew she couldn't hold onto the electro-shock weapon indefinitely. She'd have to get it the hell out of her cell—fast.

And she would.

All she needed know was a way to get to Struthers.

Another smile eased over her lips. She knew exactly what she—

"Hey, Miss Heaven," Clitina said, chopping off the plan slowly rooting in Heaven's mind. "What'chu doin' today?" she asked, leaning up against the frame of the cell.

Heaven turned to her. "Hey, Tina. Nothing much. Probably relax for a bit. Read and listen to music. I have to go scrub nasty-ass toilets at six."

Clitina made a face. "Ugh. I wouldn't clean a fuckin' thing."

Heaven shrugged. "It beats being in lockup, hon. I'm not even mad about it, anymore. It's a shitty job—pun intended, but someone has to do it."

"Mmph. You good, Miss Heaven, 'cause I know I ain't wipin' up nobody's shit. Dickalina tried that with me when her nasty-ass man came home drunk one time 'n' shitted all over himself. She gonna ask me 'n' Candy to help her clean 'im up. Candy's dumbass helped her. What kinda woman you know, Miss Heaven, gonna ask her daughters to help her wash her man's long dick 'n' the crack of his ass, when she know we both love dingaling?"

Heaven blinked. "Tina, girl, I can't. Y'all have a lot going on over there."

"Don't we, though," she agreed. "But, uh. I'm so fuckin' bored right now. I wanna get off this unit. No harm, Miss Heaven, but y'all bitches is boring as shit over here. I need me some action. I need to be where the live bitches at."

Heaven nodded knowingly. "You want to go to Four East, I bet."

Clitina bounced up and down. "Yass, yasssss, Miss Heaven. The hood, boo. You already know."

Heaven shook her head. "Girl, you a mess."

"Mmhmm. And I love it messy too," she said. "I can't wait to go out to the yard, so I can turn up with my niggas."

Heaven opened her mouth to say something, but then quickly shut it. She simply didn't have the energy. "So have you spoken to your mother?" she asked instead.

Clitina sucked her teeth. "Fuck no. She still actin' stank. I hope the rest of her edges fall out. But Candy told me her 'n' Day'Asia comin' up to see me in two weeks." She lowered her voice to a conspiratorial whisper. "She said she gonna bring me up some Sour Diesel. I told her make sure she wrap it good, too 'cause I don't want her soakin' my weed in none of her nasty cootie juice . . ."

Heaven blinked.

"And Day'Asia gonna bring a bag of Molly for Weena's fiend-ass. That bitch know she a borderline junkie, but I don't really like to tell nobody's business, so I'ma shut these lips on that."

Heaven gave her an incredulous look. "So these drugs are to do *what?* Sell? And how are they getting this stuff to you?"

Clitina gave her an *uh-duh* look. "In they cooties. Where else?" She sucked her teeth. "And no I ain't sellin' it. I ain't no dealer. I told you I like to smoke, chill, 'n' steal shit off the racks. Not sell no damn drugs."

"Oh, okay. Whew," Heaven said sarcastically, wiping her forehead. "I got worried there for a minute. I thought—"

"Tina, I need my six soups back by tomorrow," a slender, pretty Caucasian girl said, stopping in front of Heaven's cell. "*Please.*" She wore a white V-neck T-shirt, sleeves rolled up over her shoulders. One of her arms was entirely tattooed in black roses and red hearts.

Odd. But striking.

Clitina scoffed. "*Bitch*, hit the floor with it. You better slurp on these six soups between my legs 'cause I ain't got nothin' else for ya cracker-ass."

The woman's cheeks flushed pink. "Well, you don't have to be a fuck-face about it. Just let me know when you can get them to me," she said, before she quickly walked off.

Clitina scoffed. "Fuck-Face? Oooh, she lucky I'm tryna go outside right now or that bitch woulda got stomped, Brick-City style."

"It's not that serious, Tina," Heaven stated calmly. "Pay her what you owe her and let it go."

Clitina frowned. "All I asked for was *two* soups 'n' that bitch gonna tell me I gotta give her *six* back. All she gonna get is them two nasty-ass soups she gave me."

Heaven shook her head. "Tina, that's not how it works. You have to pay the taxes on anything you borrow; you already know this."

Clitina bucked her eyes, then blinked rapidly. "Um—wait for it. No. Hell, no. Anyway. Like I was sayin' before Casper came up tryna set it off. I'ma get *turnt* all the way up. I'ma smoke until my lips turn black. Shit. Weed is good for the soul, Miss Heaven."

Heaven lifted a brow and tilted her head. "You—"

The CO called out over the PA system for movement out to the Big Yard.

"Ooh, let me go, Miss Heaven. I ain't got no time for lectures right now. But you need to come outside 'n' get yo' life. These hoes already *think* you *think* you too good. And you know I already had to drag that Spanish bitch last week for talkin' shit 'bout you."

Heaven gasped. "Ohmygod! That was *you?*"

Clitina smiled, all teeth and pink healthy gums. "Mmmhmm. I got that bitch while she was real wet 'n' soapy, then swung her down to the floor by her wet hair and punched her titties up 'n' stomped her all in her—"

"But you *bit* her," Heaven stated.

Clitina gave her a look and shrugged. "Oh well, she should'na been flappin' her lips all crazy. She lucky I was being nice that night. But I let that Mexican bitch know don't talk no shit 'bout you."

"She's Puerto Rican," Heaven corrected.

"And that bitch *still* eat burritos," she snapped. "So don't go takin' up for her."

The announcement for last movement to the yard blared over the speaker again, and Clitina took off down the tier, leaving Heaven standing there like a deer paralyzed in a car's headlights, about to get hit.

THIRTY-FIVE
Kiss It Better . . .

"**Y**eah, baby. Pussy tight . . ." Officer Rawlings murmured, relieved that she hadn't given none of these other motherfuckers here any of this wet, gushy good-good.

He was becoming more obsessed with her. More protective of what was his.

It'd been a little over a month (thanks to the warden and her bullshit-ass lockdown) since he'd been inside of her, and he couldn't go another second (let alone, another day) without *feeling* her, *fucking* her.

He missed the hell out of her.

During the latter part of second shift, not only had he managed to finally get the dildos and vibrator to her, he'd found a way to have her called off the housing unit for a *medical* visit. He was doing overtime and had been able to maneuver being assigned to the infirmary.

He, his *dick*, ached for this pussy. He needed it. And judging by the way Heaven's cunt convulsed around him, she'd needed this, this good loving, as much as he did.

He began slamming into her—hard, harder, harder—making him feel as if his sole purpose at work (on this earth) was this. Being right here, fucking her, his dick enveloped in heat and mind-numbing sensations.

His breath escaped in hot gasps, and his balls tightened in pleasure as she moved against him, fucking him back.

He growled as he thrust, again, again, again.

He never wanted it to end.

He was all fucked up. She was all in his head. Had him slipping. *Hard.*

"Stop," Heaven said breathlessly. "Please. Oh, God . . . *please* . . ."

"You don't mean that," he rasped, his dick still moving in and out of her. "God can't stop this, baby. And you know you don't want me to stop this, either. Let me pump this nut inside of you." His dick brushed over her G-spot and her cunt clenched around him as she bit back a moan. "That's right, baby, grab *your* dick . . . uhh . . . this is . . . mmm . . . your dick, baby . . ."

Her juices *swished-swished* all around him. Fuck yeah. He loved fucking her from the back. Back arched, all exposed. Her ass, her pussy. He loved watching her sweet flesh open to him. He loved the way her ass shook for him, clapping around him. Loved the way her folds spread, the way the pink center—all wet and pretty—sucked at him.

He—*oh, fuck, yeah*—loved the hot rhythm that melded them together as he pounded into her, steady and deep. Loved how wet and silky her walls became every time he stroked over her G-spot.

So he fucked her hard and made her moan deep in her throat, and she became even wetter. "Oh, stop . . . mmm, daddy, stop . . ." Her body trembled beneath, her words contradicting the clutch of cunt.

"No, baby," he murmured. "I can't . . . stop. Your warm wet pussy won't let me."

Tiny goose bumps dotted her arms as he slid a wet finger in the crack of her ass, then rubbed lightly over her hole, his dick twitching as that little brown opening kissed his fingertip.

His mouth brushed against her ear. "Can I nut inside this pretty ass, baby?" he whispered.

Her hips rocked back in response. "Yes," she panted.

"Yes, what, baby?"

She ground her ass into his pelvis, then slid forward, rocking her pussy back and forth over his dick. "Yes, you can fuck me in my ass," she said in a low voice.

He groaned in her ear, then nipped at it, before kissing the back of her neck, then slowly sliding his lips down her spine until his dick slid from her body and his mouth was almost hovering over the tailbone.

Her body shuddered, and he kissed her there.

"I'm going to tongue your sweet ass, baby," he breathed out.

And his erotic words rolled over her body in shudders; her hand slid between her thighs until eager fingers spread over her clit, all slick and swollen—and she touched herself.

He kissed the small of her back again. Then his hands peeled her open and his tongue slid along her hole, and Heaven shivered to her toes and closed her eyes as he rimmed her opening and then thrust his tongue into her ass.

She gasped and her entire body spasmed.

"Fuck me in it," she murmured.

He glanced at his watch. Time was ticking away. He had to hurry this along. And yet she was so tight there. He knew once he worked his dick inside her ass, it would grip him tighter than a fist.

The thought had him ready to come. Now.

Shit. He looked down at his thrashing dick. It would take at least ten minutes—or more, to prime and ready her sweet ass for it. Time he didn't have.

He cursed under his breath, both happy and relieved that she'd wanted him to take her ass and that it wasn't loose already, but shit ...

"I gotta get back inside your pussy, baby," he groaned. "Gotta come, fast."

She shifted her body. "No, no. Let me ride you," she said, her voice a hot whisper as she reached between his legs. And when he opened his mouth to protest (being on his back took away his control, and he didn't like *not* being in control), her hazel eyes flashed a blaze of desire that caused him to emit a hot sigh when her hand stroked his dick.

His whole body vibrated with lust. And without a word, he lay on his back and watched through lust-brimmed eyes as she climbed on top of him—her pussy all open and glistening wet—then bound forward and reached between them and held onto his dick. It thumped in her hand in anticipation of her sliding her sweet cunt down onto his shaft.

Holy shit. He was really doing this. Giving her control.

He gripped her ass as she smoothly impaled herself, rocking down on it until she took him all the way down to the base. A moan escaped her. Then him.

His hips moved upward matching hers. "Yeah, fuck me," he said, then lifted his head and alternately sucked her tits.

They both moaned as her clit pressed against his body just above the base of his dick, and then everything inside of her washed out over him.

"Aah, this pussy good . . . fuck this dick," he hissed as she leaned forward and kissed him, her tongue sliding into his mouth, taking his breath, hotly and intensely—while she rode him, fast and hard.

She watched as he closed his eyes during their heated kisses. She liked him. God, she really, really did.

She fucked him wildly—with hot abandon, galloping up and down on him until his eyes rolled up in his head behind his closed lids.

She bit his lips as she came, her orgasm violently sweeping through her body like a tornado. She kept riding him, her pussy sucking him further into its wet clutch.

"God, yes, baby. I-I-I . . . aaah, shit . . . love you . . . uh, uh, uhhh . . ."

His orgasm wasn't far behind, and she covered his mouth with her hand as he growled out in pleasure, his body convulsing beneath her.

THIRTY-SIX
Wild Cookie...

Heaven sucked in her breath. Had she heard him right? She was pretty sure she had, but . . . in the heated moment the room had been spinning and she'd been moaning and all she heard was her heart pulsing in her ears.

No, no—she couldn't have heard him correctly.

"I love you . . ."

She closed her eyes. Replayed their passionate night in the infirmary, rewinding to everything before their orgasms.

"I love you . . ."

Her eyes flew open. Oh, God, no. She *had* heard him right. Those three words were the last thing she'd expected to hear from him—or any other man. Not here, not now.

That's not what she was here for.

Love.

Love . . . that little dirty motherfucking word was what got her here. She hadn't heard those words—*I love you*—from a man since . . . Freedom.

She brought her eyes closed again, then slowly opened. She couldn't deal with this right now. All she wanted to do was concentrate on reading her—

"Hey, Heaven," someone said; her tone was just above a whisper.

Heaven placed the book she was reading, *The Prisoner's Wife*, by Asha Bandele up to her chest, its worn pages (from many years of handling by countless hands) pressed to her breasts. She'd found the book on the tier and decided to read it. So far she was enjoying it.

She looked over at a square-bodied, spectacled woman with brown frizzy hair, who looked to be in her mid-thirties and was built like a Transformer, meekly staring back at her.

"Yes."

"I was wondering if I can rent out"—she glanced around the tier, making sure no one else was around to hear her— "you know. One of your . . . *toys*?"

Ever since she'd gotten her sex toys from Rawlings over three weeks ago, she'd been renting the items out to a select group of women on the housing unit. And, thanks to Greta who'd planted the idea in her head, she'd been building up a nice little clientele. She kept record of each transaction and the initial of each inmate in a journal, indicating date checked out, and date returned almost like a library card.

But this woman here, she'd never done business with.

Heaven slid from her bed and walked over to her. She stared at her acne-studded forehead for a moment longer than she probably should have, before locking her gaze on hers.

"Exactly what *toys* are you speaking of?"

The woman looked around again. "One of your *dildos*," she whispered.

Heaven tilted her head. "Well, before we go any further. I need to inform you of the terms." She paused, and the woman stared intently, waiting for her to continue. "First, you must have a clean pussy. I don't do business with women with filthy hygiene."

"Oh, I'm very clean," she quickly assured. "No bad odors. I wash and shower daily."

"Good. Second, you pay up front. No layaways, and no IOUs. You wanna *play*, you gotta *pay*."

The woman nodded. "Okay."

"Third, you must bring each rental back in the same condition it was given to you. It must be washed and cleaned."

"Okay."

"Fourth, if you bring it back late, you'll be charged a late fee— six cans of mackerel for every thirty minutes it's late. Fifth, you *must*—and I can't stress this enough—*wrap* it in a glove."

The woman nodded. "Okay."

"Six, if you get caught with it and it gets confiscated. Then it's your debt to bear. Do you understand?"

She nodded.

"Great. Now, tell me. How long are you looking to rent for?"

She leaned in a little closer, and Heaven could smell her minty breath. "Well, I was hoping for the whole night."

Heaven smiled. "Oh, you a greedy one. Huh?"

The woman's lips spread into a toothy, shy grin. "And I was hoping for that real *big* one."

Mirth shone in Heaven's gaze. "You sure you want *that* one?"

The woman nodded. "I'm sure," she said, her tone serious. "It's been one of my fantasies. To be, well, you know . . ." She paused, gauging Heaven's expression, "with a *big* one," she said in a whisper. "I've never done it with, well . . . a black man. I'd never do it in real life, though. But here—"

Heaven lifted a brow but didn't say anything, not wanting to embarrass her any more than she already was. And, well, it didn't matter what the woman's fantasies were while she was fucking herself as long as she was willing to pay for them.

Heaven put a hand up to stop her. "Say no more." She briskly walked back over and pulled out a plastic bin from beneath her bunk and pulled out Cockzilla (she kept the severely long phallus wrapped in a towel), then sashayed back over toward, um . . .

"I didn't get your name," Heaven said, cradling the towel-wrapped dildo in her arms like a baby.

"Oh, right. It's Penelope. After my grandmother."

"Oh. Well, nice doing business with you. This one here is going to cost you four books of stamps for all night." A book of twenty stamps cost nine dollars on commissary, but had a street value of only six dollars in prison. And at Croydon Hill, postage stamps and cans of mackerel were the predominant currency used.

Heaven slid the towel back the way a proud mother would her newborn baby, giving the salivating woman a peek of what she'd be getting.

Penelope's eyes widened as she sucked in her bottom lip. "Yes, yes. That's the one I want."

Heaven smiled. "Then you had better show me the money."

A few hours later, Heaven made her way down to the second tier, speaking to a few inmates as she sauntered toward the cell of an inmate by the name of Annie-Mae. Annie-Mae had been incarcerated for the last four years for endangering the welfare of a child and kidnapping and burglary. She'd taken her three children to Texas without their father's permission. And then was arrested when she refused to return to N.J. with the kids.

"What's going on, Annie-Mae?" asked Heaven as she discreetly slid into her cell. "Seems like you've forgotten how to return *my* property." Heaven placed a hand up on her hip. "You've had it out for more than four days. And *you* haven't said *one* word to me about it."

The sandy-brown-haired Albanian stood from her desk, and said in her thick accent, "I'll get it back to you tonight."

Heaven tilted her head, and her jaw clenched. "Bitch, this is unacceptable. You're cutting into my coins." She had three women on the wait list to use the sex toy, and this ho was hogging the vibrator.

The woman apologized. "I, well . . . see, I let my bunkie use it, and then . . ." She shifted her weight from one foot to the other. "And then—"

"So you *loaned* my shit out without *my* permission?"

"Sort of," she admitted. "But I was supposed to have it back two nights ago, and, well . . ."

Heaven's nose spread. She didn't have all night with this bitch. "Look. Do you have payment for the late fees?"

"Well, not at the—"

The rest of her sentence was cut off by a large can of mackerel hitting her in the mouth. Heaven split her bottom lip, then hit her upside the head with the can.

The woman's hand flew up to her mouth, and her eyes widened in shock.

"Ohmygod! You bust my lip."

"And I'll bust your skull if I don't get my shit back, Annie-Mae— with the interest you owe, because if not, I'm going to claw your goddamn eye out like I did that bitch over on Four East. You have until noon tomorrow."

And with that, she quickly slid out of the woman's cell and headed back up to the high-rises up on the third floor. God, she didn't want to resort to violence. But that was what some bitches only understood. So if she had to resort to barbaric measures, then she would.

And, for good measure, she'd sic Clitina on her ass.

THIRTY-SEVEN
Simon Says...

"What is it *now*, Lewis?" the sergeant asked smugly as he sat back in his chair and practically eye-fucked her. Instantly, his dick swelled against his uniform pants. It was second shift, a little after six in the evening. And she was practically off the housing unit to finish up her last night of extra duty, when Bitchy-ass Harris—God, she hated that bitch—(she was covering overtime again)—called her back and told her she needed to get down to the sergeants' office.

So here she was—part annoyed, part bubbly with determination; a mixture of irritation and arousal managed to flash in her expression. She'd requested to see him *over* three weeks ago, and the bastard took his slow sweet time to finally grace her with an audience. Whatever.

She had to race back up to her cell to *freshen* up a bit. She quickly changed out of her jumper and slipped on a pair of panty briefs. Then slipped on one of her baggy jumpers (well, you know—only in case she needed to slide her hand down into her panties), but she'd pulled her hair back in a sleek bun and shellacked her lips in her favorite orange lipstick. She wanted them dick-sucking shiny and deliciously enticing.

Then she rolled on a scent by Viktor & Rolf called Flowerbomb. The CO Miss Kimberly had slipped her two samplers on the sly, then placed a finger to her lips, before walking off.

So she decided to roll the perfume along the back of her neck and behind her ears, then down the center of her breasts, and in the crook of each arm, making sure the fruity, floral scent lingered around him—even after she was gone.

"Tonight's my last night of cleaning detail, Sir," she said sweetly.

"Yeah, *and?* You want a medal?"

No—just my shit. She shook her head, feeling herself go hot with anger. She inhaled sharply, then slowly blew her agitation out through her nose. "I wanted to know if I would be able to have my personal belongings returned to me"—*you know the shit you stole from me?*—"or at least my television and other devices."

Sergeant Struthers sneered. "Ho, look around you." Heaven glanced around the office, purposefully taking him literal. "Where the fuck you think you at?"

She bit the inside of her lip. "Prison," she said softly. God—why couldn't she stab him in his neck, then leave him for dead?

"That's right, prison. You bitches think you can come up in here and freeload off taxpayers'—"

"Excuse me, *Sir.* No disrespect. But I'm not freeloading off of *any*one. I bought those things that had been taken from *me* for no reason from out of *my* own damn money. *You* did what you did to me, then turned around and stole all my shit from out of my cell."

Struthers stood to his feet, shoving his hands in his pockets in an attempt to hide the heavy bulge between his legs. "I *did* to your dick-sucking ass what you wanted me to. Don't get it fucked up. Your trick-ass wanted dick, and so I gave it to you."

Heaven blinked several times, but she kept her cool. "That was some dirty shit what you did, though," she said. "And you know it."

"It's called life. And life sometimes gets dirty. And it isn't always fair. Get over it. This is my house. And in my house, you bitches do what I say. You understand that?"

Heaven crossed her arms over her midsection, and the gesture inadvertently plumped her breasts up more than they already were, pushing them upward until they strained against her jumper, her cleavage practically spilling out.

Struthers choked back a groan. He swore he could almost see her nipples, and felt his dick stir. "Now what you wanna do to get your shit back?"

"Well, I *want* a do-over," she boldly stated, catching his gaze on her breasts. She placed both her hands on her hips. Then let out an exaggerated sigh. "I don't want to be *handcuffed*, like some damn slave on an auction block. And I don't want that *ugly* CO bitch watching while I'm down on my knees worshipping you."

Struthers stared at her and gritted his teeth. This pretty bitch with the plump, juicy lips was really fucking asking for it.

"Lewis, get the fuck out my office, before I write your ass up."

As Heaven finished cleaning the last three toilet stalls, she spotted a bunch of little writings on one of the doors. She narrowed her eyes.

I NEED MY COCK SUCKED

BLACK BITCHES HAVE THE BEST ASS

I WANT SOME ASIAN PUSSY

WHO WANTS THIS BIG COCK?

STRUTHERS SUX LITTLE COCK

She shook her head, then glanced at her watch. She had another twenty minutes to go and she'd be finally finished. She sighed, grabbing the toilet brush and opening the stall—

"Where you think you going?" Sergeant Struthers said as he leered at her.

Heaven gasped, dropping the toilet brush to the floor. "Ohmygod!"

"Don't get scared now," he sneered, the pupils in his dark-brown eyes wide dots of lust and deviousness, almost as if he was possessed. "I want this dick sucked."

Suddenly, the air was so thick and heavy, Heaven couldn't breathe. She wanted this, had asked for this—a second round, but she hadn't heard him come in, and she hadn't expected him (although she had wanted him to) to seek her out *tonight*.

She found her breath. "And I *want* my property back," she pushed out, feeling more in control.

"Your shit is already up in your cell."

She tilted her head. "*All* of it?"

His nose flared. "What the fuck I just say? Don't make me regret it."

"Well then . . ." She glanced over at the bathroom door.

"It's already locked," he hissed, already rubbing over his hard dick. "Get on your fuckin' knees. I don't have all night. The next time you open your mouth, it should be to stuff it with this dick. And I'm telling you now, *bitch* . . ."

He grabbed her by the throat and forced her down to her knees. His large hand tightened around her neck. He felt like slapping her, hard, then strangling her. But he restrained himself. "Don't ever fuck with me again. You understand?"

Breath caught in her throat, her eyes widened and instantly filled with tears, yet she managed to quickly nod her head. Her pulse raced, but she didn't fear he would kill her. No. He knew what he was doing.

And when he finally let her go, his erection straining painfully tight against his zipper, she gasped heavily, feeling her cunt burst into flames as he pulled open his pants and yanked down his zipper, quickly dragging out his enormous erection over the waistband of his navy blue boxer briefs.

Heaven took a steadying breath rubbing her throat, but it did nothing to quell her lightheadedness or the ache in cunt as her inner walls flinched.

This motherfucker!

He stroked himself to his full hardness, then let the wet tip of his dick rub against Heaven's lips. His dick was at the ready, about to ravage her mouth. The feral spear about to strike. She licked at it. And then he slapped his dick across her face.

"You a pretty bitch. But I'm warning you. Don't fuck with me."

"All I want is this dick," she murmured, her tongue lolling out of her mouth. Another shiny bead of lust welled from the crown.

He fisted her hair cruelly into his hand. "Open your fuckin' mouth."

She parted her lips, and he shoved his dick all the way to the back of her throat, causing her eyes to fly open. He pulled out and then thrust his hips, forward and deep, until his balls slapped against her chin.

She felt her clitoris swell and jut from her mons, and she moaned over a mouthful of dick. With a free hand, she unzipped her jumper. She needed to get a hand inside, needed to feel, needed to brush her fingertips over—

"Fuckin' slut," he hissed over a moan; his meaty girth growing thicker than she thought humanly possible. "Swallow all that dick."

She gulped and bobbed her head, her jaw stretching to beyond what she thought possible. Saliva flooded all around his dick and her wet mouth felt like silky heat.

He viciously pounded in and out of her mouth, impaling her throat with the broad head of his dick, his pelvis banging into her nose.

She groaned and looked up at him as her hand slid down into her jumper, reaching, reaching . . . oh yes—*ooh*. There it was. Right there.

She closed her eyes for only a moment to savor him, this . . . down on her knees, powerless to him (so he thought), worshipping him (the way he wanted), devouring him (to hurry this along), moaning and humming and straining over the width of him— mm, yes, yes, yes . . .

She felt it. The swelling of his nut right below the crown, she tasted its arrival as precum glossed her tonsils. He was almost there. So much pressure building in his loins, he could barely breathe. His thighs shook from endless thrusting.

She peered up to find his face captured in the perfect sex face— strained with pleasure and disdain and overwhelming need that pissed him off.

He began pumping his hips more furiously. Deep. Brutal. Never-ending.

And then he roughly grabbed her head in both of his hands and held himself down in her neck, making it unbearably difficult for her to breathe.

"Swallow my shit," he growled. "You worthless bitch."

Heaven cringed as thick heat jetted against the back of her throat and she tasted the salt. She almost swallowed on instinct, but didn't. She let it slosh down her chin and kept sucking him, her hand easing up from out of her panties.

His eyes were still closed as he kept rocking back and forth into her mouth, his body jerking as the remainder of his orgasm sputtered out of his dick. Before he could open his eyes and pull himself from her mouth. . .

She'd jolted him.

And his huge body crumpled to the floor.

THIRTY-EIGHT
This is a Warning . . .

"For the love of God," the warden hissed, the blood in her face quickly draining as she held the smartphone in her hand and stared at the photos. She swiped over the screen to the next one, and then the next one. Three of them—all lewd images of Sergeant Struthers passed out on a bathroom floor; his flaccid dick flopped out of his underwear.

The warden's mouth tightened into an angry line and then she slumped back in her chair. "Where'd you get these?" she hissed, feeling herself drowning in a silent anger. "And where did you get this phone?" Her stomach churned. The last thing she needed was this sort of scandal right on the heels of everything else that had happened at Croydon Hill.

Heaven matched her stare. "You're not in the position to question me about where or how I got the phone. You shouldn't even be worried about the phone anyway. Your concern should be Struthers. And why he's passed out on a bathroom floor with his dick out." She paused, tilting her head. "Now that work of art, I took myself. And believe me. Anything happens to me, I will drag this place with you along with it. Not only will you and your prison be under investigation, I will sue the drawers off you and the state."

The warden felt her blood boil. How dare this bitch threaten her!

When the sergeant had finally come through, he'd awakened to a note that Heaven already had neatly prewritten and had kept on her tucked in her bra to give to him once she'd handled him— you know, just in case he'd try to retaliate.

I have pictures of you. And of the bruises around my neck from you choking me. Come after me and I'll post them all over the Internet. Then send copies to Angelica.

So far he'd called out sick for the last two days, which only made him look suspicious in the warden's eyes. Still . . .

Heaven reached inside her bra and pulled out a plastic baggy and then tossed it up on the warden's desk. "A little extra treat for you."

"What is *that?*" she asked repulsively as she . . . she blinked. "Are those what I think they are?"

Heaven nodded. "Yes. His nasty cock hairs."

The warden blinked back her disgust. She was so sickened by all of this shit that she wanted to throw up. And then for this self-serving bitch to have the fucking audacity to come into *her* office and threaten *her* was enough to make her piss fire.

She fucking knew it. Knew inmate Lewis was going to be trouble. From the moment she'd stepped off that bus and she'd witnessed the effect she had on inmates and officers—and even *her*, she fucking knew Heaven Lewis was going to be a never-ending source of angst for her.

Heaven stood and unzipped her jumper, then slid her hands inside.

The warden's eyes went wide with shock. "Miss Lewis, what the *hell* do you think—?"

"Lady, I am not interested in you," she snapped, pulling out the

Taser, then setting it on the warden's desk. "You might want this."

"How on earth did you get *this*?"

Heaven slowly shook her head. "Now, now, Warden, I may be many things. But a snitch I am not." She took her seat, and her eyes flickered toward the phone. "Not unless *you* fuck with me. And then I will have every news anchor across the country eating this up. I have more pictures where these came from, in safekeeping."

The warden gasped. This bitch was obviously trying to destroy her. She had to be. That was the only thing the warden could come up with for how much sleep she'd lost ever since she'd arrived to her prison.

Her nose flared, but she'd managed to fold her hands neatly together in front of her as if she were praying. It was deliberate. Lord knew she needed prayer. And she needed the strength not to lose every ounce of her self-restraint she had to keep from reaching in her desk drawer and pulling out her flask, then beating this bitch over the head with it—*after* she tilted it to her lips and emptied it.

She took a slow, deliberate breath. "I need for you to tell me what happened from the beginning. *Now*."

Heaven reached up and unlatched her hair clip, and shook her hair. The warden watched as it tumbled over her shoulders.

"Struthers sexually assaulted me," Heaven reiterated gravelly. "He *skull*-fucked me. Not once, but twice. And I was afraid of him." It was a lie, but she ran with it. She loathed him and yet had found herself sinfully aroused by him all in the same breath.

Still, she wanted to lure her own prey in, and suck and fuck them on *her* terms, *not* have someone else try to exert his or her position and power over her. No, that didn't work for her.

She took a deep breath and then continued. "I didn't feel like I had anyone I could go to, so I needed my own protection. And when he'd come into the bathroom I was cleaning, and then demanded I suck his dick, or else he was going to make my life a living hell, I knew I had to do something; especially after he choked me." She pointed to the phone. "There's one more picture where you can see where his handprint was around my neck. Anyway, I knew I had to protect myself, so that's when I used the Taser on his ass."

The warden's brow rose. "Yes. About that, I need to know how you got this?" She reached for it and held it by the handle.

Heaven shook her head. "It's not important. What matters is, I've turned it in to *you*. I only needed it for one purpose, and one purpose only. To bring *him* down."

The warden massaged her temples. She needed a damn drink, just a sippy-sip to calm her nerves. "Well, why didn't you report what he'd been doing to you?"

Heaven snorted. "*Report* it? To *who? You?* Another officer?" She let out a sarcastic laugh. "You know, like I do, they *all* stick together. Would you have believed me if I hadn't come in here with *proof*?"

"I would have conducted a thorough investigation."

Heaven choked back a snort. "And he would have perjured his way out of it, then eventually gone right back to being the pig he is. Who is going to believe an inmate over a sergeant, huh? *You?*"

The warden shifted in her seat. Her outwardly calm and collected demeanor masked her raging inner turmoil.

"I should fucking destroy him," Heaven hissed. "And take you down with him. But I'm willing to make a deal. And I think we'd both like to keep this quiet. Not make a big production over a sergeant degrading and sexually assaulting inmates. This way, you get to keep your cushy job and I get to move around stress-free."

She sat back in her seat, and crossed her legs. "Oh, and by the way. If the cock hairs aren't enough, I have his nut."

The warden gasped.

"Yes. Right after he came in my mouth, I let most of it spill out onto my jumper, then spat the rest out into a washcloth, right before quickly taking those pictures of him and then running out of the bathroom, leaving him there sprawled out on the bathroom floor. And trust me. I will have those photos posted all over social media. 'Hashtag Croydon Hill Runs A Sex Camp,' 'Hashtag Sergeant Sexually Assaults Inmates.' Shall I continue?"

The warden felt her hands shake. She wanted to puke her guts up.

"You little conniving *bitch*."

Heaven let out a sardonic laugh. "Yeah, I'm the conniver. I'm the bitch. But I'm not the one preying on inmates. *Your* sergeant is—right underneath your drunken nose. On *your* watch . . . "

The warden's jaw clenched, but she dared not give this manipulating bitch the satisfaction of a reaction. That's what she wanted from her. She knew it.

Heaven scowled. "All these women who he has abused in here are too fucking scared to report his ass. You want to know why, Warden? Because the bastard only preys on weak, gullible inmates who he knows he can easily manipulate and intimidate; that's why. But, he didn't know whom he was messing with when he shoved his dick down in my throat.

"Here's the thing, Warden," Heaven said as she leaned forward in her seat. "I'm not the *bitch* to fuck with," she said acidly. "And *he* . . . fucked . . . with me. I shot the man I loved in the back for cheating on me. So what do you think I'd do to a motherfucker who shoves his dick down my throat, and I feel nothing for him?"

The warden's eyes flashed with fury.

During her years as a CO, she had overheard the rumors, that Struthers had a penchant for bullying and degrading inmates, forcing them to perform sexual acts, while also tormenting them. She had always hoped that none of it was true. She wouldn't, couldn't stand for this sort of behavior. She wouldn't ruin his career, but he'd be forced to retire. She'd have to get him out of her prison, or she'd be forced to pursue other avenues. Legal repercussions. And she'd throw him under the bus before anyone had the opportunity to throw her.

The warden cut her gaze down at her desk drawer.

"Is that where you keep it? The *vodka?*"

The warden swallowed. Even though she held Heaven's gaze, and never flinched, her mind was in utter disarray. This dizzying bitch with all of her sexual energy—along with the damaging photos on the cell and the disturbing fact that an inmate had gotten ahold of a Taser—had all given her a pounding headache.

The warden sighed. She finally resigned herself to the fact that Heaven had her in a very precarious position—one she didn't like one damn bit. The last thing she needed, or wanted, was any sort of negative press, or damaging media coverage. She only had a few more years to retire; that was it. Nothing was going to get in the way of that.

Not even this bitch.

"Okay, Lewis," the warden finally acquiesced. "What is it *you* want . . .?"

THIRTY-NINE

It's Not Over...

The metal door slid open, and Heaven stepped out into the large visiting room. She was immediately slapped by noise. Lots of it. Babies crying. Kids running around being unruly. Couples arguing. Family cackling. Music playing. It was all too much for her ears. She felt a headache coming on. She didn't remember the noise level being so obnoxiously loud the last time she'd come out for a visit.

Then again, it had been on a Wednesday night—so long ago—the last time she'd come out. And today was a Saturday visit after all—one of the busiest visiting days of the week. She made a mental note to tell whoever was here to see her to come on another day next time—if there were a next time. She felt like she'd suddenly stepped out into a world circus with all the featured attractions on site.

Still, she had to admit, it was nice to get out from behind the other side of the metal doors to see how the outside world was living, even if she had to be mauled by Officer Clemmons again to do so. "Mm. I bet you taste real good, bitch," she'd stage-whispered before beginning her frisk. Then she'd roughly pawed Heaven. That fucking undercover *dyke*-bitch made her skin crawl. She'd grabbed her breasts this time, then slyly ran her hand over her crotch, trying to squeeze the front of her pussy, while the other three COs were busy searching other inmates.

"There's a can of Mace with your name on it," she'd warned. "Give me one good reason to use it. I'm begging you." She lowered her voice to a whisper, her lips barely brushing Heaven's ear. "Seeing you drop to your knees and cry out would make my dick hard." And then she laughed, causing Heaven's stomach to knot. "Now get the fuck on before I deny your visit."

Bitch.

"So glad to know you enjoy your job," Heaven replied sarcastically. "Have a nice day."

Heaven tried to shake the negative energy, but somehow she felt herself becoming strangled by it. She wanted to maim that bitch. She sighed. *Lord, help me.* She wished she could have someone stomp her wrists, and break every fucking bone in her hands. Slicing her eyeballs out with an ice pick would be an added bonus.

Suddenly, Heaven smiled. She had something to look forward to.

She quickly scanned the crowded room for her visitor. Her eyes unexpectedly welled with tears when she spotted who had come to see her. Her cousin.

Bianca.

They hadn't seen each other since her wedding. Nor had they spoken. When Heaven had gotten arrested, she'd wanted to reach out to her cousin while she was in the county jail, but her pride wouldn't let her. She'd been too embarrassed. Ashamed.

Bianca had warned her about Freedom. Warned her to be careful getting involved with him. And she should have listened. Her cousin hadn't liked him from the moment she'd met him.

Heaven didn't really think she'd come see her. Still, she'd put her name down on her visitor's card thirty days after she'd arrived at Croydon Hill.

And now here she was.

Bianca saw Heaven coming toward her and stood, smiling. The two women embraced, rocking side-to-side, so happy to see the other. Once they finally peeled apart from each other and took their seats, Bianca looked her cousin over.

"You look so good, girl . . ."

Heaven smiled. "Yeah. In spite of everything."

Bianca leaned in closer. Her skin was glowing. She looked amazingly beautiful. "How are you holding up in here? Are they treating you all right?"

Heaven glanced around the visiting area. She spotted that CO bitch from 4 East huddled at the registration desk with officer Banks talking and laughing. Over on the other side was Rasputia's twin brother, Officer Alvin, looking over in her direction with his sidekick—the tall, light-skinned officer with the big nose.

He was attractive, and she had a thing for big-nosed men. She made a mental note to find out more about him. She still needed a few good—well, no-good men—to help make her stay more bearable.

She could have sworn he licked his lips at her. She kept from licking her lips back, and shifted in her seat. "I'm okay, considering." She shrugged. "It's prison. What can I say? There are good days and bad days. I simply try to make the best out of a screwed-up situation."

Bianca nodded, and reached over and squeezed her hand. "I'm so sorry I wasn't there for you during the whole ordeal. I came to visit you in the county twice, but I was told you denied both visits."

Heaven dabbed a tear from her eye. "I'm sorry," she said remorse-fully. "I just didn't want to see anybody there. I guess I was still in shock over the whole thing. I mean. I *knew* what I'd done. I just couldn't believe I'd actually done it. I guess I was kind of in shock—still. "

Bianca slowly nodded. She understood. "It's okay, cuz. I'm here for you now. And if you need anything, don't hesitate to reach me."

Heaven smiled. "Thank you."

"Oh, and . . . before I forget. I put some money in your account. Four-hundred dollars. I hope it's enough. I called and asked if I could bring in a money order, but they told me I had to do it on *J*-something."

"JPay," Heaven said. "And, yes, that's more than enough. Thank you so much. Now enough about me." Heaven leaned back in the plastic chair. "How is that fine man of yours, and those adorable boys?"

She eyed her cousin as she beamed, feeling a tinge of envy seep through her veins. She loved Bianca, and was genuinely happy that she'd found love. Before she'd met Garrett—six feet, four inches of milk chocolate—she had been a self-proclaimed man-handler, as she liked to call herself. A nympho and *ho*, rotating the men in her life, like a set of used tires. But all it had taken was the right man, at the right time with the right amount of patience to change all that.

Bianca had met her husband, Garrett, through her brother, Tyler. They were both New Jersey State Troopers who'd been close friends for years.

"Oh, Garrett is fine. That man wants to keep me barefoot and pregnant." She laughed, rubbing her stomach. "But I couldn't have asked for a better husband."

Heaven gasped, clasping a hand over her mouth. "Ohmy-god! You're expecting again?"

Bianca smiled and nodded.

"That's great news. Congratulations. How far along are you?"

"I'm nine weeks."

Heaven smiled back, but her heart silently ached. She wanted what Bianca had—a man who fucked her good and loved her unconditionally.

"I'm so happy for the both of you."

"Thanks. And the boys are getting bigger than ever."

"And how are your brothers?"

Bianca shook her head, smiling. "Well, let's see. Tyler is doing great. Still happily married. Terrance is still in San Diego. He's divorced from Cherelle . . ."

Heaven laughed. "Oh I'm sure there's no love lost there."

"Exactly. I'm so glad he finally saw her for the skank she is."

Heaven glanced over to her left and witnessed an inmate stealing a kiss from her male visitor, her hand slithering over his crotch. Across from them, a woman slid something into another inmate's hand. *Drugs*, Heaven thought.

She brought her attention back to Bianca as she said her brother Terrance was still with the San Diego police force.

"Terrance was always my favorite," Heaven said, blinking.

"Mine, too," Bianca admitted.

"And how's Tyrell, Lamont, and Trent doing?"

"Girl, please. Still manwhores."

They both laughed.

Bianca shook her head. "And Thomas has, *yet*, another two kids."

Heaven gasped. "Ohmygod. How many kids does this make now?"

"Eight. Seven baby mothers; just slinging dick everywhere."

Heaven chuckled. "Mygod. Does that man know anything about birth control?"

Bianca let out a disgusted grunt. "Apparently not. He says he's allergic to condoms."

Heaven looked at her like she had two heads.

Bianca waved her off. "Girl, don't shoot the messenger."

The two shook their heads.

"You know," Heaven said, leaning forward in her seat. "Actually, there *is* something I need for you to do for me, if you would."

"Whatever you need," Bianca assured her.

She lowered her voice. "I have money stashed in a safety deposit box. I need for you to get it, and hold on to it for me and send me about a grand each month. That should keep me comfortable in this hellhole."

Bianca reached over and took her hand.

Heaven let out a sigh of relief. She knew she could trust her. Begging and groveling and pinching coins wouldn't have to be her plight.

"Thank you."

Bianca waved her on. "Girl, no problem. Of course I'll make sure you have whatever you need."

Heaven told her where to find the key to her safety deposit box. "Your name is listed at the bank, so there shouldn't be any problems."

Bianca nodded. "Say no more. It's done." She shifted in her seat. "Ooh, I need to use the bathroom."

Heaven pointed toward the registration table. "They're right there. Over on the left."

Bianca excused herself, then walked off toward the restrooms.

Heaven glanced toward the microwaves, before shifting her gaze over at the registration table. Sergeant Struthers walked in and stood by the table engaging in conversation with the two female officers, who giggled like two silly schoolgirls.

They probably want to suck his dick, Heaven thought, her attention being snatched by a voice in back of her. "I got my eye on you, Lewis," the male voice said low, causing her skin to prick with goose bumps. She could smell a hint of mint on his breath.

Heaven glanced over her shoulder and into the eyes of the light-skinned officer who'd been over on the other side of the room watching her.

"Should I be scared . . .?" She glanced at his nametag. "Officer Flores?"

He grinned. "Nah, be ready; that's all." Then he walked off, leaving her baffled with his masculine, woodsy scent swirling around her.

Be ready for what?

"Girl, that bathroom is a mess," Bianca said, finally returning to her seat holding two bags of Doritos and two bottles of water in her hands.

Heaven swallowed, glancing up at her. "Girl, please. These hoes coming up in here to visit are about as nasty and trifling as some of the inmates."

"So I see." She handed Heaven a bag of chips. "You still like Cool Ranch?"

She smiled. "Girl, you know these are my favorite." She took the bag, opening them. "Thanks."

For the remainder of the two-hour visit, the two women talked, laughed, and gouged on carbs the way they used to when they were young girls.

When the announcement was made that visiting was over, Heaven stood to her feet, and Bianca reluctantly did the same. It hurt her to see Heaven in prison garb, but she was relieved to see how good she looked in spite of her current situation.

"It was so good to see you."

"You, too. Thanks for coming."

"No problem, girl. I'm here for you."

The two women hugged, promising to stay in touch. Heaven gave her cousin a wave and watched her leave out the visiting area, while she made her way over to the line for the strip room to be searched.

And across the room, all Heaven felt was the heat of eyes burning over her flesh. And she couldn't help staring back into the gaze of Officer Flores, wondering exactly what the hell she needed to be ready for.

FORTY
Ready or Not . . .

Heaven found herself feeling a mixture of relief and sadness on her way back to the housing unit. She was relieved knowing she had someone on the outside that she could honestly trust to handle her money affairs, without trying to fuck her over. She cursed herself for not thinking of her cousin sooner. Bianca had always been trustworthy, even while growing up. As teens, she'd entrusted Bianca with her secrets, like getting pregnant while in college, then having an abortion, and her three trips to the clinic with syphilis once and chlamydia twice.

Not once had Bianca judged her or repeated what she'd been told. And Heaven loved her for safeguarding her secrets; never throwing them back up in her face, as they grew older and apart.

Heaven was pissed at herself for not reaching out to her all this time, but was happy her cousin had made her way up to the prison to visit.

As much as she'd needed that visit, it hurt her even more having to hug Bianca goodbye, knowing she wouldn't be walking out that door with her for many years to come.

With her right hand, she swiped at a lone tear before it had a chance to slide down her cheek. "No tears," she mumbled to herself. Crying made her vulnerable and a potentially easy target for some wolf-ass bitch lurking in the shadows for new prey. Her list of enemies seemed to be growing rapidly thanks to her still brewing beefs with that Goldie bitch and the rest of her 4 East cronies.

All over some ho who tried to force herself on her.

Heaven shook her head.

Even with the effort administration put on her to keep her and the inmates she'd fought away from each other, Heaven knew if anyone wanted to get at her, they would.

The question was when?

The corridor back to her housing unit was uncharacteristically quiet for a Saturday afternoon, which made her wonder why there wasn't a lot of movement, or the sound of other inmates within earshot. She'd been one of the last inmates to get strip-searched and had expected there'd be stragglers in the corridors.

But there wasn't.

Maybe because it's—

A strong, masculine hand came from out of nowhere and covered her mouth, nearly scaring her shitless. He wrapped a muscular arm around her, pulling her up against his surprisingly hard chest and snatching her around the corner and pulling her into a closet.

Oh, God. She didn't know if she should put up a struggle and bite his hand or scream. But then came her captor's voice, "Ssh," he whispered in her ear. His heated breath caressed her skin. "I'm not gonna hurt you."

Wait.

She'd heard that voice before. It was familiar, but she couldn't put her finger on it. Her body stiffened in her abductor's arms. It was a CO. "Relax," he said in an authoritative voice, loosening his grip, a hand lightly brushing over her left breast.

And what frightened, and aroused her, was the way his body felt against hers—lean, tall, and toned, along with his natural animal scent blended with an intoxicating fragrance. Expensive. Masculine.

Her cunt clenched.

"Didn't I tell you to be ready?"

Officer Flores.

"Are you *crazy?*" she hissed, twisting out of his grasp. "You scared the shit out of me." Her voice was breathless, and she wondered why there weren't any other COs monitoring the corridors. And she cursed herself, wondering why the hell had her panties gotten wet.

He smirked, his gaze gliding up and down her body, causing her body to heat. "My bad. I didn't mean to frighten you, Lewis. I couldn't visit, though. You were strutting, nah . . . swaying like you don't have a care in the world."

She glared at him, then found herself gazing down at the long, thick lump in his uniform pants. She swallowed. Tried to rein in her slutty thoughts. Her chest rose and fell at a rapid rate.

"How can I help you?" she asked, sounding out of breath.

"Let me holla at you for minute," he said, tugging her by the elbow and quickly ushering her into a utility closet he'd—unbeknownst to her—already made sure was unlocked.

He'd also managed to divert any other inmate traffic from coming this way. He'd had one of his cohorts send the inmates out of the strip room through another door that led to the other side of the compound where each inmate could get to their housing units. Sure, a longer walk. But it gave him the chance to make his move on the sexy enchantress. He'd had his eye on her from the moment she'd stepped foot on the prison grounds. But he hadn't had the opportunity to get at her. Until now.

Shit. He had to manipulate and practically give his left nut to make this happen. All he needed was fifteen, twenty, minutes tops.

He'd heard the rumors that she was a freak. Heard the buzzes of how fat her pussy was. How she loved playing in it, enticing motherfuckers, while in lockup.

And now he wanted to see—and hopefully *feel*—firsthand if what he'd heard about the beauty standing before him held true. He'd watched her in the visiting hall, his dick hard as steel. He wanted some head, ass, something. Shit. His wife wasn't fucking him, and he'd already fucked half the female officers—and most of their pussies were trash, any-damn-way.

He wanted some new pussy. Wild, uninhibited prison snatch.

And he wanted hers before any other motherfucker had the chance to stretch their dick up in her.

"What is it you want . . . Officer Flores?" she questioned, her gaze shifting from his dick print, pulling him from his lusty thoughts.

He stepped up in her space, causing her to take a step back, her ass suddenly brushing the wall. God, he smelled good—too damn good.

"You," he drawled.

She gave him an incredulous look, even though she wasn't surprised by what he'd said. She saw the way he'd looked at her the first time she'd been to visits months ago, and then today.

"*Me?* You don't even know me."

He leaned in closer, lowering his head; his lips a mere inches from hers. "Yeah. But I know enough to know that I like what I see, *mami*. And I want what I see. You do me right, and I'll do you even better. So what I gotta do to get you on your knees sucking this dick?"

She tilted her head coyly. She couldn't deny. He was fine, and he looked to have what might be a big, thick dick. She needed, no wanted, some new dick on her team. New dick meant a new prison sponsor. And anything she could do to make moves in this fuck-ing hellhole drama-free she'd consider doing it—at least once.

"Depends?"

He licked his lips. "On?"

She stared him in the eyes. "On what you can do for *me*. These dick-sucking skills don't come free," she snapped sassily. "And neither does this pussy. So if you're looking for a head doctor, then you'll need to slide a hundred dollars into my commissary."

"And how I know you're worth a hundred dollars?"

She arched her back, allowing her breasts to poke out further. "You don't."

He grinned, his dick throbbing, straining against the fabric of his pant leg. He wanted to fuck her. Right here, right now. He wanted her sucking his dick with her on her knees, worshipping his cock like a good little bitch. And then he wanted to bend her sweet ass over, handcuff her hands behind her back and fuck her long and hard, balls deep. And then after he finished nutting in her cunt, he wanted to eat that pussy, clean her out with his tongue and suck on those sweet tits.

"And if I wanna fuck?"

Crossing her arms, Heaven tossed her head to displace a wisp of hair dangling on her forehead. "Then you're going to need to get me on a housing unit where I can maneuver more freely." She liked being back on 3 West. But she was sick of those depressing prison bars. They made her feel like some wild, caged animal.

At least a door would make her feel . . . well, more normal. That was the beauty of being in lockup. She had the gift of a door. Privacy. Yes, yes. She wanted a steel door.

God, she couldn't believe she actually wanted a door with a food port, instead of the open bars on her cell. At least having a cell with bars afforded her a better view of the housing unit. She could see who was moving around on the unit, but it also made it easier for some hateful bitch to sling piss or shit bombs—or worse, a Molotov cocktail—into her cell in an attempt to set her ablaze.

No, no. No thank you.

A door would prevent that. Provide more safety. She was precious cargo. She needed safeguarding. Besides, she couldn't even talk on her cell without fear of getting caught.

Wait. That Coletta chick from 4 East flashed in her head. She didn't want to risk ending up with another crazy bitch like her for a cellie.

"I want a single cell," she stated. Then she licked her lips. "But, until then, I might be willing to give you a sampler if . . ." She paused, her gaze fluttering down to his crotch, then all the way down to his feet. Size thirteen, at least. He had on a pair of shiny black, military-style boots.

He rubbed a hand over his dick. The mischievous look in his eyes said he was ready to devour her, ravage her cunt, her mouth—and possibly even her ass. The idea excited her. She felt a tingling in her clit, her inner walls clutching with horny want.

"If what, baby?"

She flitted her gaze back up to his eyes. "If—"

She was cut off by the low crackle of his radio followed by a baritone voice. The officer in central control was looking for him. *Fuck.* He cursed again under his breath, then radioed in, his gaze never leaving hers, giving the officer in central control his ETA.

He glanced at his watch. He really had to bounce. They'd already been in the tiny space for almost ten minutes. Getting caught in a closet with an inmate wasn't an option. He'd kill this bitch first. Well, maybe, not literally.

He licked his bottom lip, then pulled it into his mouth. "I gotta bounce, *mami.* But know this"—his eyes darkened, making him look more predatory than ever—"you gonna be my lil' prison whore," he said bluntly.

Her hazel eyes flashed with indignation despite the heat that suddenly pooled low in her belly. "I don't think—"

He stole a kiss, slamming his mouth over hers—his plush, cushy lips and thick tongue demanding her mouth open as he framed her face with his large hands. The effect was unexpected. Potent. His tongue brushed over hers. And then . . . she felt it—his big dick. No, no—his very thick, very long dick.

Without a second thought, she ran her hand up and down the length of it. When she finally reached the head of his dick, she let out a soft whimper into his mouth. It was the size of a plum. She kneaded it, and his dick grew harder and thicker in response to her touch.

A groan slipped from the back of his throat, causing her body to reverberate with desire. Her mouth watered, and their kiss became wetter, juicier; her tongue slick heat against his. She knew then. She'd fuck him.

God help her, *him*—she'd let him spear her cunt with his long, thick sword. But she'd be dammed if she'd fuck him right here, right now.

Not when her wet cunt was desperately clinging to her cell phone—sealed in plastic and tucked inside a latex glove—by its slippery walls. God, no, she needed to remove it, before, before . . .

Shit.

Slowly, almost reluctantly, she released her grasp on his hardened dick and pushed him slightly back from her—breathless—before she reached for the button of his uniform pants, lowered his zipper and tunneled her hand into his pants, freeing him.

She needed space. Air.

Suddenly, she felt claustrophobic.

And incredibly wet.

FORTY-ONE

The Morning After . . .

"**S**o what I gotta do to get you on your knees sucking this dick?"

Heat flashed through her body as memories of her unexpected closet rendezvous with Officer Flores flooded her mind. It'd been over a month ago since that sordid encounter. Yet, the recollection of him was still fresh in her mind and had suddenly filled her with lusty desires, and now she felt her pussy warming.

She swallowed, and fought the urge to finger herself. She didn't usually like her men thin. Tall, yes. Very tall preferred. But—Lord, yes—he was tall *and* thin.

She'd make an exception, this once.

The thought of that big, long dick stretching her cunt to the seams made her tingle from the inside out. She'd never been a *ho* or a *whore*—she'd learned, many years ago, from her cousin, Bianca, that there was a difference—on the streets. But, in the words of her favorite radio personality, Marcel, on 93.3 *The Heat*—she was ready to let her "freak flag fly."

She already kept it sexy, kept it wet . . . always stayed ready. But fucking multiple men, let alone fantasizing about it, had never been *her* thing. She'd been a closet freak most of her life, beasting in the sheets only with men she'd been in relationships with.

She took dick like a pro, sucked dick like a porn-star, and knew how to make a man's toes curl. Never denying her man pleasure— any time, any place, anywhere. But that was always with one man.

But, now, since being incarcerated, her libido—*and* fantasies— was at an all-time high. All she wanted to do was fuck. Ride a dick. Suck a dick. She wanted it. Dick, dick, dick . . . and more dick; her whole body ached for it.

Officer Rawlings had unlocked Pandora's box, but it was Officer Flores who'd flung it open. And now she was ready to click on her ho-meter and turn up. She was ready to bite into more of the proverbial forbidden fruit and sink her teeth into its meat.

"You gonna be my lil' prison whore."

The thought made her pussy quiver.

Heaven glanced over at her flat-screen perched up on one of the tiny desks in her cell, catching the tail end of *Little Women: Atlanta*. She let out a disgusted grunt seeing Mama Bear. *Lying ass.* She gave Heaven a headache with all of her delusions.

"Mmph. Miscarriage my ass. But you didn't go for a D & C? Trick, your ass was never pregnant," Heaven heard her saying.

What a damn liar. And that Ms. Juicy . . . *mmph.* Heaven just couldn't with her ass, either. Not. At. All. *Trifling-ass bitches come in all sizes,* she thought, shaking her head as she reached for her remote and changed the channel to the WE network. The previews for *Cutting It in the ATL* flashed on the screen, and Heaven rolled her eyes.

God. What was this world coming to? Ratchet TV was everywhere. Seemed like Atlanta was a breeding ground for ghetto-ass reality shows.

Disgusted, she turned off her television, then rose from her bunk and turned on the radio to 93.3. She glanced at the time, and

found herself wishing it were eight o'clock already. It was Thursday.
And tonight was the radio station's segment of *Creepin' 'n' Freakin'*
After Dark, and she'd get to listen to the deep, rich baritone voice
of her fantasy man.

She chuckled to herself. Sabina would slice her throat if she
knew she, too, lusted over the mouthwatering Marcel. Mm, yes.
Lord, have mercy. She'd go to hell in a gasoline-soaked hand basket
for a night with him. Marcel, Marcel, Marcel . . . dammit. What
was that sexy man's last name?

She couldn't recall. But she remembered all the rumors. And
rumor had it he had a huge dick, and was a freak. That he and his
wife were swingers of sorts. Heaven could only imagine what
kind of heat the two of them created in the sheets.

God. What a tragedy. Heaven closed her eyes and shook her
head at the memory of hearing the murder of his wife unfolding
as it'd aired live on the radio. God, that whole experience shook her
to her core. She'd screamed in horror, then burst out in tears when
she'd heard the gunshots ring out along with millions of listeners.

Freedom had come rushing down into their living room when
she'd let out a piercing scream. He looked at her crazily when she'd
told him the cause of her distress. He thought her hysterics were a
bit over the top for someone she'd never met, or known. But, in
her mind, she *had* known him. And loved him.

She sighed, and reached for the book she'd received in the mail
the other day from Amazon. *The Real Mrs. Price* by J.D. Mason. God,
she was so behind in her reading. Seemed like she'd gotten a lot
more books read when she'd been in lockup. Maybe she should—

She shuddered at the thought.

On second thought, no thank you.

She would rather—

Sabina rushed into the cell. "Ohmygod! You're not going to
believe this."

Heaven gave her a confused look. "What?"

"Did you hear about Struthers?"

Heaven's face was expressionless. "No, what about him? Who has he fucked over now?"

"Girl, no one. I heard he is out on leave. And he won't be coming back."

Heaven feigned surprise. "*Whaaat?* I definitely didn't hear anything about that. When did this happen?"

Sabina shrugged, shaking her head. "I have no idea. They were talking about it down in the day space."

"Well, good riddance," Heaven said, raising her hand in a mock toast. "And lots of *bad* luck."

Sabina gave her a look.

"What?"

Sabina shook her head. "Nothing. Anyway. Let—"

"Hey, sweet pussycat," a voice said, cutting Sabina off.

The two women looked over toward the door, and Heaven smiled at the wiry, thin woman standing there with a big toothy grin. "Hey, Miss Janie. How are you?"

"Hey, Miss Janie," Sabina chimed in.

Miss Janie rolled her eyes at Sabina, but then smiled at Heaven. "Oh, I'm fine, pussycat."

Sabina caught Heaven's gaze, and shrugged. Sabina had no clue as to why Miss Janie didn't like her. But she didn't.

Miss Janie was a sixty-two-year-old woman who'd been at Croydon Hill since it'd opened back in 1990. Damn near twenty-six years ago. Heaven couldn't imagine being incarcerated *that* long. Hell. Ten years was torture enough. And here Miss Janie had another twenty-nine years to do before she was eligible for parole. She was going to die here. And, sadly, that realization pained Heaven. But Miss Janie, always with a smile on her face, didn't fret about that. She felt blessed all the same. And had found peace with her journey.

She'd murdered her husband. Stabbed him in his sleep, sawed off his dick, then burned the house down with him in it. She was twenty, almost twenty-one, when she'd committed what police called a heinous crime.

And what had she'd done with her husband's phallus?

Well, she'd mailed it to the married whore he'd been fucking, right before she fled the state. She'd been on the run for almost fifteen years before the authorities finally caught up with her down in Louisiana, living under an alias (Bertha Jarvis) with a new life, new husband, and three young children.

Heaven didn't know her that well, but the older woman was always friendly to her whenever she made her way up to the third tier. And, somehow, she'd decided that her nickname for Heaven would be Pussycat. "'Cause you cute as a kitten," she'd told her once, "and slick and crafty as a cat."

Heaven had almost felt offended at first, but then she'd realized it was meant as a compliment. So whenever the older woman called her that, she simply smiled. The only time she journeyed this high up from the first floor was when she had to go around and collect on a debt. When it came to her money, Miss Janie didn't care about being out of place. And the COs didn't bother about writing her up, or redirecting her. As far as they were concerned, she was harmless.

Sabina grabbed her MP3 player. "Well, let me get out of here."

Miss Janie grunted, then waited for Sabina to leave the cell. "That nasty gal right there will screw anything with two legs. E'ery time I look at her, it reminds me of an ole nasty streetwalker. And why I murdered my first husband."

Heaven gave her a questioning stare. "Oh."

Miss Janie waved her on. "Anyway, I thought I was gonna have to beat that lil' bitch's ass six cells down."

Heaven blinked. "Who, Miss Janie?"

"That lil' wild child, Clit-something-or another. Ole hot-in-the-ass heifer."

Heaven laughed. "Miss Janie, what Clitina do to get you all riled up?"

"Cheating on the Spades table, last night. Chile, I was about to reach over and slap the piss, the spit, and the snot outta her, then snatch out her tonsils. That ole black ashy ragamuffin better ask somebody. Then she got the nerve to hop up and call me an *old bitch*. I thought I was gonna have to pin my wig down real good and show her what this old bitch can do. Two—*no* three—things you don't mess over. Bingo, a game of Spades, and my damn wig."

Heaven couldn't stop laughing. "Ohmygod, Miss Janie. You are so hilarious." She wiped tears from her eyes from laughing so hard. "Well, did y'all win?"

"*Mmph*. You know we did. Me 'n' Ethel tore they young asses up." Ethel was her bunkie and gambling buddy—an older white woman who was also incarcerated for murdering her husband. She'd run him down in his tractor-trailer.

She and Miss Janie had been cellmates for the last ten years, and best friends ever since. They were the Lucy and Ethel of Croydon Hill. And two of the most feisty, fiery women in the entire prison known for their gambling and cell-brewed "prison hooch."

"Chile, I had to come up here—Ooh, them damn stairs real bad on my knees—and remind that heifer that payday was Friday. And the bitch better have my money, or interest would accrue by the day." She puckered her lips and bucked her eyes, putting a hand up on her hip. "What she think, these old hands can't go in her mouth? Let her not have my coins come payday and see what these hands do." She reached up and snatched her wig off. "Just like that. I'ma snatch her scalp off."

Heaven hollered. "Oh no, Miss Janie. We can't have you snatching off scalps. How much does she owe you?"

She readjusted her wig back on top of her head, tucking under her two long pigtails. "Let's see. This week and last week ..." She pursed her lips, counting in her head. "That ho owes me sixty dollars."

Heaven blinked. *Sixty dollars?* What the hell was she gambling for, when she had no money coming in?

Heaven stood to her feet and walked over to her locker, counting out sixty dollars' worth of goods. Ten iced honey buns, four three-pack pecan swirls, and one can of Maxwell House coffee. Twelve ramen noodles were a dollar. No, wait. She put those back. She reached for a jar of chunky peanut butter, which was worth five dollars. Two cans of chicken breasts equaled to five dollars. She tossed in two bags of Snyder's jalapeño pretzels. And since candy bars were a dollar a pop, she doled out fifteen Milky Way bars. And, lastly, she grabbed cans of mackerel— Croydon Hill's most wanted form of currency. Eight cans of mackerel were tossed in the bag.

"Here you go, Miss Janie." Heaven handed her the bag. Everything in it was more than enough to cover Clitina's gambling debt.

Miss Janie smiled, looking at the bag. "Chile, you got yourself a regular ole prison Seven-Eleven up in here, don'tcha? I appreciate you wanting to handle that gal's debt, but that ain't teaching her nothing. She needs to know how to pay up or get beat up. You hear what I'm saying, Pussycat?"

Heaven nodded. "I hear you, Miss Janie. But it's okay. It's an investment."

She grunted. "*Ummph.* In what, *trash*?"

Heaven shook her head. "Miss Janie, one woman's trash is another woman's treasure."

Miss Janie waved her on. "Chile, I don't know 'bout all that. Mmph. That ho's treasure chest ain't filled with nothing but shit. Now let me go take my *old* ass back on down the way. It's always good seeing you, Pussycat."

As she turned to leave, Heaven called her back. "Hey, Miss Janie?"

"Yes, baby?"

"I know you've been here for a long time, so I wanted to ask you"—she lowered her voice, stepping up to her—"if you knew an Officer Flores?"

She blinked. Narrowed her eyes. "Who, that light-skinned-ed fella?"

Heaven nodded.

"Pussycat. Yeah I know him. He's one of the Classification officers. Mm-hmm. Ooh, that's one pretty man." She fanned herself. "He fine, ain't he?"

Heaven shrugged nonchalantly. "I guess."

"Mm-hmm. What you *guess*ing for? Even I can see he fine. Long, tall drink of sexiness; I don't think he wears drawers to work."

Heat crept up through Heaven's belly as the memory of how his dick had felt as she stroked him over his pants. She giggled. "Miss Janie, you a mess."

"Uh-huh. Don't go snooping where the sun don't shine, Pussycat. Now what you asking 'bout him for?"

"Curious, that's all."

She narrowed her eyes, studying Heaven. "Well, don't be getting too curious. He one of the candy men."

Heaven gave her a questioning look. "A what?"

Miss Janie crooked a finger and beckoned for Heaven to come closer. Heaven leaned in, then Miss Janie whispered conspiratorially, "He the dope man."

Heaven blinked, then opened her mouth to—

Miss Janie put a hand up, and stopped her. "Not another word on that."

And then she was gone.

FORTY-TWO

Get Ready...

"You owe me," Heaven informed Clitina as they walked around the outdoor track. The weather was gorgeous. Warm, but breezy. Low humidity. Heaven couldn't resist coming out to the yard to let the sun shine down on her. Oh joy! This was what her life had become. From Central Park carriage rides to getting excited about sunshine in a prison yard.

Still, it was a nice change of pace from being cooped up in her cell. The stale air was slowly starting to eat away at her lungs. So fresh air was a welcomed break. But she'd be on guard. Ready and alert. Her blade was in her bra, in case anything jumped off. Never sleep on a bitch. Never get too comfortable.

That's what she'd learned here.

Clitina gave her a sidelong glance. "Why you pay that old bitch, anyway, when I ain't ask you to?"

Heaven shot her a look. "Did you have her money to pay her?"

Clitina snorted. "Who said I was gonna pay her ass?"

"Well, boo, that *old bitch*, as you call her, was going to beat your ass real good if you hadn't settled your debts with her. So, thank you works better."

She huffed. "That old, country bitch don't want it with these hands. I'd beat the wrinkles off her ass. I don't care nothin' 'bout her killin' her husband or how many years she been locked up with her ole saggy-ass titties. I'm from the hood, boo. I'd beat her dentures loose."

Heaven shook her head. *This ignorant little bitch.* She mentally scolded herself for that thought, no matter how true. It was obvious she was simply a product of her environment. *Don't judge her. Her mother is named after a dick, for Christ's sake.*

So she said, "Being from the hood doesn't make you the baddest or toughest bitch out in the streets. And definitely not in here."

Clitina huffed. "Miss Heaven, *boom.* Hit the floor with it. I'm *one* of the baddest. You better Google me. My rap sheet on fleek."

"And that rap sheet on *fleek* is gonna keep your ass in and out of prisons, hon, if you don't learn to fall back from the streets and that kind of mentality. The streets and the hood, boo, mean you no good."

She frowned. "So I'm 'posed to leave the hood? Hit the floor with it. What, a bitch like me gonna do in the 'burbs besides boost in they stores? Yawn. Where they teaching that at? The streets is *every*thing."

Heaven gave her a sad look. "And those same streets will turn their back on you. Look around you, Tina. Is this the life you want?"

She shrugged. "It ain't all that bad. Two of my girls in here 'n' I'm already cool with a few more bitches. And I ain't gotta hear dumb-ass Dickalina telling me she gonna put me out unless I pay rent. Where they do that at? Bitch ain't even payin' full rent."

Clitina shook her head. "I mean, I miss my sister 'n' my girl,

Day'Asia. But being in prison is almost like being on the streets. I just ain't gotta pay no rent. And anything I want, I can get. If I wanna hang out on the block, I just come out to the yard. If I wanna kick back, I can chill in my cell, or down in the day space. If I wanna turn up 'n' have me a drink, I can turn up. If I wanna roll with my girls, they got that here, too. Pills. Dope. Weed. Whatever. You want it, they got it." She shook her head again. "All I really need is some steady dingaling in my life 'n' I'm good."

Heaven gave her an incredulous look. She'd heard it all. "Bitch, there isn't shit about being locked up *anything* like being at home. Nothing. This shit isn't glamorous." Heaven swept an arm around the yard. "Look around you. Do you see any dick—or *dingaling*, as you call it—anywhere out here? No. Unless you're taking up riding a little-ass clit like it's one, there is no dick out here for you."

Clitina waved her on dismissively. "Miss Heaven, hit the floor with it. I ain't talkin' about no damn inmate. These bitches can't do nothin' for me. I see lots of dick out here—all in uniforms. At least one of 'em gotta want some cootie, or some sloppy top from an inmate from time to time . . ."

This ho will need to have lots of stock in douche kits, Heaven thought as she took her in. She had a gorgeous shape, all boobs and lots of curves, Heaven admitted to herself. Still the stench from her pussy during their first encounter had scarred her. It still lingered in her senses, and came back to haunt her every now and again.

"Anyway. I be seein' how some of these COs be lookin', like they ready to fuck. I know they be some horny-ass niggahs workin' up in here. And you know it, too. Shit. Sometimes I just wanna get my throat wet."

Well, shit, she had a point—a very valid one. Hell, she was fucking one herself. And anticipated fucking another CO the next opportunity she got. Real soon.

"But, anyway. I ain't tryna get no sermon today, Miss Heaven," she stated, cutting into Heaven's thoughts. "So what I owe you now? Who you need me to slice?"

Heaven gave her a look, an eyebrow rising. "I don't want you slicing anyone for me . . . right now. But I'll think of something."

Clitina spotted her hoodrat friends from 4 East as they made their way around the track again. "Okay. You do that. . . ."

"Tiiiiiinaaaaa!" her friends yelled.

She threw a hand up and waved over at them. "Anyway. All this walking around in circles is corny; 'specially when we ain't smokin'. I'll catch you later, Miss Heaven."

"Later, girl."

Clitina walked off, cutting across the grass, but then she stopped and called after Heaven. "Miss Heaven?"

Heaven glanced over her shoulder. "Yeah?"

"Next time, don't be bailin' no body outta shit. I know how'ta handle a bitch on my own." And then she trotted off toward her loud, rowdy friends, her ass bouncing in her teenie-weenie shorts.

"Heeeeey, bitch!" they called out in unison.

"We was wondering when you was gonna ditch that ho."

"Ooh, y'all stop bein' messy," Heaven heard Clitina respond back. She laughed. "That's my bitch."

FORTY-THREE
Magic Stick...

"Aah, shit, baby," CO Rawlings muttered in her ear as he held her by her hips—his fingertips digging into her warm flesh—and slowly he slid his dick in and out of her body. He was thick. He was hard, so, so very hard.

She hummed with pleasure as he took her from behind, her puffy, heart-shaped pussy flowering open and then closing around him.

"Mmm," she rasped. "Feed my hungry cunt with your good dick. *Mm*, yes, yes, *yesss* . . ."

His vision blurred.

"This pussy is so damn good," he said huskily, tangling a hand into her long, loose hair, pulling back on it, just enough to make her head snap back and her scalp tingle.

"Oh, baby, baby, baby," he chanted low in her ear as he rode her curves, swimming in her liquid fire. He was drowning—in her, in lust, in every part of her clutching cunt.

She trembled violently, her orgasm building into an enormous ball of roiling heat as he stroked her walls. She writhed in pure ecstasy. At the delicious pounding he was delivering. At the threat of getting caught with her panties down, hidden in a closet with *his* dick stuffed in her.

She wanted him to finish with her pussy, then take her mouth, then her ass. She wanted him to get lost in every orifice, to fuck every crevice of her core.

She moaned, her cunt juices sloshing out of her body. She couldn't deny it, he felt so good inside of her. Why, why, why . . . did he have to be such a damn good lay?

Every part of her flesh was rigid. Her breasts, the turgid peaks of each nipple, ached in pure pleasure, causing her cunt to pulse uncontrollably.

"*Fuck* me . . . *fuck* me . . . *fuuuuuck* me . . ." Her words came in rasps. "Mmm. Yes, yes, yes . . . give it . . . to . . . me . . ."

Her soft pleas were music to his ears.

"Shit, baby, shit," he murmured. "You about to make me cum . . ."

He wanted to be inside her raw. Wanted to feel every delicious inch of her pussy. He felt himself floating as she swallowed him over and over in a heated rush, causing him to bare his teeth. He struggled to maintain control, struggled to keep from toppling over, as he watched his condom-sheathed dick disappear in and out of her body. She was wet, soaking wet. And, so, so tight; so tight that he knew she hadn't had a good fucking in a long, long time.

She radiated sensuality. A sexual heat that made him crazy with want, with need, with salacious desires.

"So good," he rasped over and over in her ear.

"Mm, so . . . are . . . you," she purred.

She shivered and a soft moan escaped her parted lips, and the CO squeezed her ass, pulling her open wider to him, his dick probing even deeper into her pussy than he already was. He felt the mouth of her cervix opening and closing, suckling the bulbous head of his dick.

Another low moan escaped her breathlessly as she clutched him, milked his shaft, her orgasm coating every inch of him. She didn't want to get too used to this, but God—oh God, yes!

Then came a gasp. They'd been fucking for no more than four minutes and she was already on the verge of another orgasm. He didn't have one of the biggest dicks she'd ever had, but it was by far one of the best. Better than her last lover's. All eight inches of his thick dick stretched her just right, slid in and out of her body with the right amount of sweet burn. Stroked over her spot with delicious heat and friction.

Yes, yes, yes . . .

She threw her ass back at him, glancing over her shoulder to take him in. She wanted all of him, deep.

Hard.

Harder.

She reached back, pulled open her ass cheeks, and slammed back on his dick.

"Fuck me," she murmured. "Mmm*hmm*. Fuck me."

She curled her fingers until her nails clawed at the floor. Oh, oh, oh . . . mmm. She fought to stay unattached. And yet she was utterly fascinated by his masculinity. She glanced over her shoulder again. Her blurred gaze took in the sleek rippled muscles of his stomach, the dark whorls of hair at the base of his dick, and she came, her orgasm rushing out of her body.

His dick stroked over her spot again and again and again, brushing the ridges of her flesh, causing jolts of fire to shoot through her body. She pulled in her bottom lip, and bit back a scream.

"Spit in my asshole," she urged breathlessly. "Finger me there."

And then he did, a glob of spit pooling in her ass's puckering, sweet brown hole. His middle finger slid inside her waiting, bubbling ass and then she began to rock her body just slightly, a signal that she wanted it, was ready for it. Both holes filled and fucked.

He twisted his finger in her ass, stroking her there the way he stroked her cunt. God yes. She arched her back, basking in naughty delight as Rawlings growled. He felt it. Her heart beat—*thumpetythump-thumpthump*—deep in her guts, his dick sweeping against her walls.

The CO watched, mesmerized by the way her cunt gobbled his dick, the way her ass sucked in his finger. He groaned low in the back of his throat as her body gripped every part of him, pulling out every inhibition. She had a measure of power over him that no other woman had ever achieved. He loved that she could let go and let her lust drive her, bringing him so much pleasure.

"So good, so good," he rasped as the huge head of his erection poked and prodded at the basin of her well. He knew he couldn't linger inside her body long. He had to get back to his post. And she had to return to her housing unit.

Fuck.

He wanted to stay right here. Engulfed in her wet heat. Buried balls-deep between her slick walls. He lightly smoothed a hand over the bare expanse of her back, causing her skin to prickle with heat. Then he leaned forward and planted kisses along her shoulder, his lips melting into her silken skin.

"You all mine, baby," he breathed out, his voice thick with arousal. "You, this pussy, your body—I just wanna fuck your soul inside out, baby."

She shuddered, mere words—low and dirty—slowly pushing her over the edge of another orgasm. Closer, closer, closer . . . she was almost there.

Goddamn, she was so fucking wet.

"Oh God," she breathed out. "This dick is so . . . mmm . . . *soooo* . . . good."

Arrogant warmth spread through him. Because the dick was good. And because he already knew that it was. He'd been waiting for her to finally say it. Admit it.

He thrust hard and then slowed, sliding his dick out to nearly the tip, moving his hips ever so slowly, stirring her juices over and around the head of his dick, before plunging back in. Deep.

Tension began rising in her groin. Her pelvis tightened. And her hand automatically went to her sloshy-wet pussy as it rapidly clenched tightly around his dick.

He was panting. "Aah, shit, baby. My dirty little prison slut . . ."

Her cunt flared at the truth, at the words. She made no apologies for being wanton and shameless.

"Goddamn you, baby . . . Aaah . . ."

Head thrown back, eyes closed, neck straining in pleasure, the veins in his forehead popped out. He was in a zone. And the look on his face brought a grin over the inmate's lips. He was *in* heaven.

"Oh, my sweet fucking *Heaven*," he whispered, murmuring out her name over and over as his dick jerked uncontrollably inside her until finally—fuck yes. Holy shit—he exploded inside her, slamming his dick in as hard as he could, the sound of slapping flesh ricocheting around the tiny space. He felt the closet spin as his orgasm violently erupted from his dick.

And then he collapsed, feeling more satiated than he'd ever felt in his entire life.

FORTY-FOUR

Fuck You In My Sleep . . .

"Mmm. Fuck me . . ." came a whispered voice.

Heaven had dozed off less than a minute ago, and yet she thought she was hearing things. Maybe dreaming. But then she heard the faintest of a moan, and the slight creak of the mattress above her.

Her lashes fluttered open.

"Oh, *yes . . . yes . . .* fuck me . . ."

Heaven held her breath listening. And then came the familiar sound of wet clicking.

She blinked.

Oh. Oh. Ohhhh. *Ooh, this horny bitch,* Heaven thought.

Sabina was fingering herself.

Surprisingly, the hum of Sabina's fingers sliding in and out of her cunt didn't disgust Heaven. At least Sabina had waited until the wee hours of the night when she thought Heaven was sound asleep to pleasure herself. And yet the wet clickety-click-click sounds in combination with Sabina's low moans caressed Heaven's ears like a sensual lullaby. She breathed in Sabina's arousal.

Then swallowed.

Oh God.

Her heart beat a little harder.

The thin mattress above Heaven's head shifted. Sabina's hips thrust upward, her fingers going in deeper as she bit her lip. Dear God. Holy fuck. She was so wet, so goddamn horned. She'd overheard Heaven phone sexing again with some mystery caller.

Heaven's low dirty talk had sent a wave of sparks through Sabina's cunt, her clit engorged, its tip becoming overly sensitive. She'd winced when her fingers made contact with her clit. She'd been so turned on, so close to coming that her eyes watered.

Awed. Aroused. She'd wanted to lean over the side of her bed and watch Heaven in the dark. Watch Heaven bring herself to orgasm as she ear-fucked her caller.

But Sabina hadn't. Instead, she lie in her bunk and ear hustled, her hands freeing her swollen breasts from her bra and silently cupping them, lazily toying with her pink nipples, then pinching them into thick, rigid peaks.

Sabina didn't know how long she'd been eavesdropping on Heaven and her phone lover. But when the sordid call had finally ended, her body was nearly trembling.

Her cunt soaked.

"Ooh, yes," she murmured, replaying Heaven's sensually heated conversation in her head.

"Mmm, yes, you nasty fucker. Let me smear my pussy in your face . . . Stick your finger in my ass while you're sucking my clit. Yes, yes, yes . . . lick all over my cunt while I suck your dick . . . Mmm. I'm going to slob all over that dick, drench your balls in my spit . . ."

Click-click-clickety-click. Sabina's fingers rapidly moved in and out of her body. She was almost there, almost. She hadn't touched herself in weeks. But Heaven had ignited her need for release tonight. Oh God how she needed this. But she needed, wanted, a hard dick even more. Her pussy was tight, but three fingers stretched her, enveloping her fingers as she thrust deeper and harder.

The mattress creaked again.

Click-click-clickety-click-click.

Heaven's gaze fixed up at the gray metal over her head and inhaled. Then she swallowed again. The heady scent of Sabina's arousal began to fill the air. She bit her lip. Sabina's low moans licked over Heaven's skin, causing her pulse to race.

What the fuck was going on?

She wasn't a lesbian. Had no attraction to women. But Heaven found herself immensely turned on beyond belief.

Her hand slid between her legs. Her fingertip circled her clit, rubbing over it; her pussy going wetter and hotter as she imagined herself straddling Officer Flores, his huge dick at the hungry mouth of her cunt, her fingers wrapped around his girth as she guided him inside her quivering body.

She shut her eyes and arched her back, spreading her legs wider, pretending her two fingers were his dick instead. In her mind's eye, her hands were above her head against the headboard as he looked down at her, and watched the sight of his dick sliding in and out of her pussy, while he slid his hands underneath her ass, opening her so he could go deeper.

A moan slipped from her in response, and Sabina moaned as well. Heaven's hand stroked through her swollen folds, fingering her clit.

Click-click-clickety-click.

The wet sounds bounced off the concrete walls and echoed in their ears. Both women's fingers played their own symphony as they frantically sought to bring themselves pleasure, relief. Their cunts clamping around their fingers like two greedy fists.

Mm, yes. Erotic.

The scent of tangy, musky arousal filtered through their nostrils.

Sweat broke out on Sabina's forehead, her face straining with her impending orgasm. She rotated her hips, grinding her ass into her mattress. Closer, closer . . . she was nearing another burst of pleasure. Another soft moan escaped her. Wet fire splintered through her, her cunt sizzling like hot oil.

She moaned—a notch above a whisper; more loudly than she had anticipated—as Heaven's gasp caught in her throat, her own orgasm blooming through her body, unfurling like the petals of a budding rose.

Moments later, everything went quiet but for the sound of snores and whimpers elsewhere on the unit. Then the sound of keys could be heard as the housing officer strolled by their cell making his rounds. It was three a.m., his last time coming around the tier until six a.m. morning count.

Both women lay in their bunks, panting, their bodies flushed with pulsing heat, savoring the aftermath of their orgasms.

Sabina sucked on her cunt-stained fingers. Then listened out for Heaven's breathing. Heaven licked the tips of hers, then closed her eyes, ready to finally count sheep behind her lids. She realized she'd somehow crossed naughtily into an alternative reality. One she wasn't quite sure how she should feel about. But she wasn't going to put too much thought into it. She'd wrestle with it in the morning.

For now, her mind and body craved sleep. She rolled onto her side. Then, seconds later, restlessly rolled back over on her back. God, what a horny bitch she was.

"Heaven," Sabina whispered, breathing through her nose.

Heaven's eyes opened, her gaze snapping to the underside of Sabina's bunk.

Oh God! Had Sabina heard her over her own whispered moans?

"Heaven," she breathed out again. "You sleep?"

Heaven wanted to ignore her. Oh how she wanted to feign being in deep slumber.

But her curiosity got the best of her.

"Yeah?"

"Can I taste your pussy?"

FORTY-FIVE

Girl, Lady, Woman . . .

"Can I taste your pussy?"

The words still ricocheted around in Heaven's head two days later. She couldn't believe Sabina had so boldly asked her that. Her words had sunk deep, finding their way to her still throbbing pussy.

"*Just one night, Heaven. Let me pleasure you . . .*"

Ooh. That scandalous *bitch!*

Heaven covered her face in heated shame. Not from the question, but from her response. "Yes," she'd breathed out.

Holy fuck. She'd said, *yes!* Shocking herself, and Sabina. In a savage moment of desire and curiosity, she'd pulled back her sheet and spread her legs, revealing the mocha lips of her pussy, inviting Sabina between her legs. And Sabina's already wet cunt had gotten ridiculously wetter. Her own juices sliding down the inner part of her thighs.

Heaven shook her head and groaned. One night of experimentation, of unadulterated pleasure, hadn't turned her into a lesbian, had it?

No, no, of course not.

But she'd enjoyed it—a little *too* much. God, just the mere thought of the dirty things Sabina had done to her with her tongue and fingers still made her pussy tingle.

Dear Baby Jesus. Sabina's tongue lightly fucking her, taunting her, tasting her from the inside out had her wild, bucking and writhing. She'd dug her nails into her sheet, clawing at her mattress.

She'd closed her eyes against the rushing heat, the sensations shooting through her body. She was dripping wet, hot.

"Keep your eyes open," Sabina had urged, looking up at her through a veil of lust and lashes. Her pupils flickered with wild abandon. "Watch me."

Heaven strained to open her eyes, and forced herself to observe Sabina devouring her cunt, savoring her rich, thick taste. Her tongue and mouth working in harmony as she reached between her legs and used a hand to play between her own folds. The erotic sight caused an abject rush of pleasure to engulf Heaven. Her blood pounded. Taboo pleasure, thick and hot, pooled between her thighs, soaking into the sheet beneath her.

And then came fingers—one, two, three—slushing and stretching in and out of her cunt. She was deliciously wet. Mmmm. Sabina was so greedy for her. Her mouth watered. Drooled. She felt the ripple of Heaven's pussy as she licked and sucked at her clit. She'd stroked Heaven's velvety walls, reaching deeper to the spongy area of her G-spot. And Heaven . . . Lord Jesus, yes, yes, yes— she'd cried out. Mewled. Howled.

Ooh, wee. Every nerve ending in her cunt became alight with fire. Sweet agony.

Dirty pleasure coursed through her entire body. Everything she saw, felt . . . all heady abandon. It was, it was . . . an unexplainable type of sensation, a different sort of surrender.

"Oh. Oh," she'd gasped as Sabina used a steady rhythm to lave her tongue up and down and over every inch of her folds, her slit, her clit. Every so often Sabina's eyes drifted upward to gauge Heaven's reaction to the pleasure she was determined to give her. She'd been consumed with tasting Heaven. To give her a taste of what type of pleasure a woman could give her, of what no man would give her as long as she was behind bars.

Heaven took two deep breaths, her mind still reeling from the memory.

This shit couldn't have happened to her. But it had been. Live and direct. Sabina had snatched her breath and her cunt and had done with them what she damn well pleased, stroking in and out of her wet heat, enjoying the feel of her silky walls.

Heaven had begun biting her lip, trying to contain the sounds of pleasure bubbling out from the back of her throat, exploding into hot, dirty words.

Her hand tangled in Sabina's hair, holding her head down to meet her thrusts.

"Give it to me, Heaven," Sabina had whispered over her clit. "Come in my mouth. Flood my mouth with your sweet juices."

She'd withdrawn her fingers from Heaven's cunt and then moved her mouth down to her opening and wedged a wet finger inside her ass. The act had caught Heaven off guard and, yet, she came, hard, exploding in her mouth, on her tongue, glossing her lips and bathing her chin with her creamy nectar.

Sabina walked into the cell and saw Heaven with her head down, a hand holding her forehead. "Oh, God," she drawled, plopping down on the foot of Heaven's bunk. "Please don't tell me you're still all straitjacket crazy over what happened between us the other night. Get over it, girl. It was just a thing."

A thing? Yeah, okay—easy for her to say.

Heaven lifted her head, turning a glare in Sabina's direction. "You took advantage of me."

Sabina burst out in laughter. She couldn't help herself. That was the most—well, one of the most—ridiculous things she'd heard in a while.

"Ohmygod! You make it sound like I tongue-raped you or something. If memory serves me correctly—and it does, I don't recall *you* putting up much of a fight. Hell, you didn't put up any fight."

Heaven feigned shock. "How dare you? I was vulnerable and weak."

"Don't go getting all self-righteous now. The moment you opened your legs, you gave me the go-ahead, the invitation to feast on that smorgasbord of goodness between your legs." Ooh how sweet and tasty it'd been, too.

Heaven blushed. Heat bloomed to her cheeks. "Well, that was a one-time thing. I'm not a lesbian."

Sabina rolled her eyes upward. "And neither am I. But it's okay if you feel guilty for enjoying it as much as you did. Get over it. We're both grown women. And I won't deny that every now and again, I like to indulge in a little kitty-licking. Shit. Don't label me. And don't label what happened. All it was for the both of us was a night of well-deserved pleasure. Period. So don't make it out to be more than that. And judging by how hard you came, you enjoyed it."

Heaven rolled her eyes. "Who wouldn't," she begrudgingly admitted. Damn, damn, damn. She felt like such a hypocrite. She'd turned down that Snake chick's proposition, adamant about not going *that* way. Yet, she'd allowed Sabina to tongue-fuck the shit out of her. Lord, she hoped she wasn't going to turn into one of those confused bitches that struggled with her sexuality.

Heaven took a breath. "So I take it this is something you've done often?"

Sabina shook her head. "No, not really. Not since I've been here.

But home, yes—sometimes. I enjoy threesomes with my man." She smiled. "He gets off watching me licking a pussy while he's fucking me from the back."

Oh.

Sabina patted Heaven's hand. "Well, if it's eating you up that badly that you had so much pleasure from it, then you're more than welcome to return the favor." She wiggled her brows. "Hint, hint. I'll graciously accept your tongue, and come all in your mouth."

Heaven flipped her the finger. "Oh, I bet your freak-ass would. But not going to happen."

Sabina stood and shrugged. "Oh well. Don't say I didn't try to ease your guilt."

Heaven laughed in spite of herself. "Bitch, please. You wish."

FORTY-SIX

The Way You Move . . .

Heaven hurriedly stepped out of the showers donned in her prison bathrobe with her still wet hair wrapped perfectly in a white towel. Turban-style. She preferred showering when it was mostly empty. She liked to get in and out of the showers without all the distractions and chitchat, unlike other inmates who seemed to linger around, almost as if they were prowling. She wanted no parts of whatever they had going on.

As far she was concerned, wash your ass and go—nothing more, nothing less. She could primp in her cell if she wanted. She looked over her shoulder making sure she left nothing behind, then shuffled off in her shower shoes just as two females were walking in.

Reluctantly, they let her walk by. Then one of them muttered behind her back, "Bitch."

"Yup," Heaven snapped over her shoulder. "And I'm a bitch you *don't* want to fuck with. Now carry on."

She walked off, cursing under her breath for having said anything. That's what the hating-ass bitch had wanted her to do. Feed into her miserable shit.

And she had—for a slight moment.

As she headed down the tier, she heard yelling coming from one of the cells. "Bitch, I know you stole it. Just give it back before you piss me off."

"Bitch, shut your dirty-ass up! I ain't steal ya shit."

It was Clitina and her cellmate arguing.

"You a fuckin' lyin'-ass bitch! I want my silk scarf back."

"Eat my ass, bitch! I don't even wear silk, ho! So fuck outta here!"

Heaven shook her head and kept walking.

"Miss Heaven," Clitina called out, sticking her head out her cell. "You hear this bitch, tryna say I stole her fuckin' scarf. If I'ma steal some shit from a bitch, it ain't gonna be no fuckin' old-ass dirty scarf. This bitch dumb as fuck. I steal new shit."

"No bitch, you dumb. And so is your retarded-ass mammy for givin' you that fucked-up-ass name. You—"

Clitina charged back inside; all Heaven heard after that was, *whap! Whap! Whap!*

Then came the sound of loud tussling, and threats. "I'ma kill you, bitch!"

"Not before I kill you, you bum-bitch!"

They were both going to find their asses in lockup if they didn't find a way to fight more quietly.

Though she wanted to turn back and say something to them, she took a deep breath, and kept on walking. She had her own shit to deal with.

When she finally returned to her cell, Sabina had the privacy curtain up and was still on the phone, supposedly talking to her boyfriend (you know, the bastard on the streets living his life while she rotted away in prison for his shit) in the same spot Heaven had left her, sitting Indian-style in the middle of her bunk.

"What you mean you can't come see me?" she whispered. "Why not?"

She looked over at Heaven and shook her head as she mouthed, "This black fucker."

"This black fucker?" Really?

Heaven frowned.

"A *warrant?* For what?" Sabina rolled her eyes. "Mmhmm. Interesting. But whatever," she hissed. "Anyway, I need you to send me money . . . I don't know, like two, three, hundred . . . *whaaaat?* What you mean you ain't got it? Where's all your money? You sell drugs, nigga. I know you got it. So stop playing with me . . . uh-huh . . . Well, what about a hundred. I haven't asked you for shit . . . so do you think you can handle that? It's not like you're accepting my collect calls. I was nothing but good to you on the streets, nigga . . ."

Heaven cringed inwardly, shooting her a sharp look. There was something about hearing a white person using *that* word even if it wasn't used with the "E" and "R" at the end of the word.

The bitch still had no right to use it, or speak it. She didn't give a damn how many black dicks she sucked and fucked. Now she wanted her ass off her phone. She wanted to yank it from her ear and slap her in the face with it. But she had to grit her teeth and let it slide until she was done with her conversation. Then she'd confront her ass.

She knew it wasn't any of her business how the two of them communicated or argued. Still, the shit irked her. Maybe he accepted that shit, but she didn't.

And she planned on telling her so.

She angrily applied cocoa butter cream all over her skin, then slipped into a pair of commissary-bought pajama bottoms. She turned her back to Sabina, slid off her robe, and put on a tank top.

Then stared at the television—arms folded, and waited.

"Whatever, Raheem," Heaven heard her huff. "Fuck you. Whatever bitch you out there fucking; keep fucking her. All the shit

I've done for you and you can't even send me a few fuckin' dollars? You ain't shit. I hope that bitch you screwing is lovin' the dick . . . black motherfucker! Yeah, yeah, okay, whatever . . . like I said, fuck. You."

"Arrrrgh!" She slid off her bunk, then handed Heaven the cellphone back. "I can't believe that motherfucker hung up on me. I should have let them fry his ass. But, no—I take the weight because I'm supposed to be his ride-or-die bitch. Ugh! All the shit I've done for his black ass, and he—"

Heaven cut her off. "Um, let me ask you something. What part of the game makes you think it's okay for you to refer to him as *nigga*?"

Sabina blinked. "Excuse you?"

"I *said* what makes you think it's okay for you to call him a *nigga*?"

Sabina's eyes widened, her face turning pink. "I didn't call him a *nigger*."

Heaven's nose flared. "I didn't say you called him *that*. I know what you called him. Don't play stupid, Sabina. What I want to know is, *why?*"

"That's how we talk," she stated, shrugging. "If he isn't bothered by it, why are you? I'm not racist if that's what you're implying. I have lots of black friends. That's all I hang with."

Heaven's lids flapped open and shut several times. "Oh, so you only hang with blacks so that makes you black by proxy, is that it?"

Sabina huffed. "Bitch, I didn't say that. All I'm saying is, I'm not a racist. So don't make me out to be one. And as far as I'm concerned, I talk to my man however I want to."

Heaven sneered. "I didn't say shit about you *being* racist. But don't think because all you fuck are black men and smoke and drink and chill with a bunch of black women that it's okay for *you* to use that word."

Sabina rolled her eyes, her hand flying up on her hip. "Why? Because I'm *white*?"

Heaven tilted her head. "Exactly."

"Ohmygod! What does the color of my skin have to do with anything? I'm from the hood too."

Heaven gave her an incredulous look. "Bitch, being from the *hood* and spreading your legs, fucking *black* men doesn't give you some free pass to let the word *nigga* fall from your damn lips. I don't care in what context you used it."

"Oh, bitch, please," Sabina snapped back. "You're blowing shit *waaaay* outta context. Why is it okay for other blacks to call each other *that*, but someone who identifies with the culture, can't because they're white?"

Heaven stared her down. "Trick, the only thing *you* identify with is the whole 'once you go black, you don't go back' slogan."

"Unh-uh, bitch. Answer the damn question. Why can't I—a *white* chick—use the word in the same context as blacks use it? It's not said as a *diss* to what black men have gone through—what they still go through. It's just a damn word; it's not that damn serious."

Heaven felt like hopping up and slapping her around the cell. She tucked her hands under her thighs and sat still in fear she'd leap up and claw her tongue out. "Because obviously, bitch, you don't know shit about what the black man has gone through. So, no, bitch. If you want to call your white men *that* publicly, then do so. But—around me, don't use that word, referring to anyone with the same color skin as me. Period."

What she really wanted to say was, "You white bitches start fucking black men and think your asses are the damn door prize." But the truth was, she truly didn't care whom white women, or any other woman, fucked as long as it wasn't *her* man. And she didn't care how another woman talked to her black man. She could call him as many *black* motherfuckers and *niggas* as she wanted. But she didn't need to hear it.

Sabina stared her down, eyes wide and wild. Her whole body shook from the inside out. She wasn't in the mood for this bitch's self-righteous bullshit.

Heaven stared back. "Bitch, move along. Don't fucking look at me."

"Kiss my"—she tooted her backside and slapped it—"*white* ass, *bitch!*" Then she snatched down the privacy curtain and stormed out the cell.

"Yeah, whatever, *Becky*," Heaven yelled at her retreating back. "And the black motherfucker ain't even your man! So go fuck yourself!"

FORTY-SEVEN

Yeah, I Said It . . .

"So, like really, *dude*," Sabina scoffed, standing in front of her—arms folded, head tilted—blocking Heaven's view of the television. "So you're really *still* not speaking to me?"

Heaven stared at her. "Hell no, I'm not speaking to your ass," she snapped. They hadn't spoken since their nasty argument almost a week ago. Both women basically ignored the other, while trying to stay out of the other's way (utterly ridiculous considering how tiny their cell was). "Now move the hell from the television."

Sabina rolled her neck. "Absoooolutely, *not*. Not until we clear the air." She stabbed a finger in the air at her. "You had no goddamn right talking to me the way you did. I felt disrespected. And to even *suggest* that I'm racist was fucking ridiculous and hurtful."

Heaven sat on her bunk staring at her incredulously. "Are you fucking kidding me? *You* felt disrespected? How about how *I* felt hearing you use the word *nigga* talking to your so-called black man—or whoever the hell he is to you? And *don't* fucking tell me in which context you used it, or meant it. The fact is, *you* used it.

Then turned around and called him a *black* motherfucker? And *you* don't see anything wrong with that picture."

She scowled. "No, I don't see anything wrong with it, because I'm not a racist."

Lord Jesus. This ignorant bitch still doesn't get it, Heaven thought as she stared at her blankly. She sighed. She had bigger battles to fight than trying to educate Sabina. She liked her, but she was giving this ho the side-eye.

"Bitch, I'm *not* calling you a *racist*. I'm calling you out on the fact that when I hear a white woman call a *black* man she's fucking *nigga*, all I hear in my mind is the word *nigger*, whether you meant it that way or not. Personally, I don't care what the two of you call each other in the privacy of your own shit. But, bitch, doing that shit in earshot of others could get you dragged and stomped; that's all I'm saying. Be mindful of what you say, and where."

"So you're telling me, you've never gotten mad and called your *ex*—or any other man—and called him a *black* motherfucker or used the *N*-word—with an *A* at the end—out of anger?"

Heaven sighed. "Bitch, go have a seat. I'm black . . . *he's* black, so why would I need to point that out to him if I'm calling him a motherfucker, huh?" But in truth, Heaven had been guilty herself in the past of calling men she'd been pissed at black (with more emphasis on the word *black*) motherfuckers at one time or another in her life.

It was wrong, but she'd done it.

"But yeah, I have been guilty of it," Heaven finally admitted.

Satisfied, Sabina smugly stepped away from the television. "As I thought. So tell me this. Why the hell you mad with me—a white chick, for calling her man the same thing you and nearly every other black woman has called *her* man at some point?"

Well, she had a point. Still . . .

"I should be able to talk to my man however I want. IF he doesn't check me on it, then why should you or anyone else? I am not apologizing for what I said to him. He pissed me off. But I will apologize to you if what you heard offended you in any way."

Heaven twisted her lips. "Well, apology accepted. Still, bitches like *you* who do that shit make it out to be about race when you choose to point out that he is a *black* motherfucker. You knew he was black before he stuck his dick in you. Now get it together, because someone else might overhear you calling *your* black man—whether he accepts it or not—*that* and they might be ready to stomp your kidneys out; that's all I'm saying. Now what's for dinner, bitch?"

"Now that we've made up and we're back talking," Heaven said, leaning her elbows up on Sabina's bunk.

"Wait. Shouldn't we hug or something," Sabina joked.

Heaven playfully rolled her eyes. "No. You might try to fuck me."

Sabina laughed. "Bitch, not."

Heaven gave her a "yeah-right" look. "Anyway, moving on. Riddle me this: how many COs you think are up in here fucking inmates?"

Sabina pulled her earbuds out of her ears and pursed her lips as she let the question roll around in her head.

"Hmm. Does sucking count?"

Heaven rolled her eyes. "Yeah, tramp. Getting sucked or getting licked. It's *still* sex."

She sniggled. "Girl, you know—wait for it—eating ain't cheating, right?"

Heaven gave her a blank stare. "Is that what they're teaching these days? I'll pass on that, hon. Speaking as a woman who has been cheated on, if a motherfucker is getting his dick sucked or has his face stuffed between some ho's legs, then sorry boo, his ass is cheating; especially if he's doing it behind his partner's back. Come again."

"Ohmygod! Wait! You've been treating me so shitty lately, I almost forgot. Did you hear about Struthers?"

Heaven tilted her head, kept a straight face. "No. What about that fucker?"

"Girl, he's been out on leave. And I overheard he's retiring."

Heaven shrugged. "Good for him. One less freak to fry," she said dismissively. But inside she was smiling. She'd gotten him out of there. And she'd been able to get the warden to agree to making sure women had access to more sanitary pads and toilet paper each month, along with getting fresh uniforms weekly. And—for those inmates who came into the prison with no money and wearing no underwear—new packages of underwear when they first arrived in prison.

"Now back to the question," Heaven stated.

Sabina playfully rolled her eyes. "Cranky, eh?"

"No. Curious. Now talk." She glanced over her shoulder toward the door, then lowered her voice bringing her gaze back on Sabina. "You've already fucked two of them, no?"

Sabina grinned mischievously. "Something like that."

And Heaven had already fucked two, sucked one, and still had another few possibilities. But she had no intentions of sharing that bit of news with Sabina. The best dirt done was always alone. No secrets told. That was her mindset.

"Okay. So that's two off the top; that you know of. So how many others you think?"

Sabina frowned. "Why? You writing a thesis?"

Heaven laughed. "Maybe. Right now I'm collecting information."

"Well, I want my cut," Sabina stated, her face set in a serious stare.

Heaven grinned. "But of course. Now talk, dammit."

Sabina tapped her chin thoughtfully; her greenish-blue eyes rolling upward like Pacific waves, then washing over Heaven. "Are we talking female COs, too?"

Heaven nodded. "Yeah, them nasty heifers, too."

"Hmm. Maybe like three officers might be tryna get her lick on."

"Oh, okay, like who?"

"Oh, that's a no-brainer. Definitely Clemmons. She loves tryna feel titties on the sly anytime she working visits, or out in the hallways."

Heaven grimaced. "Freak-ass."

"Yeah. And Banks too. She's like the shower stalker. Both them bitches nasty."

Heaven shuddered. "Now how many male COs you think."

"Probably like six, maybe seven. But I heard one of the teachers, Mister Gary, been fucking this girl over on One South. He's ugly as shit, though. And he looks like he gotta little pink dick. So, scratch him off the list. He doesn't count."

"And what if he has a big pink dick; will he count then?"

She frowned. "*Barf.* Hell no. Not dark enough."

Heaven chuckled, shaking her head. "You a mess, girl. What about Flores?"

Sabina made a face. "Umm. I don't know. I've never heard anything about him fucking with inmates." *Hmm. Interesting.* "He's too light, anyway . . ."

But he has a long, thick dick.

Sabina licked her lips. "Ooh, but I wish Sergeant Braddock fucked around. I would—"

"Bitch, I'd cut you over him," Heaven susurrated, cutting her off.

"Girl, fuck that. There's enough of him to share. We can both fuck him. I love staring in his crotch when he does his tours. I'd love to straddle his face reverse cowgirl and watch you give him head. Maybe we could kiss and swap his cum."

Heaven laughed. "Ohmygod." She shook her head. "Silly. And nasty as hell."

Sabina raised a brow. "Yup. But I'm serious." She scrunched up her nose. "Ugh. Alvins. You can put that nasty fuck on the list, too."

"No surprise," Heaven shared. "He pulled his dick out in front of me one night; actually a few times when I was down in lockup."

"Ewww. What did it look like?"

Heaven groaned. "God, I hate to admit it. That fat fucker's dick had the nerve to be worthy of a ride with the lights out and a plastic bag wrapped around his face . . ."

Sabina laughed. "And from the back. Don't forget that part."

"Ugh. Doesn't he remind you of Rasputia?"

Sabina snorted with laughter. "Ohmygod. Yes, yes!"

"Would you fuck him?" Heaven asked.

Sabina ran her tongue over her teeth, then narrowed her eyes. "So it was long and fat?"

Heaven slowly nodded her head. "Very."

Sabina twirled a lock of hair around her finger. "Then yes. After I'm drunk."

They cracked up. Then for the next hour, Heaven listened intently to Sabina as she jabbered on about who was fucking whom.

FORTY-EIGHT

Chasing Pavements . . .

"*Mm*, just look at him," Sabina said, shoulder bumping Heaven as the two women stood on the tier leaning over the railing watching everyone down in the day space. "God, he is so fine," she commented.

Heaven swept her gaze over in the direction of Sabina's. She narrowed her eyes, zooming in closer. And there stood a tall, muscular man with coal-black hair he wore short and stylishly spiky on top—with a bad-boy air about him.

"Who is that?" Heaven asked curiously.

"That's Mister Panty-Wetter right there," she answered on a laugh. "Doesn't he remind you of that actor Channing Tatum, minus the dark hair?"

Heaven looked harder. He definitely did favor the sexy actor. "Yeah, but who is he?" she asked again.

"Officer Swanson. Mmm. I'd fuck him."

Heaven snorted. "Ho, you don't *fuck* white men, remember? Or has that little horny snatch of yours forgotten that fact?"

Sabina waved her on. "Girl, for *that*. I'd make an exception. I think my kitty would forgive me."

Heaven shook her head. "Girl, your ass is out of control."

Sabina kept her gaze on him. "Would *you* fuck him?"

She pondered the question, then shrugged. "Depends?"

"On?" Sabina shifted her body toward her.

She'd never been with a white man, but she could appreciate any man who exuded lots of sex appeal and swag. And for a white man, he did exactly that. And, from where she stood—looking down on him, he was damn sexy.

"On how pink it was . . . down there. And if he was circumcised or not."

Sabina made a face. "Eww at the visual; pink dick, no thank you. But, um, a dick with lots of skin—*mmm*, yes . . . *yummy*—I love nibbling on it; sticking my tongue in between the skin, then licking the head."

Heaven stared blankly at her. Then clutched her stomach, feigning illness. "Oh, God, I think I just threw up in the back of my mouth a little bit. That is so nasty."

Sabina rolled her eyes. "Don't knock it, hon, until you try it. A big, meaty dick with lots of skin is a real tasty treat."

Heaven glanced over at the CO again, then back to Sabina. "I'll pass."

"But would you pass on *that* sexy one right there?" Sabina asked as another CO walked onto the housing unit.

Heaven's pulse kicked up.

"I'd fuck him in a heartbeat," Sabina stage-whispered. "God, he's so damn fine."

Officer Rawlings looked around the unit, then up at the third tier—if he spotted her, he didn't let on, and Heaven pretended not to notice him, either.

Sabina licked her lips. "You can have Mister Panty-Wetter. I'll take Rawlings. He's the catch of all catches."

Heaven felt her jaw clench. *This bitch had better back up off him,* she thought as she gave her the side-eye. "And why is that?"

Sabina grinned. "Girl, I thought you knew. He's the warden's son."

Heaven blinked. "Say whaaaat? Rewind. He's—"

"He's all kinds of sexy," Clitina chimed in as she walked up to the two of them. "I'd give 'em both some of this good hoodie-hoodie."

Sabina and Heaven stared in question.

Clitina huffed. "Damn, y'all. Top them off. *Geesh.* You bitches cray-cray. Suck they dingalings like they were two jumbo scrimps dipped in warm butter sauce."

Sabina stared at her in disgust.

Clitina caught how she was looking at her and frowned. "Cracker-bitch, don't be starin' at me like that. You a dick-suckin' ass yourself, so don't judge me, bitch."

Sabina stepped from the railing. "*Bitch*, you don't know me. So go take your dirty-ass on before I show you what this *cracker-bitch* can do."

"*What*—?"

Heaven quickly jumped in between the two women before punches were thrown. "Sabina, girl. Don't trip." She then eyed Clitina. "Don't do it. Both you bitches play nice."

Clitina huffed. "Miss Heaven. I ain't gotta play nice with her wannabe-black-actin'-ass. Fuck her."

"No bitch," Sabina snapped. "Fuck *you*. And it's *shrimp*, dumb bitch. Not—"

Whap!

Clitina's fist reached over Heaven and knocked Sabina in her jaw. Heaven quickly got out of the way and let them fight. She knew once blows were thrown, she'd have to let them bang it out and let the COs handle it.

She wasn't trying to break a nail today. But she wanted to get back to Rawlings and this news that all the while she'd been *fucking* the warden's son. Oh, God, how delicious this—

"You fucking ugly, dirty *black* bitch!" Sabina yelled, swinging her fists.

"What you call me?" *Whap! Whap! Whap!* "You call me a black bitch, huh?"

Whap!

"Cracker-bitch! Let me show *you* how ugly this black bitch can get. . . ."

Clitina wrapped her hands in Sabina's hair and swung her down to the concrete floor and stomped her in her head, then dragged her by her hair down the tier.

Heaven cringed, feeling terrible at how badly her cellmate was getting dragged. But she kept spewing out *black bitch*, this *black bitch* that. Heaven sighed. She had to step back and let her cellmate get her ass beat on just that alone.

"That's the warden's son . . ."

Heaven couldn't believe it. A part of her didn't *want* to believe it.

"Lewis," Sergeant Braddock called out as he approached her cell. "Pack your shit. You're moving."

"Moving?" she asked, surprised. "Where?"

"Two North," he stated.

She frowned. "But why? I didn't ask to be . . ."

Oh shit, oh shit.

"And if I wanna fuck?"

"Then you're going to need to get me on a housing unit where I can maneuver more freely."

Pieces of her conversation with Officer Flores replayed in her mind. She couldn't believe he'd actually taken her serious. This was his doing. It had to be. No one else would have reason to move her to another—

Wait. Wait. Wait.

"What about my cellie? When is she coming back from lockup?"

The sergeant gave her a look, trying not to stare at her dark nipples peeking through her white T-shirt.

"Beats me. Depends on what happens at her hearing."

"But her stuff?"

"We'll handle it. Now get packed."

Her heart sank. She'd gotten comfortable over here. Her and Sabina had a nice flow and setup. *But the dumb bitch had to fuck it up fighting with that Clitina's trifling ass.*

Heaven scowled. "Are you sure there isn't anything you can do so I don't have to be moved?" She looked up at him all flirty with her sweet mouth puckered into a pout, and the sergeant nearly came on himself.

"I could," he admitted, wiping his imaginary sweat from his forehead. "But, I think Two North is where you'd want to be."

Her brow rose. "Why?"

"Single cells," is all he said, then stepped away from her cell.

FORTY-NINE

Love In the Dark . . .

Mm, yes. Heaven's cunt was so wet, so hot and horny and needy as she found herself down on her knees under a long desk in the control center of her housing unit—alternately sucking the dicks of two corrections officers (one Hispanic, the other black) while they sat back in their chairs sharing in the pleasure of her warm mouth while the rest of the inmates in her unit remained locked in their cells, asleep.

She'd been on 2 North for almost two months, and had somehow managed to snare two of the third-shift COs into her sultry web without much effort. They'd actually roguishly pursued her. Making lewd comments about her *phat-ass*, her *plump tits*, and her *beautiful made-for-dick-sucking lips* out of earshot of others.

Both had made their intentions, their wants, known. And so had she.

"You want pussy, you want head . . . then it's going to cost you . . ."

And she meant that.

Still, what she hadn't known was, the two COs had been lusting over her, slyly vying for her attention, from the moment she'd stepped on the grounds of the prison over a year ago.

They'd watched her from afar, zooming cameras in on her every chance they got. Then during her first stint down in lockup, they'd heard the rumors of how freaky she was. How she got off on flashing officers her sweet pussy whenever they'd come to her door during their shift tours.

Fuck if Officers Martinez and Corbet didn't want their nights with the sexy vixen before other motherfuckers got to her first, and she became another one of Croydon Hill's used-up hoes.

So far, they hadn't caught wind of anyone fucking her—*yet*. And now she was all theirs for the having—*and* the taking.

Her move to 2 North had been a dream come true for the two unscrupulous cohorts. They both were as dirty as they came as far as COs went; known for fucking willing—and most times *coerced*— inmates into either sucking them off, or taking turns sneaking into an inmate's cell and fucking her.

But Heaven didn't care about any of that. All she cared about was, her payment—in money, in commissary, in contraband, in extra privileges—nothing more, nothing less.

She had a cell full of commissary. And between the prison 7-Eleven she ran and her rent-to-use dildo service, she was doing very well for herself. She'd even been able to add four new items to her sex toy inventory—thanks to Officer Rawlings.

Unfortunately, she hadn't been able to see him as much since the move, but he kept minutes on her phone and they spoke whenever possible. Most recently, she'd started sending him nude videos of her in her cell fucking herself with the dildo molded from his cock that he'd given her. And it happened to be the only dildo she used (and didn't rent out).

Tonight she'd gotten a hundred dollars and cable zip ties from

Corbet—under the pretense that she wanted him to fulfill her fantasy of being secured to her bunk, her wrists and ankles tethered tightly, edging toward painful, yet, dangling on the edge of sadistic pleasure.

That's what she'd told him.

And Martinez, he'd managed to bring her two pints of Hennessy and six Carolina Reapers—a bright red pepper with a scorpion tail that was a cross between a Pakistani Naga and a red Habanero that was bred in South Carolina.

The Hennessy was for her wild child friend Clitina, who had finally gotten her wish and had been sent to 4 East after she'd finished her fifteen days in solitary for fighting Sabina.

And as far as the six bright red peppers that had a sweet fruity flavor and enough demon heat to burn out an asshole. Well, she knew exactly whose asshole she had in mind to use them on.

Clemmons'.

The warden hadn't transferred her as she'd asked her to, so Heaven decided to deal with her roguish-ass her way. She planned on making a paste with the peppers, and then . . . well—by the time Heaven finished with Clemmons, her clit and cunt and the inner part of her walls would be enflamed.

She smiled over Corbet's cock, sweet anticipation blooming in the center of her cunt. "Aah, yeah, freaky bitch," he groaned, his lusty stare locked down in his lap as she licked over the head of his dick. He was uncircumcised—a *first* for her. But she was glad the foreskin slid all the way back.

She had yet to see it in a flaccid state, which was fine for her. All she had to do was breathe on the horny fuck and his dick hardened, its skin stretched back like a tight tarp over his shaft.

"*Mm*," she moaned in response, her head bobbing back and forth from one dick to the other. Both were thick and long. And heavy. And ribbed with veins. Mm—God, yes, yes, yes . . . Lots and lots of winding veins along the top of their shafts that she trailed with her tongue, leaving wet streaks up and down the length of them.

Martinez's cockhead was shaped like a large stuffed mushroom. And leaked lots of precum that tasted sweet and salty, like a PayDay candy bar. Corbet's dickhead, on the other hand, was a giant, plum-shaped head . . .

"Yeah, that's right, you slutty lil' cunt," Martinez hissed. "Suck that fat black cock." She swirled her tongue over Corbet's piss slit, then shifted her head and slid her tongue over Martinez's as she stroked them both in each hand.

"Fuck, yeah, baby . . . nasty bitch," Corbet murmured on a groan.

She sucked and popped, sucked and popped, each dick in and out of her mouth, swirling her tongue over their piss slits, collecting the sticky treat that endlessly drizzled out.

God, she hated these crude, disrespectful bastards, especially Corbet's misogynist ass. But she loved sucking their tasty dicks. And loved when they talked dirty. When they called her slutty names and treated her like a dirty cum-whore—only when she was down on her knees. Upright, she had a problem with it.

It heightened her mental foreplay, skyrocketed her arousal. And made her wet—oh so, very, very . . . *wet*.

Tonight she felt sluttier than she'd ever felt, and she wanted to be fucked as such. She wanted them both to fuck her raw and deep, taking turns fucking her deep in her pussy until it burned and she screamed and begged. She wanted them fucking her in her ass, pumping into the loose heat, stretching it out like the Lincoln Tunnel, her asshole fucked open wide enough for a small fist—or double-dick fucking.

Yes, God, yes . . . she wanted it dirty. She wanted, needed, her pussy licked from slit to clit, her ass tongued, and to be fucked from the back on all fours with both of her arms pulled back like horse reins. She wanted it rough. She wanted her hair pulled and her ass spanked, hard, until it reddened and bruised . . .

Sadly, none of that would happen. The grimy fuckers only wanted head with lots of spit tonight. She groaned over Martinez's cock—in frustration, in hunger, in greedy need—as her hand slid up and down Corbet's shaft while she sucked and sucked Martinez; his thick, throbbing cock, pulsing in her mouth.

Martinez grunted. "Ah, *sí*, sí . . . oh *Dios* . . . fuck . . ."

Heaven's pussy clenched. Her sweet, musky scent billowed out from beneath the desk, engulfing the room.

"Damn, bitch," Officer Corbet said, his dick pulsing in agitation that this fucking whore was spending more time on his partner's dick than his. "Get that greedy little mouth over here on my dick, too."

Heaven gave him the side-eye; her focus solely on making Martinez's toes curl in his boots as her mouth brought him to the edge of ecstasy. Then pushed him over.

She'd take care of *him* next.

"Fuck, fuck . . . *sí*, *sí* . . ."

Martinez howled low in his throat as Heaven sucked and sucked, his toes curling as a gusher of cum burst out his slit, splattering the back of her throat. He ground his hips, then gripped the arms on either side of his chair as his hips rose and his body shook.

Then he whispered, stroking the side of her face, "*Quiero lamer tu coño, mi dulce puta cachonda* . . ." (I want to lick your cunt, my sweet, nasty whore.)

There was no fucking way he was going to let his partner know that he wanted her so badly. He wanted Heaven all to himself. He wanted to hold her beautiful tits in his hands and slide his dick between them and come all over her. He wanted to be the only one coming in her mouth, in her ass (if she wanted him there), and in her cunt.

He wanted her.

And he'd have her.

Even if that meant he had to—

Corbet's growl yanked Martinez from his crazy thought of breaking Heaven out of prison, and he stared enviously—jealousy slowly brewing in the pit of stomach—as he watched the object of his desires swallow Corbet's dick as he viciously gripped her by the head and thrust himself in and out of her mouth.

"Aaah, aaah . . . aaah . . . suck that shit, bitch . . ."

His body jerked and Heaven gobbled and slobbed and swallowed a glob of heated cream, then slowly licked around his head as if it were a vanilla-frosted cupcake.

Martinez gritted his teeth.

He wanted to punch this *hijo de puta* in his motherfucking neck.

FIFTY

If It Don't Fit (Don't Force It)...

"Hope them muhfuckas over there aren't trying to get in them drawers," CO Rawlings said, out of nowhere. Well, it hadn't really been random. It'd been brewing in the back of his mind of late. Not seeing her as much was fucking with him. And he saw how motherfuckers like Flores and Martinez leered at her, and he didn't like that shit one bit.

But he had to play it cool.

Still, he needed more than videos. And phone sex—from *her*. He needed to be inside that pussy, at least once a week. But—fuck, the lack of available overtime was making it difficult for him to make moves. So he couldn't get to her the way he wanted, and he didn't like the fact that she was over on 2 North with motherfuckers like Corbet and Martinez. Both them motherfuckers were snakes.

He didn't want anyone coming at his woman crazy. And he damn sure didn't want any of the motherfuckers up at the prison trying to get at her.

And if she was playing him . . . God help them both.

Silence fell over the line. And then Heaven blinked. "Excuse me?"

"Nah. You heard me," he stated, his tone biting. "Who else you fucking in there?"

Heaven frowned. "I don't like your tone. And I don't like what you're insinuating. I'm not *fucking* anyone else." Well, okay—she was lying. "But since *you* want to question me. Maybe I should be asking *you* who you *fucking*. Since you want to accuse me."

"Chill with that. I'm not fucking anyone." He paused to let his words sink in. "This dick is yours, all of it." He sighed. "My bad, baby," he apologized. "I'm fucking bugging. Not seeing you got me feeling some type of way."

She rolled her eyes. How cliché. She'd heard that line before. More times than she cared to remember. "I don't know that," she said.

"Yeah, true. But I'm telling you."

"Uh-huh. And I'm telling *you* the same thing, but you don't seem to want to believe that. So why should I?"

"You right. My bad." He blew out another breath. "It's just that . . ."

"And *why* didn't you tell me that *you* are the warden's *son*?"

There was a deafening silence between the two of them, before he finally spoke. "Who told you that?"

"Well, is it true?"

"Yeah, but how'd you find out?"

"That doesn't matter. But what matters is *you* being the warden's son. And you not saying anything."

"I'm a CO, baby. Intimately involved with *you*. An inmate. And you expected me to tell you that I'm related to the warden? Really? That's the last thing I wanted you to know, at least while you're still incarcerated."

"I understand," she said a beat later. And she really did. "I'm sure she'd lose her mind if she found it."

"Which is why she *won't*. Not until you're released. We gotta keep this on the low, baby. I'm not trying to lose my job. Or end up with charges."

Heaven bit back a laugh, imagining sitting at the warden's dinner table for Thanksgiving. "She'll never accept *this*. You. Me. You do know that, right?"

"Let me worry about that," he said.

She shook her head. She didn't know what she wanted to do with this knowing, this information, yet. She'd said nothing to him until this very moment. Why had she not confronted him before now? She didn't know. But what she did know was, she wanted to smear this news in the warden's face—that she was fucking her son, but not at the risk of hurting him.

"I miss you," he said in a low raspy voice.

Heaven finally smiled. "What you miss?"

He grinned. "What you think?"

"You miss this pussy," she said for him. *Of course you do.*

"You got me bugging, baby," he admitted. "You're all I think about. That shit ain't cool. You'll have me fuck around and bust a muhfucka in his head over you."

Heaven swallowed. She felt her heart sinking. She felt guilt rising up in her like bile. This news of being the warden's son could be used to her advantage. But she didn't want to hurt *him*.

Shit. Truth was, she found herself liking him more and more as the months went on. But she was in prison. And they'd never be able to have any type of real relationship (well, anything with substance) as long as she was incarcerated. And there were still a few other dicks she wanted to straddle down on. That was what she had to keep telling herself. She needed to keep justifying—and reminding herself—why she was doing what she was doing with him.

He was a means to an end, nothing more, nothing less. Period. She couldn't lose sight of that. But she knew she was lying to herself. He *was* becoming more. And that could pose a problem for her, for him.

"I thought this was only about sex with us. Are you saying it's more now?"

"Yeah. It is. At first, yeah—I admit, I only wanted to smash because you're fine as fuck; and that ass was looking real right. But, then . . . I started wanting more. More of you, and definitely more of the pussy; but it's not about that anymore. Fucking. I wanna build with you."

She blinked. He wanted to build with *her*.

"Maybe we should stop this," she whispered, clutching her cell. "I don't want to get hurt. And, obviously, neither do you."

"Nah. I'm not trying to stop anything. Is that what you really want?"

Heaven went still, and licked her lips, suddenly feeling them go dry. She knew what she needed in the right here, right now. But what she wanted? Well, aside from her freedom, that was a whole other matter.

She still believed in love. Still believed in the beautiful complexities of a relationship. She wanted love. Wanted to be in love. She wanted a man whom she could trust, a man who understood the intricacies of a relationship, of monogamy.

She didn't want to end up alone and lonely, becoming some old bitter bitch who sat around watching *Jeopardy* and reruns of *Oprah* and *The Golden Girls*.

By the time she got out of prison, she'd be forty—*ohmyfucking-God* . . . forty-six and childless. Her eggs dried-up raisins. She wanted a husband and a home. And two, maybe three, babies. She wanted to be someone's wife, and the mother of his children. One day.

But for right now, all she wanted was . . . to survive.

"Tell me you don't want this," he said, snatching her from her tormented musing. "And I'll fall back. But know this: If *this*—*me*—is what you want, baby, I'd never hurt you. I'ma ride this shit out with you. All I'm asking is for you to keep it one hundred with me, no matter what. And, if you're doing shit with another muhfucka behind my back, all I'm asking is that you don't let me find out about it. Respect me—as your *man*."

Whelp.

"Oh, so you're my man now?" she asked, dodging his question as she plopped back on her mattress. She couldn't answer him, not yet. She didn't want to make any hasty decisions. She needed to weigh her options. Assess what other opportunities might lay ahead of her.

Translation: Was there a way she could keep him, and still make moves?

"No doubt," he said. "Thought you already knew. But *you* tell me. Am I *your* man?"

She sighed inwardly. He wanted an answer. Damn him.

"I'm in prison. An inmate. What type of relationship do you really think we can have? It's not like I only have another year or two and then I'll be out. No. I have years to go before I'm out of here."

"I know that, baby," he said. "I'm not saying it'll be easy. Shit, this is one of the most unconventional relationships that I've ever wanted. But, I still want it. With you."

God, no, please. She'd said months ago, that she'd never be with a man like *him*. And, now, here she was, lying on her bunk feeling conflicted about her feelings—about him, about this predicament she was in.

"Listen to me," she said, feeling herself becoming irritated. Not with him, but herself. She was trying to give him an easy out. But he wasn't seeing it, or maybe he was ignoring it. Either way, he was making it difficult for her to end things.

"I'm not getting out for at least another eight-and-a-half years," she pushed. "Any chance of parole is gone now because of those two fights I've had."

"Listen, baby. I hear you. But nothing worthwhile comes easy. You're worth whatever struggles, whatever obstacles, we might face. I'm in it with you. All I'm asking is that you trust me."

Trust? She wanted it. But somehow she was starting to believe it was overrated.

She inhaled, then slowly exhaled. "I need—no, *want*—sex," she admitted. "Lots of it. But, unless I . . ." She lowered her voice to almost an inaudible whisper. "Unless I spend my entire bid in lockup, I can't get that good dick as much as I want it."

She felt him grinning through the phone. "Oh word? You think this dick good?"

"Yeah," she murmured. "Real good." She stifled a yawn. It was going on three in the morning. "Tell me what you think about this pussy? Why are you so in love with it?"

"'Cause it's like *heaven*, baby," he said real low, his voice coating her senses like warm honey. "When I'm inside of you, all I wanna do is lie up in it and float away."

What more could she say?

She simply closed her eyes, and slipped her hands into her panties.

FIFTY-ONE

Stairway To Heaven...

Officer Flores waited until close to two a.m., before he quietly snuck inside Heaven's cell and startled her. It'd been several weeks since he'd had her moved over to 2 North. Though it was still a max housing unit, inmates had single cells. He'd purposefully taken his time coming to her. It'd killed him to wait, but he'd wanted to let her get settled in—first before he made his move.

2 North was where he sold most of his cocaine. He also sold Molly and pills, mostly over on 4 East. But the majority of his prison sales were in weed. Half the inmates at Croydon Hill were hooked on the good shit he trafficked into the prison through the kitchen deliveries. A dime bag on the streets sold for fifty dollars behind these walls, and he was making a killing. And he had several civilian staffers on payroll to make sure his operation ran smoothly.

"Ssh," he whispered, placing a finger to his lips. "I'm here to collect on what you promised me." He slid his hand over her sheet-covered ass.

Heaven blinked him in, her eyes quickly adjusting to the dark, and she saw a slow blaze beginning to burn in his eyes.

She'd heard the cell door creep open, but had lain still, pretending to be in a deep sleep. She actually thought it was Officer Martinez again. He'd become her late-night pussy licker over the last several days. And she'd grown accustomed to him sneaking into her cell all hours of the night, and serving her up fifteen to twenty minutes of bomb head with his long, thick tongue.

Martinez hadn't fucked her, yet. But she wanted him to. She wanted to know what having Hispanic sausage meat felt like being stuffed between her folds. But seeing Officer Flores in her cell, his lids half-mast and filled with lust, was even better.

"And what exactly did I promise you?" she asked coyly. "I don't remember."

She tried to turn over on her back, but he stopped her, his hand squeezing her ass. "Don't play, baby," he said huskily. "You promised me a sampler."

Flores reached for her sheet and pulled it down from her body, and a low moan left him as he looked down at the lacy, feminine underwear—definitely not prison issued. He licked his lips and undid his pants, staring at the globes of her ass.

Heaven grinned seductively at him over her shoulder. "Oh, right."

A deep muscle tightened low in his stomach. "Yeah, right. Now take off them drawers and let me see what's on the menu."

"Know this," she said, her voice slightly above a whisper as she kept her neck craned over her shoulder. "You can have your sampler. But if you want more than that, then you had better come right. You only get one round of free pussy."

She tried to roll over again, and he held her down.

"Nah. I want you on your stomach. And I got you."

"Then *you* need"—she lifted her pelvis up off the bed—"to take off my panties." Ass up, he groaned. He couldn't resist touching it. He pulled her ass apart and put his face in it, inhaling her—ass, pussy. He kissed over her beautiful ass, licking along the edges of each cheek.

Then he finally pulled her underwear until the slinky material slid down her hips, and slid them off her body, and then tossed them to the floor. His dick thickened imagining what she'd look like with only a pair of stockings and garters on.

She looked like a fucking goddess. His. All his.

That's what he wanted. Her. His prison whore.

Heaven panted lightly as her body tightened. She felt it between her legs. That ache—sweet agony blistering through her cunt; he reached between her thighs and found her swollen clit. He kneaded it gently. Then slid his hand over her pussy, his palm brushing every part of her. She was wet, very wet, and hot. Damn.

And he hadn't even *really* touched her—yet.

And then he was easing his long, thick dick deep inside the tight, wet passage of her body until he was balls-deep, until she felt it traveling up in her spine—the heat, the burn. She groaned as his hips slowly seesawed up and down, his deliciously long dick, stretching through her body, her hips joining the pulsing rhythm of his.

She closed her eyes and forced herself to breathe out as she felt him go deep, deeper than any dick had ever gone, and she gave herself into the red-hot intensity of unadulterated pleasure.

Ecstasy—*mm, yes* . . .white blinding heat—permeated him as she moved her hips with his, as she took him deep. Goddamn. Shit. Fuck. He thought he'd go up in flames from her cunt's heat.

"Uhh . . . oooh, yes, yes, *yessss*," she purred.

She closed her eyes and gave her body to him not for any other reason than because she wanted to; because she felt like being a prison slut.

Beautiful . . . he whispered into her ear. *So fucking . . . sexy . . . wet . . . juicy . . . sweet baby* . . . and a string of other words that clung to every part of her as he moaned in her ear and blanketed his body over hers; his heat, his sweat—and melded every part of himself into her body.

She came. Then came again, and again, and again; her climax crashed around him, her body absorbing his thrusts so fiercely that she wanted to growl and bare her teeth. She bit down on his arm, and heard him groan in response, causing his dick to swell more inside her body, throb more.

"Yeah, that's it," he murmured in her ear, before sucking her earlobe into his mouth. He nipped at it, then sucked and licked on the back of her neck

God, she felt so fucking good; so tight, and so goddamn soft. He knew he wouldn't last long. After months of waiting, he'd been primed to have her all night, ready to finally be inside of her. And now she was here with him—with his dick in her.

He groaned low in the back of his throat. His weight pressed her into the mattress and he closed his eyes as she used her slick walls to grip his shaft, drawing the length of him in and out of her snatch until he could stand it no longer and he—

"Aaah, shit . . . motherfuck it . . . good fuckin' pussy . . ."

With a cry, Heaven clawed the sheets and bit her bottom lip and breathed in the excruciating pain, until she almost broke skin and drew blood. The fluid motion of his hips caused her to whimper. He was by far the biggest dick she'd ever experienced inside her cunt, yet her mouth was another story.

Her pussy cried out for help, begging her to free it from, from, from—oh God, oh God, oh God . . . yes, yes. Her body shook as his hands bore down on her hips and his dick quickly slid in and out of her body, stretching her, burning her, fucking her cunt raw with an exquisite pain and horrifying pleasure that she'd never experienced in her life.

Instantly, she filled the entire cell with her scent. Warm juices sluiced out of her body, wetting the sheets beneath her. His dick jerked excitedly.

Inmate or not, she was so fucking perfect. And she was his. All his. He slid his dick into her body, and drove his point home, pounding, thrusting, and hungrily fucking into her wet fire.

He pounded into her, pulling out and plunging back in, digging his hands into her hips as he sank deep inside her, retreated, then did it all over again and again and again.

"That's right, baby," he rasped. "Take all this dick, like a good little prison bitch. Mmm, yeah . . . I feel you comin', baby . . . I feel you soaking my dick . . ."

And then he bit back a groan and curled his toes as liquid heat tore through his body and exploded inside Heaven, while her own orgasm spread through her body, coating her quaking walls.

"I need two hundred dollars," she said on a moan. "Need it . . . mmm, yes . . . in my . . . ooh, yes . . . account."

He emitted a low growl, caught up in the fires of ecstasy as her walls gripped and milked him. Her pussy was addictive. She was addictive. He felt himself getting lost in her heat, his body melting over her silky curves, everything about her enfolding him into her seductive web.

"Whatever you need, baby," he murmured, reaching around and cupping her breasts. He squeezed as he slid in and out of her body. "I got you, baby."

When she looked back over her shoulder at him, his eyes were half-closed; he was buried so deep. So fucking deep. And he cursed at the delicious squeeze.

"I'ma make you mine," he whispered. "Whatever it takes." And then his body shuddered into hers. He stayed inside of her for another minute longer than he should have, then slowly pulled out.

A slow grin rolled over her lips as he stuffed his dick back in his boxer briefs, then fastened his pants. She didn't know what she was going to do about Officer Rawlings or Martinez or Corbet or Thurman, or the slew of other COs here at Croydon Hill who would eventually end up standing in line, waiting to get into the walls of her sweet cunt.

All she knew was, she'd keep fucking whoever made it worth her while.

She was Heaven.

And everyone wanted to get to *heaven*.

It wasn't in the sky. And it wasn't where souls ascend to in the afterlife. No, Heaven was here on earth, behind barbed wire and concrete and steel.

And it was right here between her smooth, sexy thighs.

Where it'd always been.

About The Author

Cairo is the author of *Prison Snatch*; *The Pleasure Zone*; *Dirty Heat*; *Between the Sheets*; *Ruthless: Deep Throat Diva 3*; *Retribution: Deep Throat Diva 2*; *Slippery When Wet*; *The Stud Palace*; *Big Booty*; *Man Swappers*; *Kitty-Kitty, Bang-Bang*; *Deep Throat Diva*; *Daddy Long Stroke*; *The Man Handler*; and *The Kat Trap*. He is the coauthor of *Sexual Healing* with Allison Hobbs. His travels to Egypt are what inspired his pen name.

If you enjoyed "Prison Snatch," be sure to check out

SEXUAL
Healing

by Allison Hobbs and Cairo
Available from Strebor Books

One

Milk chocolate perfection, that's what she was . . .

Wet need stretched through her pussy in a slow-flowing river of heat as she stepped out of her Mercedes S600, handing her key fob to the tall, lanky, good-looking valet in his early twenties. Too young. But still worthy of a sly glance. Sure, she'd fuck him in a heartbeat had she'd been another type of woman, one smutty and unscrupulous. But he was just a horny boy in her eyes, one clearly mesmerized by her beauty. However, he wasn't worthy to sniff her panties or lick around her cunt, so . . . no thank you.

She needed someone old enough to know what to do with her and her never-ending curves. She needed a man who knew how to ride her body, and fuck her down into a mattress. She suspected the young valet would be a clumsy-fuck, at best.

Still, it was flattering. His ogling, that was.

A slight smile edged its way over her glossed MAC lips as she caught his gaze sweeping over her body. Or maybe it was the backless dress with the plunging neckline—red, silky . . . and very clingy—that had him seemingly flustered, and stuttering out a *hello*. Whatever the case, she found him adorable.

She slipped him a ten-dollar bill, then tucked her purse beneath her arm, and strutted toward her destination, her hips swaying, her ass bouncing, every which way. She felt her adrenaline surging through her veins as her strappy heels clicked over asphalt, then concrete, moving toward brick and mortar.

Sublime pussy.

That's what Arabia Knight knew she had.

Breath-taking.

Heart-stopping.

Toe-curling.

Sweet, sticky slices of wet heaven that melted over a hard cock like warm honey. There was no mistaking it. Her juicy cunt was the crème de la crème. And she had a scandalously long list of lovers *and* past stalkers to prove it.

And she had a few tricks between her smooth thighs that would drop a man to his knees, and have him eating out of the palms of her paraffin-soft hands. And she knew, the minute she slid down on his shaft, rolled her hips, and clamped her walls around his dick that he'd fall in love.

They always did.

Any time one of her many lovers cried out her name or sputtered out inaudible chants, she became keenly more aware, more empowered, more inspired. Each time her pussy spasmed, and she heard them call out to the heavens or whisper sweet nothings in her ear, she knew. Her pussy was some exclusive, platinum-plus-American-Express-Black-Card-type shit. She had to laugh to herself. Men never wanted to leave home without it. It was, what she liked to call it, that snap-trap pussy. Wet. Juicy. Steamy. Dick-clutching. Skin-sucking tight.

And, tonight, she was looking to snap her trap around something good, something dangerously thick. She was a woman on a mission, a woman on the prowl. She'd worn the dress and sexy heels for one purpose and one purpose only: to seduce.

Then get *fucked*.

She always wore red when she wanted to be wild, when she wanted to fulfill her wanton urges. Tonight was the night. She was a huntress, on the hunt. She knew the drill. All she had to do was use her womanly wiles to lure her prey to her. Then strike.

Luckily, she wasn't on a hunting expedition for another lover this evening, just a one-night stand. So there'd be no need for formalities. Not at this establishment. Just hot, naughty—*hopefully* dirty—sex.

Mmm, *yes*.

This was a sex club. Her secret rendezvous place to lose herself to temptation.

Sure she was *engaged* to . . . *three* different men.

And?

Monogamy had nothing to do with fulfilling her dark desires. She was a woman with insatiable needs. Needs her three lovers oftentimes fell short on fulfilling, which left her cunt weeping, aching, to be skewered by a long thick—

Her cell rang inside her crystal-studded purse, slicing into her salacious reverie.

She ignored it.

It rang again. Then buzzed that a message had been left.

She rolled her long-lashed eyes. Whoever it was could wait. Talking on the phone was the last thing on her mind. She was on a quest for some good hard, anonymous dick. And nothing was going to distract her from the quest at hand.

Her gaze honed in on the thick mahogany doors that led to the club's entrance and her clit pulsed. Fierce passion and seduction awaited her, and she couldn't wait to get bathed in its heat. The mere thought of being awash in pleasure excited her. She felt the fire roiling along the walls of her cunt, and her breath almost caught in her throat.

Her ten-thousand-dollar-a-year membership fee afforded her access to her share of freaky fun. Shamefully, it'd been months since she'd frequented the exclusive For Adults Only club. But, tonight, she'd make up for lost time. She wouldn't squander any opportunities. She'd be the naughtiest of them all.

Filthy and wild and indiscriminate.

Her nipples tightened as she stepped inside the marbled foyer and was greeted by a tall, chiseled, bare-chested hunk wearing a silken mask. She eyed the prominent bulge beneath his loincloth, imagining her hand reaching out and languorously stretching over its girth, then caressing it. She could tell, fully erect, it would be a deliciously long, thick dick.

She imagined herself holding his dick in her hand like an ice cream cone, licking at the tip, flicking her tongue over the precum she imagined already gathering there, before swirling her hot tongue around the whole engorged head. *Damn him*. She felt herself on the verge of dropping to her knees and begging him for his cock.

As if reading her scandalous mind, he smiled, his gaze flickering over her swelling breasts. "Welcome, beautiful," he said in a deep timbre, his voice melting over her body like hot fudge, thick and rich. A fresh burst of heat shot through her cunt. She bit her lip. Then slid her hand into her clutch and handed him her gold membership card. Her gaze drifted from his eyes to his mouth, imagining her clitoris and nipples being sucked into its wet heat.

He caught a glimpse of her cleavage, again, before reaching for her card. Then he glanced at it, and she wondered what he did for a living. Perhaps he was a suit-and-tie guy by day, or . . . maybe a professional athlete. She quickly dismissed the thought. How he made his money really didn't matter. Whether or not he was a good fuck did.